FOREWORD

I FIRST ENCOUNTERED Joel Lane through his fiction - it was in the pages of the British Fantasy Society's journal *Dark Horizons* when edited by David Sutton. I then met Joel in person - David introduced us one evening when we all met up for drinks. I must admit, at that meeting I failed to recognise his name and when I asked if he had written anything Dave put me to rights. Joel was amused by ignorance but never held it against me. We became good friends, part of the Brum Balti Boys (Joel, David, Mike Chinn, John Howard, Stan Nicholls, James Brogden and I), meeting semi-regularly for drinks and then a meal in one of the numerous Balti houses in the Sparkhill suburb of Birmingham (after buying our beverages in the next-door off licence, of course). In fact we were in the process of arranging a meal before Christmas ... and then we learned the sad news of Joel's death in November 2013.

When I edited *Winter Chills* (later *Chills*) for the British Fantasy Society, I included two of Joel's stories, and a poem, in its ten-issue run, including the outstanding 'The Earth Wire' (in *WC3*). Then when he proposed a themed anthology for The Alchemy Press I jumped at the idea; *Beneath the Ground* appeared in 2002. A story of his, from *Swords Against the Millennium* (edited by Mike Chinn and co-published by The Alchemy Press), 'The Hunger of the Leaves', was selected for two Best Of annuals (best horror *and* best fantasy).

Joel was an incredibly bright and perspicacious devotee of horror and weird fiction, old and new. He saw things in stories that most of us would take an age to spot. Yet conversely when I suggested that a story of his, which I had just read, was packed with autobiographical elements, he hadn't seen this for himself. His fiction had many levels, although often rooted in Birmingham and the Black Country. Reading them was like reading a map of the tragedy of that city and its environs.

But Joel was more than a colleague in the fantasy/horror arena. He was a good and empathic friend. When my first marriage was breaking down I told Joel before anyone else. He offered not just sympathy but support, helping me through a difficult time.

As many of you know, Joel often suffered ill health himself, had his own emotional burdens. At these times Jan Edwards and I would have him round to our house for dinner and an evening of conversation (we lived about a ten minute walk apart - five minutes if you walked like Joel). When Jan and I moved away from Birmingham and couldn't meet up so frequently, and his ill health and ill-luck increased (his father died, his mother's continuing ailments), I felt as though I was letting him down. Several times he tried to come and visit but that just didn't happen...

What else? Joel and I shared a passion for music, swapping compilation cassettes of our favourite songs trying to convert each other - although our tastes overlapped for the most part. We went to gigs - sometimes with friends, sometimes just us - seeing the likes of dEUS, Flaming Lips, Echo and the Bunnymen, Drugstore, Only Ones, Tindersticks, Sparklehorse ... all the way to some of the icons of rock music: Nick Cave, Lou Reed and especially Richard Thompson. But he never converted me into a Bruce Springsteen fan.

If Joel had a weakness it was in his modesty - he didn't tell us about a major poetry award he had won, for example. But that was part of his charm.

I am privileged to have counted Joel as a good friend and I was so terribly depressed at his passing. Still am. He was only fifty, for God's sake! If there is an afterlife he is in the company of his favourite writers, chewing the fat with H.P. Lovecraft, Robert E. Howard, William Hope Hodgson and Clark Aston Smith

something remains

Published by The Alchemy Press

Rumours of the Marvellous by Peter Atkins

Doors to Elsewhere by Mike Barrett

Evocations by James Brogden

Give Me These Moments Back by Mike Chinn

The Paladin Mandates by Mike Chinn

Nick Nightmare Investigates by Adrian Cole

Leinster Gardens and Other Subtleties by Jan Edwards

Merry-Go-Round and Other Words by Bryn Fortey

In the Broken Birdcage of Kathleen Fair by Cate Gardner

Tell No Lies by John Grant

Touchstones by John Howard

Monsters by Paul Kane

The Komarovs by Chico Kidd

Something Remains by Joel Lane and Friends

Where the Bodies are Buried by Kim Newman

Music From the Fifth Planet by Anne Nicholls

Music in the Bone by Marion Pitman

Invent-10n by Rod Rees

The Complete Weird Epistles of Penelope Pettiweather, Ghost Hunter by Jessica Amanda Salmonson

Dead Water and Other Weird Tales by David A. Sutton

The Private Life of Elder Things by Adrian Tchaikovsky, Adam Gauntlett and Keris McDonald

Visit www.alchemypress.co.uk

for further details of these and our anthologies

something remains

joel lane and friends. . .

allen ashley

simon avery

stephen bacon

simon bestwick

james brogden

ramsey campbell

mike chinn

gary couzens

sarah doyle

jan edwards

paul edwards

liam garriock

john grant

terry grimwood

andrew hook

john howard

ian hunter

tom johnstone

BROKEN EYE

...child
...with videos
...on Staircase (orgy in dark)
...watched dawn through wire grid in glare
...seemed as though darkness still there

Des

Rachel — collects ...

staying with sister & child in tower block
meets young man in block, stays with them
— he collects photos & videos — ...
going back to her room in the dark, ...
runs into couple (group?) making love
on staircase
goes back to the man — he is lonely/afraid.
leaving in morning — drugged teenagers on
balcony
back to room — daylight felt like darkness
(slept for a day & then felt better)

The ... shows domination? Is it myopia or that makes films ... daylight my favourite ... voices more alive ... I'm not a voyeur ... will do ... through to the void of the ... still in the ... being heard, being ...

(1) imprisonment — bars, stone, grids — against light
(2) the eye — TV screen — light
(their eyes ate the daylight)
(3) images — compound eye — windows
(broken up into windows)

A TOURIST

... idea of freedom.

matt joiner

tim lebbon

alison littlewood

simon maccculloch

gary mcmahon

david matthew

adam millard

chris morgan

pauline morgan

thana niveau

marion pitman

john llewellyn probert

rosanne rabinowitz

nicholas royle

lynda e. rucker

steve savile

david a. sutton

steve rasnic tem

mark valentine

joe x. young

edited by
peter coleborn and pauline e. dungate

in aid of

DIABETES UK
CARE. CONNECT. CAMPAIGN.

Published by
THE ALCHEMY PRESS

First edition

ISBN 978-1-911034-04-9

The Alchemy Press, Staffordshire, UK
www.alchemypress.co.uk

CONTENTS

COPYRIGHT INFORMATION

DEDICATION

This book has been an emotional journey. Thus, to everyone who contributed, thank you for trusting us with your work.

And especially to the memory of Joel Lane. You are still very much missed.

—Peter and Pauline

among many others.

Pauline tells the story behind this anthology in her Introduction so there's no point my repeating anything here. Suffice it to say that I am privileged to be involved in this project. The response to our calls for submissions was overwhelmingly supportive. I wish to thank everyone for taking the time to contribute to this memorial to Joel Lane.

Peter Coleborn
(A version first appeared online in 2013)

ANTITHESIS

(SOMETHING OTHER)

(MOMENTS)

Fantasy/ideal ingrained in everyday life. At critical moments (turning points).
Calm, determined eyes; a strong opening hand; a shadow falling on me; arms holding me from behind.
Looking in strange faces, as into a well...

YOU GIVE ME FEVER

Truth

drove her mad — later, her
became his reality — wint
gradient of cold — wooden

Not a child, no. More
sick animal, a sick d
and pissing over the c
trying to fuck a duffe
call it a child."

could see the cold: di
the air, like lines mov

his father died,
one in
not mine. It

if you try to remove people's armour

Suit of armour outside shop.

I NEED SOMEWHERE TO HI

comic-book mentalities: mas

emphasis — text falling on

"What do they know of Engl
know?"

a baby crusted in rock

clean-shaven, cropped, per

"It shows I'm in comple
army

INTRODUCTION

WHEN JOEL LANE died unexpectedly in November 2013 the literary world lost a remarkable talent. Some of us also lost a friend and mentor.

Once we heard the news, Chris Morgan and I volunteered to help in any way that we could. His mother, whom we had met a number of literary events, was frail and recovering from a fall which had cracked (but thankfully not broken) her femur. Joel's younger brother Tom lived and worked in Weymouth. The big issue was clearing Joel's home.

Joel lived in a small terraced house which he had neglected. The interior needed to be cleared so it could be sold and the mortgage paid off. Joel collected books. And he never threw anything away.

When he first moved in Joel constructed a lot of flat-pack book cases. They quickly became totally inadequate for the number of books he acquired. It wasn't only the supernatural horror, fantasy, slipstream, crime and literary fiction - both books and magazines - that accumulated but as a poet he also collected poetry. Then there was the music. Both tapes and CDs filled cupboards and boxes. He'd frequently copy tracks for friends.

In one corner of his study was a book case piled to dangerous heights with the volumes, sometimes in multiples, of the publications in which his stories, poems and articles appeared. His mother had no room for them so they went into boxes and were transferred to our house. This was only intended as a temporary measure and once catalogued we took them to the Science Fiction Foundation in Liverpool University Library along with his awards. They are now available for anyone who wants to consult them.

Joel's imagination was always at work. Ideas for stories or poems were jotted down on anything at hand - gig flyers, envelopes, whatever. He was constantly recording phrases, making notes, roughing out poems or the starts of stories with the intention of using them later. A lot were incorporated into his body of work. The problem was deciding what happened to them after the initial jotting.

Sorting out Joel's house was like an archaeological expedition. Obvious dross was cleared away. Old newspapers, some magazines, flyers had to be assessed. Anything with Joel's neat, inevitably black, handwriting went in other boxes along with notebooks for further investigation. Everything was there, including his essays from university days. Books, some still in their original packaging, turned up in unlikely places.

We went round whenever we could and it took nearly nine months to clear the house ready for cleaning and sale. A lot of cheap paperbacks were taken, by the boot-load, to Oxfam. Others are gradually being sold, with the proceeds going to Ella, Joel's mother.

The manuscripts were a different issue. It soon became clear that there was a wealth of material that had never seen the light of day. As well as Joel's huge number of genre publications, he wrote hundreds of poems. Not every story was completed or published. It seemed a shame that all this should be lost. So I spoke with Peter Coleborn of Alchemy Press, and a good friend of Joel's. My idea was somehow to resurrect the best of the ideas and ask some of Joel's friends to finish them. Peter liked the idea.

Once all the material had been catalogued, Peter and I got together to select the fragments that we thought other writers would be interested in developing. We took the titles to FantasyCon in 2015. Not surprisingly, there was a lot of enthusiasm for the project. Writers in the horror field had a lot of respect for Joel, both for his writing and the for man himself.

One problem we had was that it was sometimes difficult to know if Joel had intended the notes to be a poem or a story.

Another was whether he had written the story, and changed the title. Some remnants had several changes of title until Joel hit on the one that reflected best the story he wanted to tell. They were an important and integral part of what he wrote. Nothing in the final product was insignificant.

One of the things we decided early on was that the proceeds of this volume would go to charity. All the authors have given their time and expertise to this project for free. All profits will be donated to Diabetes UK.

Peter did most of the initial work, liaising with writers interested in contributing, sending them copies of fragments to work with. The response was magnificent. The result is this book. There were a number of themes that recurred in Joel's work. You will find them all here. Some stories have captured the style and atmosphere of his work. Others, while remaining faithful to Joel's ideas, have fashioned something that also allows the writer's personality to show through. He wouldn't have minded that. He was always willing to advise and help other writers. If some of the stories are not rigorously perfect, it doesn't matter. Each one of them has been written as a tribute to a man they regarded as a friend; a friend whose presence is deeply missed.

Pauline E. Dungate
June 2016

JOEL

Chris Morgan

(i)

Up to a point, the world still turns on its axis.
Through the train window I could see floods,
a swan swimming across a field. In London
it was sunny, not cold, an exceptional day
for early February. Around High Wycombe
red kites were soaring and twisting, wing
fingers close and clear, something to brighten
my mood. Birmingham that evening was
still crying, soaking as I walked home from
the station. Two months since you died, went,
bowed out, and belief hasn't caught up yet.
You're gone. No more late night phone calls,
literary and illuminating, both of us laughing
before we finished. No more baltis with you
slipping out to inject insulin between starter
and main, coming back to finish your Diamond
White, discussing the new poems we'd each
brought. Gone but not gone. Twenty-five years
of knowing you has left its marks tattoo'd on
my mind, on my beliefs, just as you have
indelibly marked the world. All those hundreds
of stories and poems. Perceptive articles - not all
of them on the subject of Ramsey Campbell.
A greater intellect than me, than most of us,
carried lightly, never boasting. Helping other
writers, making the world a better place.

(ii)

So, Saint Joel? Not quite. You never know
somebody until they die and you clear out their
house because there's nobody else, and you love them.
Oh, Joel, time-squeezed between a job and a
demanding mother and writing most days. You
never found time to clean your house or sort
the maelstrom of books and paperwork. Your
National Collection of plastic carriers was no
more than an affectation, but why didn't you throw
out the mountains of used train tickets, free papers,
out-of-date leaflets. If you'd alphabetised your
library you'd have noticed the many duplicates.
Perhaps the disorder grew like a Cthulhu creature
with tentacles, too fast and eldritch for you ever
to control it. All those books and CDs and, horror
of horrors, *Buffy* videos you bought and never opened.
This is the essence of the accelerating 21st century.
And yet you read so widely and remembered it, wrote
so prolifically. Not death, then, but immortality. You
were there in every carrier bag I sorted through,
in the choice of each book I checked and boxed. You
were there, listening in the walls. Oh, how I miss you.

The Shadow

... moon ... moonlight
on wall of room in ... (room)
landlord, who reveals it belonged to man w...
his shadow — tall, broad-should...
... (?) that only at a cer...
full moon, landlord stands befor...
... landlord gives hor...
... that of a distorted ...
... window — only shado...
... turns ... 20 ... —

... 2nd year at University
(ON OTHER SIDE)
... station platform
... evening, cool
standing on one side, waiting for
... train ... with me
... flickering & staring (usual g...
... sons — family, friends)
(... boy ... age)
other side — boy sitting alone on
suitcase, hands ... out on
... , looking at the tracks —
pale, near-blond (no-one I knew ... thought I
... quiet ... knew why he
... alone ...

... brighter ... at
least less cluttered — I picked
my suitcase & crossed the
platform, sat beside him — he
looked at me — our hands touched
no-one noticed I had gone —
world behind me didn't exist —
waited, together, for the train
... going ... the opposite
... my planned journey
... but ... lamplight
...

about 1,000 words

WINDOW SHOPPING (?)

character: 20 yr-old man ...
university. Uneasy with hom...
away, familiar/alien. The h...
Highlights fading in his h...
Feels at risk/exposed
but not expecting to be seen ...
his distance. Need for ph...
Maths student ("a ...
another but not to his ...
people in this town. Past ...
when he wanted, chased by ...
Almost always rejected ...
wished he didn't have ...
"almost").
The ...
... next ...

NOT DISPOSSESSED:
A FEW WORDS ON JOEL LANE'S EARLY PUBLISHED WORKS

David A. Sutton

> *'A wonderful, lyrical and relentless story about the horrors of alcoholism. I think this is one of the best Joel has submitted to* Dark Terrors.*'*

WHEN I WAS editing *Dark Terrors: The Gollancz Book of Horror* with Stephen Jones, I kept a database of brief notes on all the shortlisted story submissions. The quote above is the comment I typed immediately after reading Joel's 'The Country of Glass' (published 1998). It's a remarkable piece of fiction and although I don't think it won any awards, it certainly should have. In the late 1990s Joel was creating intensely personal and demanding stories. And it wasn't surprising that *Where Furnaces Burn*, the 2012 PS Publishing collection showcasing more than twenty of Joel's stories, very deservedly won The World Fantasy Award in 2013.

The news about Joel's death in November of that year came as a bombshell. Joel had a great many friends and locally he had been a member of the 'Birmingham Balti Boys' (a loose and ever-evolving crowd of, usually, Midlands based fans who tramp the streets of the Balti Triangle in Birmingham in search of the elusive world's finest balti). The group had met up not too many months before we heard the numbing news about Joel, on one of our balti bashes, and learned from him that his sleep apnoea 'could be problematic'. It was a snippet of personal information that was engulfed, as these things usually are as the evening wore on, by the group's random conversations on the genre, on music, on politics, social issues, and so on. When I heard in an email that he had died in his sleep, Joel's words suddenly mushroomed in my mind as if they had been a grim prophecy. It's hard to accept that Joel, someone fifteen years younger than yourself, should depart this world before you. And that he would no longer be around, no longer offering his help and encouragement, his jokes, his formidable critical insight into the genre. And most particularly, no longer any new weird fiction from his pen...

I WAS THE first editor to publish Joel's genre writing. In the 1980s I was doing a stint as editor of *Dark Horizons* for The British Fantasy Society (six issues from 1981-1985) and in number twenty -four, (winter 1981) I published his poem, 'The Face'. This (and a non-fiction piece in the same issue) was Joel's first genre writing to appear:

Moonlight, stone and earth, and hands like claws
Tearing the prey free from the flimsy shroud.
Hunger, like nausea, forces open jaws
And makes the world seem cold. Death is not proud;
Nor is life peaceful for a starving soul.
But tragic fate answers a prayer too well:
From a grave mined as damned men dig for coal,
A face from heaven greets the face from hell.
The sleeper smiles with uncorrupted bliss,
Taken back whole into the warm earth's keep;
The robber has not heart to steal a kiss,
Nor wit to wake the past from its long sleep.
Dreaming that once the youthful face was his,
Cold though his tears be, even a ghoul can weep.

The essay in the same issue was 'Strange Eons and The Cthulhu Mythos', ably illustrated by Dave Carson. The article evaluated Robert Bloch's novel as one of a rare breed of fictions that brings 'in the macabre field a cosmology adopted purely from Lovecraft's original concepts':

> *The 'Cthuluoid' fiction of Robert E. Howard, Clark Ashton Smith and Frank Belknap Long has nothing in common with Lovecraft's Cthulhu Mythos tales save the general complexion of the style and a few eldritch names. Many such stories ... are tacitly accepted, for the flimsiest of reasons, as belonging to the Mythos; while many minor Mythos stories merely quote from the mass of Mythos lore in order to lend a spurious stamp of authority to an otherwise unremarkable concept. Thus while the list of Mythos tales stretches into infinity, an average scattering of particular stories seem to have little in common.*

As associate editor of *Fantasy Tales*, I accepted another poem, 'The Worm' in mid-1981 and at about the same time I took his acrostic, 'Book of the Dead', (obviously Alhazred's deadly tome!). 'The Worm' was published in issue eleven, in the winter of 1982. 'Book of the Dead' was left languishing a bit, and was finally published in *Fantasy Tales* issue fifteen, winter 1985.

For issue twenty-six of *Dark Horizons*, spring 1983, I brought out another piece of verse, 'Invocation', nicely illustrated by Alan Hunter. In issue twenty-seven, summer 1984, I included 'Absence'. In *Dark Horizons* twenty-eight, spring 1985, there was another poem, 'Climacteric', accompanied by a very nifty Allen Koszowski illustration.

JOEL'S FIRST PUBLISHED weird fiction short story was 'The God of Clay', which was among the contents of *Dark Horizons* issue twenty-seven. In my editorial I said, 'The God of Clay' is an evocative and surreal fantasy from Joel Lane, who I am increasingly finding is a writer of great depth and passion'. From the opening paragraph of this story, the reader is thrust into a relentless LSD trip of colour and sensations. This fantasy world seems eons distant from Joel's later work, but his fluid use of language and the dreamlike, lyrical passages evoke horror and loss, the sublime and the surreal. More E.R. Eddison and Clark Ashton Smith than Arthur Machen or M.R. James:

> *The evening sky was a hearth in which the diffuse flames of the sun's aura spread, crimson-hearted and azure-tipped, above the huddled coals of the earth. It shimmered and shifted wilfully, emitting clusters of whirling sparks like premature stars to trace illegible symbols across the already bleared scrolls of cloud. The smoke of the sun was darkening the world.*

This awareness of Joel's burgeoning writing talent on my part was in evidence because of course I had already been reading other stories submitted from his pen. I took 'The Soldier at the Gate' (a collaboration with Laurence Westwood) for *Fantasy Tales* in September of 1982. Unluckily the story never made its appearance in the magazine – I wonder what happened to this yarn? It does not appear to have been published elsewhere.

'Irene's Garden', another story I snapped up, this for the BFS, appeared in the spring 1985 issue of *Dark Horizons.* And by now Joel's writing was much more restrained. He was on his way to finding his literary voice. The story concerns the friend of a now-deceased fellow writer who strikes up a relationship with his widow and is invited to peer into the strange garden viewed from her window:

> *The creature was of my own height, but stooped, concealing a greater size. The body was abnormally thin and angular; the arms must have been very long, for the hands twisted on the ground like a piece of waste paper in the wind. I cannot recall the features with any clarity; they were not ugly, but terrifyingly strange, being masklike and rigid; the eyes were large, red-glowing and extremely beautiful, like a dog's; and the wide mouth held no apparent teeth. I reached out my left hand toward the glass, and the creature extended its left hand – at which I took a clumsy step backward, shook my head and blinked repeatedly.*

On 30th October 1983 I was immensely pleased to place Joel's 'The Dispossessed' in the *Fantasy Tales* files. At the time of acceptance the publication was still a small press magazine, Stephen Jones' editorial design and layout evoking the pulp era, in particular *Weird Tales.* But it took a while for us to use 'The Dispossessed' and it finally emerged in issue two of the paperback editions from Robinson Publishing, *six* years later, in 1989, with Dave Carson providing a full page illustration. The more nuanced urban horror that Joel has become famed for found expression in 'The Dispossessed'. The plot concerns Mark, living in a bed and breakfast in a northern town for his work away from home (I think Joel was staying in Macclesfield at the time he wrote the story). Here he is haunted by a woman he calls Marian and is infuriated with his landlord, Mr Snell's conspiracy theories and the political views that stem from them:

> *'The world is corrupt,' said Snell in a flat voice. 'The flesh of lies is dripping off the empty skulls of the spiders, the money-spinners. They have an old alien way of power, but our power of the white flame is older; and it will triumph. Out of the decaying cultures the hunger of the white flame will grow and consume the dead wood.' He sounded as if he were trying to chant, without rhythm. 'But I won't say any more. You won't see until your own eyes change.'*

Another of Joel's early tales that took some time to see the light of day (unfortunately this was always a problem with the publishing schedule of *Fantasy Tales*) was 'And Make Me Whole', which I placed on file on the 11th November 1988. It appeared after the magazine folded, in *The Anthology of Fantasy and the Supernatural* (Tiger Books 1994). This anthology provided an opportunity for us to collect and finally publish a backlog of accepted stories that had been left high and dry in the *FT* files.

Urban decay and a feeling of intense alienation feed the horror Joel creates in 'And Make Me Whole'. The title is from a line in Hazel O'Connor's song 'Will You'. The story concerns James' brittle and failing relationship with Adrian, who lives in his dead parents' house, where he was abused as a child, in a run-down area of Birmingham:

> *Generations of neglect had reduced the Victorian houses to awkward hulks... The narrow windows were smeared with dust, over whitish curtains that were obviously left shut. The window-frames were split and warped. An overgrown privet hedge, interwoven with the brambles and weeds it enclosed, walled off the front garden from the street.*

The story of the breakdown of the characters' relationship and Adrian's actual breakdown, and their final night in the house, leads the reader inexorably into the extreme horror revealed in the final paragraphs of the story. And Joel very effectively heralds the awfulness to come without giving anything away when he has Adrian say:

> *'This house is full of hiding places. I'm filling it up with things that remind me of the past. Or express things in myself that were never realised. When I finally move out I want to be clean and whole. I want this house to keep all the ugly and crippled parts of myself. But to do that, I need first to bring them out of hiding.'*

When Steve Jones invited me in the late 1990s onto the editorial team for *Dark Terrors: The Gollancz Book of Horror* (a direct sequel to *Dark Voices: The Pan Book of Horror Stories*, which Pan had axed after five volumes), it became a natural outlet for Joel's fiction. I wish we could have used more of his output, but in volume four in 1998 we published 'The Country of Glass'. Joel Lane's stories were by this time appearing widely. About this tale he said, '[it] owes something to the influences of Fritz Leiber and M. John Harrison', both authors Joel cited as major influences along with Robert Aickman and Ramsey Campbell, when interviewed by Brian J. Showers in *All Hallows*, the journal of The Ghost Story Society, issue forty (October 2005).

For *Dark Terrors* five (2000) Joel provided 'The Bootleg Heart' and in volume six (2002), 'The Receivers'. Joel commented on 'The Receivers', saying '[it] is one of an ongoing series of supernatural crime stories I've been working on for a while.' And, 'they aim to combine traditional weird elements with modern social and political themes'. That same year Joel edited, with Steve Bishop, *Birmingham Noir,* an anthology of crime and psychological suspense stories, for the Tindal Street Press.

As the twenty-first century said hello, I asked Joel if he would care to submit a story for consideration to my anthology *Phantoms of Venice*. Unfortunately he wasn't able to offer a story, but he did the next best thing, he wrote the Foreword, 'A Dream by the Old Canal'. Meticulously he gets to grips with the Janus-faced nature of Venice and reviews those scribes who have penned yarns set in La Serenissima as a taster to the selection of new stories I used in the book.

When Peter Coleborn invited Joel to edit *Beneath the Ground* (2002) for The Alchemy Press, I submitted a story with a suitable theme and it was lovely to hear he had accepted 'The Tomb of the Janissaries' for the anthology. Then later he took 'Zulu's War' for *Never Again: Weird Fiction Against Racism & Fascism* (jointly edited with Allyson Bird for Gray Friar Press, 2010). I'm proud to be among the writers Joel selected as editor.

Poet, writer, critic, anthologist, political activist. I feel certain that had Joel lived a full three score and ten, he would have added so, so much more to the wealth that is our genre. As it stands it is not hard to appreciate the impact his thirty years of writing has already had on weird fiction. I recall him saying he was working on a critical analysis of the genre; I imagined this would be a major study of the field. I wonder if this manuscript is waiting to be uncovered? And what insights it will reveal...

Joel was ever thoughtful. Never hasty to comment or rush to judgement, but incisive and measured in his views of the genre and individual writers. His first collection of weird fiction was *The Earth Wire And Other Stories* (1994), inspiringly published by Nick Royle's Egerton Press. I got my copy signed on 30th September of that year. This is what Joel inscribed:

To Dave –
The first person to publish any of my stories... With thanks for your help & encouragement over the years and with all best wishes from Joel.

In writing this piece I just dug that book out for reference, but was so moved because I had omitted to remember the considerate expression Joel had jotted down on the title page in his neat but squiggly handwriting. I thought that would be the simplest way in this article to convey Joel's generosity of spirit. I am certain that had I not been there at the time to publish his early work, he would have taken the genre by storm anyway. But it was a privilege to have been, in a very small way, a part of Joel's life.

EVERYBODY HATES A TOURIST

Tim Lebbon

AS EMILY HAD suggested, I went to her place first. She'd promised pre-drinks because the club prices were so high, and she'd hinted that a couple of her friends might be there, too. As it turned out it was just her and a tall, quiet guy she introduced as Nathan. He nodded at me and smiled. While Emily mixed drinks in her flat's little kitchen area, Nathan looked me up and down. I caught his eye and he looked away, but he was smirking. I wondered if he was Emily's boyfriend and almost called him out on his ogling. But that would have been no way to act in my new friend's home. It wasn't as if I had so many friends I could afford to throw one away.

'Jenny's just come up from London,' Emily said.

'What're you doing here?' Nathan asked. He slumped down on the sofa and nodded across at a chair. I sat, trying to put myself at ease but feeling more strung out with every moment that passed. I knew this had to change if the evening was going to work out. I had to chill if this whole move was going to be a success.

'Just having a break away from the big city,' I said.

'So Birmingham's not a big city?' He grinned, though, before I could protest. I didn't think he'd really taken offence. His smile was open and welcoming, and I decided I'd give him a second chance. It was what I was asking of life, after all.

'Jenny started at the hospital last Monday,' Emily said.

'Nurse?' Nathan asked.

'Admin.'

He grunted.

'Mojitos!' Emily said. She carried three cocktail glasses through without spilling a drop and placed them on the table between us. She dropped down next to Nathan and kissed him on the cheek. I envied her natural grace and casual beauty, but chided myself. It was way too early to start forming jealousies.

'Administration,' Nathan said, stretching the word out. He and Emily picked up their glasses and I followed suit.

'To your new life,' she said, raising her glass to me. Her boyfriend copied her.

I wanted to protest. It was hardly a new life I'd come here to find, just a calmer extension of the old one. I still had my brother and mother back in London, and the friends I'd made and left behind for a little while, and none of that would change. This was a journey, not a destination, but they were already drinking. I raised my own glass and sipped. The alcohol hit my system and warmed, calmed, and within an hour and two more cocktails it brought on a comfortable smile.

Emily was smart and engaging, and her closeness with Nathan was obvious. She put on some music. It was a folk singer I didn't know, music so smooth that his lyrics were almost subliminal. I found myself angry at the government and eager to live my life to the full, and I giggled because I was pissed in a cosy flat with new friends.

They touched a lot, then started to kiss. It was affectionate and playful, not passionate, and I didn't feel embarrassed. He made a couple of faux-angry comments about me stealing his girlfriend away from their regular Friday evening date-night.

'You'll have to just stay in and have a wank,' Emily said, jumping up and away from his grasp.

Nathan sighed heavily and sank back into the sofa. 'At least make me another fucking cocktail.'

'Come and help me choose a dress.' She smiled at me, and for a moment I wondered who she'd been talking to. Then Nathan stood and followed her past the little kitchen and into parts of the flat I had yet to see.

'Five minutes!' Emily called. 'Choose some music if you like.'

I stood and moved around the small living room, checking out the alcove filled with books. There were medical texts, some volumes of poetry, a few second-hand Folio Society volumes, and a shelf of crime novels. I'd read a few of them. Her music came from a soundbar below the TV, an iPod propped next to it, but there was also a rack of vinyl albums. I flicked through them, smiling when I saw some old nineties albums that my brother owned. The furnishing was warm and lived-in, almost familiar. It felt safe. It felt a thousand miles away from what had happened in London.

The current song stopped. I heard a strange sound coming from the hallway past the kitchen area. I held my breath and cocked my head, straining to hear another strangled cry. The silence was heavy, loaded.

My heart beat faster. A flash of violence cut through my comfortable alcoholic haze, red and glaring. The memory touched all my senses and I almost gagged.

Another song began, filling the room with movement. I drifted to the hallway, listening all the time. A door was open on the left, light spilling out. I leaned forward to look through the crack between door and frame.

I saw undulations of naked flesh, lamp-light playing across skin, the jarring, bristled glimpse of pubic hair. Sighs and giggled. The rhythmic, insistent whisper of a mattress being compressed.

I gasped and backed away, legs banging against the living room table. I was an intruder. The strange sexual thrill could not be denied - it had been months since I'd been with a man - but neither could I deny this deep sense of being a stranger.

I'd come here from London to try and *stop* being a stranger.

By the time Emily emerged a few minutes later, looking beautiful in a dark blue dress and subtle make-up, I'd had another large drink and was well on my way to being pissed.

'Let's hit the town!' she said, offering me a high-five. I reciprocated. I didn't see Nathan again until later.

I HADN'T SEEN Emily for a couple of years. We'd worked together for a while back in London, but we'd never been close. Passing in corridors and smiling, occasional chats at the coffee machine – that had been the extent of our communication. We'd certainly never been friends. On my first day in my new job we'd met again, and I'd felt a rush of relief that she was there, even gratitude. More so when she invited me out on this, my first weekend in a new city.

'So where are your friends?' I asked. We were walking towards the city centre, passing pubs bulging with people who'd soon be following us in towards the clubs.

'Friends?' she asked, frowning.

'You said some of your friends might be at your flat.'

'Oh, yeah. 'Spect we'll meet them at the club.'

'Which club are we going to?'

'Bad Mac's.'

'Oh.'

'Chill, Jenny!' she said. 'It's a great place. Friendly, safe, I know loads of people there. I'll introduce you. You'll like them.'

I smiled but couldn't help thinking she was almost issuing orders. I remembered that about her from London. Those few times we'd chatted properly back there, she'd spoken in certainties. What Emily says, goes.

The streets were dark and warm and busier the closer we got to the centre of town. I welcomed the alcoholic buzz and the way it relaxed me, putting a distance between me and the surroundings. I knew that if I'd walked through here sober I'd have found the atmosphere threatening, but now the shouts and laughs, the rowdy, singing groups, and the occasional screams, were merely the results of people having fun.

Emily paid for me to get into the club and once inside I shouted into her ear that I'd get us drinks. She nodded. Music blared and boomed, and she had to lean in close to reply.

'I'll be over there!' She pointed vaguely towards the back of the club. 'I'll be with...' She said some more but the words were lost to me. Perhaps because they were names I didn't know.

Before she left she took my hand and squeezed, an intimate gesture that surprised me. I went to squeeze back but she'd already let go, weaving her way between bodies, disappearing in a sea of flashing lights and dancing shadows. I felt a moment of unaccountable panic watching her go. It was as if she'd left me somewhere dangerous and I'd never see her again.

A group close to me started jumping up and down when a new song came on. They were all smiling, men and women alike. They were happy. One of the men caught my eye and grinned. By the time I'd smiled back, he was looking elsewhere.

I made my way to the bar. The club was dark and noisy, the music pounding so hard that it pulsed in my chest and bones, rippling across my skin. Emily seemed to like the place but it reminded me of any number of anonymous subterranean clubs I'd visited in London. The people crushed in at the bar in the same way, smelled the same, exuded a similar desperate need to get pissed as quickly as possible. A woman forced her way back through the throng, carrying several bottles of brightly coloured fluid. A hand reached out from somewhere and pawed at her breast. I gasped in shock. She grinned.

Part of me wanted to leave there and then. What was I doing here? Why was I here with people I didn't even know? Was this really the way to move on from what I'd left back in London? I closed my eyes but that made the music even louder. The heat was oppressive and slick. I thought of Emily and Nathan screwing before we left her flat, and wondered whether they'd been worried that I'd see or hear them. For some, being found out might have been an added thrill but I was suddenly certain that they'd not considered me at all.

I tried to turn, struggling against the push towards the bar, forcing my way past blank-faced people who couldn't understand why I'd leave without a drink. They all seemed to be glaring at me as if I was an alien believing itself human, or a human so lost that I was acting alien.

I resolved to find Emily and tell her I had to go.

Once out of the bar crush, I headed around the club. The large dance floor was in the centre, with tables and seating areas set around it on various raised areas and nooks. Multi-coloured lights flashed and swung but none of them could properly penetrate the shadows. I felt even more drunk than before. Dizzy. Was I already on my second circuit? I looked for Emily but couldn't find her. When I reached the bar area I started around the club again. This time I searched more carefully, trying to think past the alcohol fug. One large seating area extended back into the shadows past the end of the bar. I might have missed it the first time, so I stumbled in, passing tables laden with empty bottles and glasses and surrounded by people who were all starting to look the same. A few of them offered me smiles that fell away when they realised I wasn't who they thought. More often it was a dull stare – and I feared it mirrored my own.

I saw several others who appeared to be on their own; they weren't people I wanted to be with.

I couldn't find Emily. I kept searching, and a sense of urgency bit through my drunken state. My third time back at the bar, I wondered whether she'd got tired of waiting for drinks and started queuing herself.

A new style of music pulsed in, laden with bass and drums that seemed to surround my heart and manipulate it in a vibrating fist. Soon my heart was beating in time with the music. I coughed, one hand flat against my chest.

I can't go in there again, I thought, looking at the mass of people pressed against the bar. They seemed to be moving now, throbbing like some giant sea creature splashed with coloured lights of its own making. Naked limbs writhed like countless tentacles. Hands caressed and gripped black-clad torsos, alien starfish searching across the bodyscape.

I had no idea how long I'd been looking for Emily – it felt like hours – but it struck me then that I could leave without even telling her. She wouldn't care. She'd probably not even notice that I'd gone, just as she'd barely noticed I was at her flat while she was fucking Nathan in the next room.

Fighting against the flow of music and the weight of lasers and lights, I found my way eventually out into the street. Night was no more welcoming. The music of sirens broke the darkness, and the flashing lights out there were mostly blue.

I WAS LOST even before I started walking so it couldn't get any worse. I stayed on the main street. A dozen dark alleys tried to lure me in but I resisted their silent promises. I stepped in a splash of vomit and almost slipped. Three young men argued outside a burger bar, immature shoves never quite descending into a proper fight. A couple snogged in a recessed shop doorway, her bare arm catching the streetlight as she jerked him off.

The sirens continued singing from elsewhere. Blue lights were reflected from higher windows. I caught them from the corner of my eye, never actually seeing one. It was as if whatever tragedy was unfolding sought to keep itself from me.

I pulled out my phone and realised that I knew no one in the city. Emily and I had not swapped numbers. I tried to check out a news app but I had no reception.

'Did you hear?' a girl said as she ran past me. She was holding her shoes in one hand, feet slapping against the pavement.

'Hear what?' I asked. She ran on without replying.

'What's happening?' I asked a group of teenagers. Too old to stay at home, too young to get served in the pubs and clubs, they cuddled half-empty cider bottles and averted catching my eye. 'Hey!' I said. 'What's happening?'

'Dunno,' one kid said.

'Sounded like a bomb,' one of the girls said.

'Really?' I asked.

'Or Godzilla,' a lad said, laughing. He was so drunk he could hardly stand. 'Or, like ... a Transformer.'

I left them and walked faster. The main street ended in a wide square, and I aimed for that, hoping to find more people who knew what was happening.

'Hey!'

I spun around and Nathan was there. He dashed across the

street towards me and I felt a brief moment of panic.

'What's happened?' I asked.

'A bomb at the hospital.'

'A bomb?'

'Where's Emily?'

'A bomb at the hospital?'

'Where's Emily?' He held my arms and squeezed, and I realised that he was terrified.

'I ... don't know.'

'You came out with her! Where is she? I can't find her.'

'Maybe she went to the hospital to help,' I said, thinking that I should be doing the same. I was surprised I hadn't been called in but then I remembered I had no phone signal. Everyone was trying to call everyone else.

'No, she's not there,' he said. 'Been there.'

'What's it like?' I asked, but he was already looking away, letting go of me and turning to head off. I grabbed his arm.

'Nathan! I'll go with you. I was lost, and –'

'No,' he said, soft and quiet. He meant it. He ran away from me, disregarding me as if I'd never even been there at all. For a moment I thought of running after him, but then he was gone. I didn't know this place or these people. There was no way I could follow.

Instead, I continued to the end of the wide main street and sat in the square. Surrounded by shops, pubs and fast food outlets, it should have been busier. There were a few other people there, but they all seemed to be like me - alone, confused, silent. I guessed that we were all visitors.

What was happening in the city felt a very long way away from me.

MUCH LATER, WHEN dawn burned above the buildings in the east, I found my way to the hospital. I entered its grounds through a gate that should not have been open, approaching some of the buildings from behind. I could see no signs of damage, but on the air was the unmistakeable acrid tang of fire. Smoke hazed the air above and beyond some of the taller buildings. Many lights were on. Policemen patrolled the grounds, some of them carrying machineguns and others holding dogs.

Two of them saw me and came my way. A man and a woman, both carrying guns, both grim-faced. I held my shoes in my hand and knew that I looked out of place.

'Who are you?' the woman them asked.

'Jenny.'

'What are you doing here?'

'I work here.'

'Doesn't look like you do.'

'I was out, haven't had a chance to go home, but I thought I should—'

'Get the hell away, Jenny,' the man said. 'You don't belong here.'

I could have argued, protested, tried to convey the truth. Instead, I left the hospital grounds and heading back out onto the streets. It felt very much like a strange city and I wondered if the policeman had meant just the hospital grounds.

Sometimes, I wonder if I belong anywhere.

He's always on the edge of

– the crowd on the side
b/w stop-motion film
disco (silent film
juxtaposed)

I don't know why he
that / unless it's the
of his expression
making him seem
... dependent ...

THE CONSCIENCE OF THE CIRCUIT

Nicholas Royle

WHEN MARK MORRIS called in November 2013 to tell me the terrible news, I was waiting for a train on a freezing cold station platform. But for the setting (Godalming, Surrey), I could have been a character in one of Joel Lane's stories, many of which featured trains and railway stations, and death was never far away. (Though, for some reason, telephones featured rarely, mobiles hardly at all.) I couldn't take it in.

A huge crowd braved gales and torrential rain to get to Robin Hood Crematorium, between Shirley and Solihull, on the outskirts of Birmingham to attend Joel's funeral on 23rd December. We hugged and shook hands and slapped each other on the back, and we smiled and even laughed and shared reminiscences and jokes. We listened to moving tributes from Chris Morgan, Poet Laureate of Birmingham, and Joel's brother Tom. I also said a few words. Perhaps we met people we had never met before, people we had heard of from Joel and always wondered about but never met. A great deal of good feeling and comfort was given and received, but, there was no denying, a new and very large hole had been torn in our lives and we were all a little bit diminished by it.

That night in Birmingham, my girlfriend and I searched the streets of Moseley for a balti house. I tried to find one of the places Joel had taken me to in the past. We entered somewhere. I wasn't sure about it; it didn't look the same. I wanted to ask Joel if this was the place. The following morning I saw the bold new Library of Birmingham for the first time. I liked it, but I wanted to ask Joel what he thought. Anything to do with Birmingham, I would always think of Joel. But Joel was more than just my link to the West Midlands and, particularly, the Black Country. We had been friends and collaborators and/or colleagues for more than twenty years. We had each helped the other out of tight spots. We read each other's stories, occasionally published one another. Joel was the most amazing reader, extraordinarily generous with his feedback.

Joel suffered from chronic health problems, but no one had an inkling that his life was in danger. A sudden, unexplained death at a young age (Joel, like me, was born in 1963) presents particular difficulties for family and friends. While you take comfort from the fact that the deceased was spared, for example, a long, slow decline, would never lose his sight (as a result of his diabetes) or his mind (Joel was exceptionally intelligent), you never had a chance to say goodbye. More to the point, *he* never had a chance to say goodbye. We know from his work that he hardly lived in ignorance of mortality, but for him to go to bed one night and simply not wake up in the morning is so bewildering you really do struggle to get your head around it. What the fuck is that about?

I re-read the first story of Joel's I ever read, 'The Foggy, Foggy Dew'. Mark Valentine published it in a chapbook in 1985 and Karl Edward Wagner reprinted it in his excellent series *The Year's Best Horror Stories*. Like many of Joel's most successful stories, it's like a dream, not because it resembles a dream, with dreamlike logic and surreal imagery, but because it is vivid and absorbing and totally believable and when you look back on it you find you can hardly remember it. I'm not suggesting that this was Joel's intention, but I would argue it's a virtue. His best work was subtle and achieved its effects without your being aware of what strings he was pulling. He wasn't sly or underhand, though he did have a sly humour with a great fondness for puns, but much of the work of his stories went on, as it should, behind the scenes.

Sure, he had a roster of favourite words and images – 'smoke', 'ash', 'dust', 'fibres', 'vapour', 'scars', even 'ectoplasm' – at least one of which would turn up in most stories, but it wasn't like he had them written on a Post-it note stuck to his computer. They were just in his head, they were what he saw about him.

Perhaps one word that recurs more than any other, as I've come to appreciate on re-reading as many of his stories as possible, is 'district'. A less evocative word than 'ash', 'vapour' or certainly 'ectoplasm', 'district' nevertheless somehow seems to possess a dark, almost wintry resonance, perhaps because of the subconscious effect of reading it so many times in Joel's stories over the years. There's 'The Lost District', of course, the title story of his 2006 collection published by Night Shade Books (the story was originally published in *The Third Alternative*), but the word crops up again and again. 'Peter and his mother had moved away to another district,' we read in 'The Foggy, Foggy Dew'; in 'The Earth Wire', the title story of his 1994 collection (published by my own Egerton Press), when Geoff goes to look for his parents' house, he finds that, 'In isolated districts, violence between gangs was still escalating'; in 'The Country of Glass', a powerful story about alcoholism, 'Lang revisited the district where he'd grown up'.

Joel wrote about Birmingham and the Black Country, an area slightly to the north-west of the city characterised by a post-industrial landscape that he described and evoked with great potency. He named the districts he wrote about, those in the Black Country and in south Birmingham where he lived in a series of rented properties over the years. Names such as Clayheath, Netherton and Tipton, Acocks Green, Moseley and Yardley Wood, came to acquire great resonance for me. I wanted never to lose myself in Digbeth at night; it probably wouldn't be wise to wander up the Hagley Road, whether after dark or not. His settings were persuasively real, yet his characters sometimes doubted that. 'The landscape itself felt unreal,' finds Geoff in 'The Earth Wire', while Jason in 'Waiting for a Train' has a different but equally alienating experience: 'The landscape was too real for him to pass through it.'

For all the imagery of ash and vapour, the details are solid, nailed down. The industrial part of Handsworth is a 'jigsaw of iron and concrete' ('Coming of Age'); the canal system is 'an endless stony network that led nowhere but onto renewed outgrowths of itself' ('The Earth Wire'). But like Blake and like M. John Harrison, who once remarked to me that Joel was so good he – Harrison – was envious of his talent, Joel was also a visionary. 'The Country of Glass' is a story not only about alcoholism but also about redemption, shot through with amber-hued glimpses of the rumoured land of the title, Vitraea. Matthew Lang starts to half-see 'a kind of wavering or rippling in buildings... Worse, sometimes he'd look along a tree-lined avenue or sunlit canal and see images from his own past clotted with dust and dead leaves, abandoned... The past was not biodegradable.' Lang, German for 'long', is filled with longing; the story, one of Joel's best and most affecting, is basically Harrison's 'Egnaro', with ice and a slice. 'As the afternoon light flickered through trees like a distant candle, Lang walked through the park where he and his brother had played cricket with a tennis ball.' I now read this line somewhat differently since hearing the following words in Joel's brother Tom's moving tribute at the funeral in December: 'I have so many fond memories: going to parks every Sunday and playing football and cricket; playing cricket in the road, the telegraph pole as the wicket...'

In 'The Sunken City', one of the original stories written for his World Fantasy Award-winning collection *Where Furnaces Burn* (PS Publishing, 2012), Joel writes, unusually, about a writer, bravely electing to make him a rather pompous and arrogant character. Corin Ward, arrested on suspicion of murder and attempted murder, declares, 'You have no idea who you're talking to. I'm a man of visions. My soul is as far above that of the herd as it is above the rats and cockroaches in the sewers.'

In 'The Earth Wire', Mark unscrews a plug and shows it to Geoff. 'You know what the middle wire is? The earth wire. Right. The plug can work without it. It's just a safety device. The conscience of the circuit.' *The conscience of the circuit*. Joel's political beliefs and acute sense of justice informed most of what he did. Often, and perhaps most effectively, it was buried in his stories; occasionally it surfaced and became explicit, and with Allyson Bird he co-edited *Never Again* (Gray Friar Press, 2010), an anthology of anti-fascist fiction.

While politics, for Joel, was arguably no laughing matter, he did possess a wonderfully childlike sense of humour that would surface in his work from time to time, not quite as often as in social situations and personal exchanges. His criminal weakness for puns is revealed in the opening to 'Quarantine', another crime story written specially for *Where Furnaces Burn*: 'DC Morgan looked around the bare room. There was nothing new to see, in here or outside. "If a killer returns to the scene of the crime," he said, "does that make him a SoC puppet?"' Sometimes the humour gets darker. Assault victim Carl Bradmore in 'Incry': 'Can you hold your breath in your sleep? But it'll be over soon. Because I'm going downhill. You'd think that was easy in a wheelchair, but it isn't.'

In the absence of a cause of death in the real world, one searches for clues in Joel's fictional one. That line of Carl Bradmore's – 'Can you hold your breath in your sleep?' – while apparently throwaway must surely refer to the sleep apnoea from which Joel suffered. In the same story, the policeman narrator refers to 'a trapped rage', which he says he felt in the automatic toilet where Carl was beaten up. It's a good description for how it feels to have lost a friend unexpectedly and at far too young an age, while the line about the canal network from 'The Earth Wire' already quoted above would not be a bad metaphor for the thought processes one goes through trying, and failing, to make sense of the loss.

Same-sex relationships are common in Joel's fiction, but they aren't the whole story. He wrote equally insightfully about homosexuals and heterosexuals, men and women, boys and girls – and adolescents and adults, for that matter. 'It wasn't until their third date that the boy asked Richard to behead him' – the opening line to 'The Window' and easily the most arresting opening line to a story I can remember reading. The closing lines of 'You Don't Have to Say', originally published in *The Freezer Counter: Stories by Gay Men* (Third House), occupy similar territory and return us to Joel's fondness for wordplay: 'He stood up and pressed against me. His hands pulled at my ribs. "Neil. Neil." So I did. Wishing there was some way I could swallow his energy and spit out his unreason.' For some inexplicable reason, during the editing process at Third House, 'So I did' was changed to 'So I said it', which destroyed the joke and rendered the ending of the story incomprehensible. (Joel also wrote the most terrifying ending to a short story I've ever read, in 'Face Down', collected in *The Terrible Changes* published by Ex Occidente Press in 2009.) But perhaps my favourite passage of Joel's about men and women and the difference between them is this one from 'The First Time': 'By his mid-twenties, Gordon had all but given up on relationships. Men were like suits of armour: bright containers of darkness. Enclosed and choked by their own defences... Women were more human.' *Bright containers of darkness... Women were more human.* One wonders how revealing Joel meant those lines to be.

I was fortunate enough to publish his story 'Black Country' in my Nightjar Press series in 2010. This story, conceived as a companion piece to 'The Lost District', was reprinted in *Where Furnaces Burn*, which, while not including either his story with my favourite opening line, or his story with my favourite ending, or his story that might be my favourite of all his stories, 'The Country of Glass', feels as if it might end up being my favourite of his collections. It's a grower and a keeper (they're all keepers, let's face it). His stories don't often make me cry, but 'Without a Mind' (another of the half-dozen previously unpublished stories in *Where Furnaces Burn*) did and still does now, more so now, in fact, having acquired extra uncanny freight and poignancy. It begins:

None of this was an investigation. It was personal. Though I first became aware of it when talking with the Coroner at the Law Courts about suspicious deaths. He said that people sometimes died for no reason. In the past year, for example, there'd been a cluster of sudden deaths in South Birmingham from previously undiagnosed diseases. 'Sudden organ failure – the heart, the kidney, the liver. No obvious risk factors, no environmental cause. Maybe it's a new trend they'll find a reason for in a few years' time. At the moment the only medical verdict is that shit happens.'

I remember when the collection was still just a vague idea. Joel was writing the stories over a period of years and he would talk about them as his 'weird police stories'. I wondered if he meant they were weird stories about the police or stories about weird police. For a long time I thought he meant the latter, and I read them, one by one, as he wrote them and sent them to me, thinking, *When is this policeman going to start getting weird?* but of course he meant the former. His unnamed policeman narrator is not at all weird, but very ordinary, quite normal. He displays empathy and compassion. He is vulnerable and battle-scarred. It's the oldest mistake in the book, of course, to assume too close a link between author and narrator, but still.

Another profoundly affecting story now rendered even more powerful is 'The Only Game', first published in *The Lost District*. It's another one with a great opening line – 'On the last morning in February, Jean died again' – but it also contains the following words, with which Jean seeks to comfort the narrator after the death of his father: 'Other people are part of us. Missing them shows that we're still connected to them, we still need them. It's the love we need to hold onto. The life, not the death.'

Joel Lane – the writer, the man, a son, a brother and a friend – continues to be greatly missed.

(A version of this first appeared in *Black Static*, 2014)

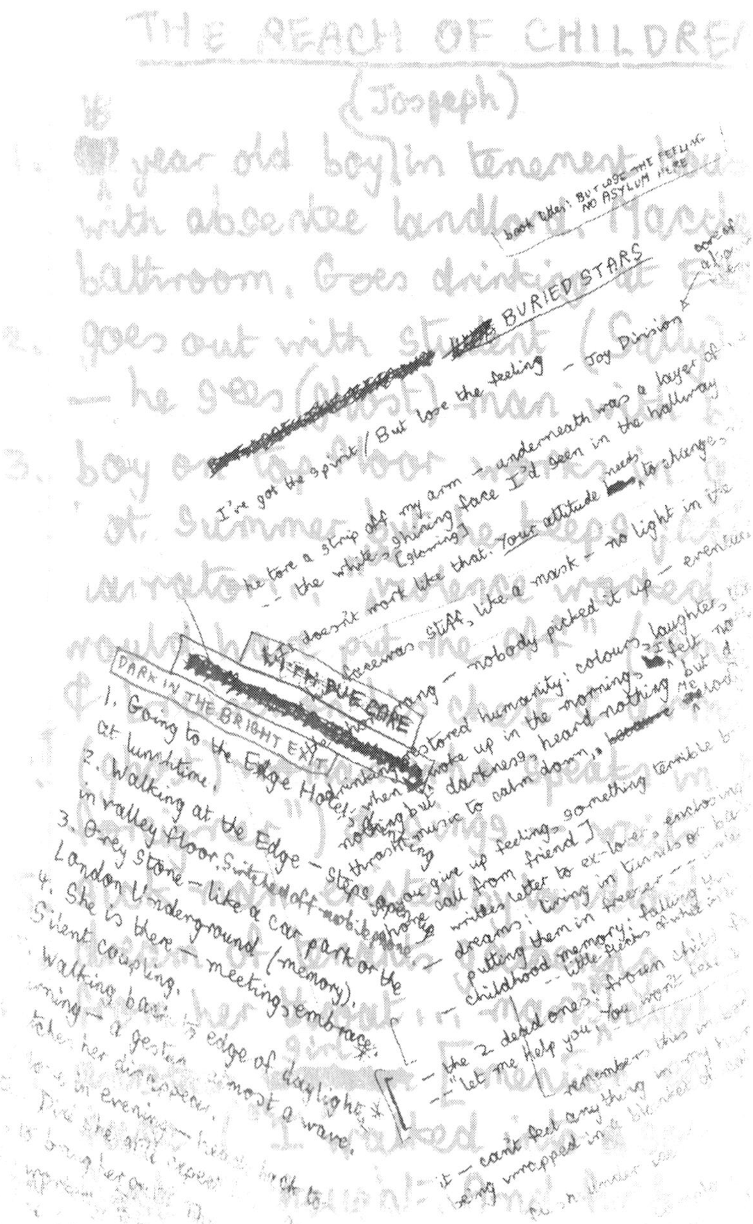

THE REACH OF CHILDREN

(Joseph)

1. year old boy in tenement ... with absentee landlord. ... bathroom. Goes drinking at ...

2. goes out with student (Sally) — he goes (lost) man with ...

3. boy on ... floor ... at Summer ...

book title: BUT LOSE THE FEELING / NO ASYLUM HERE

BURIED STARS

I've got the spirit / But lose the feeling — Joy Division

he tore a strip off my arm — underneath was a layer of ...

— the white shining face I'd seen in the hallway [glowing]

doesn't work like that. Your attitude needs to change ...

face was stiff, like a mask — no light in the ...

... rang — nobody picked it up — eventu...

... stored humanity: colours, laughter ...

... when I woke up in the morning, I felt no...

nothing but darkness, heard nothing but ...

thrashing music to calm down, ... something terrible ...

you give up feeling, something terrible ...

call from friend]

writes letter to ex-lover, enclosing ...

dreams: living in tunnels or ...

putting them in freezer ...

childhood memory: falling ...

— little flecks of white ...

frozen child ...

— the 2 dead ones

— "let me help you" — "You won't ..."

remembers this ...

— can't feel anything ...

being wrapped in a blanket of ...

DARK IN THE BRIGHT EXIT

1. Going to the Edge Hotel at lunchtime.
2. Walking at the Edge — Steps ... in valley floor, Switched off mobile phone.
3. Grey Stone — like a car park or the London Underground (memory).
4. She is there — meeting, embrace. Silent coupling.

Walking back ... edge of daylight *

...ning — a gesture almost a wave.

THE MISSING

John Llewellyn Probert

SOMETIMES IT TAKES more than losing something to make you realise how much you valued it. Sometimes it has to be returned to you broken.

That's how I feel about my memories now. The doctors, nurses, cognitive and behavioural therapists, all of them had done their best during the three months I was a patient in the unit, but they couldn't put everything back. And I'm not even sure the parts they could restore are in the right order. The only reason I know how long I was in hospital was because the admission and discharge dates were on the letter they gave me to pass on to my GP.

Cerebral trauma, the summary began. *Patient found in an unconscious state at the bottom of a flight of stairs. CT head revealed depressed skull fracture and extradural haematoma. Haematoma drained and fracture elevated by neurosurgeons. Transferred from surgical ward to neuro-rehabilitation unit until deemed fit for discharge.*

Fit for discharge.

If that was really true, it was the only thing I was fit for.

The hospital car dropped me off at my flat. I must have been here recently as part of the hospital's social rehabilitation package but my intermittent memory couldn't remember any of that now. What bothered me, though, was not so much that I couldn't remember where I lived…

It was that I was convinced I lived somewhere else.

'This your road, then?' The driver was a nice guy. He'd told me on the trip over that he did a lot of this kind of volunteer work. It made him feel he was making a difference, helping people get back on their feet again.

I stared up at the two-storey row of terraced housing and the dark alleyway beyond which, according to the sign, lay Flat No 47A.

'I think so,' I said. It did seem vaguely familiar. 'Compton Street.'

The driver frowned. 'No mate, this is Stanhope Street.'

So that was it. I relaxed. 'That's one street over from mine.'

'You mean Chapel Road?'

No, I didn't. 'That's one street over the other way. Compton Street's between the two.'

'It's not, you know.' The driver's pleasant demeanour never faltered. He was probably used to dealing with patients - with people - like me. 'Chapel Road and Stanhope Street are right next to each other. Always have been - as far as I can remember.'

As far as he could remember was going to be better than I could. And yet I was sure I had lived on Compton Street.

That alleyway did look familiar, though. At least I thought it did.

'You want me to come in with you?'

'Yes please. If you don't mind.' There was still the chance it could lead to someone else's house. I didn't want to be left, lost and alone, in a part of the city I should have known well but only seemed to be able to remember poorly at best.

'No problem.'

About half way along the alley on the left, set into an otherwise sheer wall of damply weathered red brick, was a door. I didn't expect my key to fit but it did. The lock mechanism ground against itself as if it didn't want to let me in, but finally it relented.

There were stairs leading up but they were wrong, I was sure of it. My flat was on the ground floor and accessed by a door to the right.

By a door that should have been to the right.

Nothing there.

'Something wrong?'

The only way was up, so I might as well find out where it led. 'No. No, I'm fine.'

And so it was that I found myself in my first floor flat. Now, finally, I at least remembered the layout of the single room. The tiny kitchenette on the far side, the bed to the left, beneath the tiny window that looked out onto the narrow street. The books and papers and films that covered every available inch of floor space.

'This all your stuff, then?'

Well it had to be, didn't it? 'Yes.' I picked up the magazine lying on the battered bedside cabinet. *Cinefantastique* volume ten number five, a special issue featuring Alan Jones' exhaustive, career-spanning profile of British horror film director Nick Laurence. Laurence's grinning, frizzy-haired, bespectacled face was the centrepiece of the issue's cover painting. Around him leered the bizarre monsters and lethal contraptions of his many movie creations.

'You don't sound too sure.'

I was now. Much more so, at least. I picked up a pile of photographs from the stained plywood coffee table. Front of house stills for films with titles such as *Born to be Dead, Rope Burns, The Missing.*

The Missing...

'Film fan, are you?'

I nodded and held up a still from *Darkness, Awaken!* 'Ever seen any of his movies?'

'Who?'

I tapped the name at the bottom. 'Nick Laurence. British, you know.'

'Never heard of him. But then, I don't go in for all that stuff. Gangster films, they'll do me. Them and anything with that Keira Knightley in it. Horror's not my thing.'

'Of course.'

The driver touched me on the shoulder and I flinched. 'Look, you seem a bit ... weird. Are you all right for me to leave you now?'

No, please don't. 'Yes that's fine.'

I don't remember him leaving. Maybe he was never there. Maybe he's something else I made up, or remembered wrongly. Like my street name, like which floor my flat was supposed to be on.

Like so many other things.

Between the bed and the scratched Formica of the kitchenette fittings was squeezed my tiny desk, on top of which sat my even more ancient computer. I switched it on and waited. The internet is a wonderful thing but when the device you are trying to view it on is more than ten years old it requires a little patience. I needed some form of company and as my flat seemed to be lacking a television set (stolen? pawned? never bought in the first place?) a flickering screen on which I could type would have to do.

A search for 'Compton Street' followed by the name of this city brought up no results. Fair enough, I thought. I must have imagined the name for some reason. I tried my address, 'Stanhope Street', the city name and hit the search key, just to confirm.

No results.

Perhaps the search function was having a bad day, if such a thing was possible.

Okay, let's give it something easier.

I typed in the name of this city.

No results.

Definitely a bad day. Cardiff, forty miles south, was still there. Worcester, forty miles north was still there also.

So why not this place? Why not the city where I lived?

I scratched my head, my fingertips running over the tiny bumps on my scalp where the rows of stitches had been taken out. They didn't hurt any more but they still felt strange from time to time, gnawing at my skull as I tried to sleep or if I tried to think too hard.

Like I was doing now.

I switched the computer off. That was what you were supposed to do, wasn't it? Switch it off and on again to make it work?

It could stay off for now. I'd read instead. That issue of *Cinefantastique* would do. When I had entered the flat the memory of researching the films of Nick Laurence had hit me like a blast of warm air but now it was all too swiftly receding, like tissue paper tossed on the wind, always just out of reach. Perhaps the magazine would help to solidify the memory and even bring others back.

The pages were blank.

How does that even happen? And why, if they were, had I left the magazine splayed open, cover uppermost, ten pages in? Had it been my fury at being cheated of the contents of a rare magazine that had led to me storming out and then stumbling my way down the stairs in a near-fatal death plunge?

Surely not.

My gaze strayed to the stills on the coffee table. I hadn't noticed it before but they had obviously suffered the effects of being left out in the sun, causing the colours to fade.

I shuffled through the bleached photographs. The images depicted destitute and broken people clawing their way through a blasted land, monstrous creatures emerging from well-to-do country houses, bandaged children being forced into the gutter by towering grey machines that appeared to be breaking apart the surface of the roads upon which their outsized wheels of brutal steel travelled. None of them stirred any memories within me.

I flipped to the bottom of the pile. The final three stills were blank, and the few just before them so faded I could barely make out what they showed. The rest showed pictures of ruin similar to the ones I had already looked at. Images of the desperate and the disenfranchised, of hopelessness in the face of overwhelming, crushing defeat by creatures and machines vast and incomprehensible in their inhumanity.

I had no memory of any of them.

Had I actually watched any of the films these stills had been taken from? My gaze shifted to the shelves above my desk, the ones crammed with books and DVD cases. Did those black plastic boxes contain the potential to replenish lost memory?

I took one down at random. The sleeve was white. The care with which the title had been written in black ink was almost childlike. Tiny blots showed where the pen had rested on the paper a moment too long during the careful transcription, allowing the ink to saturate the paper. Was this my handwriting?

The Missing.

The title caused a tremor of misery somewhere at the back of my mind. Faint, but enough to make me hesitate from opening the case. Had I seen this? Had it disturbed me so badly that even now my subconscious was attempting to stop me from watching it a second time?

I was about to reach up and take down an alternative but the warning not to do so was even stronger, as if to say, if The Missing was disturbing the others were strictly a no-go area.

But I had to know. Of course I did. Was this what had led to my injury, to the loss of my memories? Had the final act of my old life been to binge watch the movies of Nick Laurence, and in doing so I had ended up so traumatised that, drunk on imagery, disturbed by subtext, disorientated by metaphor, I had sustained the injury that had led to those little bumps on my skull?

The DVD case was open, the silver disc gleaming in the waning evening light.

There was no label. Just more of the meticulously neat handwriting. Title, director, and a date. Date of production? Date of watching? It didn't actually matter and yet somehow it did, if only because I couldn't remember why that information was there.

I had no television, no DVD player.

The computer, then. Even if the outside world did not wish to lend its information to the ancient printed circuits within, perhaps the disc player might work?

The machine hummed as it booted up once more and my mind hummed as I suppressed the subconscious desire to throw the DVD away. As the desktop assembled itself out of the corner of my eye I saw the issue of *Cinefantastique* I had tossed aside. The cover was now blank as well, the painting of Nick Laurence and his movies less than a faded memory. All that remained of it was what I possessed within my unreliable mind.

The evening had grown darker and with it had come a sense of claustrophobic consequence. The walls were closer, the ceiling lower. It was too dim now to see the pictures on the coffee table. Either that or they, too, had faded away altogether. My sweating fingertips threatened to drop the disc. I knew that if I did it would have vanished before it touched the threadbare carpet. I pushed it at the slot in the machine. The disc was accepted with a dull electronic grinding that reminded me of how the lock on the front door had tried to stop me coming in here in the first place.

The screen flickered. The room darkened of its own accord once more. Was it trying to help me concentrate on the screen? Or was it more concerned with further obscuring the things I felt should be familiar to me but still refused to be so?

Black screen.

Title: white letters on black.

The Missing.

Black screen again.

I sat there and waited for something to appear. Some image that I might remember. It was only after I had sat looking at my own reflection in the blank darkness for what seemed like hours that I realised that was the whole point.

weaving / tapestry loom

THREADBARE — notes

Helen, ~~[illegible]~~ weaving / tapestry artist & ...

Tracey, singer, computer operator

1) Helen & client (Tarot reading)
2) embroidery – faces
3) Helen & Tracey
4) two clients with threadbare faces
5) Helen & Michael – argument over ...
6) uses her own hair to embroider ...
7) hands shaking – loom rusty – pulls ...
   – in café, faces coming apart
8) back with Tracey, feels her own sk...
   a series of horizontal threads – th...
   interwove – you had to start somew...

Superstition is a loose thread in the fab...
— ~~not authorised by faith~~
belonged to an unauthorised bit of faith

CHARMED LIFE

Simon Avery

THE WINDOW WAS full of light. For a moment it blinded him but beyond the light he could tell there was only darkness.

Michael got out of bed slowly and pulled on his robe. His body ached. He felt ancient. The antipsychotics they'd prescribed for him left his limbs stiff with jittery tension. Now he moved like a man with Parkinson's. The trade-off was a chance at change, whatever that meant. The fog of the past few years had lifted gradually since he'd been detained here, but with that new found clarity was the comprehension of the damage he'd done to himself and to David. It was another side-effect that he wasn't entirely able to accept with any comfort.

The floor was cold under his bare feet. He could usually hear the assorted moans and cries for help from the other patients at the Tamarind Centre after lights out, but when Michael reached the window, he realised with a chill that there was only silence. He felt abandoned for a moment. He gripped the window sill for proof that the world still existed.

The view from the window offered no comfort. Beyond the glass there was no longer the familiar sight of the bland garden, nor the lights from the traffic shivering through the rain on Yardley Green Road. Michael felt a jolt of vertigo. It was as if the world was tilting away from him again. That loss of control frightened him more than he could admit to himself, much less the counsellors here.

The sketchy charcoal figures looked like burnt dolls, moving with the rigidity of insomniacs through a devastated city. It wasn't Birmingham anymore. It couldn't be. It looked like bombs had fallen. Like fires had ravaged the streets and buildings for weeks until there were only ruins. It reminded him of pictures he'd seen of Dresden, or Hiroshima. Or Aleppo. But the people were what unnerved him the most. They were marching in loose formation past the shattered black frames of buildings, beneath twisted trees and over ashen ground, beneath a starless sky. Like refugees. They were a river of souls. He could smell the smoke and sulphur. It was in his lungs already. He couldn't look away. When Michael extended a hand to the window the surface was pliant. The scene seemed to gather and coalesce at his fingers, like oil on water. He withdrew and it was gone. There was the garden again, the frosted benches, the streetlights and traffic. He heard a patient weeping quietly in the next room.

Michael returned to the bed and lay shivering in the dark. The memory of the view of the city was burned on his retinas like light. It was everywhere he looked. When he closed his eyes he saw the burned figures, the ruined city. How could he sleep after that? When he turned on his side he heard a sigh of pain, and he opened his eyes. There was a man in the corner of the room. He smelled of smoke and sulphur. His clothes were no more than rags. His face was burned almost black. Michael jolted up in bed but the alarm quickly subsided with the realisation that this was no stranger. He recognised his own eyes peering out of the devastation. It was *his* face. But he was a shadow as much as a reflection. Michael tried to move but he was dimly aware that fear had made him piss the bed. The man with his face touched his bare shoulder, leaned down and kissed him with his ruined lips. Then he turned and left the room.

In the dark, Michael's blood was a shadow. There were shallow cuts where the man had laid his mouth and fingers.

BRUISES HAD APPEARED across Michael's body the following morning. They looked like a map of a city forming beneath his skin. He decided not to mention them to the doctor. It might hinder his chances of leaving today if they thought he was self-harming. It also felt like a secret he had to keep for himself and the stranger. That moment of intimacy seemed to suggest more than he could comprehend yet.

'How are you feeling about getting back to the real world today?' the doctor asked him.

'Fine,' Michael said. 'Good actually. Really good.'

'And how do you feel about what happened to bring you here?'

He was only dimly aware of that night, almost two months ago now. He remembered the police arresting him and then being detained in Acocks Green police station. Later he was sequestered at a hospital while they scrutinised him and waited for a psychiatric evaluation to happen. Finally they'd assigned him to a psychiatric unit where he'd been detained under Section 3 of the Mental Health Act. Most of that was blur. Something had broken inside him that he sensed he could no longer fix with booze or drugs or sex. He'd lost the ability to be numbed by those things. They just felt like crawling across broken glass.

He'd thought about David a lot in the subsequent forty-eight days, about the damage he'd done to him in their flat that night. David hadn't brought charges against him but had moved out the flat once he'd been released from the hospital. The injuries Michael had inflicted upon David had healed but the relationship was a lost cause. *Like polishing brass on the Titanic,* Michael thought. The only subsequent contact from the outside world was a solitary visit from Michael's brother, who'd signed the papers to refer him to the Tamarind Centre in Bordesley Green. It was a medium secure facility providing assessment, treatment and rehabilitation for men who'd been assessed as needing care. He'd been resistant at first but then the antipsychotics had begun to work to a degree. The therapy sessions broke down a wall he hadn't been aware was there. He'd wept in front of this doctor more than once. He'd come to comprehend the perpetuating cycle of violence, and the wrong turns, poor judgement and subsequent fractured relationships. There was a fault line in his life, stemming from an abusive father in his childhood, that consequently splintered through every relationship he'd ever had. Everything after his detainment had been about discovering that crack in his life and finding a way to seal it up.

He answered the doctor's questions, glancing at the window, at the light fluttering at its edges. Then he signed the papers and he was a free man again.

THE DAY WAS cold and brittle but too bright for him. The air smelled of bonfires. His lack of sleep made everything seem like the ghost of what the world had been before his life collapsed. It shivered between the houses and the trees, and beneath the fallen leaves, waiting for him to succumb. Michael caught the bus home, clutching a holdall that contained his clothes and toiletries. Nothing was the same, but everything was. He couldn't look anyone in the eye. They all seemed to know what he'd done. The fault line might heal and scar but the shame was like an open wound. This, he supposed, was the uncertain quality of freedom.

His flat in Acocks Green was frozen like a painting in that last moment of violence, but it had been robbed of its subject. David was long gone. He'd removed his possessions and slipped quietly away, leaving behind the broken records, the shattered table and TV, his blood on the walls. By now he could be a mile away or a thousand.

Michael sat with a photograph of them in better days. It stung him that David had chosen to leave behind all of the photos but he wasn't surprised. His new life elsewhere would have no memory of the man who'd treated him so cruelly. The picture had been taken in Brighton, where the impulse to kiss or to hold hands could be indulged without fear of recrimination. You couldn't do that in Acocks Green. It was full of young men leading dogs like weapons through the estates.

He put on The Cure's *Disintegration* and indulged himself in misery for a while. Going through the motions before he put his new methods into action. He stared at David's pale, haunted face until tears blurred his vision. It was only now that he realised how much he'd loved him. He tried to lose himself in good memories from their time together but the room and the ghost of violence meant he could barely cling to them for shame.

Later he arranged his medication on a shelf and cleaned the flat, emptied all the wine and spirits down the sink. He wrote David a long letter, admitting to a lifetime of wrong turns and poor decisions. He didn't expect anything. There was nowhere to send it anyway. It was, his doctor had told him, a means to an end.

MICHAEL WENT OUT into the city centre a couple of nights later. Staying in was making him maudlin. He had no one left to speak to out here in the real world. Intense relationships were fine when you were in the eye of the storm but it was often to the detriment of friends and family. When it was over, sometimes there was no one left to console you. He'd burned his bridges before that. Violent men only had space for violent friends or victims. He wanted to go somewhere where the music might jolt him out of his mood like an electrical charge.

He'd had to change shirts twice when he'd found fresh cuts across his stomach and back. The blood looked black in the light of the bathroom. He washed them and applied Savlon. The bruise had spread too, around his entire left side. He'd touched it tenderly and thought of the window and the blackened stranger with his eyes. He wondered where he had gone. He hoped he was okay.

The Jester had been part of his coming out when he'd met David at the age of nineteen. But now he felt too old to do anything more than window shop. Later he drifted through the Nightingale and left because the music was shit, and he was feeling the dangerous urge to get drunk. Drinking had once been a means to an end too. He skirted the Basement and Subway City, hovering on the fringe, sipping water, and trying to remember when his next dose of medication was due. He ended up at a converted warehouse beneath the railway arches in Digbeth. The teenagers were all on speed, jittering from the dance floor to the darkest corners where they seemed to be searching each other for clues as to who they could be tomorrow. You could be changed by someone new, which was fine as long as you could find your way back to yourself afterwards. There was light everywhere. Light on the dance floor, light in the eyes of the slender boys at the bar, light in their mouths and their laughter. Light in their youth, in their endless energy. It made Michael feel lost, like another species. The industrial techno was like a deep throb in the foundations of the buildings. You could feel it in your blood if you wanted to. Or perhaps it was the chilled vodka he suddenly realised was in his hand. It felt like an old friend on his lips, warming his chest and kindling a fire in his belly.

There were too many old faces here for him to really let go of himself. People he knew. They gave him a wide berth, knowing what he was capable of. He realised he was searching for David but knew he'd left this scene behind years ago – the rough trade and the proto-queens and the sallow-faced youths with bruised eyes and tight jeans. Coming back here seemed crucial in some way to Michael. You had to face up to your mistakes before you could put them behind you. The aching past. Once he'd believed he'd lived a charmed life. Once, when there didn't seem to be anything to regret. But no one wanted to know about his shame or hear his apologies. He felt a sudden, vacant rage grip him. Its ferocity scared him. He'd spent the last two months learning to repress that anger.

Then, across the shivering sea of bodies, he caught sight of himself. After a moment's hesitation, Michael drained the vodka and followed his ruined face out of the building. Recognising himself felt like vertigo. All he could do was fall towards himself. The face was no longer burned. His skin simply seemed like it had been scalded by boiling water. It was red and raw and yet he seemed utterly indifferent to the attention his appearance drew. Michael pushed his way through the unyielding mass of bodies.

By the time he was outside, his shirt was clinging to the sweat and leaking wounds across his back. The cold air was like the kiss of life breathed directly into his lungs. There were others outside; kids shivering under the railway arches, either smoking dope or trying to find their way into another body under the cover of shadows.

Michael followed nothing more than a shadow past the empty factories, the boarded over pubs and salvage yards of Digbeth. He felt a wave of disorientation pass through him. Perhaps it was the vodka, or that he'd forgotten to take his medication. Everything seemed to be in sharp focus. His limbs were stiff. He couldn't walk properly on the frozen ground. He stumbled down the back streets, past clusters of derelict buildings. The encroaching winter made the city feel old again, the way it had been before empty investment and progress had transformed it into something he hardly recognised anymore. Perhaps he shouldn't resist that change. Succumbing to it needn't be a sign of limitation. Winter claimed some of the city's soul back. Out here in the cold and dark, he felt like he was chasing his.

As if reading his mind, his doppelganger led him down below street level and onto the canal towpath. Michael had walked home with David this way before but it had never been this dark. The canal was a blank space, only reflecting the graffiti on the underside of the bridges, or the shattered glass of windows on the backs of empty factories. His jittery footsteps were amplified down here. He'd lost sight of himself. He heard distant traffic from the ring road, far above him. The stars were gone. The wind was scratching flakes of sleet out of the darkness. It looked like ash. He felt adrift.

A man's voice sounded nearby. Others joined in. Michael thought they were singing a hymn but the song grew ragged and declined into a terrace chant. The breath froze on Michael's lips. He went rigid with fear.

'*Michael,*' the man said finally. The other voices petered out. There were four of them. He recognised the ringleader. Michael had bought bags of pills, coke or weed from him on a semi-regular basis. Exchanges of folded bank notes and little packets passed from closed fists in small car parks. Burgess had a grey, angular face, jagged little teeth, and a short, brittle manner. 'Michael,' he said. 'You still *owe* me.'

Michael held up his hands. 'I was put away,' he said. 'I've been out of action for the last couple of months. I don't have any money.'

Burgess pushed him up against a wall. The breath went out of him. 'Not good enough. Try again.' His voice rose and fell. His pupils were dilated. He pressed himself against Michael. He could feel Burgess's stiff cock against his leg, against his own. It was all he could think about. The sly arousal of violence. He dimly recalled that sensation. It was like a light going on in a distant room. A cycle that he'd never be able to break free from.

Fibres of rain were spread out against the soft glow of the streetlights on the expressway above them. Michael could smell alcohol and bile on Burgess's breath. There was still only one way to respond. 'Fuck you,' he said.

The first blow doubled him over and shocked the breath from his lungs. Burgess forced him upright, turned him around and drove him into the wall, once, twice, three times. He relinquished him finally and Michael fell to the towpath. The lights were shimmering like static on the still water of the canal. He could smell ashes and dead fires on the breeze. It came up out of the depths of the past. How far did you have to run to outdistance it?

The blood was warm on his face. He tried to curl into a ball. But Burgess and the others began kicking him. It took too long for him to lose consciousness.

HE WOKE ON an iron frame bed. The mattress was stained but Michael couldn't decide if it was his own blood or someone else's. When he attempted to sit up a wave of pain crashed through him. Yet there were no wounds on his body or on his face. But there were scars. Deep pronounced scars. He could feel them under his fingers. A map of pain. Increasingly it seemed like the sum total of his worth.

He had no memory of being delivered here. It looked at first glance to be a hostel but, as his eyes adjusted to the gloom, Michael began to see the others in beds around him. Charred and petrified bodies on bare iron frame beds. There was blood smeared across the corridor walls. Michael rose and moved through them quickly, his mind a forgiving blank.

He passed a small chapel whose roof was missing. The stars were gone too. A tilted cross and chunks of masonry hanging from the girders. The shattered glass beneath his feet crackled loudly in the stillness of the ruins. There were no signs of life.

Outside the wind was like static in his ears. The trees were empty and bent, black fingers scratching at the burning sky. There were cinders floating in the dark, ash falling soporifically like snow. Tattered flags were whipping in the stiff breeze.

Michael heard them before he saw them. The sound of marching feet - an empty, ragged sound. They were a black river of bodies, charred people travelling like the displaced. Refugees. But he sensed that this march had gone on for eternity, that it was like a videotape on loop. It was a migration to and from nowhere. Voices rose and fell in the confusion of static. Michael watched them pass. Some of them glanced his way, but whatever it was they saw in him wasn't alien enough to warrant a second glance, which frightened him more than anything else. They were too consumed by their own torment.

They weren't the dead, he realised then. They were the living. They were him and his friends, his family, his lovers, strangers he passed by on the street, burdened by lifetimes of guilt, grief, shame, deceit, lies, violence, disease. They were grieving, walking from one point to the next, never returning, never arriving. The tears stung his eyes. Then the wind rose and the folds of white noise seemed to envelope erasing him from the city.

THEN THERE WERE hands gathering him up. A warmth he felt duty bound to cling to. When Michael opened his eyes, the face that greeted his was a face he'd abandoned to memory a long time ago; a face he'd only find in photographs, ten years old or more. They were still on the canal towpath. There was blood in his eyes and his body felt as fragile as china. He realised he was clutching the other man's hands and relinquished them. He could hear his own jagged breath.

'Burgess has gone,' the other man said. His accent was broader than he'd imagined. It wasn't what he heard in his head, only on recordings. 'I can take you home.'

'Do you know the way?'

'Of course.' It made a sad kind of sense to Michael. *He* didn't know the way home anymore.

'Who are you?' Michael asked as he put his arm around the other man and they made their way along the Grand Union Canal. Into the suburbs.

The other man laughed. 'You can call me Jon if this confuses you. But I'd prefer you call me Michael.' His face was pale and drawn but unblemished. He'd healed in a matter of days. His eyes gave very little away.

'Why do you look like me?'

'You know why.'

It was four a.m. when they arrived at Michael's flat in Acocks Green. The streets were still. Frozen. The only sign of life was a fox bolting across a side road and disappearing into the shadows. Michael felt ashamed of the blood stains that remained on the wall in his living room. He'd intended to buy some paint, but he hadn't gotten around to it. Jon helped Michael onto the sofa and lit the gas fire. He dressed his wounds, made some tea and then leafed through his vinyl collection, selecting *Hard Shadows*, a Triangle album that had belonged to David. Raw guitars, echoes and feedback, a cold voice that always seemed to know him.

The half-silvered window
That means I can't see you
The pane you watch me through
The pain you keep me in
The frozen point of view.

Michael found himself telling Jon about David. He had tears in his eyes more than once. Jon sat on the floor beside the sofa and touched away the tears with his fingertips. When he'd exorcised himself of his memories, Michael glanced out of the window and saw light fluttering at its edges as the night gave way to another day. He felt empty, yet filled up to the brim with something he couldn't describe. All the sadness was gone. And the guilt and the grief. The withdrawal and the pills and the therapy had only been the first step. This was the last. He stared at the stranger's face, knowing he wasn't a stranger at all. Not anymore.

'Christ,' he whispered. 'I don't think I was ever this beautiful.'

'Bed,' Jon said, smiling, and eased him off the sofa and turned off the lights. He gently took off his clothes for him. Michael caught sight of himself in the mirror. The bruise covered most of his body now, the scars making patterns of intersecting paths across the purple and black skin. It was a map of his life. He couldn't see himself anymore, but he saw himself perfectly. Jon pulled him gently beneath the covers and kissed him in a haze of fatigue and desire. Michael held him tightly then slipped beneath him, let him take the lead. He knew exactly what he needed but still it was difficult. Every move they made drew blood. They cut each other with their lips, their hands, their cocks. The blood flowed and then healed, scabbed and scarred over. Bleeding and healing, bleeding and healing. It was like sleeping with someone made of shattered glass.

When Michael woke later that morning, he was dead. He was little more than a charred body, lying beside him.

He spent the day becoming accustomed to his new life. He went out and bought groceries. He bought paint and decorated over David's blood on the wall. He called his brother and made tentative inroads with him. Perhaps one day he'd track David down and do whatever he could to make amends. There was time enough for that.

When it was dark, Michael gathered up Michael's remains and took him out into the little garden behind the flats and buried him in a shallow grave. Tomorrow there would nothing left of him. Afterwards, he returned inside and fell asleep. He woke in the night and glanced around, still uncertain of his new surroundings. He felt afraid. The window was full of darkness. But beyond the dark, there was light. Acknowledging that was easy. Believing it was something else entirely.

ANTITHESIS
(SOMETHING OTHER)

(MOMENTS)

Fantasy / ideal ingrained in
everyday life. At critical
moments (turning points).
Calm, determined eyes; a
strong opening hand; a
shadow falling on me;
arms holding me from behind.
Looking in ~~for~~ strange faces, as
into a well...

YOU GIVE ME FEVER

...e drove her mad – later, her
...became his reality — wint...
...gradient of cold — wooden...

"Not a child, no. More
sick animal, a sick do...
and pissing over the c...
trying to fuck a duffe...
call it a child."

...e could see the cold: di...
the air, black lines movi...

"After his father died,
...

...ot mine. It alwy...

if you try to remove people's armou...

suit of armour outside shop.

I NEED SOMEWHERE TO HI...

comic-book mentalities: mo...

emphasis — text falling on...

"What do they know of Engl...
know?"

a baby crusted in rock

clean-shaven, cropped, per...

"It shows I'm in compl...

ANTITHESIS

Alison Littlewood

I HAD NO idea what had made me come here. The streets on this side of town were wet and badly lit, strewn with garbage the council had long since given up on collecting. Its occupants weren't much better, mindless drones going from job to pub to – well, this place. The Night Side it was called, in a flash of something that was almost poetic. The interior was anything but. Its shell of black-painted walls was scratched to let the old white shine through; strobe lights echoed the chest-deep *duff-duff-duff* of the bass. Blank faces, eyes closed, waved their hands in the air at the command of the DJ. There was a smell of beer old and new, a tacky floor and tackier chat-up lines. By the end of the night a little huddle of blokes by the door would try to scoop up whatever flesh was left over, though we hadn't reached that stage yet.

I pushed between tight-pressed bodies, their faces becoming silhouettes as the spotlights turned. The Night Side played a mishmash of tracks that was never quite up to date, though we had always liked them, since we were never quite up to date either. As I went farther in I recognised the one they were playing, one of Alex's favourites, and as if it had conjured him, I saw him across the room.

For a moment I couldn't breathe. Of course I'd known he used to come here but I somehow hadn't expected that he'd come back again, not since we split. I'd stayed away for months. The idea that he hadn't, that it didn't even trouble him, was like a fist in the gut. *Bastard.*

Lights sprayed his face, highlighting his smooth skin and neat features. He was always the better looking one of us. He took care of himself, cared enough to bother, unlike me. I could never even be arsed to shave. He used to laugh at me for that. Mostly, I liked it, the way he just laughed things off, never really taking them seriously, not letting them get to him. The pain of it now surprised me, though it was subsumed by the coldness of regret. I reminded myself that it was me who'd pushed him away, not the other way round, but it wasn't until now that I realised why. It was because he was better than me, always had been, and a part of me had always known it, even if it had been unconscious knowledge.

It still didn't stop me from wanting him. His warmth, his beauty, even his mocking laughter. And it could be better, couldn't it? *I* could be better.

I started across the dance floor, forgetting about getting a drink. I dodged between flailing arms and elbows and darkened faces, seeing only Alex standing there not focused on anything at all. Then the lights blazed out and everything changed. The girl nearest to me turned. There was something wrong with her face. Her features were normal enough for the Night Side, clownishly matte with makeup, her eyes black with eyeliner, her lips red. She looked like all the other girls in here but I knew at once she was *not* like them. I could see something in her eyes – or rather, behind them – and I flinched away and saw the lad next to her, his chin riddled with acne, and his eyes, they were wrong, just *wrong*. I didn't know why or how I knew, but the hairs on my neck and arms were prickling. Something was in here with us. I couldn't understand what it was and I couldn't name it. I only felt it was something I should never have experienced, that nobody was meant to experience. Something *other*.

I looked from face to face, seeing the same damned thing; that something-and-nothing I could feel but not really take in behind all of their eyes. The spotlights moved on and the beat began again and it all rushed back, the Night Side, the people, just as they were and always had been. I didn't know if they had changed or if I had. I couldn't see Alex and assumed that he had left.

I pushed back through the crowd, taking a blow that sent me staggering. I started to shove people aside, ignoring their cries of protest. I reached the corridor and caught a glimpse - only the back of his head but I knew it was Alex - I could see the little patch at the nape of his neck where the hair wouldn't grow, the place I'd used to kiss - and then I saw the arm around his waist and stopped dead. He was with a slightly-built guy, the way he liked them. Not like me. The man's arm tightened about Alex, squeezing his waist as they left together and I heard the drift of his laughter as they went out into the dark.

I stared after them. Everything was normal and yet it wasn't. It wasn't so much anything I'd seen as what I'd felt, as if I'd just been scorched by the embers of some kind of truth, albeit one that couldn't be put into words. The everyday faces around me had, for a moment, become beautiful. It wasn't their features, the cast of a cheek or chin; it was more as if the ordinary had been transfigured, as if something had shone through them, momentarily, from another world. And yet their eyes... I shuddered as I stepped back onto the street. It came as a relief to see it was empty now; Alex and his new friend had gone.

Guardian angels, I said to myself as I walked away with my head down, pulling my coat tighter. Whatever had happened, it had done me a favour. Alex hadn't been good for me. I hadn't liked who I became when I was around him. Yes, they must have been some kind of guardians. After all, they had just saved me from making a huge mistake.

DESPITE WHAT I'D told myself in the club - despite the *faces* - a few days later I was still dwelling on Alex. I think that's what had led me to the canal when I'd decided to go for a walk. It couldn't have been the scenery, the backs of factories with their rotting, graffiti covered brickwork. We'd come here together sometimes, and now I had no better purpose than to torment myself with the memory of him.

I half expected to see him as I had in the club but there was only a couple ahead of me on the towpath, probably in their thirties but acting younger. His tongue was down her throat, his hand on her arse. He saw me looking as he surfaced and his expression turned sour. He leaned aside and spat. She turned to glare too as I went nearer. I didn't care, just kept on going, and it took me a moment to realise that someone else was there. It was a woman, her hair dyed purplish-red and tied in a twist. She was sitting on a bench that was set back a little from the path and staring into the water – at least until she turned and saw me.

It happened again. There was *something*, not seen but sensed, blazing behind her eyes, and yet her expression remained calm. There was nothing about her that was special but for a moment everything was, and I was frozen by it. There was a presence here with us, the antithesis of this place, these people, these times. I opened my mouth to take in a breath and somehow couldn't get any air.

I was drowning. I could taste the canal. Its slimy, rank water slipped down my throat. I spun away from her, all of it, and suddenly the pressure was released. My lungs worked, gasping in the dank air as if it was purity itself. I stumbled back the way I'd come, finding it strange that my clothes and hair were completely dry. I only looked round once I'd reached the steps leading off the canal bank. The red-haired woman was still sitting on her bench. I could just see her feet, twitching to some tune in her head, and I somehow knew that whatever had visited me there was gone.

The man beyond her was still glaring at me, his girlfriend too, her arms crossed across her sagging chest. His mouth opened and the word formed – *fag* – and I saw that his hand was curled around something. A rock? I couldn't tell and didn't want to know. I headed away. All I felt was some kind of loss. There was nothing extraordinary, now, about the day. Grey clouds closed in over the grey streets, shutting in the damp and the faint smell of rot. Still, what remained to me – again – was a sense of relief. I somehow knew that something had been averted; that something had intervened.

IT WASN'T LONG before I came to a decision. I still didn't know what the hell it was I'd seen but it didn't matter; an element of it had stayed with me, seeping into my system and beneath the skin. I was changing, becoming something new - I hoped something better - and I was ready to move on. I was heading into the city, to stay a couple of nights with a friend. I wanted to sit back from it all, take stock of my life, and after that I might even leave for good. The moments I'd experienced felt like glimpses of hope, little threads of gold that were only visible because the sun had broken through. I wondered if they had been trying to make me happy in some way. I'd always thought that wasn't something I was designed to be, but now I wasn't so sure. I'd seen something different; maybe I could be different too.

I lowered my rucksack to the station's gritty platform, realising only then that the past wasn't about to let go so easily. The place was all but abandoned - few trains stopped here now - but, somehow, Alex was there. He was with his new boyfriend and their arms were linked, their thumbs tucked into each other's jeans pockets. That, more than anything else, made me angry. It was something I'd used to do.

Alex glanced around and his eyes narrowed. I caught the dark implacability of his stare, the one that always said more than his words ever could. His other half whispered something in his ear and Alex's lips twisted into a contemptuous smile. I had seen that smile before, many times, and I hated it. A sudden memory rose: of the day we broke up, the day I wiped it off.

I looked down at my hands, at the faint trace of scar tissue lacing the knuckles. It had faded more quickly than the memory of Alex's nose splitting under them. I formed a fist, squeezing tight, and for a moment I almost saw blood dripping to the cracked asphalt.

I closed my eyes, forcing myself to think of the faces I'd seen, the privilege I'd been granted, the fact that they'd somehow lifted me, set me apart. I took deep breaths, telling myself that I was a better person without Alex.

I started as a train swept through the station, an express

service joining places that were more important than this. There was something wrong with the faces I glimpsed through the windows.

It was there again, that sense of something ordinary but beautiful. This time, all of their eyes were the same - dark, blankly shining, like peering into a deep well and catching sight of black water below. They opened their mouths as if they were screaming along with the shriek of the train, and then there were only windows. And it was gone.

I turned and looked at Alex. His back was turned but his new boyfriend was watching me with a steady glare, his chin resting on Alex's shoulder. I couldn't look away. Molten anger stirred inside me. Didn't they know what I'd seen? Hadn't they felt it at all? Those things had looked upon me - *me* - and now this arsehole thought he could stare at me like that.

I stepped towards him. A shadow had fallen across me and its coldness had taken hold. I had a brief sensation of hands on my arms, trying to hold me back, but the rage had risen again like an old friend and I threw them off, dimly registering that there was no one there, couldn't be anybody there.

It didn't even matter. When everything else passed, the rage remained. That was what happened and it would always happen because that was who I was, who I'd always been.

Alex tried to pull his friend away, calling out, but I ignored him and I swung my fist into the new guy's well-shaven face. The last vestiges of the vision I'd seen evaporated. I was myself again, free to do what I wanted at last, and I did. I felt his cheekbone crack under my fist. I pushed Alex back, punching his friend in the solar plexus and kneeing him in the ribs when he doubled up.

I lost it for a while. When I came to I was shoving the man's face into the asphalt, rubbing it from side to side to erase whatever remained. Alex, somewhere behind me, was making odd, high-pitched sounds. His boyfriend wasn't. He wasn't making any kind of sound at all.

For a moment I couldn't focus and then a discarded crisp packet skittered down the platform. I realised that a breeze was rising; the rushing in my ears was the sound of a train.

I stared at the back of the lad's head, wondering what his face had become. Would it be different now? Something other – the opposite? I didn't want to see, didn't need to. I knew what I'd done. Everything was sharply delineated, as if I'd awoken and was seeing clearly for the first time in my life. Perhaps I was. I'd never had a guardian angel. How could I? What had possessed me to think I had? Those things – they hadn't come for me. They weren't trying to protect me. They were trying to stop me. It was the others they'd been trying to protect and I was the thing they had to protect them from.

Except they hadn't, had they? I closed my fist and blood dripped to the cracked asphalt. I'd had a chance to turn from this, to change, to be different. Those brief moments had been a gift of a kind, even if they did not belong to me, but I'd failed to seize a single one of them.

The train was squealing and shrieking to a halt. Alex shrieked too, calling out for help. I didn't look around but I imagined the faces in the windows, the same look of horror that would be on all of them, their eyes glassy and blank. Suddenly I wanted to turn the body over after all, to see its staring eyes and whatever it was they held, but I did not. I knew what it would be. My own reflection staring back at me, the expression on my face something cold and grey and dead.

BROKEN EYE

... with videos
... on Staircase (orgy in dark)
... watched dawn through wire grid in glass
seemed as though darkness still there

Des

... staying with sister & child in tower
... young man in block, stays with
— he collects photos & videos —
... back to her ~~room~~ in the dark
... into couple (group?) making love
on staircase
... back to the man — he is lonely/afraid.
... in morning — drugged teenagers on
balcony
back to room — daylight felt like darkness
(slept for a day & then felt better)

(1) imprisonment — bars, stone, grids — against light
(2) the eye — TV screen — light
(their eyes ate the daylight)
(3) images — compound eye — windows
(broken up into windows)

... idea of freedom.

The ... shows ... domination

is it myopia or
that makes films
... sunlight my favourite
voices more alive ...
I'm not a voyeur, ...
will do ... sand burrow
through to the soil of
... towards me, still in the
... loving heard, being ...

EVERYBODY HATES A TOURIST

DIFFERENT ...
1) couple ...
2) solitary ...
3) girl in ...
4) bomb ...
5) like an alcoholic
don't care ...
6) not sure ...
alien that ...
is human
being so ...
an ...
7) dance ... tourists ...

DARK FURNACES

Chris Morgan

IT WAS ONE of those years when my marriage to Elaine was under pressure. Each of us suspected the other of seeing somebody else. Wrongly, but by the time hindsight delivered sense and clarity to us both, damage had already been done.

Not long after I was promoted to DS, I was briefly seconded to a station in the Black Country - more officers than usual were on sick leave and there was an upsurge of suspicious deaths. Nobody was suggesting a direct connection. It was that time in late February when your memories turn over and open their eyes - you could blame the weather or Valentine's Day. The area was one of the polluted badlands between Brierley Hill and Stourbridge, full of old factories, most derelict. Some had been demolished, some left to collapse under their own weight of memories. No longer were the drop-forges working. No longer was steel strip being rolled and coiled, then chopped up and pressed into small anonymous shapes vital for industry. It was a semi-urban district with no name, no clear centre and no live music.

I'd left our Vauxhall with Elaine and travelled by bus, a long, spiritless journey; there was no Panda car available.

DI Tutt, who I was reporting to, had found a place for me to stay. 'It's nothing much but it's close.' Most landladies won't take police - too much coming and going at unsocial hours.

The room was worse than I could have imagined, with damp patches on the walls, a lumpy bed and problems of access after midnight. It wasn't even close to the office: half an hour's walk through a cheerless late winter that a glazing of frost couldn't make anything but ugly. There were too many locked factory gates, shuttered shops and boarded-up houses.

The investigation was out of the ordinary; I'd already got a name at Acocks Green station for being the one willing to tackle strange cases. This time, young men were dying. At least six in four months. We could have classified them all as suicides and saved ourselves a lot of legwork, but some computer nerd cleverer than Tutt had suggested that crimes were being committed.

Tutt was a skinny and wrinkled old man, arrogant, set in his ways. When I went out with him to talk to relatives of the dead I could see that he was going through the motions, doing sufficient to keep the superintendent off his back and tiptoe his way through to a pension.

After the sister of the third deceased said, 'No, he wasn't depressed, but...' and Tutt failed to press her with a follow-up, I felt I had to do more. It's a feeling that all young policemen have, an idealism that's gradually eroded away by experience and disappointment.

'But what *had* changed?' I asked her.

'No spark,' she said. 'He seemed dead inside.'

I ignored Tutt's sigh of exasperation, kept watching the sister's face. 'How did it happen?'

Her face hardened. 'I blame the girl. Not a regular girlfriend. A one-night stand. I didn't recognise her but I've seen her around since. Goth make-up, small and thin. Baz picked her up in the pub. I was there with a couple of mates, saw them go off together. In the morning he was different. It was like his fire had gone out.'

'How long was this before he took the tablets?'

'Three or four days.'

Back in the car, Tutt said, 'Why are you trying to complicate it? A suicide's a suicide.'

I told him I'd like to go back and ask a few more questions about the others.

'If you must – but you can do it on your own and we can't

spare you a car.'

It took me three days. Yes, I was working long hours. There was little else for me in that god-forsaken bit of the West Midlands except work. I knew nobody within fifteen miles except Tutt and he didn't choose to socialise with me. It was mutual.

By day I spoke to friends and relatives of the six - which became seven the day after I began my solo enquiries. By night I hunted for the Goth girl in local pubs.

Very quickly it became obvious that she was part of the mystery. In addition to Baz Hawkins, three of the others had been seen leaving pubs with her and presumably had sex with her. They had all died within a week of that. Verdicts of suicide had been recorded in the earlier cases. Two, including Baz, had OD'd, one had cut his wrists in a hot bath, one had jumped from the open top floor of a car park. In the other three cases the Goth girl was not mentioned: perhaps it was just a lack of witnesses. I read the autopsy and post mortem reports with some care, searching for hints of disease, for any physical cause. There was nothing. I spoke to the pathologist, who could add no more to what he'd written.

Yet in every case there'd been a mental change, a sudden passivity or lack of interest in home, work, life itself. Some of the seven might perhaps have been suffering from clinical depression (though none were being treated for it), since five were out of work and four had broken up with girlfriends in the previous month or two. Correlation, I had to remind myself, is not the same as cause.

Goth girl had been seen in two or three local pubs. I drank in all of them, purely in the interests of the investigation, of course, though none had a drinkable real ale. I was looking for any signs of her and attempting to get into conversation with regulars, without asking too many questions or looking like a copper. My starting point was trying to find an agreeable place to stay that didn't cost too much and allowed me to come and go at odd hours for my 'shift work'.

There were Goths around, almost always in groups. It very

soon became clear that my quarry was always, initially, alone. Her name might be Sophie. She was small and thin, perhaps anorexic, with facial piercings as well as the excessive eye make-up, black lipstick and a streak of purple or turquoise in her long dark hair. She wasn't on the game. I knew that because I'd spoken to a few of the local prostitutes. They didn't know her; one offered me her basic service free if I fancied it. 'I always like to give the cops a hand.'

At The Green Man I got chatting with a jovial elderly man whom I'd noticed before, sometimes serving, sometimes sitting in a corner near the bar.

'You must be police,' he said.

'Must I?' I'm reluctant to admit it when I'm off duty, though it's not easy to differentiate. Am I ever completely off duty?

'Come on, lad,' he said. 'It takes one to know one.' He was broadly built, bald and fat-necked, limping to favour his left leg. Perhaps sixty, perhaps older: his face was too plump for wrinkles.

'You did your twenty years then bought the pub?' It isn't a rare career combination.

'Yes. Twenty-five. '

We chatted convivially for a while before he said, 'You've been asking about Sophie.'

'You know her, then?' I asked carefully.

'She's been in here. I'm Tom Buckler.'

I told him my name and he nodded as if he knew it anyway. There had to be local networks; he probably knew Tutt. After we'd shaken hands, his enveloping mine, I said, 'You must know what she does.' Not a question.

'I know what I've seen and heard,' he said. He paused and I got the feeling that he was calculating, weighing something up. 'And I know you're looking for digs, better than the dump you're in. There's a spare room here, upstairs, if you want it. As private as you like, with your own staircase and outside door.' He mentioned a weekly rate half what I was paying.

My instincts told me to take it. And I knew I could do with a good night's sleep. But I didn't want to leave The Green Man to fetch my stuff from the B&B a few streets away in case Sophie arrived. 'Okay,' I said. 'Tomorrow –'

'She won't be in tonight. We can both relax. You go and tell Mrs South you're leaving. I'll get the bed made up fresh.'

'You know a lot about Sophie,' I said. And about me, I thought.

'More than you do.' I expected him to laugh, dewlaps rolling and eyes crinkling, as he said that. But he didn't. 'Tomorrow night,' he said. 'You'll see her then.'

THE GREEN MAN'S spare room was even better than I'd hoped: clean, quiet and comfortable with a bathroom and toilet. It had windows overlooking the side passage and rear garden. On a table was a vase of fresh carnations.

After three nights of fitful dozing, I was almost asleep on my feet. You could blame the days of legwork and the three pints of bitter as well. I slept deeply.

I woke briefly at three according to my watch. Sitting on a chair, watching me, was Tom Buckler. There was just enough streetlight edging around the curtains for me to resolve his bulk, only three or four feet away, unless it was part of a dream – the watch-checking and Tom's presence, both.

He said nothing. I said nothing, and I fell asleep to wake refreshed at eight.

At the station, Tutt was in meetings and I was mostly writing reports and checking facts over the phone.

The one time I got to speak to Tutt I told him I was staying at the pub run by Tom Buckler – 'an old friend of yours.'

'No friend of mine,' he said with a sour expression and a tone close to vehemence.

Because nobody wants to have you as a friend, I thought without quite vocalising it.

'Have you cleared up the suicides yet?'

I told him I was hoping to speak to the young woman involved with them all.

He made a sceptical noise and shut himself away in his office.

Perhaps it was just to make it look as if he was working hard on a Friday afternoon, wasn't about to slip off early and didn't expect anybody else to do so, either.

I had no reason to rush away. I was not sure that I was going to find Sophie, despite Tom's confidence. And it made me wonder what the problem was between the two old men.

The pub was already busy when I arrived at 6:30 after a quick and tasteless burger. Sophie wasn't there. I went upstairs to shower and change. At seven she still wasn't there. I ordered a pint and sipped it very slowly, doing my best not to look as if I was an anxious guy hoping his date would turn up. And I really didn't want to get into a conversation with somebody else. It was becoming noisy and smoky. I'd already given up smoking by then and it made me want one – just a single draw.

At about nine I saw her. She was there without warning, might have stepped out of a corner for all I knew. The clothes and make-up were black and there were more shadows about her than you would expect.

I pushed through the crowds and intercepted her. 'Are you on your own tonight?'

She nodded.

'Let me buy you a drink,' I said.

I got her a half, which looked like a pint in her hand, and we leaned against a shelf just wide enough for glasses. The ambient noise made conversation tricky. Also the fact that she was the best part of a foot shorter than me. She said her name was Sophie and she lived – or had lived – fairly close. We talked about music, groups she'd seen. She told me about some stuff she'd done – a term, or it might have been a year, it was difficult to catch everything she was saying – doing art at a college in Wolverhampton, lots of shop work.

Tom was busy serving and chatting at the far end of the bar. He wasn't looking in my direction but I knew he'd seen me get her a drink. There was more to all this than he'd told me. I was in a difficult ethical situation. I didn't want to question her without admitting who I was and what I was doing. It was impossible to talk properly in there.

'Do you want to come outside with me?' was the best I could manage.

We went out, into the alleyway beside the pub. I pushed the door to behind me and looked round to make sure nobody else was there to hear me interview her.

By the time I turned back she'd opened her blouse. No bra. Her breasts were almost flat and both nipples were pierced. I could count her ribs.

'No,' I said, 'that's not what I'm after. I need to ask you some questions. I'm a police officer.' As I fumbled my warrant card out of my wallet I saw her trousers sliding down.

'You can have me,' she said, 'while you ask.' Her pubis was shaven and an intimate piercing glittered.

'Please put your clothes on. I want some information about...' It was a watershed moment. I'd like to have summoned a WPC and a squad car, but this was in the days before mobile phones. Then there was Sophie. She was not my type, being too scrawny by far, and I knew I could be sacked for an affair with a witness or a suspect. But she was intensely desirable, her mouth slightly open, the tongue showing. There was a siren-like quality to her. She had something for me, something precious and unique. I could take her up to my room and nobody would know. Together we could go to places I'd only imagined, experience wonderful... I forced my mind to take a sideways step. Sophie was dangerous and not really cute. All at once I could see why so many of the locals had been drawn to her, and the magic was working on me, too. I had a pretty good idea of what she'd done to them. I'd like to say I thought of Elaine at that moment – but I didn't.

'Please hold me,' she said. 'Let me hold you.'

I felt so desperately sorry for her that I nearly agreed. 'I have to ask you questions about Baz Hawkins, Dylan Lang, Adam Sandars and the others. You know who I mean.'

'Yes.' She'd rearranged her clothes.

'You met them all in pubs?'

'Just this one.'

'And you came outside with each of them?'

'Yes.'

'Do you want to tell me what you did to them – and why?'

For the first time she showed hesitation. It was impossible to read emotion through her mask. After a long pause she whispered, 'I need it. Just ask Tom.'

But I couldn't take her back inside and ask Tom. I told her I would take her to the station for further questioning. When I slipped the handcuffs onto her she didn't struggle. I wondered if her small hands would slide through even the narrowest setting. We walked to the station – it seemed the best way. It took us thirty minutes through thin freezing drizzle. There were no problems.

The duty sergeant was Jeff Kirby, a decent guy who'd taken the trouble to chat to me. I explained only what I needed to, and we got Sophie into a cell. She gave her surname as Smith but she had no ID on her, so it was easier to accept it without fuss.

For an address she mentioned The Green Man. I asked if she was normally there overnight.

'No, I suppose not,' she said. 'Not really. But I have to keep going back – it's Tom Buckler.'

'Oh, God, not him,' said Kirby. He wouldn't say more.

I pressed Sophie for some sort of clarification but it didn't come.

We put her down as no fixed abode.

Back at the desk, out of Sophie's hearing, Kirby asked me, 'Is she connected with all the dark furnaces we've had lately? I know you're looking into them.'

It was a local police term for dead bodies, he explained, rather more apt than usual.

'Perhaps,' I told him.

I walked back to The Green Man, where they were closing up. Tom wasn't visible, wasn't available they told me.

In the morning there was trouble.

When I got to the station I was told that Sophie Smith had disappeared from her cell during the night. No sign of a break-out. No hint of an inside job by Kirby or his overnight deputy. It was inexplicable. Kirby had gone off duty but Sergeant Frohawk was there and had the details, such as they were. Tutt and Furneaux the superintendent weren't in, it being a Saturday.

I said I'd sort it out and trudged back to The Green Man. By now the route was so familiar I could have walked it blindfold; perhaps I should have, the views were so depressing.

Tom Buckler was in his office, up a different flight of stairs. He didn't seem totally surprised by my news. He spun his chair round to face me.

'Why come to me?' he asked.

'You're at the centre of all this. It's your pub she keeps returning to. You know more than you've told me.'

'Maybe.'

'We can't let her roam around, Tom. Somehow she's sucking the life essence out of young men. We don't want more deaths. She said I should ask you. So exactly what do you know about it? Can you stop her?'

'Dear God,' he said, 'mea culpa. I knew you were going to arrest her and I hoped steel bars might hold her. I never meant to...' He was shaking with emotion.

I wasn't sure if he was crying or not. Men - especially coppers - aren't meant to notice other men crying.

I put my hands on his shoulders. Our faces were only a foot apart. 'Will you stop her?'

'You know what you're asking?'

'I think so,' I said. 'You started it. You can finish it.'

I WAS STANDING at the bar on Saturday evening, keeping watch on the door, when she came in, looking exactly the same as the night before. I saw Tom go up to her and escort her out. Perhaps half an hour later he was back, moving a little more deliberately. He sat by the bar. His face had a blank, dazed expression. Something had gone out of him. There was no spark, no fire. One of the bar staff spoke to him and he ignored her.

There wasn't much I could ask - it was obvious what had

happened. I went up to him anyway. 'Tom?'

Gradually his focus returned from some far-away place. He looked at me, said nothing.

'Thanks, Tom.' I tapped him on the shoulder and went up to my room. I wondered what he would do, how much internal strength he might have.

The next day was Sunday. I could have travelled back to Acocks Green to see Elaine. With public transport being even worse on Sundays, I decided not to bother. Instead I phoned her at home, tried several times from different phones before I got her. We chatted. It was something.

I spent most of my day at the station, finishing my report. Of course, it wasn't complete. It said what it had to say. The cluster of suicides was a temporary occurrence, very nearly over. A young woman who might have been a contributory factor had left the area. I hoped I was right. I didn't refer to Sophie by name, and I played down her role.

Fortunately, Jeff Kirby was one of the few staff on Sunday duty, and we agreed to agree that she'd been released without charge. It would save all kinds of trouble. And I asked him again about Tom Buckler.

'There was a scandal a few years back over a missing girl,' said Kirby. 'Buckler could have been disciplined, or even charged, but he resigned, took his pension.'

On Monday, DI Tutt, having glanced at my report, said, 'You should have listened to me. You've been a waste of space this last week. If I want young officers with fancy ideas instead of competence I can find plenty locally. You can go back to Acocks Green.'

There wasn't much I could say.

Fortunately, Sophie never turned up again. Tom did, fished out of the icebound Stourbridge Canal a few days later. I went to his funeral. It was well attended, and plenty went for refreshments at The Green Man after the ceremony. Neither Tutt nor anybody else from the station was there. I thought I noticed extra shadows in a dark corner of the room, but I couldn't be sure.

BROKEN EYE

Gary McMahon

IT WAS THE kind of place where even a prisoner might feel caged. Somewhere you only went to live if you were trying to climb up the economic slope, or had already slipped down the other side.

A squat tower block situated on the outskirts of the city with featureless concrete walls and blind wire-meshed windows. A place of broken dreams and ripped-up promises.

Naomi often wondered what had happened in her life to bring her here. There had been no great fall, no major event to which she could pin blame. Her slide had been slow and gradual; a downward journey she'd barely even noticed until she was standing on the cold walkway outside her sister's flat, trying not to weep.

'Come away from the window. I don't like the gangs to see the lights.' Sally brushed past her and shut the curtains, her face pale and expressionless, her fingers thin and pale as they went about their business. 'You know what it's like out there at night … the bastards are like moths drawn to a flame.' She smiled but it looked out of place, a bad fit on her naturally dour features.

Naomi nodded, clenched her hands into fists to ease the pain in her knuckles, and sat down on the tatty sofa. She massaged her hands, hoping it wasn't a sign of arthritis, the condition from which their mother had suffered before her early death.

Polly was playing with a couple of cheap plastic dolls on the carpet, making them dance. The Child stared at the dolls, calm and focused in a way that her mother rarely was. 'I'm hungry,' she said, without looking up.

'I know, baby.' Sally crossed the room, bending her knees as she passed by her daughter and reaching down to ruffle her long dark hair. 'I'll make you some supper. How about a nice jam sandwich?'

The girl shrugged, glancing up from her play. 'That's all you ever give me for supper.'

Naomi averted her gaze, watching the silent television screen. A solemn-faced newsreader mouthed the latest atrocities or government cuts or crime statistics. Closing her eyes, she wished that she could see something better.

She stood and walked to the living room door, placed one hand on the edge of the door and held her breath for a moment. She needed to escape but there was nowhere to go in the tiny flat. 'I'm going for a walk,' she said.

'I wish you wouldn't.' Sally's voice was small and lacked an echo. She returned from the kitchen holding a plate for her daughter. 'It's night.' She nodded, as if that single statement explained everything.

Naomi opened the door and went out into the cramped hall. 'I know. But I need some air.' The flat was so small they could talk to each other from separate rooms without ever having to raise their voices.

'Don't go off the landing.'

'I won't. Or maybe I will. I might pop downstairs and visit Callum.'

Her sister said nothing. Her silence was enough of a rebuke.

Naomi left the flat and hurried along the external landing, her black pumps making a soft brushing sound against the concrete. She paused at the fire door, then pushed it open and entered the tower block's internal stairwell, hoping the lights were working tonight. The bulb above her head flickered as if in response and she hurried down the stairs to the next level. Holding her breath against the stench of piss, she took the final set of steps two at a time and burst through the door onto the landing below.

She let out her breath and staggered to the railing, looking down at the car park.

A group of kids was hanging around near the roofless brick bin stores. They had with them a couple of mountain bikes, probably stolen, a scooter and a dog on a frayed rope leash. They were smoking vapes and speaking in loud tones, their voices competing with the tinny music coming from the weak speakers of two or three mobile phones. The dog's bark was fractured, as if it were part of the tune.

For a moment she struggled to see the kids as human. They belonged to another species. They were alien to her, unknowable.

She turned away and crossed the walkway, knocked on Callum's door. The wood was old and scarred; it hadn't seen fresh paint in years. The handle had been doused in lighter fuel and set alight by some unknown arsonist, the flames merely discolouring the metal before they burned themselves out.

The door opened slowly and a small, narrow face topped by a short shock of dark hair peered around its edge. 'Oh … hi.'

'Can I come in? It's cold out here.'

The thin face nodded, and then retreated as the door opened wider.

Naomi went inside, shutting the door behind her, following Callum's narrow back along the bare hallway. The carpet was frayed, the wallpaper was faded, but the place was clean and it didn't smell as bad as she imagined a bachelor's flat should.

'I was just in the middle of something,' said Callum as he entered the living room ahead of her.

When she walked into the room she saw videotapes scattered all over the floor, a lot of the cases lying open and some of the videos set aside. Similar videocassette boxes lined the cheap chipboard shelves on the grey walls. Some of them were in boxes with artwork and titles but others were housed in blank cases.

'I'm trying to catalogue them, to keep a record of what I actually have.'

'Wow, that'll take you ages,' she said, staring at the vast collection.

'I've got plenty of that. Time. More than I need, actually.' He grinned. He looked good when he smiled, his face opening up, his eyes sparkling.

'Has anyone ever told you that you're weird?'

'All the fucking time.' He smiled again, and this time she joined him. 'Coffee?'

'I'd love one.'

He went into the kitchen, switching on the light and filling the kettle, making busy noises as he prepared the drinks.

Naomi squatted down and examined a few of the unboxed videos - horror films she'd never heard of, low budget thrillers, odd, banal titles on dried-out stickers peeling away from cold plastic cases.

'Do you even know how many you have?'

'No.' He'd returned with the coffees - both black, no sugar. 'I get new ones every week. People pass them on to me because there isn't a resale market in video tapes. It's all DVD and limited-edition Blu-ray these days. Nobody will touch tape. Nobody except me. You wouldn't believe some of the shit they give me, sometimes without realising what it is and other times on purpose.'

She took one of the cups, sipped the hot coffee. 'Like what?'

'Oh, like homemade porn, CCTV footage, King-of-the-Gipsy street fights ... all kinds of crazy stuff.' Steam wafted gently across his chin from the cup poised at his lips.

'That's a bit scary.'

'Which part?'

'All of it...'

'The porn's the most disturbing. Fat middle-aged couples wobbling their beer-bellies and cellulite in front of a camera when they've had a few too many pints down the club.' He did a fake shudder.

Naomi laughed but deep down inside, somewhere she didn't like to examine too closely, she felt a chill as something small and icy turned over in her stomach.

'You want to see some?'

'Fuck no,' she said. The thing that had turned over inside her sat up, its interest piqued. No matter how much she objected, that part of her was curious to see what Callum was talking about. 'No,' she said again, firmer this time.

Callum shrugged. 'Sit down, if you can find a seat.'

She tip-toed through the tapes and lowered herself onto the sagging sofa, hearing it creak as she did so. Callum sat down beside her, making sure that he left a slight gap between them. She didn't mind if he moved closer; she knew he would anyway, once he felt more confident. The last time she'd been here he'd kissed her. Tonight she felt like going a lot further.

'How's your sister and the kid?'

'They're fine. The usual. Sally's stressed about having no money and Polly is defying everyone by doing well at school and keeping herself out of trouble.'

'Good … that's good.' He slid closer.

Naomi tried not to smile at his clumsiness.

His leg brushed against her thigh but he didn't move it away.

'No need to be so coy,' she said, putting her cup down on the floor at the side of the sofa.

'What?' His face took on an expression of shock. His short blonde hair looked dark in the dim light from the lamp in the corner.

'Come on … let's not mess around. You like me and I like you. Remember last week?'

He nodded. 'I haven't thought about much else.'

She placed her hand on his knee and squeezed.

He leaned in and kissed her neck, moved up to her mouth and whispered something unintelligible between her open lips.

They fucked on the sofa, in the soft light of a second-hand lamp. At one point she thought she might tumble off onto the floor and break a couple of video tapes. She wondered, briefly, if he would stop what he was doing and scold her. Then she realised that he was so intent on love-making that nothing could have interrupted his rhythm.

Afterwards, she took out her cigarettes and they smoked in silence. The lamp went out with an audible pop.

'Shit. That bulb's been threatening to go for ages. I don't have a spare.'

She watched the lit end of his cigarette trace glowing veins in the air, soft patterns and traceries that held her gaze like a magic trick. 'It's fine. I like the dark.'

Not long after that they ran out of things to say. Rather than prolong the awkwardness, she got up and put on her clothes. 'I have to get back.'

'Will I see you again soon?' he asked from the sofa, his face a small, unstable blur now that the cigarette had burnt out.

'Maybe. I don't know.'

He didn't respond and suddenly she wished she had not been so flippant. Of course she would see him again. What else did she have here? Who else was there to give her comfort in this jail, this tower of cell blocks - one perched atop another? But it was too late, she couldn't say anything like that, not now. The moment was gone.

Callum did not make a move to see her to the door so she let herself out. She hadn't expected him to escort her off the premises, or walk her home, but she thought he might at least have got up to say goodbye. Instead, as she traipsed along the hallway, she heard him rearranging his videos - the dry clicking of bones on the carpet.

The stairwell seemed darker than it had earlier. Either the bulb here was on its way out too or it was simply an illusion brought on by her mood. She almost turned back but the thought of Callum crawling around naked amid his videos put her off.

As she climbed the stairs she heard a soft whisper - several whispers, in fact, merging into one. When she turned the corner at the half landing, she saw them there - two bodies so closely entwined that they resembled one large, contorting figure. Or were there more than two of them? It was difficult to tell. She thought they might be teenagers, indulging in an orgy where they thought no one could see.

Their dry gasps and whispers raked at the air like dull blades. Random limbs moved sinuously, like snakes; clothing was pulled aside to expose patches of shockingly white flesh. She tried not to look but they drew her eye. She was unable to work out exactly what it was they were doing but the act in which they were so intently involved was surely sexual.

Naomi eased past them and climbed the last few stairs to the fire door, glancing back only as she pushed open the door and felt the cool night air rush in to touch her face.

There was nobody on the half landing. Whatever she had seen – or thought she'd seen – was gone.

She let herself into the flat, making sure that she made as little noise as possible when she locked the door and slid the bolts into place behind her. Creeping into the darkened living room, she didn't see her sister until the other woman spoke.

'It's late.'

Naomi sat down on the sofa. 'I know. I needed some space, that's all.'

Sally lit up a cigarette and began to smoke. She didn't switch on the light, just sat there, staring into the gloom.

'You're not my mother.' Naomi said. 'I can do what I please. I'm a grown woman.' Her words were intended to hurt.

'Then act like one. Shagging that lad – that druggie – isn't exactly mature, is it?'

Naomi didn't know what to say, how to respond. So she let the silence cover them both like a blanket.

When Sally finished her cigarette she stood and walked to the door. Turning, she said 'I'll leave you to sleep.' Then she left the room, pulling the door shut behind her.

Naomi pulled the spare bedding out from under the sofa and made up her bed. She stripped down to her underwear and climbed under the blankets, wishing that she had her own duvet, her own flat. It seemed like a lifetime ago when she'd lived in a place that she could call home. The meaning of the word was becoming fuzzy around the edges.

The curtains were open a couple of inches; Sally must have been looking out for her. She stared at the gap, thinking that the wire security grid on the window looked like tiny sketched prison bars. As sleep crept over her, she thought about Callum and how his eyes looked like small television screens. The screens shattered as she watched, becoming faceted. Shining but creating no light.

She woke up thinking that there was someone else in the room but when she looked around she saw that she was all alone. Not much time had passed as she dozed on the sofa but it felt as if she had been lying there for days. Her back ached, her legs tingled with the beginnings of cramp. She sat up and swung her legs off the sofa, standing unsteadily, as if she had forgotten how to walk. Sleep clung to her like webbing; she could almost see its wisps before her eyes.

She walked over to the window and looked down at the car park. There was nobody about; even the gangs of teenagers were absent. They must be looking for trouble elsewhere tonight.

She had the overpowering urge to see Callum, to say something to him that would dispel the strange feeling between them she had sensed earlier, when she'd left him scuttling amid his videos. He was the closest thing to a friend that she had, and the thought of alienating him filled her with a heavy dread.

Feeling cold and heavy-limbed, she quickly dressed and left the flat. She hoped Sally wouldn't wake up until she returned. That tension, too, was becoming unbearable. She had the feeling that Sally was jealous of her, of the way she could come and go without having to answer to anyone, her lack of responsibility. Sally had a strange idea of freedom. Naomi would love to have a small hand to hold, tears to wipe away, a daughter to care for instead of trying so hard to look after herself.

She entered the stairwell and headed down. The light was off now but she could see vague shapes ahead of her – the concrete steps, the thin metal hand rail, balled-up chip wrappers and empty beer cans.

When she reached the half landing she saw them again: the figures coiled about one another, their limbs entwined to an extent that disturbed her. As she moved past them, arching her body awkwardly to ensure that she gave them plenty of room, a small, white hand shot out of the dark bundle and moved its fingers in a come-hither motion. Was it inviting her to join them or simply reaching out to be saved? The dark oval of a head turned her way, peeling out from the central mass but she could make out no eyes. A mouth struggled to open but no sound came.

She didn't believe in ghosts but what else could they be? Spectral remains, of emotions rather than people. Lonely phantoms of unfulfilled desire.

Naomi hurried onto the next part of the staircase, heading for the way out. Out on Callum's landing, she gasped for air. Her eyes were watering and she felt a pressure on her chest, an emotion that she was unable to name. Everything was rushing in and pulling away at the same time: it was a sensation of simultaneous attack and retreat. After a few seconds of breathless panic, she started to feel normal again, her heart rate slowing, the blood pumping at a natural rate through her veins.

She'd changed her mind, she didn't want to see Callum again tonight. But the thought of having to walk once again past those copulating/merging shadowy figures on the half landing forced her onward and she approached his door.

The door opened when she pushed it. Callum had failed to secure it after she'd left, or perhaps he'd had another visitor in the meantime. Whatever the reason, the door was unlocked. She ghosted along the hallway, drawn towards the flickering glow of the television in the living room.

Callum was lying on the floor, naked. He still had an erection. There was fresh semen on his hairless belly. His eyes were open but he saw nothing - they were glazed over, as if laminated. His skin looked blue in the spastic light of the television. There was a length of rubber hose knotted around his upper arm. A used syringe lay nearby atop a video case bearing the title 'Motel Hell'. She noticed for the first time how large his feet were, and how his little toe on each foot was longer than the others.

On the television screen a man swinging a chainsaw, wearing a severed pig's head as a mask, was chasing someone. The sound was so low that it was just a dull noise. The colours were muted and fuzzy round the edges, like those in her dreams.

There should be tears, she knew, but none would come. This was pathetic rather than sad, a sorry waste of what could once have been a life and had become nothing more than an existence. Clinging to old videos as if they were fragments of reality, a crippled soul trying to convince himself that he didn't need to live because he could watch other people doing so instead. Life by proxy; social engagement via video.

None of this had worked because if it had he wouldn't be laying here, dead on the carpet, his erection dwindling even as she watched – a dying snail scooped brutally from its shell.

Naomi had no idea what to do. She didn't want to call the police because there would be too many questions, and despite her inability to sleep she was tired, bone tired. So she walked away and left him there.

This time there were no figures on the half landing. The stale air smelled of salt and rotten fish, a vague hint of the ocean. She wondered where they had gone and wished now that she'd responded to that beckoning hand, perhaps reached out and taken it instead of running away. Who knew where it might have led her?

Back inside Sally's flat, she finally felt a release of emotion but it was a small thing, not really worth much in the grand scheme of things. Still there were no tears. She walked over to the window and waited for light to appear in the sky. It didn't take long. It never did.

As she watched the approaching dawn through the wire grid on the glass, her eyes eating the daylight, she was gripped by the notion that she could see out through every window in the tower block simultaneously: a compound eye, like that of a spider. The sensation didn't last for long. It was a strange kind of vision, a lie told to her brain by her senses, and nothing more.

She turned away from the window, from the growing light, and returned to the comfortable darkness of her life.

STAINED GLASS

John Grant

THERE ISN'T A place you can put memories where they'll be preserved forever. Time chars and twists them until they become events that never were. Which is not, of course, to say that they don't exist or that things didn't really happen that way, but in some other time and some other context.

Anyway, this is as best as I can put together my memories.

OUTSIDE, THE STREETS were almost silent except for the tiny distant sounds of other people's TV sets. It seemed everyone who hadn't gone to London to demonstrate against Thatcher's Poll Tax was watching it on the box, like it was *Match of the Day* only more likely to get exciting. Me, I'd been intending to catch the coach at five in the morning and join the rest of the crew on the march, but I'd been up half the night with what seemed to be a mild case of food poisoning. Long bus rides and mild cases of food poisoning don't go together.

This was about three months, maybe four, after Ellie had left me. Being unemployed will do that for you. I say 'left', but I was the one who'd had to do the leaving. She was still in the flat that I couldn't help but think of as ours. It'd be hers once the papers went through. I wasn't going to contest that. The court had told me I wasn't to go anywhere near her, even though I'd never raised a hand to her - would never dream of doing so.

I'd moved into a shared house with my brother Alan and a few of his friends. I was a few years older than the rest of them - quite a few years - but they didn't let it matter much.

They were all in London. I hoped they'd be okay. The cops were getting more and more like Thatcher's Private Army these days.

By the middle of the afternoon I was feeling a whole lot better. I climbed out of bed, drew back the curtains without hurting my eyes too much, and had a shower. By the time I'd got myself dried and dressed I was actually starting to get hungry.

There was a big pot of stew on the stove waiting to be reheated when the others got home, late and presumably ravenous, but aside from that there was nothing in the house that looked edible except a few slices of leathery bread in the fridge.

I reckoned I could safely get as far as Sunny Gavaskar's shop at the end of the road. His name wasn't really Sunny but everyone called him that, even his own family, because of the cricketer. He had a very beautiful daughter, about twenty, whom all of us knew better than to do more than smile at politely.

I came home with bread, cheese, low-fat spread, a can of soup and a couple of spinach pakoras. Oh, and a couple of big bottles of red plonk for when the rest made it back, plus a bottle of the cheap Scotch he sold – well, the label said it was Scotch, anyway.

While I waited for the pakoras to reheat in the microwave, I switched on the TV to catch the news.

The screen was filled with struggling people – cops on horseback, cops with shields, girls and boys in jeans, older men and women trying determinedly to pretend the fighting wasn't happening all around them, banners being held high, banners being torn down, the shouting turned down low so we could hear the newscaster telling us what was really going on.

My nerves had been a bit shot, since Ellie. I sat there looking at what was obviously well on its way to becoming a riot, pakoras momentarily forgotten, and squinted at the screen in an effort to see if Alan and the others might be anywhere in the middle of all that tumult. I was certain from the start they'd be in hospital by now, trampled under some horse's hooves, or banged up in a cell for 'resisting arrest'.

The microwave pinged.

I fetched the pakoras on a plate, plus the bread and cheese. As an afterthought I brought the synthaScotch, too, and a glass for it. I never did get as far as the bread and cheese.

Ten o'clock, they'd said they hoped they might be home. There was no chance of that now.

After a while, I lost track of time. The synthaScotch was mostly gone. I kept watching the TV, where they'd 'interrupted normal service' to keep us 'informed of developments'. I knew the talking heads were talking, but for the most part I couldn't understand what they were saying.

That was when I dropped the glass.

It was an old brandy glass, a flimsy thing someone had picked up in a junk shop. As I tried clumsily to catch it, it shattered.

I looked down stupidly at the bits and pieces of shining glass on the faded green carpet, at the deep gash across my wrist.

Must bandage that up, I thought. Got to get it clean first, though.

I filled the basin in the bathroom with warm water, leaning against it as it filled, then put my hand into it. It was as if someone had flipped a switch to turn the water red.

People are going to think I tried to kill myself, I thought. They're not going to believe in a freak drunken accident as I tried to catch a falling glass.

If anything, the water in the basin seemed even redder.

Well, I thought then, why not?

I could pretend to myself Ellie would relent, but I knew that wasn't going to happen. I'd lost her, had always lost her, would always lose her. She'd married a typesetter with a promising future ahead of him, but the future had evaporated before our very eyes. I knew I should retrain for something new but it had seemed easier – the path of least resistance – to live off her for a little while as I considered my options.

We all make bad decisions. That was one of mine. Now there was another path of least resistance opening up in front of me.

I started running a hot bath and went back into the living room to get the last of the synthaScotch and a nice big sharp fragment of the broken glass.

That's the most recent time I can remember of my dying.

AFTER THE PIT roof collapsed and in those agonising final moments as I fought for breath while it seemed that half a mountainside was crushing my chest, I found myself looking at stern columns of crabbed print. Underneath me was an overstuffed brown leather armchair.

'Petherton,' said a voice from the far side of my newspaper. 'Harry!'

I forced my mind to clear itself of the smell of coal dust and the sound of other men screaming. Me screaming, too. Everything would be okay in a few minutes once I'd acclimatised to wherever I was.

'Harry, old boy, did you fall asleep?'

And then the new memories began flooding into me.

Henry Petherton, Harry to his friends. I was a cabinetmaker – or, at least, I'd started as one. I was now the proud owner of a string of cabinetmaking shops across the country. I'd married well – to Eleanor, younger daughter of a duke. It was because of that marriage that I, a mere artisan, a nouveau riche, found myself accepted at places like the Arboretum Club. I read *The Times*. I went to MCC cricket matches and sat in the members' stand.

And I did so all the more often now that my Ellie was dead, taken from me by the Spanish flu two years after we'd thought the danger had passed.

We never had children.

I spent most of my evenings here at the club, trying to grow old gracefully, trying to get drunk without it showing too much, trying not to be too obviously a widower.

'Would you like another brandy, man?'

Warner pulled down the top of my *Times* and looked at me comically over it, head to one side like a jack-in-the-box.

'Silly question,' I said, putting the paper away.

While he was telling old Humphries to bring the drinks, I looked at him affectionately. Before Ellie died he'd been just another acquaintance at the club. Afterwards, he's taken me under his wing. I'd bitterly resented it at first, but his good nature had melted my resistance. Now I thought of him as a brother.

Humphries brought four glasses, two with brandy in them, two empty, and alongside them on the tray was a carafe of what I assumed to be water.

'I want to try an experiment,' said Warner in his usual playful way. He fancied himself somewhere halfway between Arthur Conan Doyle and Harry Houdini.

'So long as nothing explodes,' I mumbled. Although my knee had kept me out of the conflict, I knew rather too much about explosions. We all did.

'No fear of that.'

He passed me a brandy and took one for himself.

'Just a sip now.' He looked at me earnestly.

I swirled the liquor in the usual way, sniffed it appreciatively, and obediently sipped.

Warner nodded. 'Now try this.'

He'd poured a little of the water into one of the empty balloons.

I held it up to my nose. Not water but gin. Why ever would Warner think I wanted to drink gin?

Just as I had with the brandy, I took a small sip.

The stuff didn't taste as bad as I remembered.

'What does it taste of, Harry?'

'Gin.'

'Anything else?'

I took another sip and shook my head.

But then I paused.

'Not just gin,' I said. 'There's something…'

'Brandy, perhaps?'

I stared at the glass as if it held a secret it was refusing to reveal to me. The firelight caught the colourless liquid and gave it a touch of redness. Something from an earlier existence was nudging at my memory.

'A little … perhaps. Maybe they didn't wash this snifter

properly.'

Warner laughed. 'Of course they did.'

'Then—?'

'It's the shape of the glass. The only thing we ever drink out of these balloons is brandy. So when you drink something else from them your mind tells you to expect one thing while really you're tasting another. It's the same if you're blindfolded and someone tells you they're feeding you an apple when really it's an onion. You taste the apple. Tonight you're sipping gin but you *think* there's a little bit of brandy taste in there as well, because that's what the glass is telling you. Want to try it with some milk? I'm sure Humphries could be persuaded to rustle up a pint of milk from the kitchen...'

I waved him away, chuckling despite myself. He was like an eager puppy. 'I've heard bad things about milk.'

We spent the rest of the evening together, alternating brandies and gins - why not? - and talking about all sorts of things that weren't important. The rest of the members in the club that night were doing much the same. It was Derby Day tomorrow, so a good deal of the talk was about horses. I fancied the sound of Humorist and, although I wasn't much of a betting man, I reminded myself to put a few guineas on him in the morning.

Around midnight, Warner, his face bright red, announced he was going to spend the night at the club. 'I can't tell the difference between the brandy and the gin any longer.' We both thought that was incredibly funny.

Ignoring his advice that I should do the same, I set off for home, a mile away.

It was a windy night, but I decided to walk rather than take a cab. The cold air, so refreshing after the heat of the day, might clear my head a little.

Away from Warner and his pranks and jests, my mind inevitably turned to Ellie again. We'd had eighteen good years together, and still I saw her as the girl I'd married, light on her feet and bubbling with laughter. And then came the awful flu, and her face becoming greyer and greyer, and at last the laughter was forever silenced.

I never even noticed the waggon that came careering round the corner as I crossed Blunt Street.

The last thing I knew was the sight of a hoof plunging through the gaslight towards my face.

BEFORE THAT THERE was the Welsh mining village, of course, and before *that* I think it was the year I spent guiding people up the sides of Swiss mountains and pretending that yodelling came naturally to me. (I always yodelled very quietly for fear of starting avalanches, but an avalanche got me all the same.) I was flying home to England from Italy on the Comet airliner that went down in January 1954. I've been murdered more times than I can rightly remember, died in battle likewise, and sometimes taken my own life, as I did on the day of the Poll Tax riots.

Always I start a new life with memories of all the living I've done up until that moment, including the loss of darling Ellie, by death or separation.

Am I creating a new world each time I find myself alive again? Or am I taking over other people's bodies, complete with their memories? I don't think so. How could Ellie be part of all their existences?

And it *is* the same Ellie in each remembered life. She's bright and clear in my memories every time – not just her appearance but the sound of her voice, the whisper of her sighs.

I met her once in the flesh but I'm doomed never to meet her again, always just to remember her for however long I'm granted in each of my new incarnations. Sometimes I'm lucky, as with Petherton, who was given a matter of mere hours to mourn his bereavement. More often it's a few months. But always I know death won't be far away even if I don't know when exactly to expect it.

And always I hope, just for the first few seconds of a new existence, that this time I'll be in time to find her.

I WISH THIS were a false memory, but I don't believe it is…

I was riding home at night in a strangely empty train. We'd left the lights of the city behind some while ago, and all I could see outside the window was darkness – not even the lights of farmhouses or villages or cars on country roads. I'd finished my book so there wasn't much else to do except sit there.

I stared at the window's shiny black.

And then things began to change. There *was* some light – lights, rather. Not the lights of windows or cars but pale white flames on the hillsides.

Soon there were more and more of them, until I could make out the landscape between them. At first I thought they must be underground fires, that some vast labyrinth of coal mines must have ignited, but the flames were white and they moved like mist. Maybe it was just a trick of my eyes but I could swear I saw silhouettes of figures dancing around them – by the time I tried to focus on them the train had gone dashing past.

Some of the figures, if I really saw figures, had horns, if I really saw horns…

I was travelling in the jolting train through a landscape that might have been imagined by Hieronymus Bosch.

Unless it was *me* doing the imagining. Had I fallen asleep in my seat? Was I just experiencing a particularly pointless nightmare?

Not even a nightmare, because I was shielded by the glass of the window from any threat the dancing figures and the spectral fires might present. I was just a spectator.

The window shattered into a crazed pattern of a million pieces, held together by its interlayer.

At least, that's what I thought for a moment had happened.

In reality, the train had plunged into a tunnel.

I'd travelled this route often enough before and we'd never gone through a tunnel. At the time that didn't concern me. I was just glad I couldn't see the dancing spectres or the pale flames.

Worse still, in that instant just before I'd realised we were in a tunnel, I'd seen my reflection repeated countless times in the fragmented window. When the blank darkness of the tunnel came, my reflections seemed to be drawn swiftly into the glass, as if I - all the many me's - were being absorbed by it.

Suddenly we were out of the tunnel and into brightness. City streets and orange-lit overpasses. I'd be getting off in a couple of minutes. I stuck my book in the pocket of my anorak, zipped up and made for the doorway. Familiar sights streamed past outside. The unknown moorland with its silent fires seemed to belong to a different world. I'd seen Hell - or a version of it, anyway - and lived to tell the tale. One day I'd joke about it in the pub.

But when we got to the station it was empty, just as the train was.

I'd stepped out onto the platform before I noticed the place was completely deserted.

This couldn't be. It was *never* quiet here. At the very least there'd be a goods train gasping like a pensioner on a distant platform, waiting to be loaded or unloaded. Yet tonight there wasn't even litter blowing across the lines.

I turned to jump back into the carriage, but it was too late. The door was firmly shut and the train was slowly beginning to slide away in a squeal of rails. I watched a row of lit but vacant windows moving past me, and then the train was gone, the red lights of its rear dwindling into the distance.

I clapped my hands, shouted.

Just echoes.

I couldn't stay here.

Out on the street it was the same. There was a brightly lit Dixons opposite and I could see all the hi-tech gear inside it. Someone had chucked a brick at the window or hit it with a hammer, because there was a star-shaped pattern right across the middle. The Burton next door was the same except that its plate glass had been assaulted twice. The display dummies, impeccably dressed, gazed at the damage with a genial lack of interest. The vandals had done a better job with the bus shelter just down from there; the orange streetlights made the drooping glass look almost fleshly, like the tanned and sagging skin of an old beach bum's throat. Cars with smashed windscreens were parked haphazardly, toys tossed aside by a bored toddler.

The pavement was covered in shards of glass. I picked my way carefully through them in the direction of home. There were bloodstains, too.

The street looked as if, only minutes ago, it had been the scene of a mighty riot, but then a hand had reached down from the skies and plucked all the combatants away. Not just the people. The emptiness was complete. I could sense that I - the intruder - was the only living creature here.

Or so I thought.

After a long while I left the city centre and the shops behind. I was perhaps three-quarters of the way home, where the street ran alongside the old canal for a stretch, when a movement caught my eye.

There was someone kneeling on the canal bank, reaching out towards the water.

I broke into a run.

As I got closer, I could see it was a child, or a young woman. The streetlights were few and far between out here but I could see she was wearing a long, pale, threadbare dress. Untidy dark hair fell around the face she turned towards me as I approached.

I pulled to a halt, wheezing.

'Boy, am I glad to see another human being.'

She stared at me, saying nothing.

'I mean, back there—' I waved my hand in the general direction of the city centre. 'It's like a battlefield, except everyone's gone.'

Still she was silent.

I saw she had a glass in her hand, a bulb like a brandy balloon but made of thick, intricately cut crystal. The lip of the glass was gilt, as was the rim of its base. She'd obviously just been filling it from the canal.

'You can't drink that,' I said, hearing my voice rise in panic. 'You'd find yourself in hospital. If you lived that long. There's all kinds of shit in there.'

She smiled at me, shaking her head slowly.

For a moment I wondered if I might be wrong. Everything else was so screwed up tonight, nothing was as it should be. I knew that in the real world the canal water was full of heavy metals, ordure, chemical runoff from the factories upstream, if the current's sluggish, oleaginous movement could be called a stream. But this didn't seem like the real world, even though I could smell the city's grimy air and feel the hard pavement beneath my feet. Perhaps where we were, the woman and I, the canal water was as pure as a mountain spring's.

Except that I could *see* the water in that crystal goblet of hers. Even in the gloom, it was obvious the stuff was murky and menacing.

'No, honest,' I said, searching for words. I stepped towards her and made to knock the glass from her hand, but she deftly pulled it out of my reach.

Close up, I could see how skinny she was. It was obvious the thin dress was the only garment she had on, and it seemed to be pressing itself to a skeleton rather than a flesh-clad body. For all that, I was attracted to her - perhaps because she was the only other living being I'd seen since getting off the train. No. Since getting *onto* it.

One last try. 'Don't drink it.'

'It's safe enough.'

Her voice was full and rich, well educated. It didn't belong with the waif in front of me.

'What do you mean?'

She held up the goblet. It seemed now to have a light of its own, an inner smoulder. The liquid in it still looked lethal.

'The glass,' she said.

'Yes, I see it.'

'It changes everything that's in it.'

I just stared at her, mouth open. I should have guessed it earlier. She was nuts. One of the street dwellers we were all supposed not to know existed, the sad crazies enjoying the benefits of care in the community - which meant a hard bench or the underside of a bridge before an early death came along as the greatest kindness of all. Maybe I should just let her drink the water, allow her to make her exit.

But I couldn't do that.

'Look, I—'

I was going to tell her I could offer her a place for the night, that I'd not hassle her, I'd take the chair, perfect gentleman me, she could get a good night's sleep and in the morning a shower and something to eat, but she pre-empted my clumsy, embarrassed, embarrassing old-world speech by lifting the ornate goblet to her lips and drinking deeply of the clouded canal water.

I think I expected her to drop dead in a heap in front of me, puffs of smoke coming from her mouth.

Instead, she smiled at me again - a curiously alluring smile that, like her voice, was at odds with her skeletal form.

'I told you, the glass changes whatever it holds.'

She held it towards me and I could smell its scent, faint on the air. It was like Turkish delight - no, rose water. I began to laugh, feeling something like fear tightening my breathing. It was like some bad joke about believing your own shit smells like roses.

'What does it taste like?' My voice sounded hoarse.

'Like whatever you want it to taste like,' she said. 'But it's not what it tastes like that's important. It's what the goblet gives to it. Im*parts*.' She grinned at the pomposity of the word. 'Try it. You'll see.'

I recoiled. I couldn't understand why she wasn't rolling on the ground, clutching her guts and puking.

She took another gulp herself and offered the glass to me again.

'You can live forever.'

The woman was crazier than I thought. I knew I should just leave her there and keep walking until I got home, if home was still there on a night like this. Something stopped me. The prospect of solitude, I think.

'What's your name?' I said, as if the mundane question would restore a little rationality to the world.

'Eleanor,' she said. 'Ellie.'

'Do you have a home?'

'Oh, here and there.' She wafted a hand. 'Mostly there.'

'Family?'

'No longer.'

'Friends?'

'You. Once.'

I was out of questions, out of words. Had I ever encountered her before? Had I ever encountered *any Eleanor at all* before? Probably, yes, in a shop or at a ticket counter or in one of those other brief interactions where you forget a person's name as soon as you turn away from them, but I was sure there was no one I'd actually known with that name. And yet, now that I looked at her again, at her slanting shoulders and her moist, expressive eyes, I did feel some tug of familiarity. We were connected in some way, I suddenly felt sure, even if this was the first time we'd met.

'Drink,' she whispered, her mouth so close to my ear that I could feel her breath.

So I took the goblet, and drank.

The filthy canal water tasted like finest brandy.

Even so, I spat the stuff out as soon as I realised what I'd done. I'd swallowed a little of the muck before the reflexes kicked in, but maybe not enough to actually kill me.

'Who are you?' I gasped, bending over with my hands on my knees.

'Ellie,' she said. 'I told you that.'

'And you're immortal because you drink canal water?'

'My life will last forever.'

'You'll never die?'

'That's something different.'

'And me?'

'It'll be the same for you. Now.'

'Who are you?' I repeated.

'We've always been connected, you and I, only you've never noticed it. We always will be.'

A bright full moon had come from somewhere to peer over her shoulder at me. I squinted against its light as I looked up at her and for a moment I caught a glimpse of the person she might have been – the tumbled hair, the ready laughter, the occasional wistfulness, the generous smile, the eyes shining with intelligence. But something, somewhere along the line, had strangled that existence before it had ever been born.

I found myself craving to reverse whatever had happened, to restore that future to her.

She smiled again, and turned away.

Before I could stop her she'd thrown the goblet far out over the canal. It went into the turgid water with hardly a splash.

Without thinking, I charged after it, going up to my waist almost immediately. I lunged out, trying to swim, but that just splashed some of the canal water up into my face, my mouth.

The bottom dropped away from under my feet and I was floundering, making things worse for myself.

I looked back towards Ellie but she wasn't there any longer. The canal bank was empty in the moonlight.

My head went beneath the surface.

I'VE BEEN A boxer and a welder and a gymnast and a gladiator and a bouncer and a monastic scribe and a professional hit man and a university literature professor. All these, and thousands more besides. I've lived for centuries and in many different centuries. Each time I die I've no idea where or when I'll be next, except that I'll always be a few months too late to be with Ellie. When I almost recognised her down there by the canal on that almost-forever-ago night, this was what I realised: that we would always be destined to be together but that somehow the destiny would never be fulfilled. All of her companionship that I'd ever be able to enjoy would be the memories I had of her in each new segment of my life.

Somewhere, before I met her on the canal bank, I destroyed her without ever being aware that I'd done so – without knowing who she was or even that she existed. A chance action that I'd never realised could have affected a stranger. A burst of laughter as the person passing me on the street was trying to cope with grief. Seizing a taxi on a rainy night that really belonged to someone else so that they missed their plane and with it the life they should have had. Any of a countless number of things I could have done to bring misery to someone else without knowing it.

What I saw through the train window – the eerily white fires and the dancing figures – I thought at the time it was the landscape of Hell. Now I know better. That was just Hell's foretaste, the welcome mat spread out at Hell's door.

What Hell really is, is having a life in which you see your own reflection repeated over and over as in shattered glass, never enough of it to be all of you, an eternity of things that might have been but never will be.

Everywhere I am I'm haunted by my own ghosts.

THE INNER EAR

Marion Pitman

Is it myopia or fear of daylight that makes films less than
    music?
twilight my chosen scene, voices more alive than faces.
I'm no voyeur, but an eavesdropper.
Sound burrows through to the coil of the inner ear
where the lost voices still move towards me,
still in the process of being heard, being taken in.

A face may fade
to nothing but the memory of a photograph.
The sound of a voice: tone, pitch, rhythm,
even without words,
remains elusive but intense.

Daylight is a mixed blessing,
bombarding the mind with input:
colour and movement, shape and size.

Twilight brings relief,
voices still resonating in the inner ear;
music distils experience,
not dissipated among five senses
but concentrated all in one.

And sound travels slowly, into the ear, the mind, the
    memory –
we cannot shut our ears –
and all the while your voice is there,
keeping you alive in my mind.

THREADBARE

Jan Edwards

THE TAROT ARE old, furred at the corners, their faces worn and their once gilt edges scraped to beige from decades of shuffle and lay. The spread is a tough one; easy to read but a bastard to explain without sounding like the ides of March. Seven of Swords on top of the Devil. King of Swords. Ten of Swords. I flip over each card and stare at it in turn. What can I say? Divination-chill runs up my arms, raising goose flesh that I rub away from habit.

Angela leans forward to examine her future. She has *resting-bitch face,* hardening into petulance. 'What do they mean, Helen?' she asks. 'Swords are bad aren't they?'

She seems primed for something hitting the fan, which makes it easier to say what needs to be said. 'Change,' I tell her. 'And challenges. The Devil is lack of confidence in making decisions. The Seven is … uncertainty. Gossip. Spite. Betrayal. You need to watch your back. The King is a man of intellectual confidence and the Ten is an unexpected end to a project. An ending - one that you didn't expect.'

The younger woman reaches across the table - puts her hand over mine - leans in close and whispers, 'It's you causing all of this. I know you called him. You called Michael.'

'I have no idea what you mean.' *Shit! She's* that *Angela.* I lay the final card, scrunching my toes, tensing my gut, anything to prevent my hands from shaking. *The Tower: there you are, you little bastard. Full house in the all-out war on the Angela stakes. Couldn't happen to a better person.* 'The Tower represents conflict. The tearing down of everything that surrounds you. Angela, you do know Tarot is about what may be and not what is to come? Whatever is seen here can change because free will has…'

'You screwed him. I heard you!'

I struggle to recall when I last spoke to Michael much less fucked him. 'I've had nothing to do with him for months. Whoever you heard Michael talking with, it was *not* me.'

'Bitch! I didn't come here to have you spout crap at me. All this is shit.' She rises, pushes my hand back and sweeps the cards away in the same movement. 'Not as much shit as you'll be getting if you don't keep away.'

The cards tumble, scrambling into the shelter of table and chairs. I am on my knees to collect them almost before they finish falling, knowing my neglected rugs are ingrained with dust and grit and cat hair. When I hear the front door bang I sink back on my heels. One card lays propped against the table's pedestal leg. The Tower. I pick it up - frowning at the fresh fold across the diagonal, adding angles to its painted lightning. *Damn it. I'm sorry, Gran.* Her cards, as tradition dictates, were a gift - or to be more precise a bequest. They are ancient. Venerable. Now defiled.

Oliver Catwell unfurls sleek red-brown limbs and comes to rub against my cheek, chirping his cattish comforts.

Angela Bateman is obviously trouble in designer heels; she is known for it. I would never have agreed to the reading had I known who she was. If she'd beaten me around the head with a brick I could not feel more damaged. Stroking Oliver Catwell's ears for luck I scoop up the rest of the cards, almost missing the stray hiding in a fold of the rug. I tug it free, half expecting to stare Death in its bony face. But this is yet another sword and I feel if not relief then a sense of completion.

'Le Trois,' I whisper. 'Heartbreak. That figures.'

Laying the rescued deck on the table, I cover it with its purple silk cloth and go to make tea. I would much prefer coffee, with a slug of brandy, but know it would keep me awake until dawn.

The stoneware mug, the one with the moulded dragon curled around the belly, is tactile, almost animate when filled with warm liquid. Wrapping both hands around it eases the 'reading chills' and stops the anger shaking through me. Aggressive clients are nothing new but Angela's visit is about a lot more than tarot. Whether the warning is from Angela herself or from Michael is not clear. It hardly matters – I could not feel more violated.

I wander into the workshop where the paying work is done. Two looms dominate the space and both are strung and weighted with commissioned pieces. I sit at the larger of them to check the pattern already emerging across the frame. A wall hanging of stylised flora and fauna in the medieval manner is a melange of merino wool and silk. My own preference is for a far less structured style. But a commission this size pays the rent for several months.

My feet ply the treadles, prompting beams to shunt back and forth. Their comforting clack-a-chunk is like a warm plaid falling across my shoulders and I work without conscious thought, allowing the rhythm to sooth ruffled calm. Retreating into that trance-like pleasure where only the coloured yarns and clacking beams hold any reality, Angela's ill-aimed venom is eradicated with the physicality of weaving. I think of Michael and what might have possessed him to hook up with 'Miss Leopard Print and Jimmy Choo's', this Angela creature, with her red-rimmed, hunted eyes.

The beams sway to a halt and I prop my forearms on the cross bar to examine progress.

Flowers? (Pansies to be exact.) A chintzy confection complete with pink ribbon curled between them in a Victorian-posy motif. *Pansies are the blossoms of visions and projections,* I think. *Curious. And really, really, not the plan.*

The clock has crept around to three a.m. and I don't have the energy to unpick the weave, nor begin to wonder why I would have created this nonsensical piece of Victoriana.

Sleep. I need sleep. New day – new perspective.

MY DREAMS HAVE followed the same trail for days. Following the fox past the Greet Inn, that isn't there anymore, and along the Warwick

Road toward Tyseley close to where Michael lives. A never ending trudge through dark, rain soaked streets lined with petrol stations and windowless blocks of industry, fabricated from pallid, angular metal. Nobody walks with me, or even passes me by. No one ever does. Cars wash along the street, interspersed with buses and lorries that fill my nostrils with their soot and diesel stench. Their slipstreams tug me towards the kerb's edge, rush headlong to traverse this featureless concrete and tarmac hinterland, and reach the sparkling promise of the city centre. I leave the commercial sector behind me, stalking through parallel lines of Victorian terraces in red brick and pebbledash, weaving my way through a slalom of dumped armchairs and flaccid black bin bags, which rustle beneath the caresses of wind and rats. I am walking past his door. His windows, curtained and dark, show no hint of what might be inside. They never have, and I don't ever want to know – except tonight. Tonight is different. Tonight I step up the impossibly tall steps and lay my hand on the door. My fingers stretch out and bend at the knuckles. My nails morph into curved arcs of honed ivory that claw slowly down the face of the blue painted door, once – twice – three times. The fox barks from the street ahead, summoning me to follow, and together we walk into the night.

TRACEY BRINGS ME coffee, kissing me lightly on the cheek and bends to examine the weave. She turns to look at me with confusion in her eyes.

'They're faces.' She touches the uppermost flower. 'Michael Thurso. No doubt about it. And this one … is this Angela?'

She is right and it makes me twitch. 'I should never have allowed that woman to cross the threshold.'

'Why on earth did she want a reading from you in the first place?' Tracey asks. 'Just to start a row?'

There is no answer. I gaze at the woven faces. My dreams have been filled with Michael for weeks. Michael the contradiction, filled with spiritual energy, yet cynical as hell. 'It was her easy way in,' is all I can say.

'Well, from what I've heard she's a total psycho. Keep the doors locked. I'm pulling a long shift tonight so I won't see you until much later, sweetie.' Tracey drops a kiss on the back of my neck, caresses my head, strokes her thumb and forefinger around my ear from helix to lobe. I want to bury my face into her neck and let her make it all better – but she has to work and I have things to start; things to end.

The door closes behind her and I pull out my phone to select Michael.

'Helen,' he murmurs, 'I was just meaning to call you.'

'If that would be before Angela got here? You're too late.'

'Oh…'

I swivel round to face the weaving. Reaching out to tap the faces with rictus fingers, nails snagging strands like a harpist noodling at their strings – uncertain of what song will fit the mood. 'Oh?' I said. 'Is that it? Your latest screw just paid me a visit and all you can say is 'I was going to call'?'

'I didn't send her.'

'Yet somehow she knew where to come.' My fingers tighten, nails gripping slackened threads. 'I'd never betray what I've seen in a reading.'

His breath whispers across the phone and away into the silence.

'She doesn't know though, does she,' I continue. More silence. 'Can't you trust her?'

'I don't do trust, Hel. Not any more.' His voice is a husk, as though unused for far longer than the half minute since his last sentence.

'Yet you're screwing her.'

'That's none of your business.'

'No more than I am any of hers... Look. Michael. You and I? Big mistake. That was the past. This is now. Get over it.'

'I am over it. I can do what I like and you can't judge me.'

I hear his breathing harshen and I sigh. He has never accepted that our twelve month marriage was one huge error of judgement. 'Going to bed with someone isn't done for the sake of getting away with it,' I tell him. 'If you do it because you mean it, fine. If you don't mean it, why bother?'

The moment plunges into the abyss of a disconnected call. I place the phone face down, not wanting it to ring again.

Silk and wool strands straggle up from the surface of the tapestry where my nails snagged the wefts. Floral eyes, noses and mouths are obliterated by ragged holes that resemble cigarette burns - damage stabbing deep, baring the warps' pale tram lines running top to base.

I feel a brutal urge to bind their wounds, to heal them. Never mind that they hate me, that I hate them. My hands move beyond my will, plucking hair from my own head. Long brown strands, silken - slippery - glistening still with life as they slide into the bodkin's unwinking eye.

I tack and sew. Folding strands into place and securing them with stitches so fine they are barely visible to my naked eyes, grafting features into each flower face. My fingers are muscular pink spider-legs stalking across the material's tattered web of warp and weft but my mind, my eyes, my soul, are wandering.

Darkness creeps into the room and still I sew, pulling strand after strand from my temples, suturing each hank as it is torn from the root, faster and fumbling. Finger tips sore - scalp raw and bloodied. I feel no pain - all the while transferring viscous red to needle and finger tips and tapestry faces.

The waking trance finally relents. I am exhausted, my hands resting limp on my thighs, mouth dry and eyes stinging. My heart is erratic, breathing laboured. I fight down the panic and stagger into the next room to reveal my Tarot, frantic for the certainty they can bring me. I turn up three cards. Death and Judgement do little to calm me with their changes and retributions. But the Three of Cups are a salve - celebrations. All will be well.

I go to bed. It's wide and cold and I wish yet again that Tracey could change her shifts. Oliver Catwell is no substitute but when he snuggles into me I breathe in his dusty warmth, and sleep.

I AM IN A street. Not the same street as in the previous night's vision. The bright neons and goldfish bowl frontages are Ladypool Road's Balti Mile. Glimpsed interiors are painted in golds and reds and purples contrasting with snowy cloths. Cutlery glitters before empty velvet-backed chairs. Around me cold rain patters onto the paving stones spotted with pale blots of long-discarded gum and waste paper whispers along the edges of the walls. I cup my hands against the window glass and peer into the depths. Tracey is there. She waves and I am sitting beside her. At the next table Michael and Angela scoop Jalfrezi with dough torn from pillow-sized naan. Michael reaches back to clasp Angela's head – and forces it forward into the steel balti dish. As the girl's struggles grow feeble he laughs at me. When I step forward to stop him … I am in the workshop. The rear wall is missing, opening up to the night with rain lashing across the loom. I begin to weave but the clack-a-chunk is forfeited for squeak-a-clunk. Rust patters across the back of my hands. The shuttle sticks, flaking, shredding, cutting threads, slicing yarn, splitting hairs…

I SIT UP, rigid, panting, my face and neck and breasts are wet, but with sweat now – not rain. Oliver Catwell is glaring at me from the top of the dresser.

'Sorry Olly.'

He opens his mouth wide to expose his pink throat and yellowing teeth in a silent rebuke before he stalks away.

I roll off the mattress and move across the room to pull the curtains aside. Rain is slanting across the sickly orange spread of the street lights and friend fox trots through. He pauses to look up. Our gazes lock briefly before he is melting into shadows without seeming to move and I wonder if I am truly awake.

A car pulls into the drive and Tracey is dashing for the front door.

TRACEY IS ALL concern. 'What have you done to yourself?'

She sets a bowl of warm tea-tree tainted water beside me and pulls a wad of cotton wool from the pack, dipping it into the liquid and wiping my scabbing scalp with gentle strokes. Her other hand is clasped around the back of my neck to hold me steady and I flashback to the balti house with its naan bread and violence. I flinch away from her ministrations. I feel stretched –

febrile – my skin taught and rough to the touch, the lines around my eyes and mouth deepened like vertical threads of my loom worn free of weave though the friction of stress.

'I needed fine thread…' I whisper, clouding my fear with mundanity.

She glances toward the loom, frowning at my red-stained repair. 'Those waking dreams again?'

I can only nod.

'Oh sweetie. Is it Michael? You have to cut him loose.' She gestures toward the ugly repair. 'Getting rid of that would be good.' She smiles reassurance and takes my hand. Our fingers interweave and the world feels clean.

I swivel around to face the loom and take up my stitch-pick, cutting one tiny thread at a time, deconstructing the night's work. A literal act, but I have to start somewhere.

Tracey carries on dabbing.

We finish together, gathering the detritus of swabs, scabs and scarified art and consign them to the embers of the log burner.

In bed Tracey pulls me close, spooning, her arms close around me, her breath warm against my right ear.

GUIDED BY THE fox, I am drifting back to Tyseley, past the furniture shop and left into Seeley Road. Darkness is interspersed by occasional halogen lamps which shine a false sense of security for passers-by that never exist, when the cul-de-sac ends at an iron fence. The fox slips through flaking railings and vanishes into a waste land of scrubby trees beyond. There is a car, an old Volvo, its tail backed up to the fence. As I move closer the glow within is brightening, flaring, outlining the figures within. A man. A woman. Unmoving. Flickering luminescence highlights their features. Michael and Angela are staring at me. Flames caress their faces and still they sit. I cry out but can get no closer, watching their faces engulfed by flame, blackening, melting, distorting, collapsing into themselves – nose first and then eyes, lips, teeth. Imploding like the celluloid heads of the birthday-gift dolls that my brothers had tortured: fixing them to lighted candles, melting them from within, gaping holes dripping globs of plastic, until there is nothing left but blackened fragments attached to charred torsos.

I'M AWARE OF sirens passing our window, projecting blue tongues of cold fire across the ceiling's white expanse. Tracey stirs to pull me closer still and nuzzles my hair. 'You're cold,' she murmurs, 'and your hair smells of smoke.'

The Shadow

it takes room in moonlight
on wall of room in (room)
landlord, who reveals it belonged to man
his shadow — tall, broad-shoulde[red]
(only) that only at a ce[rtain]
full moon, Landlord stands befo[re]
landlord gives hon[...]
that of a distort[ed]
window — only shado[w]

The Dream — 2nd year at University
(THE OTHER SIDE)
railway station, platform
early evening, cool
standing on one side, waiting for
Inter-City train — others with me
bickering & staring (usual group —
persons — family, friends)
(boy) (luggage)
other side — boy sitting alone on
suitcase, hands folded on
his lap, gazing at the track —
pale, near-blond (no-one I knew
thought I
so quiet, I knew why he
was alone....

[illegible] heightened, or at
least less cluttered — I picked
my suitcase & crossed the
platform, sat beside him — he
looked at me — our hands touched,
no-one noticed I had gone —
world behind me didn't exist —
waited, together, for the train
that was going in the opposite
direction to my planned journey
[illegible] but [illegible] lamplight
[illegible]

[illegible] to recall [illegible] more, [illegible]
[illegible] stopped by
[illegible]

about 1,000 words

WINDOW SHOPPING (?)

Character: 20 yr-old man
university. Uneasy with h[is]
away, familiar/alien. The [illegible]
Highlights fading in his [illegible]
Feels at risk/exposed
but not expecting to be seen
his distance. Need for [illegible]
Maths student ("[illegible]
another but not to his [illegible]
people in this town. Past [illegible]
men he wanted, chased [illegible]
Almost always rejected [illegible]
wished he didn't have [illegible]
"almost").
The summer [illegible]
[illegible] next [illegible]

dreaming them when they change

THE DARK ABOVE THE FAIR

Terry Grimwood

EVEN IN THE HEYDAY of the British seaside, this particular travelling fair had already gone to seed; its paint peeled, its scenic railway a rattling death-trap, its ghost train a clunky monstrosity about as frightening as Watch with Mother. *It should have curled up and died decades ago but, dead or not, it's here today. And I know why. Nothing to do with its rickety, rolling schedule, nothing to do with coincidence.*

The fair is here for me.

It's set up on The Common, as it was half a century ago. Every year it was the same, a three-week stopover, which encompassed the height of Westerton-on-Sea's holiday season. The season included August Bank Holiday and, like those of old, this one is overcast and wet.

Another wonder is that The Common is still The Common. In my day, Westerton's residents generally avoided the place. It was scabby, scruffy and speckled with litter from the out-of-towners' cars that congregated here for picnics and other less salubrious pastimes. I'm surprised a property developer hasn't made a golf-course deal with someone on the council and turned it into a set of exclusive, seaside apartments.

But they haven't.

And here I am.

There are few other punters in sight, just the rattling near-empty scenic railway and the peeling yellow-and-orange roundabouts. There's music. The Kinks' 'See My Friend'.

And beneath it all, beneath the rattle, rumble, siren-wail, and air-rifle clang, I can hear the fair's rotten heart, its beat, synchronised exactly to mine.

IT DIDN'T ONLY happen in Brighton and Margate and exotic places like that. It happened in Westerton-on-Sea, in 1965, the year after the biggest and most notorious Mods and Rockers scrap of all. Yes, it happened here, in what was once a fishing town and, at the time of the battle, a high class seaside resort (that's what it called itself anyway). When Westerton looked in the mirror it saw Hove, or Frinton.

Westerton was not *common*, like Great Yarmouth or Blackpool.

Westerton was *genteel*.

Except for the travelling fair of course – that wasn't genteel. It was tolerated because it brought in money, even if that money came from the sticky, grubby hands of the sort of people Westerton didn't normally welcome. It was only for three-weeks, after all.

Westerton had another thorn in its side. Us. Its youth. Youth that, in the opinion of its residents, would have benefitted from a spell in the army. Youth who spent too much money on clothes and those wretched scooters they charged around on all day, when they weren't lounging around in the Sea Vista Café playing dreadful music on its jukebox.

We all came from good homes and had loving families who made sure we had a decent upbringing and a fine education, the sort of education that had already landed many of us well-paid jobs. A fat wage packet, and a train line straight into London, meant that me and my friends were always at the forefront, the trend-setters, the Kings and Queens of Westerton Youth.

We were Mods, in case you hadn't worked it out. Lambretta owners to a man, our rides replete with mirrors, badges and gleaming chrome.

Oh, and my name's Michael. Back then, my dad owned Westerton's sole plumbing company.

SO, AUGUST BANK Holiday Monday, 1965, the year it was moved from the first to the last weekend of the month. There was a westerly breeze, so it wasn't hot, even when the sun peeked from behind the clouds.

Where were we? Lounging around in the Sea Vista Café. The juke box was playing The Animals. My three best mates were there: Tony Harper, the local bank manager's son, slight, quick and neat; Sheila Weir, gorgeous and definitely the property of the last of our little clique, Bobby Chambers. Good looking fella, Bobby, all blond hair, blue eyes and square jaw. Likeable, though, as long as you didn't take the piss. There were others, of course, laughing, joking around and annoying the café's more sedate clientele. Karen Whitley was there as well. She wanted to be my girlfriend. She was pretty and kind-hearted, but she could never be my Great Love, and I knew it even then.

It started at around three in the afternoon.

There was a sound, a deep rumble that became a jagged roar. It rose in volume until it drowned out first our voices then Eric Burden's, and rattled the café's big plate glass window. Motorbikes, a dozen of them, black and chrome and ugly and, yeah, I'll admit it, terrifying.

Astride the bikes - Rockers.

They slowed and swarmed on the street outside the café, then shuffled their machines in to park around our Lambrettas like Apaches circling a wagon train.

Don't get these fellas mixed up in your head with Hells Angels. They didn't have long hair and big beards and they didn't wear German helmets or decorate their leathers with Iron Crosses. In 1965, Motorhead wasn't even a twinkle in Lemmy's eye and heavy metal could only be found in a steelworks. This gang was clean-shaven, their hair Brylcreamed to within an inch of its life. They wore leathers, based on US Air Force flight jackets and laden with scores of motorcycle badges.

There were girls with them too. Half a dozen, all wearing the same leathers and jeans as their fellas.

The Enemy.

They milled around outside for a bit. Then came in.

The place didn't erupt into a fight. There was no sudden silence like in a western when the stranger enters the saloon. Cups chinked as normal, the espresso machine hissed. But the atmosphere did tighten. The other customers were suddenly in a hurry to finish their sausages and chips, and leave. Behind the counter, Charlie, the owner, frowned and puffed himself up to his full, inconsiderable height.

And us Kings and Queens of Westerton? We stayed put, and were suddenly very quiet. We had never been challenged before and apart from the odd little scrap and some pushing and shoving, we had never had to fight. It was easy to be tough when there was no opposition, but suddenly we were faced with a herd of characters who looked very battle-hardened indeed.

They ignored us at first and crowded around a couple of vacant tables near the window.

Maisie, the waitress, went over and took their order. Her voice was small and she looked scared. The gang told her what they wanted; not polite but giving no reason to be challenged or thrown out. We huddled into ourselves and tried to carry on, but bravado was in short supply.

There was no music playing. One of us needed to go to the jukebox. I was single, no official girlfriend to weep over my grave, so I squared my shoulders, reached into my pocket for some coins and stood.

At the same time, one of the bikers got up, chair scraped noisily back. He didn't even look at me, but strode across to the machine before I could get anywhere near it.

'The Last Time' by The Rolling Stones.

From that day forth I have hated The Rolling Stones.

He looked at me and grinned. He had a missing front tooth. He raised his eyebrows – a small gesture but a challenge. *What are you going to do about it?*

Humiliated, I went back to my mates.

'Next time, get up there a bit quicker,' Tony snapped at me.

'*You* do it next time,' I said to him.

'Yeah, I fucking will,' he growled.

'Hey,' Charlie snapped from behind the counter. 'That's enough of that language in here, Tony.'

Tony coloured up. The Rockers sniggered.

I wanted to get out of there. So did the others.

'The Last Time' faded away. Another silence, which was odd because the Rocker must've selected only the one record, which meant that this was a game. This was the start of it.

Tony wouldn't look at me. I got up. So did one of the Rockers, a different one this time; slight-built, fair hair. We made it to the jukebox at the same moment.

Leo Tolstoy wrote about chance and whim. There's a lot of it in *War and Peace*. Yeah, I've read it. Years after that Bank Holiday, though. I didn't time my rush to the jukebox to coincide with the Rocker's attempt. It just happened. Just the way Leo said it could.

He held back. I swear to you. He held back for a fragment of a second so that I could get there first. Money in, no hesitation on my behalf, and The Animals were back. I looked at the Rocker. He looked at me. The stare was intense, and it went on too long. Then I went back to our table. There was a lot of back-slapping, and triumphant stares over towards the window.

The Rockers shook their heads and laughed some more, not caring about our victory. They mocked their representative a little and I saw him go red, but that was it.

So Stalemate. They were by the door. Our scooters were hemmed in by their motorcycles. We needed to get out.

Bobby's girl, Shelia, was the one who said it. 'We'll just have to get up and walk past them. They're not going to start any trouble in here.' Weren't they? I admired her confidence, or was it naivety?

We all took deep breaths, got to our feet and made for the door. The Rockers watched us coming. Except for the fair-haired one. He kept his eyes on the plate of sausage and chips in front of him.

Close. I could smell leather, I could smell cigarette smoke and I could smell grease and oil and sweat and the strong, cheap perfume of the girls.

Then we were out into the pale sunshine and huddled together on the prom. I sighed out my relief. Until I noticed Tony's expression. I turned to see the Rockers emerge from the café. They set off across the road. Straight towards us.

'We'd better run,' Tony said.

'Fuck that,' Bobby said. I could see that he was scared, but trying hard to be tough. Not just a pretty face was Bobby. He glanced at his girlfriend. 'You'd better get out of it, Sheel.'

She stepped up to him and took his arm. Brave girl, braver than me because all I wanted to do was get as far away from that place as I could. But it was too late. The gang were almost on us. And I would never have deserted my mates.

'What do you want?' Bobby said. He stepped away from Sheila and stood in front of us.

'Nuffink,' said the gap-toothed character who had beaten me to the jukebox. 'Just some of that sea air.'

He smirked.

'There's plenty of seafront,' Bobby said.

'Yeah, well, we like this bit.'

'You can't have it.' I said, wanting it over with and wondering how much it was going to hurt.

'Fuck,' Tony hissed.

The gap tooth raised his eyebrows, then grinned and glanced at the others who had formed an arc about him. He nodded, and in they came.

It wasn't so bad, not at first. I suppose my own blood was up. Adrenaline, anger, fear, I don't know, but I went straight for the leader and grabbed at him. I remember the feel of leather in my hands and how cold it was, I remember the violence of the collision between us and how we were rammed close to each other and he was suddenly simply a human being and not frightening at all. I remember that he stank of sweat and cigarettes and his breath was foul. Then we were forced apart. I slipped and his boot flicked towards me and there was pain, a lot of it. It exploded outwards from my right side and I went down onto the pavement, which seemed to slam into me like a dirty, grey train. Another impact and suddenly I couldn't breathe. There was no air, only a horrible, agonised blank where there should have been taste and oxygen. Another kick. This one dulled, not the same shocking explosion as the first one. I curled up as feet shuffled around me and people shouted and swore.

Someone else went down onto their hands and knees. It was the fair-headed boy. He looked at me, and I saw blood dripping from his lip. I sucked in a breath. It hurt. Everything hurt. I struggled to my feet. Aware that at any moment someone could pile in and beat the shit out of me, but the battle had become a rout and I glimpsed Rockers running in pursuit of my mates, as they disappeared down the beach.

I stood. The Rocker looked up at me. He shook his head and said, 'This is so fucking daft.' He extended his hand towards me and without thinking, another of old Leo's moments, I took it and helped him to his feet.

'Thanks,' he said.

I shrugged.

I saw the Rocker girls still standing across the road, watching. The boy rubbed his lips with his sleeve then reached into his pocket and offered me a cigarette. I took one. 'Ta,' I said. 'Michael.'

He nodded. 'Simon.'

'Don't get mixed up in this,' he said as he took the first drag. His accent was different to the others. He sounded ... educated. I suppose that's what you'd call it. 'Motorbikes. They're my bloody downfall. I started going to the Ace Café, in London, you know, where all the Rockers go, and somehow I got drawn in. It was Nick, he's a powerful bugger, you know, persuasive...'

I assumed that Nick was the one who had kicked me.

'It's because he thinks I'm posh,' Simon said. He seemed in no hurry to leave and, to be honest, I wasn't in a hurry to go stumbling off down the beach to find the others either.

'What do you mean?' I asked. The cigarette was comforting but it hurt my chest and burned my throat, and my ribs were on fire. I wanted to sit down but suspected that that would make the pain even worse.

'My dad, he's a doctor. I suppose that sounds posh to people like Nick.'

'He still let you join his gang,' I said.

Simon chuckled, an old sound as if he had suddenly aged by twenty years. 'I'm a sort of prize. I make his gang different from the others. He's always boasting about Lord Bloody Simon. That's what he calls me.'

'Why … why don't you just leave the gang?'

He stared at me, hard. That stare, it made me uncomfortable, but I held it because there was nothing in the world I wanted more at that moment than to hold that stare. It drew me in, made me— Christ knows, what it made me feel. I remember it though. Every second of it. His eyes were blue and for those hours, days, seconds, the whole world was blue, and dark at the edges, like burning paper.

'I don't want to,' he said at last and broke the moment. Then I swear I heard him say. 'At least, I *didn't* want to.' Perhaps he didn't say that at all. In my memory he did, and still does.

'I'd better find my mates,' I said. My voice sounded dry and so bloody ordinary.

'Yeah. Look, lay low until we're gone. We'll be around until tonight. Okay? And Nick and the others are looking for a fight. There's some nasty bastards among them. Don't try to, you know, get your own back or anything. Nick's … well, he's a nutcase.'

We'd have called him a psycho these days.

'FUCKING SENT HIM down,' Tony said. 'One fucking punch.' He held up his fist. The knuckles were grazed. There was even a blood stain. 'Split his lip. Blood everywhere.' He sounded out of breath. They all did, my mates and our girls. I found them by the pier, bruised, grazed and huddled about one of its huge freshly-painted iron legs. There were no amusement arcades on our pier. There was a concert hall and, would you believe, an art gallery.

So, Tony was the one who had hit Simon. I was oddly angry about this, even though he was one of the enemy.

There was a lot of talk when I first arrived. Slaps on the back for me, and loud bravado, which quickly ran out. Karen shuffled over to me and tucked herself under my arm. The action annoyed me further, although I tried not to let it show. I wanted her to leave me alone. The sea raged and hissed over the shingles, waves bounced against the sea-buried legs of the pier. The light dimmed to grey as the sun disappeared behind yet another cloud. The scant warmth was sucked from the air.

I noticed straight away that Bobby didn't join in the war stories. He sat, arm about Sheila, face like thunder, brooding.

'Where shall we go?' someone asked, more to break the atmosphere than because they wanted a plan.

'The fairground,' Bobby answered.

'No,' I said. I didn't often argue with Bobby, none of us did, but Simon's warning was still fresh in my mind. '*They'll* be there.'

'Scared?' Tony said. He was, despite his bravado. He wasn't the only one.

'That's why we should go,' Bobby said. 'No one comes here and thinks they can do what they fucking like.' I'd never seen him like this. He ground out the words. He was breathing hard. He wanted blood.

'You weren't the one who got a kicking.' I grunted in pain, and not just for effect. 'And Nick—'

'Who the hell's Nick?' Bobby said.

'Their leader. He's bloody dangerous. I was the one who took him on remember?'

'Yeah,' Tony said. 'I saw that, before I punched—'

'How do you know his name?'

I didn't like Bobby's stare. I didn't like the suspicion it contained. We were lifelong friends. We were supposed to trust each other. I should have told them, but I couldn't.

'I heard someone shout to him.'

'I'm going to the fairground,' Bobby said. 'Even if I have to go alone.'

'I'll come with you.' Sheila gripped his arm, frightened but determined.

'Me too,' Tony said. The rest all chimed in bravely.

'Of course I'm coming,' I said.

We started to get up, not easy for me, because the pain was

getting worse.

'Not yet,' Bobby said. It was almost funny, everyone frozen, halfway to their feet, as if we were playing Simon Says...

The world, blue, burning at the edges...

'Let's get our scooters. Then we'll meet back here at about seven. Right?'

Right Bobby.

'Bring whatever you can get your hands on. Know what I mean?'

We knew. And now we were all scared.

LIKE I SAID. My dad was a plumber, so there was plenty of metal pipe stacked up in our back yard...

NONE OF US spoke as we parked our Lambrettas and walked into the fairground. Anyone looking at us must have wondered what was wrong - it's hard to act naturally when you have a length of pipe stuffed down your trousers or a knife hidden in the inside pocket of your jacket.

We strolled with studied nonchalance past the shooting gallery, the dodgems and the waltzer. Music blared from the speakers; The Yardbirds, The Beatles, The Kinks' 'See My Friend'.

Bobby led us deeper into the fair and we all followed. We glanced left, right, looking for the enemy.

My own fear was complicated and deep. My own fear was tangled up with the pain in my side and the weight of the metal pipe tucked against my right leg, and the dread of the coming fight. And Simon. I had to find him, and warn him. I don't know when I had decided that. But he was going to get hurt. We had knives and clubs and Bobby was after blood and we would do what he said because we didn't know how not to, and we were together and none of us wanted to be left behind.

There was no sense to my need to protect Simon. I didn't know him. I had swapped a few awkward sentences with him. We had smoked together.

He had stared at me, and I, at him.

And the world had turned blue and burned.

'This is a bloody useless,' Bobby growled. That's how I remember it, a growl, heard by all of us, even though we were being pounded by noise; music, the dodgem siren, the drone of the generators. He growled. Sullen, angry. 'We should split up. Come back here in twenty minutes, here, by the dodgems, yeah?'

Yeah.

I was off, quickly, before anyone else could volunteer to come with me. Karen, especially. She would have given her eye teeth to be alone with me.

My side hurt so badly, it made me dizzy. The lights stung my eyes. There were people, too many, blocking my way, bumping into me, swirling around me.

Then a shout. Louder than the rest of the noise.

And I saw them; a clutch of leather jackets by the shooting gallery, cigarettes hung precariously from their lips, sneers firmly in place. And they were moving towards me. Five of them, all coming for *me*. Five sets of fists and boots. One of them broke into a run. He carried a bike chain. Christ, they were armed as well.

It was impossible, too many people, too much pain. I could barely breathe. My side...

I fumbled for the pipe, tried to force my hand into my trousers. The waistband was too tight. I hopped and blundered through the crowd and almost fell. Then a hand grabbed my arm and propelled me forward.

We barged and battered our way towards a gap between stalls. The gap was dark and narrow. I knew without looking that the hand belonged to Simon.

WE STUMBLED TO a halt, suddenly outside the fair on the edge of its temporary car park. Behind us, light and noise. Ahead, the gathering dark, the shadowed huddle of cars, a few people making their way to and from their vehicles.

Simon still held my arm and still clutched the chain in his other hand.

We were both panting, breathless. The pain in my side was

intensified by every gasp for air.

'I ... I thought... I thought you were going to wrap that round my head,' I said.

I heard his laugh. 'I don't know how to ... I've never hit anyone...' His laugh became a cough. He released my arm so he could double-up and recover.

'You have to get out of here,' I said, my breath steadier now. 'Bobby ... my lot, we're armed...' I wrestled the pipe from my trousers.

'Bloody hell, Michael—'

There were shouts, movement, dark shapes that tumbled from the side entrance we had just escaped through. They stood for a moment, looking round. Simon grabbed my arm again and we ran, stumbled between the cars, slipped and scrabbled over the scrubby, stony ground, towards the woods that bordered The Common.

Then I heard motorbikes, a brutal, animal roar that turned my soul to ice. I glanced back to see their headlights sweep over the cars as they weaved towards us.

We plunged into the trees. I gripped Simon's hand and felt the tightness of his about mine. We crashed and stumbled through the undergrowth. The darkness grew more complete. We ran blind, tripped and careered over fallen trunks, bracken whipped at our legs and grasped at our ankles.

The night was sliced open, became a tangle of light-blackened claws, a jagged web of white and dark. The motorbikes roared behind us, one of them in the woods. Nick, it had to be Nick, the mad one, driven by whatever mindless need for revenge, violence or destruction that pumped the blood through his veins. He was close. I could smell the bike's exhaust. I could smell petrol fumes. I could smell Nick's hate.

We crashed out of the dark suddenly back in the fairground and next to the generator lorries. We ran again. The crowds were thinner here but quickly growing more dense, until we were once again in an obstacle race. At least I couldn't hear the motorbikes anymore.

The dodgems, we had to get to the dodgems, and to the others, my friends, allies. I wasn't thinking.

I led the way now. I hauled Simon behind me, my hand tight about his. Unheeding. Too frightened and desperate to understand.

'Mike! Over here!'

I saw them: Bobby, Tony, all of them, looking hunted, frustrated. I lurched into the light. Tony grinned and took a step towards me, Karen beside him. Bobby made to speak, to ask where I'd been? Had I found…

'He's all right,' I said, meaning Simon. 'He's not like—'

I wrenched my hand free. I sensed Simon take a step back.

'Fucking traitor,' Bobby spat at me. 'Fucking—'

He had no words. None of them had any words for what they had seen. Nor did I. All I saw on their faces was hatred and disgust. My lifelong friends. We were children running and laughing in the playground. We were the Kings and Queens of our town. Me, and these the people who I loved.

And who's love I needed more than anything.

I swung round. I still had the iron pipe in my right hand, my free hand. I can't remember all of it, only the first moments, the anger and the need and the way Simon staggered back but didn't go down straight away. I remember his face. The blood. His wide, bewildered eyes. Blue they were.

...and the world burned at the edges.

RIGHT HERE. THAT'S where it happened. By the dodgems.

I got away with it. There was confusion, it was dark.

You can bury the truth only for so long; weeks, months, decades. You can bury it but it will slowly claw its way back the surface.

Like a splinter.

The others managed to drag me off and we slipped away.

Our gang didn't survive long after that night. They all kept the secret though. I respect them for that. Me, I joined up, ten years in the army. Quickest way out. Eventually, I found a wife and we set up home a long way from Westerton-on-Sea. We were happy. No kids. For the best. Seven months ago Natalie noticed blood in her urine. Happiness is never everlasting.

A good life then, but formed about the tumour in my soul, layers of lies and guilt that could never stop its slow, relentless spread. I didn't cry at Natalie's funeral. I'm crying now. I have a mobile phone. Bloody thing, too awkward for my clumsy fingers. Only one number needed though, the same one, pressed three times.

Police.

I killed someone.

GREY CHILDREN

David A. Sutton

HIS GRANDFATHER HAD told him that *he* would never go into the workhouse. Robert was in Selly Oak now, as his grandfather had been when he had suffered a major stroke - only it was a hospital, no longer a workhouse. He'd been treated and sent home; half broken.

Times had moved on. The hospital's bricks and mortar were the same Victorian bricks and mortar, the edifice unchanged but for cosmetic accoutrements. Long, dark, cream painted tunnels for corridors, hollow with mutterings and cries, echoes from its past, perhaps. Wheeled in from the ambulance, Robert found himself waiting; dreams and delusions carrying his thoughts.

In a moment of lucidity he thought, 'This is the place people die. This is where granddad started dying'. He said, 'Am I going to –'

The trolley rolled along the linoleum-lined corridors but the pusher didn't speak. Neon tubes above on the arched ceiling overhead whizzed past, shiny slim rockets. He was halted in the passageway.

Another shunt of the trolley... Shunt... And then a quiet room and clattered curtains to hide him from the world.

'Uhrr.' The pain was suddenly there again but muted by some sort of pain-killing drug. Robert tried to recall what had happened to him, an accident or something...

No nurse. No doctor in attendance to ask. It didn't matter. He knew he was dying. Like granddad. Only better. There'd be no post-hospital life as a half disabled old man, with a left arm, left face, left everything, immobilised.

'Do up my shoelaces, boy.' Memories ... or dreams.

Robert, half in, half out of consciousness, recalled the past, a past or a dream. A yellow girl, the ugly man, things better kept hidden. The dark, invisible sibling who stole granddad's eyes, and then told him tales from the war while cold crinkled fingers loosened his belt and searched within the inner fabric.

Vivid in the boy's memory, the tales he had been told. Flares of light, booming percussions, shredded tinsel and body parts flailing in explosive detonations. Times from the war, tales and horrors. And the pain that came with the squeezing blue-veined wrinkled hands inside his trousers.

The pain was intensifying but no one was near. Robert closed his eyes. He had been left to die. Fourteen years. Fourteen years. Repeating it would not increase the offer. Fourteen was going to be his sum.

Opening his eyes, there was a pleasant woman gazing down at him. The room's light was dim, subdued. The pleasant woman was staring as if she saw phantoms before her eyes. Then, 'Let's get you up to theatre.' A pause as she looks at a clipboard—'Robert' —out she goes, the boy ignored.

'*Nurse!*'

Too late. Robert was alone again. The pain had diminished to an insignificant nag but fear stood in its place. Something not right was happening inside.

The boy glanced down at his torso, his legs, his feet. Their shapes under the open weave blanket that tried to keep him warm. But he was cold, very cold. His granddad hadn't gone like this. He had gone in a whisper, a pause between breaths. His earlier stroke disabling enough to allow the following heart attack to stealthily creep through his arteries and veins and...

No time for guilt. No recompense for Robert. For a deathbed apology.

He threw off the nice blanket. His thin, naked body, pale, almost a dead zombie thing, waiting. His thoughts disembodied, not an accomplice to the transformation. A phantom rising from him, a spirit, a ghostly grey wraith. Insect-like. Rising, slimy, unfolding, a white nymph birth from within his insides. Robert was a recumbent pupa, a shell to be discarded once his mortal fluids had dried up.

SHE IS FIFTEEN, for gods' sake. Her pussy oozing blood, oozing her ripeness. She has real clout now. Her parents - arguing in the living room - unaware of movements, changes, slippages, new paradigms within her mind and body. 'They'll go to church this Sunday', she knows, 'they'll take the wafer and pray and murmur and sing. They'll confess their—'

Sin.

The 'sin' she wanted to commit was not to be confessed and not a real transgression. Their family priest, in his robes of authority, was in a robe of sin. The robe of child molestation and debauchery. She's seen the news; and the way their priest looks at her. She thinks their secret ways must not be allowed to become an excuse, to be listed as a minor contravention available for absolution.

She thinks about her father. Dour, not close with her mother. Only cold, with mom. Lucy's bedroom should be a sanctuary. There was only that one time, years ago. He'd rubbed something into her down there. And lay on top of her, heavy enough to take away her breath.

Father never enters her room now but she thinks he still wants to ... and probably will soon unless she takes steps.

Her mother, doomed, alone, alienated. She makes the bed, tidies up. Trappings of normality. She has friends, yes. But she's not telling what she knows about father. Her friends are mere buffers from which to hide the hidden truth about him.

Both parents go off to work in the evening, after their argument, and Lucy is left alone.

Night bears down.

Night is when the essences arise.

Lucy, nearly a woman, reaches for a pair of scissors from her dressing table. They are nail scissors, small, but do the job of scything a sheaf of golden hair from her head.

Fastened on her dressing table mirror are the pictures of former adulation. Cliff Richard. Her mom kept all her copies of *Mirabelle*. Page-clipped, she had kept the pop star in a scrapbook. Lucy suspects the child she was is now dissolved.

She looks at herself in the mirror. Blond hair, round face. Eyes wide apart, lips dry and pale. Spots. Blemishes. Her eyes are bright, but fevered. She clicks off the bedside lamp and the bedroom stills into shadow. In a drawer which she slides open slowly, she removes the soft clay doll she had fashioned. It looks not much like anything, except perhaps *Morph*. But not open and friendly like the television character. More ancient, hostile; its eyes are not wide, amusing, staring. Its eyes are blank buttons from her mom's sewing basket. Odd, pearlescent, reflectively dead. That doesn't matter.

The girl wraps her cut hair around the doll and presses it into the soft clay.

On her dressing table an old enamelled tin wash basin waits. She places the doll within. A bedpan for a bed. She squirts lighter fuel on the doll and strikes a match.

The flare lights up her bedroom for a moment before the stench of burning hair and fluid permeates the room. She opens the sash window to release the smoke, which drifts above the clawing shrubs in the back garden.

And the visitor enters.

BIRDS ARE SINGING. Robert can hear them as the glow slips from him. The glow moving across the ceiling, a fat white form swathed in bristly hair, crawling away with a rustle.

THE STREETS OF the suburb are always a night country. Narrow terraced housing trace two lines along the slender street. The black cloud sky merges with the grey roof tiles which makes a bower of the sky and buildings. The dwellings are merging into their front yards and pavements in their dereliction. The houses are uniformly dark, windows cracked or broken, hollows of greater darkness glowering over the crumbling street. They represent, for those that live within them, and in their neglect, families failed by society, or families abusing neighbour, and the social mores re-defined, without taboos.

Lucy walks along the thin street. At her shoulder her demon lover. His hand, or some appendage on her shoulder, guides her. The street ends in a railway arch, and beneath it a path to a canal cuts away from the street. The grey thing turns her and they walk down a muddy slope onto the towpath.

Oily black water laps the muddy reeds as if a recently passing narrow-boat had churned up the water. On the towpath white-painted bollards mark her passage beside boarded up factories, thin, rusted corrugated iron sidings scraping against themselves in a breeze. The girl is aware that her guide is turning her again, through a scrub of hedge and into the rear yard of one of the canal-side factories. A lopsided security light hangs high up from a wall, its tepid sallow glow illuminating a yard vile with a detritus of carpets, sodden cardboard, cans, bottles, condoms and needles. Some failed administrative duty had allowed the electricity supply to continue long after the disused factory's abandonment. And provided an inadvertent spotlight on the sordid nightly machinations below. Discoloured silver extractor pipes curved out from the building's upper storey and brown shit stains on the brick walls match those on the leaky seams of the pipes. Lucy is guided over a trampled-down chain link fence and onto an adjoining towpath.

Together the couple step aboard the narrow-boat moored there, constricted like a coffin. They enter a low cabin as the boat mimics their movements, rocking to and fro. Darkness shrouds the innards of the boat but she can feel coarse cloth under her feet as her shoes slip off. Before she can turn, her companion has thrust her violently onto the floor. Her breath draws into scream, but is sucked away in fear as he rips at her underwear. His violent motions make the boat sway from side to side and the grunting sounds made by Lucy's nymph lover echo around the wooden superstructure. She feels moistness between her legs, her blood mixed with its sperm, she turns her face away, squeezing tears from her eyes. Then the rape is finished and she falls asleep.

WHEN LUCY WAKES her companion is a cold shell beside her. She pulls down her skirt and puts back on the remains of her pants.

Lifting him, he's light, a cold weightless grey shell, dusty and empty, a faceless carapace with nothing inside. She carries him off the boat onto the towpath, planning to cast his body into the black scummy water. Her eyes are cold with malice, but she hesitates. And, supporting him in her arms, she heads for home.

Her body feels strange, her companion has insinuated itself into her. Soon, he has become one with her, in her arms now metamorphosed into her grey child. Stunted, a still-birth starved of oxygen; the beetle has replaced itself with a dead changeling. A withered human face, a baby's face, cruelly crumpled and gaunt.

Yet there is movement in its pathetic white fingers.

When Lucy arrives, her house is hemmed on the street by other terraces, tall soiled brick structures blending into the sooty sky above. She approaches the front window and peers through net curtains into the yellow light. Her mother stares out, puzzled, catching a fleeting glimpse of something. Surely, Lucy thinks, she can see her own daughter and the child, frozen cold and in need of warmth. She rattles the loose glass of the window and it sounds as if winter branches strike the glass as brittle bones. She is akin to a ghost rattling the shutters of an old, old mansion, beseeching entry. Seeking retribution for past abominations.

Lucy sneaks a look upon the bastard child in her arms. It opens its stolen lantern eyes, yellow whites and golden irises. She turns the child to face the window and knows her mother's heart will soften when she sees it and Lucy will be let in. Her father will pay the price and mother will be happy.

Lucy cuddles the child and hums a lullaby and rattles the window. Behind the glass her mother moves back, distracted, worry lines upon her brow. She draws the curtains behind the nets, obscuring the light and warmth within. Undaunted Lucy moves to the front door and raps the knuckles of one hand against it while cradling the child. And the infant, she sees, is smiling, its ugly pinched face transforming from cockroach to angel.

He's always on the edge of

– the signal on the b/w stop-motion film

disco (silent film)

juxtaposed

I don't know why he

that / unless it's the

of his expression

making him seem

– if he depended on

THE TWIN

James Brogden

TAKE A BREAD stick. Wrap a length of strong string - parcel twine, maybe - around it once, twice, three times. Pull the string hard at both ends but don't let the bread stick spring loose from the coils; watch the inexorably tightening cord reduce it to crumbling shards, a helix of shrapnel.

This is his thigh bone.

The climbing rope fastens hard at the point where his foot is trapped against the rock, tangled around his leg as he dangles upside down, penduluming against the cliff face with the weight of his own body providing the traction which pulls it tight, tighter, tightest - and then comes the popcorn-cannonade of shattering bone. His whole leg looked like a marshmallow twist.

Candy is dandy he thinks, *but liquor is quicker.*

The pain is appallingly, unimaginably huge, huger than the rock-face above him: a towering, monolithic grey mass which might reach down at any moment to swat him out of the world. Too big to comprehend in its entirety. It is so big that when the anchor point tears free and he crashes a dozen yards onto the ledge below he barely feels it, or the tumbling slide down a hundred feet of scree slope to the valley floor, to lie face down in bog, sedge-cut.

A stunned moment. He puts his mouth to the black saturated peat and begins to scream. He vacuums up every particle of agony out of his body with the bellows of his lungs and screams them into the muffling moss. Bits of brokenness spray out on the spit of his breath as he howls and howls and howls until his throat is broken too, and nothing else can come out of him except a dry rasping, indistinguishable from the wind in the sedge around him. He screams himself hollow into the earth, and passes out.

But the scream sticks.

The ground captures his scream, holds it, binds it and preserves it in the particulate matrix of acidic, anaerobic peat; and something quickens, deep in the slow, cold womb of the mountain.

HE CAN'T RECALL how he made it to the cave. It's not much of a cave, in truth – more a wide crack in the cliff face – but it is some shelter from the elements. Outside, gritty snow dances on skirries of a mercilessly iced wind driving down from the higher slopes and settles in pale, bloodless scabs amongst the tussocks of bog grass. As his eyes adjust, he sees a human shape silhouetted against the opening.

He tries to speak – to ask *Where am I? Who are you? Help me!* But his throat makes only a dry clicking sound.

The figure turns at this, becoming a curve of shoulder and head, a nose briefly forming into profile and disappearing again into lumpen shadow as it turns and regards him.

'No,' it confirms. 'You have no voice.'

Its own is familiar but he can't place it. Out of habit he tries to speak again, makes only a dry sound, and claws the stone in frustration. It is only then that he realises his broken leg – jutting out in front of him like a bent pipe-cleaner – doesn't hurt in the slightest. He panics then, fearing that his spine is broken, gasping, croaking, kicking out with his good leg (which works just fine), while his bad one flops uselessly. Mobile, but utterly useless. He can even hear the broken ends of bone scraping against each other like grinding teeth *but still there is no pain.*

His shadowed companion nods. 'You gave the one to me with the other.' It shuffles closer, grunting with the effort, and continues in lower, more intimate tones: 'You cannot call for help. There are men on the mountain looking for you but you will die of exposure long before that happens unless you and I can agree on one simple thing.'

He shrugs and waves his arms around wildly. *Anything! Anything!*

It shuffles closer still and now he can smell it – the fetor of the bog, of black, rotting peat and moss and stagnant water. Its eyes glow a dim red within deeply hollowed sockets. It is close enough to whisper in his ear. Its breath on his cheek is cold.

'What I have taken from you – what you have given to me – you will never seek to reclaim.'

He can place the voice now. It is as alien and familiar as listening to the sound of oneself recorded on an answerphone. It is his own voice. It has stolen his voice and dragged him here to die.

In sudden, terrified rage he lashes out, punching the other in its face. His fist sinks deep into a spongy, stinking mass, scratchy with twigs and leaf-matter, and encounters something small and hard which he instinctively grabs at before pulling back with revulsion. The other collapses backwards and he lunges for the cave opening, pulling himself along with his three functioning limbs and the fourth dragging behind like a disjointed tail, out into the snow. The sky is bright and hard as he hauls himself over the ground using clumps of wiry rush-grass. He is certain that the other will be coming after him, and he tries to scream despite knowing that it won't work but helpless to do anything else. He looks back over his shoulder, expecting to see something rotting and moss-begotten shambling towards him, but there's nothing. Just snow-scabbed grass and the dim, drawn-out sounds of gurgling agony echoing from deep inside the rock.

He realises he is clutching something tightly in his fist, which is black with slime. He opens his fingers and sees a stone – nothing special, just a simple stone – but he remembers how it had glowed when it had been the other's left eye, so he closes his fist again and begins to crawl.

THE CAST WAS cut off with heavy shears crunching through the fibre-glass and tugged apart like a thick crust of cocoon. Through the widening gap, something black gleamed. He wanted to shout to the doctors *Stop! Wait! No, something's wrong!* But by then they'd pulled it fully apart and his leg was there – dead , wizened and glossy black like mummified oak, his knee a writhen knot, his toes blunt pegs – a stillborn limb.

The hallucination was momentary and then his real leg was there, pallid as a grub, soft as marshmallow and studded with metal pins.

Of course, he couldn't have begged them to stop because he had no voice with which to beg. He hadn't spoken a word in the months since the accident. He'd communicated through notes easily enough but hadn't been able to so much as grunt, either in pleasure or pain.

There were weeks of physiotherapy. They warned him not to overdo it in his eagerness to be whole but his inability to feel discomfort actually set his own progress back. He was unable to tell when he was pushing himself too hard and causing himself harm. Doctors quickly ruled out any physical damage to his throat and suggested that the psychological trauma of the accident was the cause of his muteness. He humoured them as far as was able but in the end how could he tell them what had really happened? His husband Steven supported him as far as he was able, but in the end how could he live with a partner who could give no understandable reason why he would not say a single word to him? When they had sex for the first time after the accident, he even came in gasping silence, like someone suffocating in outer space. No matter how hard Steven fucked him, there was no pain, and no way to express it even if there were.

He became reckless in the search for his missing pain. He found men who would take money to find inventive ways of damaging him – and quite a few who would do it for free. There was never anything sexual in it – not for him, anyway. He told himself that he was not being unfaithful.

He took to cutting himself just to see if it would make any

difference. He was careful, clean and, above all, discreet, because he knew what Steven would say. There was an inescapable fascination in watching the flesh part from either side of his blade as if eager to release the redness within – just so long as it remained red. Because the more he did it, and the deeper he cut, the darker it looked, until he began to suspect that what flowed close to his bones wasn't blood at all but peat-black bog water, the life-stuff of mountains.

But complacency bred carelessness and one time the spurting would not stop. He got himself to a hospital in time to save his life, but not his marriage. There were recriminations, tears, pleas and promises, and an ultimatum: get his shit together or to pack his bags.

He decided to get his shit together.

His one consolation in all of this was the stone that he had stolen from the other's eye. In the deepest cave of his most shameful moments he would take it out, because it *glowed.* The worse the excess to which he subjected himself, the brighter it glowed, and in its glow he saw such beautiful things: lake-reflected mountains, ice-falls like cascades of molten diamond, alpine lilies crowding inaccessible ledges. He knew that this was what the other was seeing because the visions were sometimes occluded by ghostly lashes that made them flicker, and ghostly tears that made them dim. He would be able to track the other by identifying those locations. When he decided to go back to the mountains, he was unsure whether it was to claim back what was his or to return that which he had stolen.

HE REACHED THE summit of the hill and paused to take in the late autumnal view, whose mixed pastel colours blurred into the worn-out sky. An ether of chill drizzle swirled around him, the droplets seeming to tremble on the verge of forming shapes, as if afraid of what they might show. In the valley a few stripped trees reached out thin limbs.

But he felt only a slow contentment. It was wonderful to taste hill-fog and climb out of it into hidden sunlight – to walk, after months of lameness. Watching the writhen trees, he remembered the malformed creature that he had left behind. Something dark in the darkness of clay, his half-born brother.

And here was the high valley and the cliff and the cave at its base – but he didn't see the other at first. He took it for a particularly bent and weather-beaten tree, crouched and staring into the mirror-black pools of bog water. As he approached, it rose – so slowly, bracing itself on its bent knees and grunting like an old man as it unfolded itself.

The walker was shocked at what he saw.

His twin resembled nothing so much as a living cadaver: gaunt, all knuckles and knotted joints, his flesh the glossy black of mummified leather. But it was also grossly, agonisingly misshapen beyond any dream of symmetry. It looked like it had been broken on a rack, then rebroken for good measure. Its empty eye socket gaped, its jaw was askew, its spine was no less contorted than one of the trees below, and scars scars scars ran everywhere. Its breath wheezed as it regarded him. He knew that every movement was an agony, and envied it.

He held out the stone that was its eye, offering it on his palm. *Here.*

It spat on the ground and glared at him. 'You think to *swap*, is that it?' it slurred. 'As if we are boys in a school yard trading marbles?'

He mimed clutching. *You stole from me. I stole from you. Fair's fair.* He proffered the stone more forcefully. *Take it.*

'I stole *nothing!*' Its vehemence was costly and it reeled, gasping. 'You squandered it! Puked it from your mewling mouth like an infant! So your voice went with it – did you think that there would not be a cost? Pain is an energy,' it continued, weakened by its exertions. 'And like all energy it does not die. It merely changes from one form to another.'

And then he understood how his twin had become so mutilated, where his own pain had gone – the pain of all those sordid trysts and all that self-harm. It was here, staring at him, like a twisted portrait of himself. The pain which had given life and, when taken away, made life unbearable.

Fine then. He tossed the stone away and stepped forward to claim back what was his.

IT TOOK STEVEN a while to discover exactly which path Anthony had taken up the mountain; they were many and labyrinthine. He wasn't even sure exactly why it was he'd decided to follow in the first place. The cynic in him suspected that it was to catch Anthony in the middle of one of his unspeakable liaisons, although why come so far out into the middle of nowhere? The better angel of his nature said that it was to keep his lover from harm, fearing that he'd finally come to the end of what he could endure and had decided to do something stupid and final. The mountain was large, he wasn't much of an outdoorsman, and by the time he finally saw what Anthony was doing he was almost too exhausted to react.

In the midst of an open expanse of upland moor, he was wrestling with something dark.

For a moment Steven was seized with the surreal impression that Anthony was waltzing through the bristling rushes with a tattered coat on a broken hat stand for a partner. He forced his aching legs to keep carrying him up the last slope, but the ground was boggy and sucked at his feet. The staggering, struggling couple bobbed in and out of view as he lurched forward. His last snatched glimpse was of them tumbling to the ground.

He heard the splash quite distinctly.

Steven yelled in wordless denial and arrived at where a figure lay face down, half-submerged, and motionless in a pool of black water. He threw himself in, gasping at the freezing cold of it, and dragged Anthony's limp frame to ground which was only slightly more solid. Sobbing, praying, cursing, he checked for breath and pulse, and wept when he found both.

'You're alive!'

Anthony coughed, spewing brown bile. 'Doesn't feel like it,' he groaned.

Steven stared. 'You just—'

'Talked. I know.' He reached up to stroke Steven's cheek. 'Thank you,' he whispered.

Steven stared harder. 'Your eyes...'

'What about them?'

'The left one's turned brown.'

Anthony had no more breath left to spare in response to that, so simply let himself be helped up.

'Can you walk?'

'Just about, I think. Everything hurts.' He flexed his fingers, hands, arms, shoulders, back, and hips – grimacing and gasping at each strained movement. He turned to Steven and grinned. 'Everything hurts!'

Leaning together, they began to pick their slow and careful way back down the mountain.

THROUGH THE FLOOR

Gary Couzens

I DON'T DANCE so much these days. Whether that's not wanting to be reminded or fear of the music itself, I'm not sure. Part of it's knowing I'll never be as good as James. It was less than a year ago we first met. I remember, I'd just gone into a nightclub. I hadn't even bought a drink. He was standing at one of the dark tables in front of the dance floor. A tall man, quite thin, dressed in a black t-shirt and jeans. He remained absolutely still for about ten minutes, watching the dancers. There was something angry in his stillness, a tense feeling. Suddenly he emptied his glass and slipped onto the dance floor. The music shivered through his limbs; he was caught up in it like a floating candle on a river. I knew I had to speak to him.

I was at the bar when he finished dancing. I'd bought myself a vodka and orange by then. Normally, if I came here on my own, someone might hit on me, might not take no for an answer so I'd be polite, smile, let him down gently. But tonight I was left alone, sitting on a stool by the bar, my fingers toying with the hem of my dress, my shoe dangling from the ends of my toes. Even the barman didn't try to make conversation, going on to attend to others on this over-twenty-fives night. I must have given out that vibe. But as I drank, I glanced over my shoulder at James. As the music reached a pause, he left the floor, his forehead gleaming with perspiration.

Maybe he sensed I was looking at him. He reached the bar next to where I was sitting. Closer up, he was clearly older than I'd assumed at first, with grey at his temples and flecks in his hair.

'Hi,' he said as he waited to be served.

'Hi,' I said back.

He glanced at my half-finished drink. 'Looks like you're sorted for the moment.'

'It's just the first one.' Most evenings for the last two weeks, since Mike died, I'd sat at home with a bottle and had drunk it all, sometimes spending part of the night puking into the toilet bowl. I'm not sure how I got through days of teaching Year Nines while hung over, but I did. I reckoned if I was going to drink myself into oblivion I might as well leave my flat to do it. I was on my own, as if I deserved to be. As if I were toxic, tainted.

'Oh, right. I'll get you another then.' He held out his hand. 'James.'

I took it. 'Bridget.'

He pulled up a stool. We sat there, talking, until midnight. Neither of us felt like dancing so it was one round after another. I passed tipsy without reaching unpleasantly drunk, and he matched my vodkas with pints. I found myself saying more to this stranger than I had to anyone else on a first meeting. I wasn't sure if he was simply being friendly or had sex in mind. I wouldn't have objected to that connection, even just for one night. If only to prove I could still feel something.

About my job, he said, 'Christ, I could never be a teacher. I'd murder the little shits, first chance I got.'

When he found out exactly how much older than me he was: 'Jesus, you mean when I was a teenager, smoking dope and getting laid, you were shitting your nappy up in Birmingham?'

He was bisexual, he said, had been more or less entirely gay in his teens and at University. Some people he knew had cut him off when he began to have relationships with women. He'd married one but it had been a disaster, lasting barely two years, fortunately with no children. The financial crash had lost him his job and he'd had to sell his house and move into a one-bedroom flat three floors above a shop in Aldershot town centre, which cleared his debts. He worked temp jobs when he could find them, while sending out his CV.

I told him my story. Mike had been the deputy head, nineteen years older than me. I'd had an affair with him for two years. I'm sure our colleagues had guessed what was going on, and maybe his wife did too, but they all turned a blind eye. All good sense told me we weren't going anywhere and he wasn't going to leave his wife, children and grandchild for me. But still we continued, sex driven by need at any opportunity we had. And then, one day, he died – looked the wrong way when crossing a road and a car hit him.

'You know,' I said, on my third vodka and orange by then, 'I've never said this to anyone, but I wonder if he did it deliberately.'

'You think so? Did he have depression?'

'I don't know. It just seems so fucking unfair. Just something at the back of my mind. It's a shitty reason, but at least it is a reason.'

We left the club just before one o'clock. As soon as we were on the pavement outside, the cold air hit me. I doubled over and was sick. James held my hair away from my face.

'Sorry,' I muttered. 'I'm sorry.'

'That's okay. Get it all out.'

My cheeks filled and more vomit splashed on to the paving slabs.

'How are you going to get home?' he asked.

I straightened, dabbing at my mouth with a tissue from my handbag. 'Got the train in. Farnham.'

'There aren't any trains running now. Have you got the money for a taxi?'

'I – I think so.'

He walked me to the taxi rank outside the now-closed train and bus stations. I was wobbly in my heels but the air was clearing my head.

'Go home and sleep it off, Bridget. Nice meeting and chatting with you.'

I waved at him through the window as the cab drove off.

THE FOLLOWING DAY was Saturday and I stayed in bed until late morning with a thumping headache, still queasy but no longer being sick. *I must stop doing this.* It wasn't until lunchtime that I found James's business card in my handbag. He must have slipped it in there when I wasn't looking. I was too embarrassed to call him, wondering what impression I'd made in my drunkenness. But, late that afternoon, I phoned his mobile and he answered.

The following day we met in Aldershot town centre and had a coffee at Costa. As we sat at a table by the window, I said, 'Sorry I got so drunk. I wondered if you'd ever want to talk to me again. You must've been thinking, who's that stupid drunken bitch?'

He waved my objection away. 'We've all been there. When your life hits the floor, where can you go?' He leaned forward. 'I liked talking to you. I wanted to talk to you some more.'

His flat was only a couple of minutes away, above a travel agent's. The window of the shop next door was starred with taped-over cracks, glass like spilled sugar on the pavement. A group of three Nepalese women, all of them under five feet tall in brightly-coloured full-length robes, walked slowly past. As I followed James up three flights of stone steps, I was glad I was wearing flats rather than heels. I said as much. Standing by his door, he glanced down at me. 'They suit you better.'

As soon as we were inside his flat, we were in each other's arms, his fingers clutching at me through the fabric of my skirt, scrabbling for the zip.

ON MONDAY MORNING before the first lesson, I came out of a cubicle in the staff ladies. Alison was standing by a basin, leaning forward slightly as she put on her lipstick. 'Hi, Bridge. Good weekend?' She pressed her lips together.

'Yes, thanks.' Alison was the first friend I'd made at this school. 'I met someone.'

'Ooh. Tell me more.'

I told her an edited version of the weekend as I washed my hands. I hadn't drunk anything after going home from James's flats so I had no headache that morning.

Alison straightened, picking at her trousers, slipping her hand inside her blouse to adjust her bra-strap. She chuckled. 'What am I going to do with you, Bridge? You and your older men. Are you going to see him again?'

'Yes, I will.'

'Good for you. An older man for me would be a bloody pensioner.' She gazed at herself in the mirror, made a moue. 'I've got young Mr Hotchester in my class in half an hour. Sitting in the front row, too.'

'He's in my class this afternoon.'

'How one student can be so ridiculously good-looking, I don't know. Like two angels shagged and he was the result.' She sighed. 'I may have my silver wedding next year and be old enough to be his mum but that doesn't mean I can't window-shop now and again, does it? He's not old enough for you though, eh?'

DURING THE WEEK, James and I texted each other. In the evenings after I'd finished marking, I did treat myself to a glass of wine, but not the whole bottle. I went online before going to bed, and some evenings we had a conversation via Facebook or Skype. But come Fridays, I made the five-minute train journey to Aldershot. Sometimes, we went back to the nightclub, or we'd eat at one of the restaurants in the Westgate Centre and see a film at the cinema there. On the Saturday and Sunday we'd lie in the double bed that took up most of the space in the bedroom, or take the train to London and go to an exhibition or the theatre. Sometimes he'd cook for me, or I'd cook for him on the two gas rings in the tiny kitchen, or sometimes if we both felt lazy we ordered a pizza or a Chinese.

He played me music, at first Bob Dylan, Bruce Springsteen, Leonard Cohen. I thought, *My Dad listens to these,* but kept quiet. When I half-seriously complained they were all men, he tried me on Joni Mitchell and Laura Nyro. I tried him on younger singers I liked, such as Thea Gilmore and Laura Marling. But he kept returning to Joy Division. 'Love Will Tear Us Apart' haunted me:

Ian Curtis's vocal, semi-muffled, far away, dark things trembling under the surface.

On an impulse, we went to ballroom dancing lessons. It didn't surprise me that he was good at it. But I tried to do it better, moving him as he held me, his hands pressed firmly to my waist. He led, I followed, but as the instructor said, you needed both to make a dance.

I WAS AN only child. My parents still lived in the house in Birmingham I grew up in; I spoke to them on the phone weekly. I visited them about once every other month, taking the train and staying for a weekend, longer during the summer school holidays, sleeping in my old room which was kept much the way it was when I moved out. They didn't know I'd been sleeping with a married man for two years and I wondered when I could take James to meet them. I said I was seeing him and left telling them he was almost their age for another day.

When James and I had sex, he always began by taking off my glasses, lifting them from my head and gently resting them on the bedside unit facing inwards, sightless eyes witnessing my being taken. He preferred me in leggings rather than a skirt or dress. Trousers were best of all. He liked the effort of unfastening zips, unhooking belts, lifting me slightly so that he could pull them down. He was less concerned above the waist and usually left my bra on, sometimes my top as well. I'd take them off myself, almost as an afterthought. He would always undress me, never I him, carefully draping my clothes over the back of a chair. When he'd finished with me, he'd quickly take his own clothes off, not caring where he scattered them. By then he was fully erect.

After sex, we lay together in that double bed until the early hours before sleepiness caught up with us. Streetlight orange came into the room around the thick curtains along with the noises of passing cars and shouts from below. At those times, we talked.

'Pretty much everyone thought I was gay at school,' he said one night. 'Catholic boys' school. I got a lot of shit, as you can imagine. This was the time of Thatcher, Section 28 and all that. I got beaten up a few times too.'

I said nothing, only listened. I lay behind him, my nipples brushing his back, one hand on his shoulder. This was something he had to let out.

'The priests, they ignored all of this. Wankers. Probably literal wankers too, especially if there was a boy with a cute arse around. But then there was Simon. School captain, hot as you like. He came on to me. I thought he was taking the piss at first, but it was genuine. Thought I'd pass out right there and then.

'It had to be secret. He had a girlfriend from the Catholic girls' school nearby. Heard a few stories about some of the nuns there too, I can tell you. Simon was shagging the best-looking girl in the fifth form – that's Year Eleven to you youngsters. She went on to be Head Girl, and word was she was spreading her legs for someone else Simon didn't know about. But she and Simon were an A couple, if ever there was one. But in the meantime, he and I were doing it.

'I wanted to fuck him, really fuck him. Hard. Up the arse. It was like an ache. You don't know what that's like.' He paused, swallowed. 'But he wouldn't. Never mind that we'd tossed each other off and I'd blown him a few times. It was like that didn't count, realised that soon enough. A year later we both left school and I haven't seen him since. Maybe he was on Friends Reunited when that was around. Maybe he's on Facebook. I don't really care.'

'Too painful.'

'Right, after all this time. Hopefully he's some fat bald cunt with a harridan wife and awful kids. I'd like that to be true.'

He fell silent. I continued to stroke his shoulders, leaned forward to kiss him on the cheek.

On another night, I found myself telling James things I'd never told anyone else, or not all at once and in so much detail. My childhood, growing up in Birmingham with my parents. I was a solitary child with not many friends. I told him about the best friend who, when we both moved up into secondary school, found a new circle to move in and with their assistance cut me out. There was the boy I lost my virginity to, during a party at a girl's house while her parents were away. We were in a room upstairs: he came as soon as he was inside me. And Mike: how our affair had been conducted at my flat, or once on a summer evening on the back seat of his car pulled up at the side of a country road. And once in an empty classroom, bending me over a desk and fucking me from behind, the risk of discovery exciting us all the more. As James listened, he brushed his hand over my shoulder blades, one of them trailing down to the small of my back, the touch of his fingers like branding.

'YOU KNOW, IF only you were a boy,' he said.

I couldn't help but laugh. 'James, I'm a woman. Boobs. Curves. Never in a million years do I look like a boy.' He didn't reply, seemed vaguely disappointed.

I'd always had long hair, tying it back or pinning it up at work, loose to my shoulder at other times. But one day I looked in the mirror at the hairdresser's and told the woman to cut it short. As I walked up to James's flat, I was conscious of the weight of hair I couldn't feel any more, the cold breeze tickling the back of my neck. But James was delighted with the result. When we had sex, he entered me from behind and nuzzled my nape and kissed me there when he came.

I SPENT MOST weekends with James in his flat. After a while, I kept some clothes there, beginning with changes of underwear in a drawer, then tops and trousers hanging in spare cupboard space. Then I left toiletries in the small cabinet in the tiny bathroom. It felt like a stage had been reached when I kept a toothbrush in there, even more than when he had a copy of his front door key cut for me.

ONE NIGHT, I dreamed I woke up in the middle of the night. Tiptoeing so as not to disturb James, I used the toilet. I slipped back under the duvet. James always slept naked and for a while I watched him as he lay on his side, breathing quietly, as the sky lightened outside the window on a summer Sunday morning. His arm was raised up and I counted the curls of dark hair in his armpit. And then I saw, along his side under the armpit, a line of small dots one above the other. I looked closer. A line of small mouths, or other orifices, opening and closing, gasping for air or whatever atmosphere they breathed.

I woke with James's hand gently on my shoulder. I blinked; it was full daylight outside. 'Slept well, I see,' he said. He was standing, still nude, leaning over me. For a moment, I thought to tell him of the strange dream I had, but didn't. He turned, idly scratching at his pubic hair, as he paced to the bathroom and ran a shower.

A LITTLE LATER, he said, 'Can I bugger you?'

Not *I want to fuck you,* which Mike had said the first time. It was oddly touching that James asked me first.

This time he undressed me completely, the top half first. I glanced up during the process. He was blurred without my glasses but I could make out the end of his tongue poking from the corner of his mouth as he concentrated on my trousers. He let out a little sigh as he succeeded in freeing me, and then with an air of ceremony placed his thumbs on my hips and tugged down my knickers. I raised my legs so that he could remove them entirely. He draped all my clothes carefully and neatly over the back of a chair.

'Back in a minute,' he muttered. 'Stay there.'

He returned from the front room with a cushion, pushing it under me to raise up my bottom. His hands on my hipbones, he adjusted my position, this way, that. I sensed he'd planned this for some time. Then he went into the bathroom and returned with a small jar of Vaseline. He scooped out a large glob with his fingers, working it stickily into my anus. 'Okay?' he said as he lay on top of me, resting his hands on my forearms. And then he entered me.

He sighed as he moved over me. I was full, with something I

couldn't pass if I wanted to. He reached under himself between my legs and stroked me with his fingers, but I had little arousal. He began to thrust, pushing himself deeper inside me, as if trying to take root. His gasps became louder. 'Oh God...' And then he thrust deeper still, shuddered and came.

He lay on me for a few moments, then withdrew from me. He kissed me on the temple. 'Thank you. Thank you so much.'

IN THE STAFF Ladies' I stood and adjusted my tights, picking at a piece of fluff stuck to my skirt. 'Hi,' said Alison as I came out of the cubicle. 'James treating you well?'

'Yes, I'd say so.'

'You don't sound so sure.'

I couldn't get anything past her. I'd been quiet, a little unsettled, for the rest of the weekend. I'm sure he noticed but didn't say anything. He'd had his wish and I'd been the means of achieving that ... so where would we go next? I stood glancing at myself in the mirror. I'm not sure I'd have recognised me from only a few months earlier.

'If you don't want to talk about it...'

'No, it's fine. I'll be all right.' I reached inside my handbag. After weeks of wearing no makeup, I began to put on lipstick.

THE NEXT FRIDAY, I turned to James in bed and kissed him full on the lips.

'Bridget…?'

We rarely kissed, except a companionable one on the cheek when meeting or departing. I slipped my arms about his neck in a clinch and pulled him to me.

He turned his mouth away. 'What are you doing?'

'Shhh,' I said, and kissed him again. 'I want to fuck you this time.'

'Bridget, don't...'

I rolled him on to his back, as surprised as he was by my own strength. Straddling him, I took his wrists in my hands and moved them up to my breasts. 'So you like them, James?' He nodded, gulping. 'Not so much like a boy, am I?'

'No...'

I released one of his hands but he kept it in place as I reached down and guided him inside me.

James leaned his head back, mouth open, a string of saliva uniting top and bottom teeth. 'Bridget, don't...'

He softened, and slipped out of me.

I said nothing, still straddling him, looking down. 'James, it's okay. It doesn't matter.'

'It's not fucking okay!' His face was reddening, veins standing out in his forehead. 'Get out! Get the fuck out!'

'James, I'm sorry.'

'Get your things and get out!' He pushed me away, so forcefully that I gasped as I slid off the side of the bed. I landed on the floor, on my side.

I stood up. 'James...' He turned away from me.

Dressing hurriedly, I went down the stairs, stumbling down the road to the station. The last train had gone so I caught a taxi home.

It was only when I was in my own flat that I let the tears come, thumping the wall so hard that I bruised my knuckles.

I CALLED JAMES four times the next day but only picked up his voicemail. 'James, it's me. We've got to talk. Call me back. Any time of the day or night, just call me.'

But he never replied. I left it until Sunday, then took the train into Aldershot. I was prepared for it to be all over, and at least I could recover the clothes and possessions still in his flat and give him back the key. There was no reply to the doorbell so I let myself in.

The flat had been tidied since I'd been there last, the bed made. I found James in the bathroom. A rope was tied in a slip knot around his neck, holding a plastic bag over his head. He'd also tied his arms behind his back. He was leaning forward, the noose tight. There was a strong smell. As he'd hung there, for how long I'll never know, he had voided his bowels.

I knew he was dead but I didn't call the ambulance for some time. I sat on the sofa, blinking rapidly, unable to swallow, as the sun moved across the sky, finally shining directly through the window into my eyes.

I WAS SURPRISED to find out that James had left everything to me. His parents were dead and the only relative I could trace was an aunt who hadn't heard from him in over twenty years. He wasn't in contact with his ex-wife. I spent several weekends clearing out his flat so I could put it on the market. I kept some of his CDs but couldn't bear to play them more than occasionally, the Joy Division one most so, so I put them in a box at the bottom of a cupboard.

I often wonder if that last encounter had precipitated what had followed. He had wanted control and I'd wrested it from him. But I also think this was something he had planned for some time. He'd clearly researched a relatively clean method of taking his own life. I found out later that he'd put on an adult nappy under his trousers, no doubt knowing he would soil himself, out of consideration for whomever would need to tend to his corpse.

Could I have done anything to prevent it? I don't think so. Once he'd set himself on that course, nothing would deviate him from it. Depression is like that. You don't want to end it all. You want the pain to stop.

He'd asked where you could go when you reach the floor. He'd answered his own question: you go through it. Where to, I don't know. Some day perhaps I'll find out.

TODAY I DREAMED of James. I was in his flat. He was sitting in an armchair, clothed, his hands on his knees, leaning forward, watching me intently. I was lying full length on his sofa, nude. I'd kept my hair short – it was as if that was some last part of James left in me – but in the dream it was long again, pinned up, my fingers were interlaced behind my head. A Goya pose, a naked maja. I was wondering if he liked what he saw, how my breasts lay, if my hips were too broad, my bottom too heavy. Under one of my shaven armpits, there was a line of dark dots, tiny mouths, opening and closing.

LOST

(i. m. Joel Lane)

Pauline Morgan

I stand amidst the debris of your life;
You never threw anything away but let it
Accumulate around you, just as
Your mind never lost the snippets,
The ephemera that most forget.
You didn't know whether an object,
An idea would be just what was needed.

Beneath the layers, the detritus of fifty years
I find the hidden the nuggets, brought home
Lost amid time's accumulations, just as the gold
You would have shaped into poems, stories
But which now will never be unearthed,
Buried forever in darkness.

Around me, shelves are stacked with
Your passions. Amongst them the books,
The CDs, the DVDs you bought
That remained unwrapped, unused
Like the ideas still packaged, sealed within
Your mind, forever out of reach.

FEAR OF THE MUSIC

Stephen Bacon

I DON'T DANCE so much these days. Whether that's not wanting to be reminded or fear of the music itself, I'm not sure. Part of it's knowing I'll never be as good as James. It was less than a year ago that we first met. I remember I'd just gone into a nightclub. I hadn't even bought a drink. He was standing at one of the dark tables in front of the dance floor. A tall man, quite thin, dressed in a black t-shirt and jeans. He remained absolutely still for about ten minutes, watching the dancers. There was something angry in his stillness, a tense feeling. Suddenly he emptied his glass and slipped onto the dance floor. The music shivered through his limbs; he was caught up in it like a floating candle on a river. I knew I had to speak to him.

At the bar he drank slowly, the neon painting pink beads of sweat onto his face. He put down his empty glass and I caught the bartender's eye and asked for it to be refilled. He turned and for a few moments he just peered at me with those intense eyes before finally nodding. 'I'm James.'

The club was stifling so we stood near the fire-door and made small-talk. Though the conversation was two-way, I could tell he was half-distracted, his eyes never leaving the dance floor, like he was searching for someone amongst the strobing figures and lurching shapes. I studied his face as I talked, admiring the angular features, sensing something potent concealed in the hollows of his eyes. He began to blink and sigh. It felt like he was drifting away from me so I suggested going for a dance. He hesitated for a second, and at that exact moment the opening guitar from The Cure's 'A Forest' came throbbing through the speakers. We were off.

He was just as energetic as before, especially towards the climax of the song, his limbs pulsing and spasming like he was possessed. His technique reminded me of how Ian Curtis danced in the 'Transmission' video, only James seemed more fluid, more naturally gifted, his movement totally in tune with the rhythm of the music. I couldn't take my eyes off him. The image was mesmerising. I tried to emulate his performance and he flashed a smile at me, seemingly pleased with my effort. By the time the song ended and the next one came on I was breathless and spent, and we stumbled back to the fire-door. Not long after, we left.

He had a flat in Digbeth in the shadow of a railway bridge, on the corner of Moseley Street and Pickford Street. The brickwork adjacent to the building was decorated with graffiti, lending the place a contemporary, cartoonish quality, at odds with the remnants of industry that remained visible beneath the modern veneer. The flat was as cold as the grave. Its walls were cluttered with album covers and posters of films by Jean-Luc Godard. Scrawled in paint on the wall above the bed were the words: *And those who were seen dancing were thought to be insane by those who could not hear the music.*

Within minutes we were fucking on the bed. He had a pale, hairless body, muscular at the shoulders and biceps, toned thighs; the physique of someone naturally athletic rather than one acquired at the gym. When he came he shuddered violently, his breath rattling through my eardrum like a train. He clung to me and exhaled a deep sigh. It sounded desolate, fractured. We lay under the covers and slept until dawn.

James cooked us breakfast the next morning. I felt oddly awkward, quite unsure why. I'd had plenty of one-night stands. But with James it felt like I was on the brink of something *life-changing*. He wasn't even my type really. But there was an intensity to him I found alluring.

I was just finishing my coffee when I nodded towards the words scrawled above the bed. 'You can't half bust some moves on the dance floor, yourself.'

He glanced at the quotation and smiled. 'Nietzsche.'

'More original than the one about gazing into the abyss.'

He didn't speak for a moment. I could hear the traffic out on the road, the gurgling of the radiators in the flat, a squeak of floorboards from upstairs.

'How you dance says a lot about how you view life. You can tell a lot about someone by watching them dance.'

I pursed my lips. 'But they just might like a song more than another.'

He frowned. 'No, it's more than that. Most people dance exactly the way they live their life. Or, in most cases, they don't *live* – they just exist.'

I thought about the way most dance-floors looked; people shuffling like zombies, hopping and moving around in time to the music. I thought about how James had danced the night before; the enthusiasm, the passion, the sheer unadulterated enjoyment of his own body gyrating in time to the beats of the music. It felt vivid and pure.

I knew then that I wanted to spend all my time with him.

WE SAW A lot of each other in the next few weeks. Most times I stayed at his place. Often we walked miles along the banks of the canal, stopping for a drink in some of the pubs scattered along its route. We talked about anything and everything. It felt like the more I discovered about him, the further I felt myself spiralling down into his personality. He told me about how he'd survived childhood leukaemia and the impact the disease had made on his life. During the early stages of its diagnosis, his father had walked out on them. James had never seen him again. He spoke about all the time he'd spent in hospital, separated from the rest of his friends, in the end almost forgotten. He seemed to feel embarrassed by his survival, as if he had invented the whole story, bitter and apologetic.

By the end of the summer James and I were constantly morose. The weather had changed. Autumn came with a bite. Frost glittered the dead leaves underfoot, mist hung low over the canal. Afternoon darkness seemed to descend with a vengeance. The news was filled with reports of students being attacked in the area, one of whom nearly lost an eye after having acid thrown in his face. Streetlamps were dimmed by the fog that choked the streets. By the time winter arrived I had started to feel dislocated by the weather. Christmas came and went in a warm rainy haze. To counter the melancholy mood, James started messing around with drugs. One night he brought home some pink tablets in a plastic bag. He'd bought them off a lorry driver in the pub, imported from Eastern Europe apparently. We took a couple on the last Friday in February. When we came to, it was early March.

Even now I can remember how quickly the rush came on. I felt an intense tingling sensation in my legs. I could feel my heart racing, hear a roaring in my ears. My vision was flecked with sparkles of light. We both collapsed on the bed in a tangle of limbs.

I woke after a few hours, nauseous and shivering. I sat up on the bed. James was gone. I could hear voices outside the room, indistinct and monotone. There was a hum within my chest, like a deep bass that I could not hear, only feel.

I stood and opened the door. Instead of seeing the living room I was expecting, I was faced with a long corridor which ended at another door. It was freezing cold. I could see my breath in front of me, tiny ghosts of thought escaping the confines of my head. There was music coming from beyond the door. I walked the length of the corridor and opened it.

The room was dimly lit. It had a high ceiling and arched windows covered by blinds. People were dancing in the centre, the sight of which was startling. There must have been about thirty of them, gyrating in time to the music, which was loud and upbeat. I was confused by the whole situation. I asked someone where James was but he just looked at me and shook his head. I negotiated my way through the melee to the back of the room where a closed coffin was propped up on some trestles. There was a framed photograph of James on top of it. At that moment it dawned on me that this must be a dream. Although - thinking about it now - surely that means that it must just have been a hallucinogenic vision brought on by the drugs, because when you're having a dream you never realise you're dreaming, do you?

I grabbed hold of a girl near me and shouted to be heard over the music. I felt dislocated, puzzled by the fact that there was a coffin in the room. She wiped the sweat from her face and explained that this was James's wake. She told me that he had been killed walking home from the pub one night, stabbed in the neck. I felt sick. My vision was lurching. Maybe it was the lighting and music. I looked at the dancing people, desperate to recognise someone but all the faces appeared identical, waxy and featureless. It was awkward because I was the only one not dancing but my limbs were like weights. No matter how much I wanted to join in, my body wouldn't let me. I sat down at a table in the corner. It was covered by a starchy white tablecloth and I fingered some dark stains around its edge. I watched the coffin for a while, wondering if I should open the lid and check that James was inside.

Just then I felt something in the pocket of my trousers. I pulled out a short-bladed knife, instantly noticing the dried blood caked on the serrations. I knew then I would never be able to dance the way that James wanted me to.

THE NEXT FEW weeks passed in a blur. It was suddenly May, the month of the general election. Opinion polls were suggesting that the hung parliament would be over, that reports indicated Labour could be heading for a majority. James was excited at the prospect of the coalition government's demise. He spent the evening of Thursday 7th May in a maelstrom of nerves. I fell asleep at 11:45, just as the initial results were coming in. James woke me at 7:30 the next morning, ashen-faced and bleary-eyed. He looked like he'd aged ten years overnight. The election results were devastating - a Conservative majority.

James took it really hard. In the following days he became

more and more bitter. His eyes took on a dull, dampened hue, his chin grizzled with stubble. It was almost as if he had become disillusioned with society.

'It's the apathy that gets to me,' he said. 'Not the ones voting for the Tories but those that can't even be bothered to turn up at the polling stations or fill in the postal votes.' There was anger beneath his tone. He told me that people were more likely to vote in the final of a pop music reality show than a general election. By then his cheekbones were prominent.

His mood had not improved. He told me he had been taking more and more of those pills from the Latvian. He was wracked with visions, usually of his own death. In the majority of these he had been murdered by people who professed to love him. I sensed a degree of paranoia creeping in to his behaviour. He began going out on his own, not telling me what he had been up to, not caring that he was alienating me with his secrecy. He told me that I was part of the problem, he'd known it from the very night we had met. He could see it in the way I danced. I was as listless and dead as the rest. I wondered how much of it had been brought on by the drugs he was taking. One day I came to his flat and found him sitting at his kitchen table, scrawling notes into a writing pad about how the media was influencing the public, how Labour's plans to break up the stranglehold the banks enjoyed, and how imposing energy price-caps, would have been good for the country. The walls of his flat had been plastered with newspaper headlines illustrating how they were scaremongering the public into hating certain races and cultures.

Meanwhile the attacks in Digbeth had escalated. A Muslim student had been abducted and had had his hands mutilated in what newspapers called 'a tit-for-tat crime', A travellers' camp on the outskirts of Aston had been the victim of calculated arson attacks. The newspapers screamed about IS suicide bombers and the dangers of allowing Syrian refugees into the country, while on page four they'd spread celebrity gossip about Kanye West and Kim Kardashian. It seemed like there was no longer any middle ground for news.

One night at the end of May I went for a walk and found myself on a bridge that spanned the old railway tracks. It was a warm humid evening so I sat on the railings and drank a can of Fosters, watching the light from James's window, wondering what his fevered brain would be working on now. It was almost as if his efforts in life were to compensate for the apathy and ennui of others. Everything he did, he did with enthusiasm, spirit, purpose.

An hour later I wandered over, all the more brave for having consumed the four-pack of lager. He opened the door and peered at me for a moment, as if trying to place me. This hurt, but I managed to mask it. His eyes had that dull glassy look that only downers give. Once his brain had allowed him to recognise me, he invited me in.

His computer was on, the screen displaying text in a language I had never seen before. On the table beside it was a map. None of the place names meant anything to me. It was a confusion of gradients and crisscrossed streets. In the centre was the symbol for a church, surrounded by labyrinthine pathways that seemed too randomly confusing. The word REVERENCE was written on it in James's spidery style.

He offered me a drink but looked relieved when I declined. I asked how he was. He seemed to consider for a moment before saying, 'Getting better.' Even though he was only in his thirties, I could see grey flecks of whiskers on his chin. His eyes were hollow and distant, like gems I could vaguely remember owning.

He talked about the area's random attacks, how the newspapers were selective in their reporting; manipulative fuel for the fire. He told me how three days ago an elderly woman had been found dead in her flat. She had ingested almost a litre of bleach. James held up a copy of yesterday's paper which showed the photograph of an Asian man whose shop had been targeted by vandals. It made great pains to point out that the man was originally from Leeds, the same city as one of the London 7/7 bombers.

'It's in their interest to join the dots for us,' he said. 'Feed us the news so we understand their message. It doesn't matter if it's true or not, all that matters is we accept it.'

There was a pile of leaflets on the table next to the map, most of them glossy and colourful, some of them hand-printed and mono.

I asked what he'd been up to. He ran his fingers through his hair and glanced around as if trying to remember.

'I'm sick of people making no effort,' he said at last. 'I didn't survive my blood cancer to just sit on the sofa and watch television. There has to be a purpose to things, otherwise life is meaningless. We all have our roles to play.'

I tried to tell him to relax, tried to make arrangements to go out with him at the weekend. He shook his head. 'You're just like the rest. Happy to remain in the flock, content to do as you're told.'

He wouldn't calm down. I asked if he was till taking the pills from the Latvian. He laughed and said they were the doorway to his new church. He could only get there when he took them. He spoke about a friend of his who ran the church. 'Simon's full of ideas, tired of being passive instead of active. He has a vision of how life should be and he needs everyone to follow it.'

I pointed out that one man's ideology was another man's oppression. At this he grew angry. He told me to leave. As he was ushering me out, I managed to nab one of the flyers off the top of the pile whilst his back was turned. He stood on the threshold and hesitated before closing the door. 'You should try another pill, Gary. The last one didn't suit you but the next one might.' I didn't want to antagonise him further so I accepted the plastic bag. I said goodbye and turned into the warm night.

THE FLYER HAD the word REVERENCE stencilled at the top. Beneath it was a black and white photograph of a church, followed by another of those strange maps of a district I didn't recognise. It detailed nearby landmarks as a museum and something called a camera obscura.

I returned home, morose and regretful. Seeing him like this

had made me feel weak, ineffective. I yearned for him to like me. It was only then that I realised how much I admired his sense of verve. I envied him for possessing the thing that I truly lacked – *life*. For half an hour I prowled my flat, flicking through the TV channels, ejecting every CD that I tried to listen to. Eventually I gave in and fished the pill out of the plastic bag. I washed it down with a shot of vodka.

At first nothing happened. I sat on the sofa in silence, staring at my reflection in the blank television screen. I took out the flyer. After a few minutes I realised that I knew the location of the church. I recalled the lost places on the map, wondering if I had ever really forgotten. My legs felt wobbly but I managed to stand and leave the house.

It was raining, the dampness darkening the bricks of the buildings, creating glistening Rorschach patterns on the walls. Each step hurt the balls of my feet. I walked onwards, following my memory as I hurried towards the church. The streets were deserted. As I saw each landmark, my memories of them formed. Soon I was at the gates, looking up at the ancient stone edifice, daunted by its imposing spire. I had the most intense sense of deja-vu. I could hear music coming from its walls.

The path was overgrown with briars and thorns. I fought my way through the thicket with little to show other than a few tears in my jeans. The door was made of solid oak, weathered and pale with age. I rattled the iron handle but the door was locked. I knocked on it but the sound was deafened by the music from within. Frustrated, I wondered around the side of the church to where an iron bench was positioned just against the wall. I managed to stand on its sagging wooden seat and peer in through the mullioned window. My view was obscured by what seemed like centuries of dust and grime but I could just make out the parishioners inside. An overwhelming sense of dread crept over me then for all the people inside looked as if they were pale figures moving around, like wax mannequins come to life. Even their clothes were as milky as their skin. I watched, fascinated. They were lifelike enough to be real. The church was devoid of pews, the floor had been cleared to make way for its congregation. The music was still very loud and the figures were dancing violently, just as James had done on the night we'd met. My eyes searched the crowd. I spotted him on the far side, moving in that unmistakable dance-style I had so admired. I stared for a moment, hypnotised by the spasming bodies, absently disturbed by their waxy appearance.

Just then my attention was seized by a flickering from the front of the church. I saw the orange bloom of flames around the altar. It resembled the wavering petals of some monstrous flower. The congregation seemed to form a line, still gyrating. The rhythm was haphazard and random, as if each person was moving to a different beat, but the animation was shared by all. One by one they moved towards the fire, stepping into the flames, the heat bending their limbs, destroying their bodies. I could not tear my eyes away. They disappeared into the orange blaze. I blinked the image away but even as I closed my eyes I could see the waxy figures in my mind, dancing, forever dancing, while I did nothing but stand and watch them burn.

I CAME TO on my sofa. It was day. My muscles ached as if I too had spent the night dancing. But I knew this could not be true because I didn't have James's skill. I was not able to hear the same tune as he heard.

I hurried to his flat. As I drew near I saw the crowd loitering behind the police tape, noticed the reporters speaking gravely into the pointed television cameras. Lighting rigs had been erected behind them, bathing his apartment block in stark pale definition. I eavesdropped on the reporters' conversations: a man in his thirties had been found dead in his flat. A post-mortem had revealed the strange circumstances surrounding the death. It appeared that the man had died sometime around a week ago. Forensics had confirmed that a fire had occurred, originating within the body of the deceased, apparently without any external sources of ignition.

I turned away. My head was pounding. I felt the warm sun on

my arms. I knew I would never meet anyone like James again. His passion for life, his utter determination to make the most of things meant that I would probably always feel inadequate in comparison.

There has to be a purpose to things, otherwise life is meaningless. We all have our roles to play. I think about this every day and wonder if I'll ever meet anyone that will revere me in the same way I loved James. I very much doubt it.

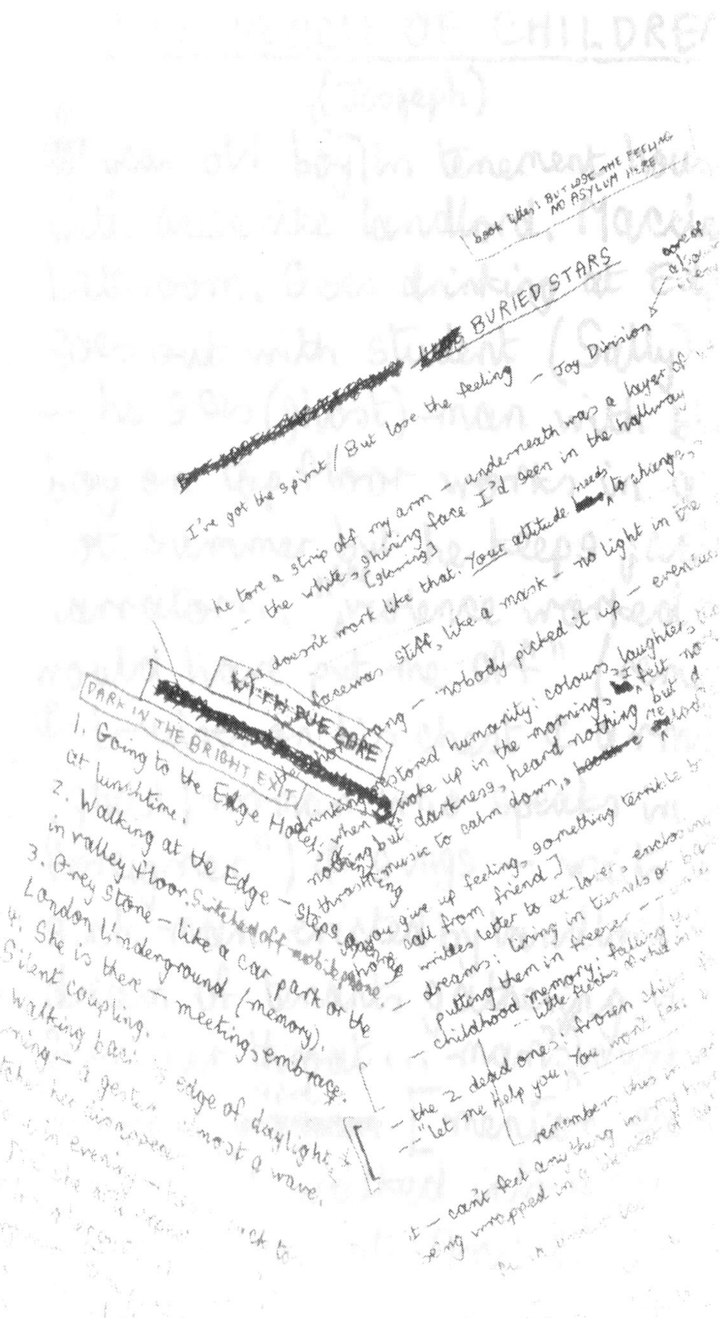
book titles: BUT LOSE THE FEELING
NO ASYLUM HERE
BURIED STARS
I've got the spirit / But lose the feeling – Joy Division
he tore a strip off my arm – underneath was a layer of
– the white, shining face I'd seen in the hallway
[glowing]
doesn't work like that. Your attitude needs to change
face was stiff, like a mask – no light in the
ringing – nobody picked it up – eventu
WITH DUE CARE
DARK IN THE BRIGHT EXIT
1. Going to the Edge Hotel, drinking at lunchtime.
2. Walking at the Edge – steps in valley floor, switched off mobile phone.
3. Grey stone – like a car park or the London Underground (memory).
4. She is there – meeting, embrace. Silent coupling.
walking back edge of daylight,
a gesture, almost a wave.
coloured humanity: colours, laughter
woke up in the morning, I felt no
nothing but darkness, heard nothing but
thrashing music to calm down,
you give up feeling, something terrible
– call from friend]
– writes letter to ex-lovers, enclosing
– dreams: living in
putting them in freezer
– childhood memory: falling
– the 2 dead ones: frozen
– "let me help you, you won't
– can't feel anything in my
being wrapped in a blanket of

BAD FAITH

Thana Niveau

THE FOX STARED at Derek with cold, cloudy eyes, its body in pieces. Tufts of rust-coloured fur drifted in the steaming air like feathers. From the shadows, something growled at him. A dog. A big one by the sound of it. Derek edged away from the kill, watching until he reached the corner, but the dog didn't appear.

THE PUB WASN'T crowded. A scattering of old men sat nursing ales at separate tables, weighed down by the heat and their solitude. A portable fan propped on the bar stirred the dense air without cooling it.

Derek ordered a pint from Paul and stood at the end of the bar, too listless to move. He watched the quick, repetitive movements of Paul's hands as he worked, doling out drinks and gathering up empty glasses. He moved like an automaton, the sweat stains beneath his arms the only evidence that he was flesh and blood.

He pulled on the handle to fill a glass with something dark and frothy for a man in a high-vis jacket. The neon yellow seared into Derek's eyes like a contagion of the sun and he turned away. He scarcely noticed that Paul had returned to his end of the bar.

'Did you hear about that burglar?'

Derek pressed his pint glass to his forehead but the beer was too warm to cool him. 'What burglar?'

Paul grunted. 'The one you didn't hear about.'

'Sorry, no. What about him?'

'Busted into the wrong house, he did. Dog fucking tore him to pieces. Police had to take him out in buckets.'

Derek swallowed. The beer felt like wet cement in his throat. 'Jesus.'

'I heard about that,' the yellow-jacketed man said a few moments later, as though the news had taken time to penetrate the sweltering air to reach him further down the bar. 'Serves the bastard right. Wish I could have seen it.'

Derek winced. 'Surely no one deserves *that*.'

But the man nodded, his expression cold and serious. 'Fucker broke the law, didn't he? Got what was coming to him.'

Paul was keeping quiet. Bartenders wisely never let themselves get drawn into discussions like this. He moved some glasses around as he pretended to be busy, a silent robot again.

Derek couldn't stop thinking about the dismembered fox. Had it been the same dog? Had the fox been alive when it was torn apart?

'Just seems like a bad death,' he said. Burglar or not, he couldn't help feeling it was an awful way to go.

But even his noncommittal response seemed to aggravate the man. He moved closer, the blazing yellow of his jacket like the spreading of flames in a house fire. Derek flinched at his nearness. The man armed sweat off his forehead as he set his empty glass down on the bar with a thud. 'You know why people break the law? Because they're fucking criminals.'

Derek took another swallow of his beer. It tasted like canal water. 'That's like saying people die because they're corpses.'

The yellow man didn't know how to respond to that. He frowned as he thought about it, then turned away in disgust, muttering something under his breath.

'What happened to the dog?'

Paul blinked at Derek. 'Huh?'

'The dog. What happened to it?'

'Put down, I guess,' Paul said with a shrug. 'Vicious thing like that.'

The yellow man laughed, a sharp, nasty sound. 'You looking for a pet, boy?'

Derek ignored him and finished his drink in one long swallow. It did nothing to quench his thirst. He'd heard about dogs that were trained to fight. Their owners made them vicious. Beat them and fed them steroids and amphetamines. Probably this poor dog was one of those. Once he'd even seen a dog with a swastika tattooed on its chest. There were good people in the world, he knew, but sometimes it was hard not to lose faith in that.

'Well, see you,' he mumbled, giving Paul a desultory wave as he left.

Outside, the sky seemed to be melting. Sweat trickled across his scalp and ran into his eyes. He scrubbed it away as he made his way down the street. It looked different in the heat. Forsaken.

Even the flat looked different, as though someone had been inside and changed things. Andrew wouldn't have done it, and anyway, he was still at work. Derek thought of the burglar and did a quick walk-through, but nothing appeared to have been taken. There wasn't much to steal in any case.

He clambered into the shower but even the water from the cold tap was like soup, warm and cloying. He was dozing on the couch afterwards when he heard the barking. It was a low, muddy sound, as though reaching him through dense fog. He pushed the curtains aside and saw motion outside in the darkening streets. Dogs. They were everywhere.

The pack was running, driving a group of people before them. Long pink tongues lolled between the razors of their teeth.

Derek drew back, startled. The dogs must have sensed his motion because they stopped at once, like a flock of birds shifting mid-flight. They stood perfectly still and only their heads turned to regard him. The movement was unnatural. *Alien*. They stared at him, eyes gleaming red, breath steaming in the heavy air.

The people they had been chasing stopped too. But they didn't run or try to get away. They stood where they were, staring down at the ground, like toys that had wound down. Derek could see that some of them had been bitten, chewed. The wounds looked black. Flesh hung from them in scarlet tatters. Still, none of them moved.

He turned away and closed his eyes, shutting out the scene. The barking resumed and he heard the scraping of claws on the pavement as the pack began to run again. The sound was drawing nearer. His eyes flew open at the sound of the front door opening and he blinked in wild confusion to find himself back on the couch. The dream had fractured. Before he could feel relief, however, he heard the fading echo of a howl.

He sat up, watching helplessly as a tall, thin figure advanced towards him. It was only a silhouette in the darkness. Its body was human, but he recognised the shape of the head as something else. The pointed ears, the long snout. It reached a long arm for him and he screamed, batting the hand away.

'Hey, it's just me! Calm down.'

The light came on and Derek saw that it was only Andrew. His partner looked terrified.

'Are you hurt?' Derek asked, grabbing Andrew's hands and turning them so he could see the arms. 'Did they attack you?'

But Andrew only looked baffled, shaking his head, his eyes wide. 'I don't know what you're talking about. Did *who* attack me?'

Derek scrambled to his feet and flung the curtains aside. The streets were empty.

THE NEXT EVENING he eyed his surroundings warily as he made his way home. He stopped by the place where he had seen the dead fox the day before but no trace of it was left.

He peered down alleyways and side streets, expecting to see dogs lurking there, waiting for him. He couldn't shake the image of those terrible red eyes, that icy breath pluming from snarling mouths.

Andrew wouldn't be home for hours yet and Derek didn't want to be there by himself. He hesitated outside the pub, not really wanting company but not wanting to be alone either. He stood outside, peering in through the window. The yellow man was standing by the bar as though he'd never left, his lips writhing in conversation with Paul.

A man and a woman sat near the open window, eating something Derek couldn't identify. It looked as though it had been scraped off the road. He watched in horror as the woman plucked a long white hair from her mouth. She showed no disgust. She just resumed eating, her eyes as dead as what was on her plate.

Derek's stomach gave a lurch and he walked on.

The streets were deserted and the hot air pressed down on him like the weight of the ocean. Cloying, stifling.

From somewhere in the night came the barking of a dog. Derek froze in his tracks, listening. Soon it was joined by another, then another. Like a wolf pack joining the howl one by one, more dogs added their voices to the chorus.

Derek moved quickly, turning down the street that led home. He felt stalked, pursued. He peered into the swarming shadows of car parks, the coiling nothingness that lurked in the passages between houses. The barking echoed as if from the sky, coming from everywhere all at once. He strained to hear beyond it, listening for the sound of running feet, of untrimmed claws clicking on the pavement, the snuffling of animals on the hunt.

As he passed houses he chanced to look inside one. The curtains were splayed, the window open wide. At first he couldn't believe what he thought he'd glimpsed – it seemed *wrong*. So wrong that he was compelled to backtrack, just to check that his mind had indeed played a horrible trick on him.

But it hadn't.

Inside the house, an elderly couple sat staring blank-eyed at a wall, completely still. For a moment he thought they were dead. But there was a stiffness to their posture that suggested they were deliberately holding the pose. Or *being* held. Like puppets awaiting manipulation. But what disturbed Derek most were the dogs. The room was packed with them. All breeds, all shapes and sizes. They too were perfectly still. They stood staring at the couple, as though waiting for something. A sign.

Derek felt his stomach lurch as he noticed the wounds. Both people had been bitten and their bare arms sported hideous open wounds, black and raw like the lips of the dogs who had chewed them. There was blood on the muzzle of the nearest beast.

A strangled little cry escaped Derek and then there was movement in the house. The people turned their heads, a synchronised, mechanical act. They looked right at Derek without seeming to see him. But the dogs did.

Before they could respond, he ran.

Behind him he heard the noises he'd been afraid of hearing, the sound of their pursuit. Growling, snarling, panting, they chased after him as he pelted along the street.

He saw similar tableaux in other houses as he ran, people frozen like statues in houses full of dogs. How many were there? How many could there possibly be?

When he reached the end of the road he hesitated, not knowing where to go. He didn't recognise his surroundings. The streets were a maze to him. Choosing a direction at random, he found himself in a cul-de-sac. All around him the barking continued but it was only a single dog that ultimately confronted him, its fur glossy and black, its eyes gleaming like rubies. He couldn't look away and he couldn't move as the dog approached, walking calmly up to him. There was no sign of emotion behind its eyes, only cold instinct. He found himself holding out his arm, offering it to the creature.

The dog sniffed him once before placing its mouth on Derek's arm, sinking its teeth in, slowly and deliberately. When the fangs scraped the bones within, Derek screamed. The pain broke the spell and he fought back, yanking at his arm. Blood fountained over them both as he pulled away. The dog stared at him for several moments. Then it licked the blood from its lips.

Derek fled, running past the dog and back into the night.

The bite throbbed and burned, and one glance showed him an ugly wound, the flesh savaged. Dark blood pumped from it in sharp jets and he clamped his hand over it with a cry of pain. The unseen pack fell silent for a moment, and then began to howl. Had they tasted him through the bite? The thought made him lightheaded and he stumbled as he continued in his flight. A left turn took him along a curving lane of darkened shop fronts and he saw a sign for the train station. Had he come so far? He felt as if he'd been running for hours.

There was no sign of the pack, only the humid night echoing with their barking. He couldn't remember the way home. But did he want to lead the dogs there anyway? What if Andrew had already let them in? Could he taste Derek's blood also? Lost and confused, Derek ran for the station, desperate to find other people, anyone who might help him.

As he plunged into the station, the din behind him began to fade. The concourse was crowded with people and he let go of his arm as he waved frantically at them.

'Help,' he gasped. 'Please help me.'

His arm was caked in blood and more was pooling on the floor at his feet. He was beginning to feel faint. The crowd swam in his blurring vision and he sank to his knees.

'Hospital...'

He shook his head, fighting the dizziness. The people were eerily silent. When he looked up he saw that their heads were the heads of dogs. Steam misted from their snouts as they turned, as one, to regard him. They looked hungrily at his arm, at the ragged black wound. The torn edges of the flesh moved like a mouth, opening and closing. Sounds came from there, a kind of dull whimpering.

One by one the people began to drop to their knees. They placed their hands on the floor in front of them and crept towards Derek. There was nothing behind their eyes. No reason, only cunning. Nothing like life. His heart lurched with horror, but he couldn't move. The pressure on his injured arm sent a river of blood across the floor, and as it reached them, the dog-people lowered their heads and began to lap at it.

His arm was twitching, shuddering. The mewling inside it was gaining in strength. Now he could feel the fur at the edges of the wound. The dog in his arm was trying to get out.

Derek tried to scream but his mouth seemed too large to form words. His tongue felt thick and heavy. He lowered his head and saw himself reflected in the blood.

Behind him, the doors swished open and he heard the padding of stealthy feet as the pack began to circle him. His last thought was of Andrew. Through his fading consciousness he could see his partner sitting in the front room, staring in frozen horror at the dogs that surrounded him, the dogs draining him of the rest of his life.

Maybe it was true after all, that people died because they were corpses.

WINDOW SHOPPING

David Mathew

VERY SOON, I suspect, the man who carries tools will knock on the glass and want to know what I'm doing here. Perhaps he will be polite but firm; he will insist on knowing my business, while making it clear that he would not be discharging his duties if he kept silent and then something happened that he had failed to challenge at the time. Then, in the course of leaning down to speak through the window that I will lower, he will see the laptop on the passenger seat and the puppy in the back, asleep as she is on a nest of towels and blankets.

My observer must be one of the school's grounds-men. He has circled the car four times now, not getting closer on each occasion, but achieving his circumference at a faster rate on each pass. Every time he orbits, he is carrying a different tool - most recently a shovel - and I try to imagine what he must think. The car park abuts one of the school's playgrounds, after all, and I have parked in a space near the chain link fence that separates the two functional areas. Every time a bell rings a different year group is released, and seventy or eighty children begin a twenty-minute play session a matter of metres from the passenger door window.

He must think I am window shopping, but I'm not. I'm waiting for my stepfather to emerge from the building, his meeting completed. As soon as I see him, I will make a show of hurrying over to the entrance. I might even stand beside him, hip to hip, and ease an arm around his waist to support his weight. I will claim his briefcase. I will help him back to the car, moving as slowly as he needs to in the aftermath of the operation on his feet that has required me to drive him to this school in the first place. As we leave the property, I will hope to see the grounds-man. I will offer him a wink.

But Mark surprises me. I have returned to the essay I must write and submit this holiday, with the laptop now spread-eagled on my knees, when the car boot opens behind me. In the sudden wash of cold air from outside, Doris wakes and protests with a single yelp. Mark has exited the school by a different door and has circled around to me unnoticed. I haven't heard the tapping of his walking stick and being crept up on like this makes me feel unaccountably ashamed.

'You were quick,' I tell him. 'How did it go?'

'That's the mortgage sorted out for the next six months,' he replies. 'Home, James!' I start the engine. 'Did you get any work done?' he asks, clicking the seatbelt buckle into place.

'A bit,' I lie. 'And Doris has been asleep all the time you were in there.' The puppy wears a harness that is locked into one of the back seat's safety slots. All the same, now that Mark has returned, Doris strains against the belt in an effort to reach her pack leader. The way that Mark ignores the bitch makes her want him more: she italicises her body on the back seat.

UNIVERSITY HAD LURED my friends away from our pleasant town. At the end of our exams we had scattered in different directions, to institutions of learning across the land. My maths result having been no worse than the other two, I had chosen a Widening Participation university as far east as a train line would take me, to study a subject that I learn in the same mechanical manner with which I had mastered 'Frère Jacques' on the recorder at Lower School.

Now I am back early for the long summer break, with a weekend job in a bakery to fund the occasional evening's entertainment, and a chauffeuring role that I had not anticipated, my mum being too busy with her own work to drive her husband around between appointments.

'I can't complain,' I tell Andy Brett, over a pint. 'They're putting me up, room and board, for twelve weeks. All they're asking is I drive Mark around in a car I enjoy driving anyway. And take the puppy to the park for her socialisation twice a day. It's okay.'

The venue is a pub called The Doghouse, next door to a plumbing supplies store called Dirty Hose (unbelievably enough), which was called something else the last time I was in this part of town. But then again, so was The Doghouse. The last time I was here it was known as Slide, and it was gay.

I am only surprised to see Andy Brett here in the way that I am surprised to see anyone I know. (I would have been amazed to see him in Slide!) Separated by ability streams at school, we had never been good friends but smoking on the school premises had bonded us. He used to do motor mechanics when I had a free period on a Wednesday. We would often meet in an alcove by the outdoors cupboard where they kept boxes of tennis balls and shot putts and javelins.

'Do you live this way then?' Andy asks.

'No. I was looking for Slide.'

Andy nods his head. 'Went bust. So you're a benny on the loose then? Don't stun me much, mate, I must admit. Thought as much.'

'Really. It must be the tattoo on my forehead.'

He doesn't acknowledge my sarcasm. 'There's another one, though,' he comments. 'Do you fancy another pint?'

For the first time I realise that Andy must have been drinking – and with a degree of dedication – before I met him by accident tonight. Now that I focus on them, his eyes are wanderers, loose in their puffy orbits.

'No thanks, I have to drive. Another what?'

'Trade bar,' Andy answers. He concludes his pint with a wipe of his chops and an air-ripping belch. 'Go there myself, time to time. I'm not a poof, like. Just watch the girls chatting themselves up. Gimme the *right* fuckin' 'orn.'

I hope the set of my lips and my tone suggests emotional coolness bordering on fragility. 'Fancy that,' I say to him calmly.

'Do you wanna go?'

'*I'D* DO IT. *I'd* pretend to be a Muslim. Get myself involved - get close to the boss. Then *bomp*. Lets his hair down, I'm fucking *in* there, mate. Put a spanner down his throat, the cunt. I'll give *him* twelve virgins in Heaven, mate. Won't have a working cock time I'm finished with him.'

It's nearly nine o'clock in a bar I don't know - and it's actually *called* Trade. The trade is threadbare - easy on the eye but nothing more - and because I have the car, a Coke or a Becks Blue is all I dare order. By very stark contrast, Andy Brett is totally abandoned by logic - he is wasted. We're not long in Trade before I start to regret agreeing to accompanying him here. I have to collect Mark from the bowling alley at ten; it's not worth driving home if I have to leave again as soon as I get there. Instead I am obliged to listen to Andy's smeared diction and vociferous views.

'So where's your boyfriend?' he asks me at one point. 'Is he here or in Norfolk?'

'Neither. I haven't got one.' It's not so much that I think I owe Andy an explanation; it's more that I'm bored and that talking will kill a few minutes. 'We had to part. He couldn't keep his pencil in his pocket.'

Andy takes a moment to digest this. When he eventually laughs, a smoke-coloured bubble appears at his left nostril.

'Gotcha. We're all the same.'

'*I'm* not,' I protest. 'I was faithful to him. I even gave him a third chance - *two* indiscretions - but he doubted I'd end it. And there's nothing worse than being thought of as predictable. So I changed the locks, metaphorically speaking.'

'So who do you fancy tonight?'

'...in what way?'

'In the shagging way, of course. The revenge shag.'

'No one. I have to pick up my stepfather at nine-thirty. I volunteered.' I lie about the pick-up time in order to plant the seed that I'll be leaving shortly.

'Where from?'

I explain about the bowling alley. 'He's in a league – they play every week. Just a practice tonight so he'll have a few beers with his friends.'

'Well, that's only a few minutes in the car. You could still get your end away.'

I laugh. 'As easy as that, eh? You're an expert all of a sudden.'

'Well, they have glory holes in the gents. They can't make it *much* easier for a quick one!'

'No, they don't!'

'Go and look if you don't believe me! I think it's between stalls three and four, but it might be two and three. Pop your piece in the hole and see who tickles your fancy. Anonymous.'

'Yes, I know how a glory hole works, thanks very much. I just can't believe they'd have one in a town pub – it must be against the law.'

Andy shrugs. 'Maybe it is, I don't know. But they had 'em last time I was here.'

By standing up I bring a smile to Andy's face. 'I need a pee,' I tell him.

'But I bet you check it out while you're there.' He also stands – for a second I think he is going to accompany me to the gents. 'I'll get another drink while you're away. Do you want another soft one … in a manner of speaking?'

Although I've already taken in more liquid than is comfortable, I decide 'One more Coke, please – just a small one' and then I leave the table.

As I cross the bar I see the grounds-man – the man who carries the tools – the man who works at the Lower School where my stepfather had his meeting this morning. The man who looked at me strangely while I waited in the car with a laptop and a puppy…

The grounds-man is playing a machine that is wider and taller than he is. He inserts a two-pound coin and a jingle sounds – the theme tune of a quiz show popular with some of my friends at university.

An urge to explain is overwhelming. I stop in my tracks, not close enough to him to be a pest, but close enough for him to notice me in his peripheral vision. Once he has slapped a large button marked C, a tone sounds that makes it clear he has selected the wrong option.

'Can I help you?' he asks with a Spanish accent. He turns to me slowly in a manner that is both sultry and rather excitingly menacing.

'I wanted to tell you what I was doing this morning, in the playground.'

'…I beg your pardon?'

'Well, not *in* the playground - *near* the playground. I was parked and you were working.'

'I don't work,' the grounds-man interrupts.

'At the school.'

He shakes his head briskly. 'I don't work at a school. I gamble.'

'But I saw you, mate!' I protest.

He takes a step towards me. 'You didn't see me this morning. You've never seen me before this moment.' His breath is sweet with what I take to be wine consumption. 'And after this moment you will never see me again, I would think. Now. Was there anything else? I intend to play this machine until I win what I've put into it. So if you'll excuse me…'

And he turns his back on me once more. Bewildered and obscurely hurt by his rejection, I head to the toilets. It is not as if I had expected the beginnings of a lifelong friendship with the grounds-man, but his behaviour has bothered me. If he doesn't work at the school, what was he doing there? Stealing tools? *Pretending* to work there in order to get closer to the children?

I enter the toilet cubicle that is third in line. I lock myself in. Sure enough, as Andy had said, there is a hole in the partition at waist-height. In fact, there are two - one on either side of the space. Theoretically, someone in the third stall could indulge in anonymous fun with someone in stalls two and four - simultaneously, even.

Suddenly the idea is intoxicating … but I am here to urinate, so that's what I do.

Except...

EXCEPT I HEAR the door to the main bar open – there is a wash of bass and a storm of cymbals and synths – and I know that someone has entered the gents. I know who it is as well. I can picture the grounds-man; he is looking for me. Although I don't understand his technique of seduction, he has made a virtue of confusion. He knows that his aloofness has made me want him.

I'm almost breathless. He enters Stall Two, on my left as I stand facing the cistern (although I have finished emptying my bladder). A few seconds pass. There is nervousness but it's the good kind of nervousness. It stretches the front of my trousers.

Do I dare?

'Are you shopping?' his whispered voice asks me. I can only just hear him.

'Yes.'

He slides two fingers through the glory hole and makes them wiggle.

'Follow me,' he whispers – and he withdraws his digits. But he has invited me over and it would be rude to turn down such an invitation.

The hole is a little low for me. By widening the space between my ankles, I am able to aim my erection through the gap. If you want to consider *vulnerable moments,* I might suggest that this is about as vulnerable as life throws at you.

The grounds-man starts licking the end of it. Within a few seconds I have relaxed; I've stopped worrying that we will be caught – the management must be aware of what goes on in here, after all. When he takes it into his mouth, I know that there is nothing else to think about.

It does not take long – I have never been able to hang on. The grounds-man spits into the toilet bowl and whispers, 'I must be going.' When he whispers, I note, his Spanish accent is lost. Perhaps it had not been a true accent in the first place.

He unlocks his door. 'I have to go the bowling alley,' he

explains in his normal voice. 'My stepson is picking me up at ten. It's been exciting. See you!'

I wait for Mark to leave the gents. I wait a long time.

CLAN FESTOR

Liam Garriock

We think that a man who does evil to us and to his neighbours must be very evil. So he is, from a social standpoint... Evil in its essence is a lonely thing, a passion of the solitary, individual soul... He is simply a wild beast that we have to get rid of ... rather with tigers than with sinners... In truth, he is merely an undeveloped man.

Arthur Machen

ON A WEEKDAY in late October 2014, when the days were darkening and leaden clouds coldly engulfed the skies, fifteen-year-old Chloe Carnegie disappeared as she was walking home alone from school. She attended St Thomas of Aquins High School yet lived in Granton, so she always took the number eleven bus to Trinity then caught the number sixteen to Lower Granton Road, although on rare occasions she took a different route to visit a friend's house. She had been following this routine since she was eleven and her parents, though initially uneasy with her new independence, gradually became accustomed to her travelling on her own.

Depending on the traffic - always a blight in Edinburgh - she was normally home before five, and always told her parents if she were going elsewhere after school, called them at the last minute if her plans changed. On the day that she vanished the only trace of her was the mobile phone and her music player, both found smashed to pieces on Boswall Road near Wardieburn. They had been stamped on with incredible violence, as though Chloe's kidnapper had trampled them in a psychopathic rage.

The police are not expected to allow their emotions to get in the way, yet even I wondered how colleagues can stifle their feelings when they are confronted with the sight of a human being butchered beyond belief, or talk with a traumatised child who has been raped – to not acknowledge to themselves the shocking things that mankind can inflict to his fellow species. Such things would be enough to encourage one to leave the force for good, and often I really wanted to, to shut myself away from the world and ignore its horrors and miseries – but that is never the right thing to do. Is it?

As is natural when a young person disappears under ominous circumstances, her anxious parents poorly masked their fear before the flashing and filming cameras as they quietly spoke into the dumb microphones before them. A photograph of her – the lovely quintessential smile of a blue-eyed girl with a thick mane of auburn hair – was reproduced on the front page of local newspapers and on posters that appeared throughout Edinburgh.

As a newbie on the plain clothes squad I was part of the team detailed to find the girl. It was my first missing person's case. For the first week we turned up nothing. Every abandoned building from Muirhouse to Leith was searched. The stench of fish lingered in our nostrils hours after we had left the port. Only the graffiti of odd and eccentric figures and faces gave mocking leers at us.

We even extended our search sites beyond the north of the city to the Old Town and beyond her school. We questioned her friends and teachers. Chloe was a cheerful, obedient girl – according to the teachers at St Thomas – but as with many youngsters, she often misbehaved when stern eyes wrinkled by crow's feet were not watching. Often, this amounted to little more than texting under the desk during class. We examined her locker, finding nothing of interest that may have aided us in our search.

ANOTHER WEEK PASSED and still we were no further on in

locating the abducted teenager. Our investigations had taken us to the district of Pilton, an unsavoury place that even the most hardboiled of thugs from neighbouring towns would be reluctant to enter. And most of us, too, despite being trained in dealing with the brutes of the human race, preferred to keep clear of the area. Yet a few of us were more tolerant; after all, they were only human beings - like ourselves; human beings that had succumbed to the dark side of existence and thus embraced the primal myths and fears fabricated to justify their destructive nature.

Several gangs used to inhabit Pilton and proudly claim it their own turf. Gang members engage in alarming behaviour, ranging from smashing car windows to attacking passing pedestrians, robbing pensioners, and even raping girls.

Then a new gang had taken up residence in Pilton, infuriating the natives. This new bunch was not the average type of delinquent. They were obsessed with the occult, with Satanism. Their leader was a robust-looking man in his late teens or early twenties, one Josh Wallace. He had a permanent sullen scowl, we heard, even when in a happy mood. Somehow, he exerted some sort of power over the youths of Pilton and many members from the other gangs, and some from neighbouring areas, too, abandoned their tribes to join Josh's. It did not sit well with the leaders of those other respective groups as their numbers became depleted.

Our attention quickly focused on this new mysterious group that occupied Pilton and we began to suspect there was a connection between them and the disappearance of Chloe Carnegie.

Chloe's parents became increasingly distressed at the lack of any trace of her; the police commissioner felt obliged to tell them some of our suspicions, but because she was concerned that they might misunderstand, might take the law into their own hands, we kept quiet about our interest in this new gang that had taken over Pilton. They probably wouldn't have known of this gang if a snooping journalist hadn't first informed them.

We monitored the gang for days. According to our informant, they were called the Clan Festor, and contrary to their outward appearance – typical black clothing – they did not worship Satan. We discovered that they worshipped an 'entity' called Festor, an ancient demon that was apparently responsible for most, if not all, of humanity's horrors, miseries, and fears. So we informed. Many times in the past, it was alleged, sacrificed virgins to it. Could this have been the explanation for Chloe's abduction? Were these hoodlums going to sacrifice an innocent teenage girl to some ancient demon?

The thought of Aleister Crowley wannabees parading around a sink estate in the north of Edinburgh was as fantastic and unreal as the idea of a primordial demon prowling said streets. Nevertheless, regardless of how outlandish our case seemed, we had to take action. When we had gathered all the evidence we could, we stormed into the lair where their practices took place – a derelict warehouse just off West Harbour Road. The youths were cuffed and bundled into vehicles. I took the time to observe their little den. Amidst the aged dust and rot there were satanic images scrawled over every surface, predominately in red. There was an altar beyond, with wax candles burning and flickering as wisps of wind blew in from outside through gaps in the eroded walls. And on the wall behind the altar I saw the repulsive drawing of a shapeless mass with the suggestion of horns. This must be their god – Festor. Although the group claimed they were not Satanists, the image had a Satanic quality to it. Despite the crude rendition, it looked as if it was drawn from an actual model though I assumed that whoever had drawn it had merely copied it from a picture in a book – I hoped.

I climbed to the second floor of the long-disused building. The stench of scented candles and burnt-out cigarettes become stronger. In addition, I smelled the acrid odour of vinegar, almost making me vomit, and I had to cover my mouth as I proceeded through the sodden, dirty rooms where further crude drawings of occult monsters were scrawled over the walls. I spotted a picture of Tilda Swinton tearing at her dress from Derek Jarman's *The Last of England.* There were also numerous cut-outs of grotesque art, the work of the visionary artists Austin Osman Spare and Rosaleen Norton. Strange creatures, chimeras of men and demons with serpents for phalluses.

I entered a room with a filthy mattress on the cold floor; on it was a copy of *Witchcraft Out of the Shadows* by Dr Leo Ruickbie, and some dog-eared paperbacks by Colin Wilson. The repulsive vinegar smell was stronger here and I almost laughed when I discovered its source - fish-and-chips wrapping on a wooden table in the corner.

There was no trace of Chloe Carnegie so I returned downstairs, feeling disgust and depressed.

The creatures depicted on the walls haunted me as I left, as though they were hitching a ride on my back out the rotten darkness into the outer world.

LATER AT THE station I left my colleagues to process the youths we had arrested. They were then incarcerated while we waited for their parents to arrive before we could question them. Meanwhile, I scoured the internet in search of Festor. I'd seen images of him behind the altar in the warehouse. But I couldn't find anything that matched, no mention of this Festor in any mythology or religion or even in the obscurest cults and sects throughout time; only Baphomets that seemed to stare at me from the screen with an expressions of sardonic triumph. This led me to believe that Josh had simply made the creature up, conjured it from the depths of his perverse imagination.

When we interrogated the youths, they were either silent or stubborn, all of the gang members. So we focused our attention on Josh, the self-styled high priest. Josh was older than the others. He was offered counsel before questioning but he refused. According to him, he had no parents. He seemed to take great pride in flexing his muscular, brawny arms and his abdominal and pectoral muscles were clearly defined beneath his tight, sleeveless T-shirt. Brazenly, he took out a cigarette but before he could light it I snatched it away and put the packet out of his reach.

'Rules,' I said.

I asked him if he knew a Chloe Carnegie.

'Chloe? Aye, I ken her. She's my girlfriend.'

I was taken aback at this. They knew each other?

'Girlfriend?"

'Aye, but she's ma *secret girlfriend.*' A smile crossed his face, a smile that revelled in forbidden pleasures.

'Secret girlfriend?'

'Aye. We've kenned each other a long time. Then I discovered Festor, the one absolute being who embodies all that's wrong with the human race. We began to worship him and he telt us that we didnae need tae be good. He made us embrace our true selves. She an' me shagged with all the fiery passion and shame of a thousand suns. We cut each other and supped one another's blood, and we enlisted others to join our clan and spread the word of Festor, cos I'm his avatar. Through me Festor spreads his power.'

I couldn't tell if he was boasting. And as much as I found it fascinating to hear him speak of his god, his take on the nature of man, the truth was, I was deeply repulsed by everything he said. How could anyone believe that mankind was nothing more than a savage beast that ultimately succumbed to base and horrific desires? After all, we had created thousands of marvels that have enriched the world with culture. I couldn't swallow it. It went against everything that I stood for, that I believed in.

'There is no Festor,' I told him. 'No record of him on the internet.'

'That's cos naebody wants to know about him. They'd rather keep him dead and buried cos he speaks the truth. He's there, alright, in the hearts of everyone. He's the one who puts dirty pictures into your mind, who makes you pick up the knife and fire the gun.'

'What mythology is he from? How d'you know about him?'

'He spoke tae me, whispered his name into my heid. And anyway, and he *has* been worshipped by everyone throughoot history – but secretly – by the Japs, the Vikings, the Chinese, Babylonians, Celts, Sumerians. Everyone who has blood on their haunds and lust burning in their hearts.'

I returned to the subject of Chloe. 'Where is she?' I asked. 'What have you done with her?'

He ignored me. 'Dinnae look sae shocked, mon. You must've wanted to destroy that woman you see undressing across the street, go over to her house and totally *destroy* her like there was nae taemorrow? That's what I did wae Chloe. She *loved* every night and day I gave pleasure tae her. Can yae just imagine her sweet young body being invaded by ma blood, an' her wriggling and squirming with delight like a worm? Can ya?'

He continued to drone on. I wanted this horrible man locked away for life. No, I felt fury that capital punishment had been abolished. Some people deserved the death sentence, deserved to hang – or have poison coursing slowly through their veins, to writhe in agony as they prayed for death to come. I stopped, reprimanded myself – that was no better than someone like Josh, who worshipped a savage and evil demon.

I knew that the warehouse had been thoroughly searched and no trace of the missing girl had been found amidst the grime and decay.

Since this was my first missing persons' case I felt a weary sense of hopelessness and futility that, during the course of those two weeks, seemed to have piled up like the Tower of Babel. There was no choice but to release the youths into the custody of their parents but we wanted to keep Josh under close watch, with not one moment out of sight.

I was sure he had done something to Chloe and I was going to make sure that he didn't get away with it, or harmed anyone ever again. Justice should be an inseparable limb of man.

But we needed evidence to charge him or we'd have to let him go, too.

THE NEXT MORNING I went to Chloe's home in Granton to speak to her parents. Her mother's eyes were red and swollen with grief. I asked them if they knew Josh Wallace. They denied recognising the name. When I told them that he claimed he and Chloe were in a relationship their sorrowful expressions changed into disbelief and anger.

'Our Chloe? Having sex? What are you talking about?' Her mother choked out the words as her equally distressed father wrapped arms around her, attempting to comfort his wife.

After a moment I said I needed to inspect Chloe's room again to see if I could find anything that might have been missed. Her room was a typical teenage girl's room, with bright wallpaper on which posters of the latest boy bands were mounted. There was a computer notebook (*Why hadn't this already been taken to forensics?* I thought) on the chest of drawers, and a dresser with a makeup kit and accessories. I imagined that her mother had tidied it as it was all immaculately placed. I poked into every nook and cranny at first finding nothing of interest. Then I had discovered a scrap of paper hidden behind the dresser. On it was a weird illustration, something which surely pertained to the cult. It looked like a human heart – adorned with horns.

On the obverse side were the handwritten words:

My heart is forever yours now, Chloe, and yours mine. Let nothing sever our sacred bond that others will never understand. You and I are special, Chloe. We know what man's soul truly yearns for, and it is something which he may receive soon. May Festor smile upon us always.

Your eternal lover, Josh

As I read, my feelings polarised. I didn't know whether to show the note to Mr and Mrs Carnegie. Before I could decide, Mrs Carnegie came into the room. She saw the piece of paper, read it over my shoulder, and cupped her mouth in shock and disbelief. Then before I could stop her she snatched it from my hand and tore it in half.

'I dinnae believe it. I dinnae. You planted that there. You're trying to villainise my daughter. Why? My Chloe's a good girl. She would never do anything like this. Get Out!' She was screaming.

I gathered the pieces of paper and slipped them into an

evidence bag. Mrs Carnegie suddenly hit me, started shouting again. Fortunately, Mr Carnegie rushed upstairs to calm her down.

'I think you better leave,' he said, restraining his now weeping wife. As I did I heard Mrs Carnegie tell her husband that I was trying to paint their daughter as a Satanist.

I WALKED WEARILY to the station. My emotions battled one another. What was I to believe? That this fifteen-year-old girl, an innocent her parents' eyes, was a secret devil-worshipper?

Reluctantly, Josh Wallace was set free. There was no choice. But by releasing him, I hoped to follow him, see if he would lead me to Chloe.

He returned to Pilton where he then headed back to the derelict warehouse. Some of his brainwashed hoodlums were waiting for him. I kept a watchful eye on the place from the shadows. I wondered whether I would witness genuine paranormal phenomena that night or merely the pretext of a black magic ceremony, where the kids sacrificed an animal. Luckily I had a clear view of the room in which they gathered and could see the teenagers who, I imagined, were listening to Josh recite the incantations to Festor, in hopes that he would manifest. Then someone else entered the room. It was Chloe Carnegie.

I decided not to move, not yet. For the moment I simply watched. Chloe still wore her school uniform, now dirty and torn. She was smiling as Josh, her supposed boyfriend, took her by the hands and passionately and slowly kissed her. The other youths merely stared at them. When the two young lovers stopped kissing Josh escorted her to the altar, where she stripped off her clothes. None of the boys behaved as teenagers would normally when they see a nude female. They remained still, like statues. Chloe lay on the altar. Josh produced a dagger that looked impressively ancient. With shock and horror I realised what was likely to happen next. Sense urged me to make a move but I felt as though I was held in a malignant trance, unable to do anything except watch as a young girl was sacrificed by one she apparently loved. Josh continued to chant, praying to Festor.

Then a group of youths crashed the room - obviously the furious leaders of the other gangs - interrupting the ritual, yelling, cursing Josh. They wielded an array of lethal weapons - bats, knives, broken glass bottles. One had a pistol, which he pointed at the dagger-wielding Josh. Breaking free of my trance, I gave a shout, wishing I had backup. I stormed into the building, shouted 'Police!' and told everyone to drop their weapons. The pistol fired. In a moment of rage, I tasered the dog-faced thug holding the gun and when he was down on the floor I put the boot in, repeatedly. Everyone froze, staring in incredulity - I was a policeman, after all.

Then Josh drove the dagger into Chloe's bare chest.

I snatched up the gun and shot Josh. He collapsed against the wall, against the drawing of Festor, tainting it with his blood. Chloe hadn't screamed when the blade plunged deep into her breast.

She simply moaned as if with pleasure as life slowly left her body.

MY COLLEAGUES WERE horrified - and perplexed - by my actions that night. I can hardly blame them. I no longer know who I am, what I stand for.

Although we searched hard, we could find no information on Josh Wallace - no parents or relatives living in the Lothians, or anywhere else for that matter. No residential address. We're not even sure if Josh Wallace was his real name. All we know is that he was a violent youth obsessed with the occult who sacrificed his young girlfriend to his bloodthirsty god.

When the internal enquiry convenes next month I intend to tender my resignation. I find the whole idea of law and order, of authority, something of a farce. I know that the demon will never be smothered. I've stopped reading newspapers. I no longer wish to read the daily tragedies that afflict the world or see the young sweet face of one who has fallen victim to the cruelties and evils that the world offers us.

SWEET SIXTEEN

Adam Millard

IT WAS BEHIND the kitchen bin that Angela found the first of them. A thick-bodied creature, a full two inches across, with spiny short legs and a dark - what she assumed was a - head. It looked like something from an awful science-fiction movie, the kind Paul would make her watch, despite her abhorrence of the genre. Though she knew this thing, *whatever* it was, was not otherworldly. It was larvae of some kind. That of a beetle, perhaps, or some weird butterfly. Watching it crawl across the kitchen floor - she could hear its minute legs clicking against the linoleum - Angela shuddered. It was one of the most disgusting things she had ever seen.

She could smell it, too. Of rotten earth and spoiled vegetables - it reminded her of the dead fox she had once discovered at the back of the shed. Yes, this thing also carried the stench of death despite being wholly alive.

After watching the thing crawl inexorably across the floor for several moments, Angela knew it didn't belong there. Quite where it *did* belong, she had no idea but she knew she wouldn't be able to concentrate or relax knowing she had allowed the thing to go free.

She straightened up and walked across the room never once taking her eyes from the peculiar insect lest it secrete itself away in some hiding place only to emerge again later when she least expected it. Tearing a piece of kitchen-roll from its dispenser, she returned to the thing and hovered over it, not quite sure how best to approach it.

'What *are* you?' she muttered. If Paul were here, he'd probably be able to tell her but unfortunately the creature wasn't able to provide her with an answer. If it had, she would have run from the house, screaming plaintively and not stopping until she reached her absent boyfriend's house a mile away.

Several minutes passed and Angela grew more discomfited. It was just an insect, far more frightened of her than she should have been of it. There was no real reason why she should feel so unnerved by the creature, other than her uncertainty as to what the thing was. She had never feared spiders or carpet-beetles or any of the myriad creepy-crawlies which were ubiquitous around the house. Her mother always called upon her to ensnare the house-spiders which came crawling out of the woodwork, and she would do so without any hesitation whatsoever, usually utilising the trusty old glass-and-postcard technique.

But she had hesitated, now, because this thing was far too big for the glass-and-postcard technique. She would cleave it in half if she even attempted it. *Then I would have two of the blighters to dispose of*, she thought.

'Okay,' she said, breathing deeply and inching ever closer to the huge larvae with its thorny legs and incongruously black head. Then she brought the kitchen towel down and enveloped the grub, shuddering as she did so. For a moment it seemed too big for her hand and she struggled to pick it up. Inside the tissue it continued to writhe and Angela could have sworn she heard the thing shrilly squeal as she tightened her grip.

Confident she had it suitably captured, she stood and carried it across the kitchen to the back door. It squirmed – and *screamed?* – in protest as she transported it out into the garden where she set it down on the dewy morning grass and watched it wriggle away toward the Busy Lizzies.

Outside it was already warm, shaping up to be another hot day in a long line of them and, as Angela made her way back to the house, a smile stretched across her face. Paul was coming around later and she had a very good idea what they would be getting up to while her mom was at work and they had the house to themselves.

Her smile faded quickly, however, as she stepped back into the kitchen to find three more grubs exactly like the one she had just removed, crawling and writhing across the kitchen floor.

'You've got to be shitting me,' she said, before pulling three more kitchen-towels from the dispenser.

PAUL ARRIVED JUST after midday, sweaty and topless. Whether this was intentional, Angela didn't know, and neither did she care for it had the desired effect. Standing there in the kitchen sipping blackcurrant squash from plastic blue tumblers. They talked about the larvae Angela had found in the kitchen that morning and what it might have been.

'Probably beetle larvae,' Paul suggested as he held the plastic glass to his forehead in an attempt to cool himself down. 'You'd be surprised how big those things can get. You should have taken a picture with your phone before you launched them out into the garden.'

'I didn't *launch* them,' Angela laughed. 'I placed them very carefully down next to the border.'

'Such a brave girl,' Paul said. 'Next you'll be wrestling gorillas in the Congo.'

Angela playfully punched him on the arm and he almost spilled his drink. 'If you'd seen the size of those things, I bet you'd have run for your life.'

Paul pulled her in to a tight embrace with his free hand. 'I would have led them all out of here like the Pied Piper of Hamelin,' he said. 'Did you know I was a flautist?'

'I did *not* know that,' Angela said, knowing full well that her boyfriend had never picked up a flute in his life, let alone played one tunefully. 'Have you ever thought about joining an orchestra?'

'Have *you* ever thought about joining the circus?' He flinched as if expecting another light jab from Angela, and she would have obliged had they not been in such close quarters – not that she was complaining. Paul was clammy and musty, as if he had run the mile to her house, but he felt good pressed against her and she quite liked the sweaty smell permeating the kitchen.

She placed her tumbler down on the kitchen counter without breaking the embrace. Paul did the same.

Then they were kissing, their bodies entwining. Paul's tongue slipped slowly in and out of her mouth and she breathed into his, hoping this was the moment, the moment the last three months had been building up to. Next week she turned sixteen – sweet sixteen – and all of her friends had already done it. She didn't want to be the one left behind and she knew Paul was the one. It was inevitable, really.

Paul pulled his head back, gasping for air, his eyes rolling as if he was already in the throes of some intense orgasm. 'We should go upstairs,' he said, breathlessly.

Without a moment's hesitation, Angela said, 'Yeah, we should.'

Then it was a race, a game to see who could reach the bedroom first, who could get undressed the quickest.

Surprisingly, Angela won.

IT HURT A little at first but Paul, who assured her it was his first time too, was sensitive and exceedingly tender. She knew he would be, and along with the pain, her anxiety also waned. It then started to feel nice – a lot nicer than she had anticipated. Paul's gentle thrusts rocked the bed and Angela pulled her pillow down to stifle the moans over which she had no control. She couldn't believe this was happening.

At school on Monday she would tell her friends Bethany and Sara how considerate he had been, how he had sought reassurance – *'Does it feel okay? Are you okay? Tell me if you want me to stop.'* – and how they were in love and this wasn't just some messed-up game that teenagers were wont to play. Bethany and Sara had both lost their virginities (at least, *Bethany* had; Angela wasn't so sure about Sara, whose parents were devout Catholics) and so it would be nice to compare notes with them, to be able to join in the sex conversations without feeling like an intruder or some sort of fraud.

'That feels so good,' Paul panted, easing himself in and out of Angela. 'Does that feel good?'

Angela moaned from beneath the pillow. Paul quickened his thrusts, eagerly seeking his first climax of the afternoon. Angela, for some inexplicable reason, could think of nothing but the grubs she had discovered in the kitchen that morning. They had been so ... thick and spiny, their bodies segmented and chitinous, and there had been so many tiny legs beneath, rushing to get away, to return from whence they came.

His penis is one of them!

It was ridiculous but in that moment Angela believed it. She could feel it squirming inside of her, a thousand minute barbed legs scratching away at her vagina wall. Pain returned once again, superseding any pleasure she might have been feeling a moment ago.

His thrusts became quicker as Angela's moans were mistaken for ones of pleasure and not utmost terror. One of those *things* was inside her and she knew it was trying to break off, to come away from its host so that it might better explore *her* body.

She screamed - at least, she *thought* she did - and then there was only darkness as Paul's orgasmic convulsions intensified, and the larval penis spewed its vile secretions into her.

WHEN SHE WAKENED, Angela had no idea what had happened or even where she was. A cursory glance around the room relaxed her slightly as she recognised the pink wallpaper, the shelf of plush bears, the bookcase filled with trinkets and snow-globes. She was in her bedroom, lying atop her bed, but what had happened? How had she come to be there? Beyond the drawn curtains she saw daylight, which meant...

Paul! She had been with Paul and they had been in bed together, doing ... *things*. Things which had been nice to begin with but had quickly soured. Things which she was going to brag about to her friends but now would keep to herself, for Paul must have left. He must have left her - halfway through? - because she wasn't doing it right, or –

Fuck, did I fall asleep? That was far worse than not doing it right. Falling asleep during their first time? That was a deal-breaker, the kind of thing that should never happen. 'No, no, no, no,' she repeated over and over again as she swung her legs out of the bed and –

She fell silent as her foot came to rest against something warm, something which shouldn't have been there. When she looked down and saw Paul lying there, eyes wide open and staring up at her accusingly, the bloodstained jewellery box lying at his shoulder. She screamed.

It was a scream which seemed to last forever.

SHE HAD KILLED him. Killed *her* Paul with the jewellery-box from the bedside table while he made love to her so tenderly – and then she had blacked out. There was no other explanation for it. She had felt the larvae inside of her and snapped, and Paul was dead. *Her* Paul. Paul whom she would marry and spend the rest of her life with.

'He looks a little like Paul McCartney; don't you think?' she had once asked her mom. Bethany and Sara thought so, too. A young Paul McCartney.

And now he was dead and lying on her bedroom floor, his head stove in with a worthless wooden jewellery box, his eyes already glassy and dried blood caking the corner of his mouth.

Murder. That's what it would be called. Angela didn't want to go to jail. They do things to people in jail, unpleasant things, things that'd make your eyes water and your blood turn to mercury.

'Fuck!' Angela screamed at the top of her voice. Then she was moving; she was dragging Paul's body across the room. He was heavy but in that moment Angela had the strength of ten men. She couldn't go to jail, not for murder, not for killing her Paul. She dragged the body across the landing and down the stairs – *thunk, thunk, thunk, thunk* – for she'd had an idea. A sick and twisted idea which she would probably never be able to live with, but what choice did she have? She had to get rid of the body.

She had to get rid of Paul's body and pretend none of this had ever happened.

AT THE BOTTOM of the garden, upright and half-buried already by dense shrubs and overgrown ivy, was the wardrobe. It had sat there for many months as the earth began to swallow it up and the foliage consumed it. It had been too large for the car and so taking it to the tip had been out of the question. When her mother suggested leaving it at the bottom of the garden – 'for now, at least until we can find a bloke with a van who'll shift it for nothing' – Angela had helped her carry it down there, to the space at the back of the greenhouse.

She looked at the wardrobe and then at Paul's lifeless body as it lay beside the greenhouse, wrapped in an old plain blanket from the airing cupboard, one her mother wouldn't miss. Like some sort of mummy. 'Shit!' she sobbed. Even though the sun was beating down and there wasn't a breath of wind, Angela shivered at what she was about to do. She pulled her dressing gown around her, fastened it tight, and took a deep breath.

She heaved the wardrobe door open, pulling as hard as she could to free the bottom of the door from the brambles which had grown up around it. She managed to open it about halfway – plenty to fit Paul's covered body through – before collapsing to the grass in a flood of tears.

This isn't right! This isn't right and you know it! She should go to the police station, the one up at Snow Hill. They would help her, wouldn't they? Not incarcerate her, for she had done this unconsciously. Without intent and because ... because she had believed his penis to be a beetle larva.

She didn't know how the law worked but she knew that a boy – her *Paul* – had died from a wound she had inflicted upon him, had died in her bedroom because she had clobbered him with a jewellery box. West Midlands Police were unlikely to need any more proof as to what had happened there that afternoon. She would be sentenced for murder, sent to jail, do not pass go, do not collect two-hundred pounds.

She wiped the tears from her eyes and climbed to her feet.

Paul fit just fine in the wardrobe. Who would have thought it?

WHEN THE DAY of her party arrived, just seven short days after she had murdered the love of her life, Angela was unsurprisingly not in the mood for festivities. How could there be a party? How could she celebrate her coming of age after what she had done? And yet she knew that by calling the whole thing of not only would she incur the wrath of her mother - who had gone to great lengths to make sure her daughter had a wonderful day by laying on a terrific spread and pinning balloons and decorations all around the house - but she would also be placing herself under the microscope. No one, other than Angela, knew what had really happened to Paul. He was simply missing as far as the police were concerned. The way they saw it, it was not unusual for a sixteen-year-old boy to disappear off the grid for a week or two. Maybe, the police had suggested, he'd gone to stay with a friend for a while. The fact that his parents were divorced made it easier, for the police hadn't yet managed to make contact with Paul's father. Maybe Paul had gone *there*.

Maybe Paul's in the old rotting wardrobe behind the greenhouse, Angela had thought when her mum told her that Paul's mother had provided her with an update. *Maybe he's out there rotting along with it, teeming with worms and chitinous beetles as they swarm over him, eating the flesh from his bones.*

The party was in full-swing by mid-afternoon but Angela couldn't wait for it to end. Already she wanted to be alone in her room, suffering for what she had done. She deserved to suffer. She deserved the unbearable agony she felt crawling around inside her, like the grubs from her kitchen. She deserved - she *wanted* - to die for what she'd done. Perhaps that was the only way out.

The only right way to grieve. Just the perfect amount of suffering.

'Great party,' Sara said, sidling up next to her at the buffet table. Angela hadn't yet eaten anything but she was aware of the myriad eyes upon her. Everyone was wondering what was wrong with her. 'What's the matter with Angela?' they were probably saying. 'Did she murder Paul and stuff him in the old wardrobe in the garden?' they probably weren't saying, but who knew what they were *thinking*. Angela had to pretend everything was fine and standing at the spread her mother had put out for her and her friends at least made it look as if she was interested.

'Thanks,' Angela said, picking up a sausage roll and, after a cursory inspection, taking the smallest of bites from its corner.

'Everything cool with you?' There was no suspicion in her friend's tone, just genuine concern.

'Yeah, cool as a cucumber,' Angela said and immediately regretted it. She had never said that before and it was such a ridiculous thing to say under the circumstances. She felt like everyone was watching her, listening to her every word, waiting for her to trip up so they could escort her down to the local police station. It was silly but that was how she felt, and curious missteps like '*cool as a cucumber*' weren't going to help fucking matters.

'Look at them all.' Sara pointed to the dance floor, which wasn't a dance floor but the kitchen without the dining furniture. Bodies swayed and danced there, swinging hips and chatting to those within earshot. There were only a dozen or so people in the cramped kitchen but it looked like more.

It looked like a hundred. A *thousand*. And the way they moved – writhing and squirming – caused bile to rise in Angela's throat.

They look like insects, she thought. Like the kitchen grubs, all segmented and spiny. She watched as they merged, became one organism, then separated once again to form an army. Some of them sprouted wings while antennae emerged bloodily from the foreheads of others. They buzzed and chirruped and danced around, their new appendages moving in time with the music.

This can't be! Angela thought. *This isn't real!*

On the floor in the centre of the kitchen, at the feet of the dancing insect-people, crawled the larvae. Twice as big as the ones she had removed a week earlier, they too seemed to be dancing and gyrating to the music. It was a nightmare – it had to be – and one Angela wanted to wake from instantly. But no matter how hard she tried, she could not shock herself back to consciousness the way she often did when she was having an unpleasant dream.

Three of the insect-people began to fornicate right there in the kitchen. Spindly legs tangling with spindly legs. Some of them even snapped off and fell to the makeshift dance floor where they were kicked around by the other revelling creatures. A dark-brown moth-woman leapt up onto the countertop and began screaming plaintively. A huge beetle, with more legs than it had any right to possess, tugged at the moth-woman's wing, urging her to get down. The wing tore away and a thick black ichor began to seep from the fresh wound.

I'm going insane! I'm going nuts and I deserve it!

'Angela!'

Someone was calling her name and, judging by the tone, not for the first time. Angela blinked away the gruesome image and when she opened her eyes she was relieved to discover Sara and Bethany standing next to her and no sign of the insect-people who had, a moment ago, been tearing up the kitchen floor.

'Are you *okay*?' Bethany said, her face contorted into something like genuine concern. 'You ... you just went *blank*.'

Angela had to get a grip. She was being haunted, not by the tangible but by her own immeasurable guilt. 'I think,' she said, staring down at the table and the vast array of food there, 'I think I just need some fresh air.'

'In that case, hang on just a sec,' Sara said. 'We've got a little surprise for you.'

Just then, the lights dimmed and the almost deafening music faded to silence. Angela took a deep breath, for she knew what would happen next and, despite feeling incredibly uncomfortable with the whole situation, she managed to force a smile onto her face. Her friends the dancers – just mates from school and not the mutated insect-people they had been a moment ago – gathered around, eagerly awaiting the arrival of the cake.

'You didn't have to...' Angela said, trailing off as her guests began to sing 'Happy Birthday', tunelessly and not quite in unison. From the living-room came her mother. She must have gone out to fetch it, Angela thought. Her mother had conspired with her friends, managed to keep the cake a secret, and here it was, all prettily iced and covered with candles.

Happy Birthday to you!
Happy Birthday to you!
Happy Birthday to Angie!
Happy Birthday to you!

And Angela was, for the briefest of moments, happy, but that changed as she noticed, upon the approaching cake, innumerable bugs, crawling over the icing, eating away at the prettiness to reveal a savaged human head. Blood dripped from the silver cake -board, the candles, the empty sockets of the human face staring reprovingly out at her.

'Blow out your candles,' urged her mother as furious applause replaced the singing.

'I'm going to... I'm going to be sick!' And Angela, who had done everything she could to remain composed throughout the party, finally rushed for the back door and the garden beyond.

SHE DIDN'T STOP until she reached the shed and even that didn't seem distant enough from the house. She was seeing things, or rather things were mocking her. It was an endless nightmare, one in which she was awake and at the mercy of everything. Defenceless against the insect-people dancing in her kitchen, and then the cake which she knew was an ordinary-looking cake to everyone else in there - but to her it was a monster, the thing from under the bed made real.

They're going to lock me away, she thought, lowering her head closer to the path as more bile rose in her throat. *And not in any prison, in some secure facility for the mentally perturbed. It's a cocktail of pills and padded walls for you, Angie, and make no mistake about it.*

She closed her eyes, inhaled deeply through her nose and out through her mouth, and soon the sickness dissipated, though she was left with a raw burning in her throat as if she had been drinking diesel all afternoon and not just lemonade. From the house she heard the music start up once again. At least her friends were having a good time.

Upon opening her eyes, she came face-to-face with yet another nightmare. One of the beetle larvae was there just a few inches in front of her own head and it seemed to be appraising her, trying to figure out if she'd had enough yet, or if madness was still a few steps away.

'No,' Angela said, no more than a whisper. She pushed back onto her haunches and straightened up. She turned back to the house and that was when she saw them. Thousands – millions – of them, scattered across the sun-dried lawn like Hell's confetti. Chitinous beetles as far as the eye could see. They crawled over the path, over her mother's prize bird-feeders, over the rockery beside the pool, over everything, and the noise they made was almost deafening. Angela clapped hands to her ears just to mute it. 'No,' she said once again.

She backed away from the beetles, which seemed to sense her apprehension and decided to up the ante by crawling toward her with more urgency.

'Just leave me alone!' she screamed. 'Just leave me the fuck alone, please!'

The beetles, now joined by worms and a cloud of dark moths, continued their approach, and it was all Angela could do to remain on her feet. She knew if she went down they would get her. They would swarm over her and feast until nothing remained but bones and ripped clothes.

Without turning, Angela walked backwards along the garden path. Why had no one come to check on her? Where were her friends? Where was her mother? Where had all these fucking *monsters* come from?

When she was level with the greenhouse, she knew she had no other alternative. The house was too far away, and there were far too many insects blocking her path, but the wardrobe – Paul's *coffin* – was only a few feet to her left.

It was her only chance, her only means of escaping the insects and the horrible fate they had in store for her.

She lunged for the wardrobe, knowing what lay within, knowing it was no worse than what would happen to her if she remained out there in the open.

If every human being on earth has their own personal Hell, Angela had found hers within the guts of an old, discarded wardrobe.

SHE PULLED THE door shut as best she could from the inside; the brass knob was on the outside, so a half-inch gap, roughly the width of her pinky finger, remained. There was nothing she could do about it. She could only hope that the grubs didn't notice the wardrobe and if they did, that they were too large to slither their disgusting bodies through the crack.

The smell inside the wardrobe was awful. Angela could feel Paul's body behind her. Even though it was covered over with a blanket, she could feel the cold beneath and the stiffness of its limbs.

Not realising she was doing it, Angela chanted nervously. *This isn't real, this isn't real, this isn't real*. But she knew that it wasn't a dream and if it wasn't real, then she was going crazy. If she was going crazy, then an old abandoned wardrobe at the bottom of the garden was probably the best place for her, even if her lodger was her dead ex-boyfriend.

How long Angela remained there, not moving, hardly breathing, she didn't know. In that moment she was only aware of two things: her own racing heartbeat and the grotesquely swollen boy behind her. Her Paul.

Don't you think he looks a bit like Paul McCartney? From The Beatles?

The Beatles… The Beatles … the beetles are in the wardrobe! Angela could feel them crawling across the tops of her feet, up her shins, and then there were cold hands upon her, gripping her by the wrists, holding her in place.

A voice said, *Hello, Angela. Miss me?* though not out loud. This was inside her own head where all the bad stuff was happening. But the cold hands were not inside her head, and neither was the penis growing against her back, feeling its way around as if independent from the body to which it was patently attached.

Angela opened her mouth to scream, but a cold hand came up to stifle it. Dirt and maggots filled her wide-open mouth and she gagged as she tried to expel the disgusting things between Paul's rotting fingers.

This won't hurt, Paul said breathily as the thing that was his penis detached, dropped to the wardrobe floor with a meaty thump and began to crawl up her right leg. *It's not your first time, is it?*

Now Angela did scream as the cold rotten thing crawled up, and up, and up…

BURIED STARS

Simon MacCulloch

I PUT THE phone down, cutting him off in mid-sentence.

The smell of disinfectant in the public phone box reasserts itself sharply, reminding me that it has been there all along, a cold, lifeless presence underneath the illusion of human closeness created by my talking. Now the only remnant of any kind of contact is the names and numbers of taxi firms glaring silently at me from their little cards, daring me to admit that I've got nowhere in particular to go. Outside the broken windows, the tree-lined street is white frost and black ice. Cars and vans hiss slowly through slush.

All right, so Michael's had enough of hearing about my bad dreams. It would be easier for him if I was over it, so he assumes that's the way it is, and tells me we'd have a better chance of picking up our relationship again if I didn't still feel the need to act like a wounded bird all the time just to get sympathy. Wishful thinking was always his problem.

Well, he's welcome to it. Tim and Andy's New Year's Eve party is less than a week away now. Maybe I'll meet someone new there. I dial Tim's number, struggling a bit against the growing numbness in my fingers. *When the hell are they going to fix the connection in my flat?*

'Tim speaking.'

'Hi Tim. David.'

A pause. 'Hi David.'

'How's things?'

'Fine.'

'Listen, I just wanted to check I'd got the details of your New Year's Eve bash right. Same time and place as last year?'

Another pause. 'Sure.'

'Well, I guess I'll see you there, then.'

'Okay David.'

A click, followed by the antiseptic whine of the vacant line as Tim hangs up. The receiver almost slips out of my now bloodless, cold-filled hand as I replace it. I look at the taxi cards again. They're about half the size of the ones Tim, in his rather old-fashioned way, always sends out weeks in advance to invite people to his end of year party. I didn't receive one this year and he didn't even bother to make a pretence of asking me if I had. So, he hadn't invited me and the tone of his voice tells me he'd rather not have been cornered into doing so now.

Walking home, I feel the first crumbs of another fall of snow, or hail, like polystyrene, bounce lightly off my face. I don't twitch or flinch – my face has become as stiff as a mask in the cold of the rising wind.

THE OFFICE WON'T reopen until the New Year. I keep myself to myself in my flat for the next few days, listening to music. Joy Division supply a core of sound wrapped in emptiness. Ian Curtis tells me over and over that he's got the spirit but loses the feeling. With each replaying it sounds less like a confession or a lament, more like a neutral statement of fact, devoid of emotional colour. Is that how it is, being a ghost?

At night, I dream I'm living in a basement, which becomes a tunnel down which I'm chasing someone. There's a chest freezer in the basement/tunnel and I know that when I catch the someone I'll put him in there, where his face can look up at me from under a surface of ice, never changing.

Outside, the chill continues. Every hour, when I can be bothered to listen, the radio repeats a forecast of steady low temperature, more snow and sleet. The news that precedes these tired prophecies, that may as well be mere observations, is scant. The world is half asleep, under a sheet of apathy. Even the crime reports seem to be given grudgingly, as if to say yes, another of those, what else did you expect? Nothing really happens when nothing ever changes.

So I put on my coat and gloves and balaclava and take myself into the monochrome pseudo-outside (the city never feels like real outside, it's too enclosed by itself). Perhaps if I can make it as far as the reservoir before the rigor mortis grip of the air and the gangrenous chewing of the freezing slush at my toes force me back, I'll be able to breathe more freely, think more constructively, work something out.

Parts of the reservoir have frozen over and a couple, a man and a woman I think, are skating on it, despite the warning signs. Or despite the suggestion of warning signs. I see when I get closer that the nearest one has weathered to an illegible blur. Now that I think about it, it looks too detailed to have been such a simple injunction - and did this stretch of water really freeze often enough to warrant such efforts? Of course, it had probably only been bye-laws, fishing restrictions - what made me think it was a warning against skating?

The couple skate towards each other, smoothly and (from where I'm standing) noiselessly, then away backwards in a mirror image movement. The white of their faces clashes against the black of their clothes. The black of their clothes clashes against the white of the ice. The white of the ice clashes against the black of the trees, the black of the trees clashes against the white of the sky… I look away, my eyes stinging with the merciless contrasts, my head dizzy. I regain focus by gazing into the tangled dark under the bridge over the end of the reservoir, where I can just make out the used condoms floating like pink sausage skins.

When I next look at the couple, they've stopped, closer to the shore and are looking back at me. Their faces are expressionless, too bone-white to have any blood left in them at all. The hand that I'd thought of raising in acknowledgement stays motionless at my side, dead as a frozen fish. I don't need to communicate with them. They can't cross the barrier between ice and earth, can't cut into the dark loam of living with that alien razored footgear.

They're trapped apart from me, from life, like reflections.

No, I think as I turn and trudge away, not here, not now – but something in my recollection of their rigid gaze translates that into 'not yet'.

As I leave the reservoir behind, the buildings encroach on the sky once more, squeezing its whiteness brighter and denser. Behind that must be packed the heavier white of more snow. But then black again, the colder, breathless black of space with the crystal white of far stars embedded in it, their long-travelled, long-outdated light (if they changed, we wouldn't know for years, centuries) still more than razor-sharp and more than antiseptically clean.

Back at the flat, I switch on the fan heater and wait for the pain when the circulation returns to my fingers. It takes its time coming and I start to make myself a coffee to help it along. I fumble a cup, drop it, and it shatters on the tiles of the kitchen floor. Picking up the shards, I barely feel one of them cut my hand, but see a pale pink slit open below the thumb. I experience a moment of panic before the expected blood begins to ooze out, sluggishly, as if mixed with ice.

I quickly apply a sticking plaster to the reluctant wound. Giving up on the coffee, I resort to the refrigerator. Two cans of Special Brew eventually warm, loosen and gently untie the knot in my stomach. I think of a corpse being endowed with a semblance of health by an infusion of embalming fluid. But then I've never been convinced that I really enjoy the taste of Special Brew.

A DAY (OR is it two?) later, the electrician still hasn't called to fix the phone connection in the flat. Of course he'd promised to come right after Christmas but really that meant right after the Christmas/New Year holiday. Work may expand to fill the time available, but inactivity exists in its own infinite space-time continuum. After another sandwich lunch I go out to the phone box again. The pavements are patched with greyish ice, walking over which demands a tentativeness that produces a sense of detachment from the ground.

Keith is supportive. He even asks me about my dreams without my having mentioned them. I tell him they're much the same.

'I'd say you need to get out more but I know you try. No-one seems to be seeing much of each other this Christmas anyway. Just the pissy weather, I suppose.'

We talk about the pissy weather for a few moments. I think of the ice on the reservoir, with little flecks of white in it like buried stars. I tell him that I think I may be finished with Michael.

'Perhaps that's for the best. Michael's okay but maybe not what you need just now.' When I ask him what he thinks I need just now, he pauses before saying: 'Someone to rub your feet,' and we both laugh.

After we hang up, I remind myself that Keith spends some of his evenings manning a helpline. So you could say he's a professional sympathiser and nurser of wounded birds. The afterglow of our laughter winks out. I decide to get a second opinion.

Craig's line is scratchy, his voice fainter. He complains of a hangover. I wonder if that's the result of a party or just the pub, but don't care to investigate. When I mention Michael, he sounds impatient. 'So, did you ditch him or did he ditch you?' I try to explain that it isn't that clear-cut and perhaps neither of us is quite ditched yet.

He interrupts with, 'That's your trouble. Drift. You know that, don't you? No grip. You let things slip away.'

'Gripping might not be the best tactic when someone's telling you you're too clingy.'

'I meant get a grip on your own feelings. Look, David, I've seen you in this kind of situation before. You pity yourself the way you are but you won't try to imagine being different. The other guy's supposed to take you as he finds you and bridge the gap. It doesn't work like that. *Your* attitude needs to change, not his.'

I start to say something half-joking about having to find my feelings before I can get a grip on them or change them but my money's run out.

'Okay,' Craig breaks in soon as the beeps stop. 'Sorry to lecture. Look, don't lose touch, all right?' The line is dead before I can answer.

Picking my slippery path back to the flat I tell myself that the way I feel isn't right or wrong, just a fact. I peek charily at the memory of last night's dream, hoping it has faded. It hasn't. And here still, too, is the white, shining face I saw in the hallway when I stumbled out to escape the dream, though the hallway must have been within it. The only part of the face that emits no light is the eyes. I remember once when I was recovering from a serious booze-up, a companion told me that my eyes looked like two pissholes in the snow. I didn't find it very funny then and I don't now. Inside, I put the heater on full, but can't get warm. I think of flesh under ice.

THE NIGHT CLUB where I meet the boy isn't one I've been to often, not one that any of my acquaintances use, which is probably why I chose it. Even alone, though, drinking in public seems to restore a sense of humanity. Coloured lights, music, and laughter form a chaotic whirl whose dynamism seems directly opposed to the monochrome rigidity of underlying reality.

It's funny, my describing Steven as a 'boy'. He might only be a few years younger than me. Perhaps I've been feeling my not-so-great age too acutely recently. Breaking up from someone can make you sensitive to that sort of thing.

Anyway. We drink, we chat, and I try not to be too self-conscious over the obvious fact that I'm picking him up. Inevitably, we stop at the all-night supermarket for a couple of bottles of cheap wine. Back at my flat, the heater whirring, I put Bowie's *Young Americans* on the stereo and we attempt jokes about just how bad the wine has turned out to be.

'Antifreeze', I say.

He answers, 'Why not? It'll help break the ice at parties.'

When I look away instead of replying, he asks if he's said the wrong thing. I tell him it's just that parties aren't a good subject with me at the moment. Then I regret it – what am I doing, playing for sympathy just like Michael kept telling me?

Perhaps I rush things a little after that, to avoid conversation, but he doesn't seem to mind. Some people respond well to being sucked off, others just don't – Steven is in the former category. Within a few minutes, he comes in my mouth. Then we lie together, both lightheaded with the sense of release. Our mouths laugh silently as we kiss.

Later, he tells me a bit about his childhood and eventually I'm able to bring it out – not the dream but its source, the originating memory.

'It was on just such a night as this…' I begin, and he chuckles softly, obligingly. 'Actually, if it had been as bloody cold as this it might never have happened. There were four of us – I was twelve, the eldest. We decided it would be fun to go to the pond after dark, mainly because we'd been forbidden to go near it by our teachers. They knew the ice was tempting, and thin. In the moonlight, it still looked tempting. We didn't have skates – we were happy just to sit down and haul ourselves along on our bottoms. I stayed near the shore and told the others to do the same. Ian was the other one from my class. He must have thought it wasn't too late for him to take over leadership of the expedition from me, if he showed a bit more daring. So he slid farther out and urged us after him. The others didn't need much urging, and it was only my reluctance to follow Ian's lead that kept me where I was. I sulked around the edge and after a minute or two I'd stopped even looking at them. I studied the ice beneath me.'

I'm not looking at Steven. I barely feel him put his hand on my shoulder. My own hands are numb and I can't feel anything at all below the waist. The blanket that half-covers us both could be frost.

'The ice… The ice was beautiful. It made even the dirt, the imperfections in the water into something ordered, motionless – something imperishable. The deeper I gazed into it, the more I could imagine I was looking into a cosmos where time had ceased to exist, fixing everything in perfect stasis.'

I pause, but Steven neither speaks nor moves - or if he does, I don't hear or feel it.

'Since then, I've tried to recall the exact point when the screams of excitement from out on the pond changed to screams of fear. I can't do it. But I can't believe I was so absorbed in my vision that I didn't respond almost instantly to the change. When I saw they were in serious trouble, I jumped ashore and ran like hell to get help. I know it was the only sensible thing to do and enough adults told me the same later that night, and in the weeks that followed, especially after I started having the dreams. It was enough to save Ian. The other two were past reviving and died before the ambulance came.'

The boy in bed with me must be hugging me. I'm aware of a tightness in a way similar to the awareness of hot water around a hand from which the blood has gone. At the instant of immersion there's a change of sensation, but at one remove, beyond a barrier, with no feeling of heat.

'Almost instantly. That's the best I've ever been able to convince myself of. But that isn't what bothers me most, now. It isn't even the fact that my first thought, when I realised that the ice had broken under them, was "serve them right". That was natural enough, I suppose, and I was only twelve. But I still see them staring up at me, frozen child faces under masks of ice. And they're beautiful. Preserved beyond change. I didn't want the ice to break. But after it had, I think some part of me wanted it to end the way it did, for all of them. Certainty. Peace. Once, when they were trying to make me feel less bad about it afterwards, my mother told me that the ones who died had "gone to a better place". I've come to believe it. No more struggle, or fear. When something's beyond change, there's no more responsibility for it. You can only let it be. So now, when I dream of chasing someone through an underground maze, so that I can put him in a freezer and preserve him under ice, I know if I let myself think about it after I've woken up that it's Ian I'm chasing. To finish the job.'

After this, Steven must be trying to say something

sympathetic, lots of sympathetic things, because his voice goes on murmuring until I fall asleep. But I'm not listening. I'm realising that Michael and Craig *were* wrong about me, at least on that point. I'm not really a sympathy seeker. My self-pity, if you want to call it that, is too rigid and elaborate a structure to leave any room for others. I don't want to be rescued and comforted. I want us all to be buried.

In the morning, Steven leaves his phone number. I take it out into the dawn frigidity and pin it up with the taxi cards in the phone box. Maybe he'll help someone, some time.

ON NEW YEAR'S Eve, I sleep till almost noon. I tell myself I'm making up for the sleep I'll lose when the bloody fireworks wake me at midnight tonight, spattering the calm sky with their motley ejaculations, breaking the dead quiet with their crackling celebration of random survival. But something is already telling me that I won't hear them tonight. And that won't be because I'm going to Tim's lousy party – I'm not.

The dreams don't come. I know that's not because they've gone. They've only gone from inside me. When you give up feeling, something terrible breaks loose. I'm not the one doing the chasing any more.

Joy Division remind me too much of vulnerability. I take refuge in death metal, drowning my thoughts in an undifferentiated barrage of cold, focusless rage in which rhythm has become wholly asexual and melody no longer exists. It calms me. Even if the phone could ring, I wouldn't hear it now.

By evening, I've drunk the last of the alcohol in the flat and go out to buy some more. Other pedestrians weave and totter on the slick pavements, uncertain as lost children. I barely glimpse their faces. The entrance to the off licence is surrounded by noisy youths whom tradition dictates we call 'revellers' for this one night of the year. I cross the street and pass by.

There are no more shops. As I near the reservoir, the street lamps space themselves farther apart and peter out. I walk on, feeling nothing but cold, seeing nothing but darkness, hearing nothing but the memory of discord. Two figures wait motionless at the end of the lane. There are no fireworks in the sky now, only the colourless long-dead light of the endlessly retreating stars. Some things survive in a different way. They wait, above the clouds, under the ice. Whatever else changes, they don't.

I walk back to the flat. I know they're following me. It's too late to vary the plan now. It always has been.

I haven't left the heater on; it's already as cold inside the flat as outside. I switch on the light and turn to look at them. In the light the glow of their faces is muted so that I can almost see the frozen child features under the adult masks. Their bodies are muffled to shapelessness in dark heavy overcoats, their hair, if they have it, hidden by balaclavas; but they've removed their gloves. One of them raises and extends its forearm in my direction, as if preparing to shake my hand, or offering me help. It pulls back the thick coat sleeve as far as the elbow, revealing more grey-white skin. I'm reminded of the smell of antiseptic as the doctor swabs my vein, the glint of the needle. 'You won't feel a thing.' This time I can believe it.

The figure uses its other hand to take a knife – or is it a razor-sharp icicle? - from a pocket and apply it to the raised forearm. The skin peels back slowly and steadily, exposing a layer of white crystals underneath. I understand now – not flesh under ice, it doesn't work like that, but ice under flesh.

The figure holds out the knife to me. My turn. There will be no more surprises. I know that they've been there along, the seeds and the harvest of entropy, complete in themselves and immutably perfect. Buried stars.

AND ASHES IN HER HAIR

Simon Bestwick

THE FIRST THING Gray saw wasn't her, but the fire. It was almost dead but still pouring out black smoke that reeked of burning plastic even through the closed first floor windows of the canteen. A moment later, the girl stood in the vacant lot beside the office.

According to the last census, there were no homeless people in the city, but her dark hair and oversized coat were dirty and ash smudged her pale face. Her hands were almost black with it. As he watched, the optical illusion knelt to sift the ashes through her hands, then anoint her face and hair with them. If they burned her, she obviously didn't feel it.

'That is *disgusting*.' Nadine stood over him. 'Haven't you called the police?'

'She hasn't done any harm.'

'Irrelevant. A: she's trespassing. B: what impression does it give our customers?'

They were a call centre; customers didn't come there. But that would have been *irrelevant* too. The lot was owned by the company, even though they'd never made use of it, and no-one else could.

The girl was looking up. Her smoke-grey eyes, startlingly visible even from that distance, met his for a protracted second. Then Nadine was talking into her mobile. Another brownie point for her monthly review: *how have you shown initiative?* When Gray looked back, the girl was gone.

THE LONG JULY evenings at least made Gray feel as though he hadn't sacrificed every day-lit minute to the corporate gods. It was still light when he got home, but Nikki was already at her alley corner opposite his flat. They acknowledged one another's existence with a nod; more than Gray's neighbours did. She was in her late thirties and lean. Her face showed signs of hard living but careful make-up hid the worst of them, and a ragged vulpine charm did the rest.

He got the vodka from the freezer, poured a slow, oil-thick measure and looked down at her through the blinds. They'd never spoken – he only knew her name because he'd once overheard a client use it – but this was probably the closest he had to a relationship outside work. If that counted.

He thought of cooking something – an omelette, maybe – but couldn't face tackling the heap of dirty pots in the sink. He rang out for a pizza instead, spent the evening munching it and sipping vodka while trying and failing to watch one of several DVDs.

Something flickered in front of his eyes, then flew at his face. He grabbed at it, felt the moth flutter in his palm, hairy and soft. He threw it outside and pulled the window shut. Below, Nikki looked up at the sound. Gray stepped back out of sight.

He left the pizza box and the glass beside the sofa but put the bottle back in the freezer before he went to bed.

HE DREAMT HE was walking through streets like the ones that surrounded the call centre. Old mills and builder's yards, takeaways and offices, vacant lots and derelict pubs. Apartments, too – some abandoned half-built in the last financial downturn, others completed but unoccupied. It was night but there were no streetlights, no lights in windows, no cars on the road; the only lights were from fires dotted about the landscape, the flames like long pale fingers reaching up into the dark. He tried to reach the fires, hoping there'd be others there, but could never seem to find them.

Then he turned and saw the girl from the vacant lot. He

opened his mouth to speak but she put a finger to her lips and shook her head. She took his hand and led him through the empty streets. Her fingers were soft. He thought he felt something like desire.

At last they entered a car park behind an office building. A bonfire blazed in the centre, silhouetted figures huddled around. He couldn't see what they looked like in any detail, and for some reason Gray knew that was something to be thankful for. The girl's grip tightened on his wrist and the texture of her fingers had changed. They were brittle and hard, and crumbled. He woke as he turned to face her.

THE DREAM STAYED with him through the rest of the day at work and with it a feeling of mingled fear and wanting. At the morning briefing Nadine told them all they were to 'be vigilant' and report anyone starting fires in the lot – or any unauthorised persons in the lot at all – at once.

He dealt with a succession of customers. Some were incapable of understanding the simplest point he told them, while others were determined to argue over each of them (and then, usually, complain about the length of time they'd spent on the phone.) Others, aware they were free to talk to him as though he were vermin as long as they stopped short of outright abuse, took full advantage of it. The only good thing was that one customer was so argumentative Gray didn't get off the phone until long after his team's scheduled coffee break had come and gone; since he had to take a break every three hours, it meant that when he wandered into the canteen at last, he had the place to himself.

The canteen was a small back office, once used for filing until the company directors started having the documents scanned. Gray took his usual place, a chair by a small window overlooking the vacant lot. It had been an abandoned pub until six months ago, when the developers had begun knocking it down. They'd been three-quarters of the way through the job when the money had run out and they'd stopped.

Some of the lower storey's walls still stood. The space inside had been half-cleared of rubble. In a corner of the clear space, he could see a small, bright fire burning. Gray felt a sudden leap of hope and a moment later the girl was there, circling the fire and watching, waiting for it to burn down. And then she stopped and looked up. Her eyes were wide and he couldn't look away. Finally she turned and went back to pacing around the fire. Gray looked at his watch – it was time to get back. He left, passing Nadine as he did.

The day ground by. At last he wandered home through the evening sunlight, waving to Nikki as he came home. She nodded back. In his flat he looked down at her, and wrestled with the temptation to go across the road. It was far from the first time he'd wanted to. There were other places he could have gone, had he wished, and bought the same thing. This was different. This was someone he knew. Sort of. It might have felt like something more, but that was an argument against it, really.

He kept the windows closed when it got dark despite the heat, to keep out the moths. He saw them flutter round the streetlamp above Nikki, remembering a bat he'd once seen in a park at dusk, weaving the same pattern around the tops of the trees, over and over. It was the same as him. Up in the morning, go to the office, suffer through the day. Then home, to perform the same dance of guilty desire over Nikki, never acting on what he felt. Drink, eat, kill time without purpose, then sleep. Each day was like pushing a reset button: start again, allow the pretence that something might change, while knowing it wouldn't. Except that somehow, with the girl, it had.

That night, he dreamt of her again.

'HAVE YOU GOT a moment?' said Nadine.

Gray felt his stomach clench. 'Um, sure.'

'Log yourself out, then.'

He felt the others' eyes on him as he followed her. *Blood in the water. Someone's going to get bollocked, maybe sacked. Poor bastard. Silly cunt. Glad it's not me.*

Nadine shut the meeting room door, sat across a desk from

him with a pad. 'So, I understand there was an incident yesterday.'

An incident. 'I'm sorry, I don't know what you –'

'Trespasser,' she said. 'Next door.'

'Oh. Right.'

'This is just a fact-finding exercise,' she said. 'Can you confirm that you were present at the briefing, where you were informed you were required to report any unauthorised people to your line manager?'

'Yeah,' he said. No use denying it. Best to say what they wanted to hear in the right places, get it over with more quickly.

'What is your understanding of this requirement? Do you understand the impact this could have on colleagues? Do you understand the impact this could have on the service to our customers?' At last Nadine was finished. 'All right,' she said. 'Next steps. There'll be a decision on how to proceed. This could mean no further action or it could mean a further meeting under the company's disciplinary procedures. But that's all for now.'

Half an hour later, Nadine called him back into the meeting room to inform him he was being invited to a disciplinary hearing on a charge of serious misconduct for failing to report intruders on company property. It was his right to be accompanied, et cetera. She gave him a letter with the date and location on it and he went back to his desk. *Invited*; he wondered if he should tell them *I'm washing my hair*.

The day's end couldn't come fast enough: in a few hours he wouldn't have to kowtow to Nadine as though she were some tinpot god, or pretend the job, or anything about it, mattered. He felt as if he was being poisoned slowly, but there was no other source of food or water than what the poisoner gave. He was dying inside; but how else could he live?

WHEN EVENING CAME, he didn't go home. He thought of the bats in the park, the moths around the street lamp. He'd had enough of weaving the same trapped pattern over and over. Tonight, he'd try to break it.

He couldn't decide where to go. Or perhaps, deep down, he knew what he planned to do, and just waited to reveal it to himself.

He left the office and wandered the streets, seeing places he knew from his dreams, but lit still by daylight. He did so for well over an hour until he knew that everybody - even, and most especially, Nadine - would have gone home. He then walked back towards the office. Or, more precisely, the vacant lot. On his way, he bought a disposable lighter from a newsagent.

The previous fires had left black stains on the concrete. He looked around and found pieces of old lathing, dead leaves, newspaper, plastic sheeting and packaging, and shied them all together into a heap. He lit a twist of newspaper with the lighter and thrust it into the pile, stepping back as it began to burn. A cone of black smoke swelled out, tainting the dusk. He coughed, eyes streaming, feeling dizzy.

The last light crept away; the streetlights blinked on and shadows poured into the lot. Gray felt foolish. What had he expected to achieve? The best he could say was that he'd found a slightly different way of wasting an evening. As he turned to go, the girl stepped out of the dark to block his way.

Gray opened his mouth but, as in his dream, she put a finger to her lips and shook her head. She circled round the fire towards him and in a moment she stepped out of the coat she wore. Heavy and stiff, it briefly stood unsupported before it collapsed, like a discarded chrysalis.

Beneath the coat, the girl was naked except for a pair of military-issue boots. Like the coat, they were too large for her, padded out with newspaper to fit. She slipped her feet out of them and went to him, her hands on his shoulders.

Beyond the fire the dark was absolute; no streetlights, no lights in windows. The only illumination was from the fire - it was the landscape of his dream. That enabled Gray to shed the last of his inhibitions and clasp the girl's narrow waist. She was very thin - he could feel the ribs beneath her skin. When she kissed him he tasted ashes on her lips, but he didn't care.

WHEN HE WOKE, his first thought was that the whole encounter had been a dream. Then he realised he was lying on bare concrete by the fire, his trousers round his ankles. He pulled them up, looking around, but there was still no other source of light.

At first he thought he was alone but then saw the girl kneeling on the other side of the fire from him. She'd pulled the coat back on – it spread around her like a pair of rumpled wings. The upturned collar formed a cowl that hid her face. She seemed to be looking into the flames and at first Gray didn't think she registered his presence. Then she looked up, and shrugged off the coat once more.

Gray didn't move; couldn't. His mind refused to accept the shrunken blackened figure, composed of charcoal, twigs and melted rubber, as anything other than an effigy. And yet it moved, and he knew with certainty that it was her.

There was movement in the dark – and the others came. Other charred things, their substance comprised of the discarded, the lost and burnt. They approached, surrounded him. The girl crabbed around the fire towards him.

He wasn't sure if they spoke, as such, but there were whispers. Fragments. *Not to have a self. Nobody can take anything from you, you simply* are. *Take only what you need to keep going.* He didn't know if he heard them outside his own head or if they'd originated anywhere else.

They crouched in the light of the fire, studying him. Gradually his fear ebbed. Had they meant him any harm, they would have attacked. It wasn't until the girl reached his side and took his hand in her charcoal fingers that he realised their intent.

'No,' he said. They flinched back. He stood. The girl gripped his hand tighter but he managed to twist free. He heard things crack and break in her hand.

He ran at the group ahead, bracing for impact but encountered no resistance. He blundered through the darkened streets, hands out ahead of him. At some point – he was never able to define when – he saw streetlights glowing, and lights in the windows of blocks of flats. From nearby came the sound of traffic on the main road. He stumbled towards it.

NO MORE FIRES were lit in the vacant lot, and when the disciplinary rolled around he escaped with a verbal warning. The following night he crossed the street outside his flat and accosted Nikki.

Partly it was the thought of having sex with her in the cold alley – it would be the closest thing he could think of to replicating the encounter with the girl – but in fact she had a flat in the adjoining street. He tried to make small talk but she shut it down. Perhaps she wouldn't have if he hadn't lived next to her beat: she needed to keep a certain distance.

It was enough, in any case, for a while. He slept with her twice a week at first, then later once (more a financial consideration than anything else). He built within himself a routine of need that would last for a while.

He never saw the burnt girl again, and after the encounter in the vacant lot he only dreamt of her once, the following April. He was wandering the same landscape, but it had changed. More of the buildings were in ruins, gutted or demolished. And there seemed to be fires burning everywhere. He saw a block of flats in flame from the lowest to the highest floor, a beacon in the night.

At last he reached the door of a ruined house, and pushed it open. Leaving the fire behind him, he climbed the broken stairs. The landing was bare of carpet, boards rotten, holes in the floor. He went along it to the door at the end, which swung open as he reached for it. Firelight shone through the glassless window and crept across the bedroom floor. The girl sat on the end of a bare metal bed-frame, holding a baby. As he came towards her she stood, and held it out to him.

He woke. It was still dark. The room seemed empty but it felt as though someone had just been there. Gray had almost convinced himself it was only the aftermath of the dream when a wail came from the foot of the bed.

For a long time he stood over the tiny swaddled shape that lay there, blurred and indistinct in the grey pre-dawn. Whether left for him as a punishment or gift, he didn't want to see what it looked like. But at last - drawn, moth-like, by the desolate need in its cries - he switched the bedroom light on and took it in his arms.

Embroidery / tapestry loom

~~Embroidery~~ / tapestry artist & clair

singer, computer operator

— notes

1) Helen & client (Tarot reading)
2) embroidery – faces
3) Helen & Tracey
4) two clients with threadbare faces
5) Helen & Michael – argument over pi
6) uses her own hair to embroider
7) hands shaking – loom rusty – pulls thre
– in café, faces coming apart
8) back with Tracey, feels her own sk
a series of horizontal threads – th
interwove – you had to start somewh

Superstition is a loose thread in the fabric
~~unauthorised by faith~~
belonged to an unauthorised bit of faith

THE PLEASURE GARDEN

Rosanne Rabinowitz

IT'S DANIEL'S FIRST day back at Cornmarket Publishing since the company moved. He now has a walk to Vauxhall followed by a half-hour train journey to the new office in Teddington. It could be worse for travel time, he thinks, but it's out in the sticks of zone fucking six. More money to pay out just to work.

Though it's not far from his home in Kennington, he's not been around Vauxhall station for ages. Years ago, he actually lived in this area, squatting in a square off Harleyford Road. There was no Vauxhall bus station then, and nothing like that bizarre steel wedding cake of a building near it.

As the train pulls away from Vauxhall, he sees that the old New Covent Garden market has been completely torn down. His household used to raid the bins there for the vegetables they cooked in the community cafe. He used to go clubbing around there too, mainly at the Vauxhall Pleasure Garden just near the market. What a dive!

Thinking about the years he lived around here kindles a warm yet sad feeling. Gigs and parties at the house on the corner, new friends, an opening of his world. That was when he started to think of himself as gay. He met the first man that he really fancied and wanted. Jon was a sensitive guy who liked poetry, too.

This must be what nostalgia feels like, he thinks, but he resists its pull. He's doing okay now, isn't he? Freelance work is varied but steady, and he has his own flat. Well, a shared ownership flat at the edge of a 'regenerated' council estate, advertised as 'cutting edge', which might refer to the poorly finished work tops in the kitchen. Everything was falling apart, even when it was brand new. But hey, he can afford it, it's close to central London and the light is good.

No, the good old days weren't all rosy. Getting evicted was never fun. Being skint wasn't much fun either. And he didn't expect to feel isolated within an 'alternative' society where straight coupling was still the norm beneath the decorative tattoos and weird big hair. Much of that time he was nursing a broken heart, then getting out of his head and into someone's trousers to forget it.

Sometimes, he just had to get away. That was when he crossed the Vauxhall roundabout to get to the Pleasure Garden. It was a passage into another world.

The morning has taken on a crumpled, soiled feeling. It's the end of winter or the beginning of spring. The sun shines but it's a watery excuse for sunlight that never fulfils its promise. His unopened *Metro* lies on his lap as he continues to look out the window.

Then he's not sure where he is at all. The train is passing between two huge building sites. On both sides, unfinished buildings rise, one after another in a jagged skyline of cranes and hoardings. Builders in orange jackets scurry through the site, cranes hoist their loads. Battersea power station is surrounded by another spidery network of cranes, and it's missing one tower.

Could this be where he used to walk every day? And where the fuck has the Pleasure Garden gone?

Duh, of course it's been torn down along with the market. He begins to think about that 'dive' with regret now that he knows it's lost forever.

'Dubai on Thames...' he hears a bloke in front of him say to his friend, who is wired up with earphones. They both nod.

The morning sun flickers in bars through the girders of incomplete buildings. The effect disturbs Daniel, the sort of thing likely to trigger the strobe-lit ocular migraines that bother him when he works on computers too long. He starts to look away but then sees someone on the top floor of the unfinished block nearest the track, loping along the framework. No orange jacket, no builders' protective gear. A slender man in jeans and a white t-shirt, cropped steel-grey hair but youthful face and stance.

Daniel thinks he knows that man...

From the Pleasure Garden, almost thirty years ago. But the man looks the same.

Then the train stops. Daniel is aware of a distant beat. For a moment he thinks it's music, then he realises that it's the building works.

'Shit, not again,' someone says. 'How long are we stuck this time?'

But Daniel is glad for the pause. The man outside has kept pace with the train and now pauses in his peculiar morning run. He leans against a vertical girder, one long leg hooked around it. He frowns as he surveys the landscape in front of him.

Then he meets Daniel's gaze, and returns it with a half-smile. His lips are parted slightly, and he extends his hand – just as he had done years ago.

A jolt of arousal hits Daniel as the memories wash over him.

He places his hand on the window, fighting an urge to pound and shatter it.

The train starts up again, leaving the man behind.

As his train lurches towards Teddington, Daniel remembers the back room at the Pleasure Garden. A grotty club with crap music transformed into its antithesis: a place lit by embers of touch and truth.

DANIEL HAD BEEN dreading the commute to Teddington but when he arrives he is also horrified to discover that the company has imposed a 'hot desk' regime. One of those stupid ideas imported from the US, along with the habit of turning nouns into adjectives and vice versa. As a regular freelancer he would normally return to the same desk where he had his own drawer. But that's all over. No drawers at all. No place for his mug, photos, bags of Hot Java Lava or sachets of herbal teas. *Nada.*

Daniel also discovers that his favourite editor has been made redundant.

He's given a whole supplement on waste electronic and electrical equipment to copy-edit and lay out, which has to be ready for tomorrow.

But he can't concentrate on *WEEE*. Not when he's remembering the man from this morning and what happened at the Pleasure Garden decades ago. The past floods into the present, filling his head like the drugs he used to take.

STRONG ARMS HOLD him from behind and he's being taken. Others are there, watching. But watching isn't only passive. It can be active, it can be a caress. He looks into strange faces as they witness his gratification. It's like gazing into a well. The water below might satisfy his thirst, or it might drown him.

A shadow falls on Daniel as someone new draws near. Calm determined eyes meet his. The man extends his hand and opens it.

Daniel clasps it. The man behind him tightens his arms, kisses his neck with surprising tenderness. The steady look of the man in front of him touches his skin, spreading its warmth deep. The man doesn't speak but Daniel sees the offer he makes in his eyes and his parted lips, feels it in the grip of his hand and the movement of fingers around his. We will give you pleasure and delight. We can take away your pain ... for a while.

Then a door opens. The face in front of him is shocked by light, then lost in shadow. Other people push in front of Daniel. There's a fight, or perhaps it's the police.

THEY STILL RAIDED gay clubs in those days. The police wore gloves, 'protection from AIDS'. Fools. He once saw a copper wearing washing-up gloves. Couldn't the Met even give its minions proper gloves? No, it wasn't all peachy then.

DANIEL GOES THROUGH his tasks on autopilot as memories and daydreams jostle for his attention. His heart hammers when he yields to fantasy: go back to Vauxhall to find the man and feel that strong hand in his again, and then...

Right, find another photo of old fridges. Lots of them, chucked in landfill somewhere. Then clean up those multiple clauses.

Autopilot does its job very well. His first completed pages need only a few corrections after they've been to the production editor.

He goes out for lunch, finding a bench on the riverside path. All he hears now is the rushing water of Teddington Lock but his mind plays a pounding counterpart, full of monotonous pre-techno beats and plastic vocals.

They played that 'hi-energy' disco shit all the time at the Pleasure Garden. Just because he was gay didn't mean he had to like it. Punk and indie was what got him dancing. He used to love going to the Bell in Kings Cross, where gay guys and girls went to dance, flirt and shag. They were young, they were poor … and determined to have a good time. They liked the pub prices and DJs that spun a playlist of punk and glam, laced with soul and hip -hop.

One night the DJ put on Joy Division's 'Love Will Tear Us Apart' as the closing number. It was probably a joke on her part but it brought Daniel together with Jon.

But Daniel fell much too hard for him. Some would call it 'love' but it was just an illness, worsened by its moments of elation. When the relationship finished, he just couldn't bear to be in the same place as Jon. He tried to have fun dancing with friends but Jon would walk in with someone else and all enjoyment drained from the night.

So he went to the Pleasure Garden, which wasn't the kind of place where people passed out leaflets for lesbians and gays to support the miners or demonstrate against Clause 28. It was just a place for guys to come and dance and fuck other guys. There was a back room for the latter. People went at it in the Bell, too, but having a room set aside for sex changed the whole game.

He'd been going to the Pleasure Garden for months before he dared open the door to the back room.

And once he was in there, he didn't think about Jon at all ... for a while.

He's been with others since, but no one else moved him in the same way – unless you count that nameless man from the back room. The same man he thought he saw this morning, dancing high above the ground. Youthful, but not young. Just as he appeared decades ago.

Did anyone else on the train clock the guy? He doesn't know because he was looking out the window. But he's sure that man is as real as the river in front of him and the bench he sits on.

He has a tentative plan to meet his friend Barbara tonight. Perhaps she'll fancy a drink and a nose around their old stomping grounds. He met her on a job several years ago and discovered that they had both lived in the square at different times.

He suggests a Vauxhall-based drink in a text message, hinting he might have a prospect to check out. He's been the token Dutch boy by her side on many nights while she cruised some dyke bar, so it's her turn to be a fag hag of sorts. He chuckles as he clicks 'send'.

Then he closes his eyes. Imagine finding *him*. His strong hand, opening in his. That feels more tangible than the work waiting for him.

He finishes his sandwich and heads back.

On his return, he finds someone else occupying his desk. A brash young thing with an elaborate three-pointed beard and three laptops spread out in front of him. Daniel's notes and printouts have been pushed aside.

'Sorry, mate,' the hipster boy says. 'But it's finders, keepers round here. Morning, lunchtime, whenever.'

'I'm not your mate,' Daniel snarls as he struggles to retrieve his things.

Then he pauses. For all he knows, this wanker could be the half-price replacement for his redundant editor. 'Sorry. I mean, I apologise for snapping at you but I left my work on the desk and I'm not used to the new system.'

Three-Beards spreads his hands in a kind of shrug before he turns his attention back to the four machines on his desk.

THERE'S A LOT more to get through on the *WEEE* supplement so Daniel ends up working late. Finally he's out of there.

The train goes over the river and the reaches of Richmond Park, stopping at a string of semi-suburban stations, until it reaches Clapham Junction. Daniel stares into the deepening evening as the train makes its passage through the Nine Elms corridor.

The cranes stand still and silent now, neon-lit company names suspended in the sky. Ruddy stars mark the heights, forming constellations. To the east, the red construction lights at Elephant & Castle also gather. He thinks of master-builders from beyond the stars descending on the humble roads of South London.

Barbara's not responded yet but he decides not to go home. He walks away from the busy train station for a look around his old square. Every corner and pavement outpost is now covered with greenery, the rickety schoolyard play equipment in the middle replaced by another community garden - back in the day, the squatters were planting the first garden on a wasteground just off the square. It's all looking good now. Perhaps he should have stayed here but he needed to move at the time.

On his way to the site he finds a pleasant little pub with real ale.

Barbara finally rings, asking him about work and his new office.

'I spent all day writing about *WEEE*!' He draws out that triple E.

'You poor thing!'

'It could be worse. I could be writing about *shit*. Anyway, why don't you come south for a pint? I've just stopped off at a pub in Vauxhall and it's okay.'

'Never mind the pub. Who's this guy you're after?'

'I met him at the Pleasure Garden years ago. In the back room. Then I saw him ... near Vauxhall Station on my way to work.'

'The Pleasure Garden? I haven't been there in years. I have so many fond memories... Women's night on Mondays, and a women's fetish night once a month.'

'It's all gone, the whole place has been torn down. It's no

Pleasure Garden where I am, just a pub on a side street between South Lambeth and Wandsworth roads. Good beer though.'

He remembers posters about the fetish night. It's hard to imagine a leather-clad Barbara cracking a whip but then people always laughed at photos of him when he wore a Mohican.

'What a shame about the Pleasure Garden,' she says. 'Even though I've not been for ages I always imagine it's there for me – if I fancy a night out.'

'I felt that way, sort of. It's a long shot about that guy. Really, I just felt inspired to have a drink in the area after passing through it this morning.'

That odd regretful feeling that is *almost* pleasant. Not nostalgia, really.

'I had some great times there,' Barbara says. 'And it was handy for staggering home. I wonder what it looks like now. I hate the way places just disappear and you forget them so easily.'

Then he has an idea. He's not sure why he didn't think of it before.

'Tell you what ... we've both raided those big bins at the market, even if it wasn't at the same time. We know what it's like to crack a squat. How about doing something like that now? Let's get into the site and find some Pleasure Garden memorabilia since we both have warm and fuzzy feelings about the gaff. There might be something in the rubble. Or we can take photos.'

'That's *mad*. I like it. But I'm too tired after work to come down from Hackney and climb over walls tonight.'

'Fair enough,' says Daniel. He has a feeling he'll end up exploring alone. Maybe it's for the best.

They talk about meeting another time. Daniel orders another pint. He turns off his phone, though he's not sure why.

He was good at breaking into places when he was young, especially when they made it more difficult to get to the bins. This time, though, he's looking for much more than free fruit and veg or even bits and pieces of Pleasure Garden.

There must be extensive security for such a high-profile building project. But a vast and sprawling site like this will also have weak spots and places to get in. He knows how it's done.

After he leaves the pub he walks along the walls bordering the site trying to remember where the Pleasure Garden used to stand. So much has changed. Even then, the Pleasure Garden had been an ugly 1970s-style place.

It wasn't a quaint old gaff like the Vauxhall Tavern across the roundabout on ground once occupied by the real Vauxhall Pleasure Gardens in the eighteenth and nineteenth centuries. But the Pleasure Garden pub seemed to mark some true down-and-dirty realm of revelry bang in the middle of the industrial zone.

He pulls his hood up and starts to walk the perimeter. At last he finds a place where there's a gap between boards. One is loose. Perhaps some other vandal has been working it free. He moves the board aside without much noise.

He's wary of security guards but doesn't see their hut or HQ. He picks his way past stilled machinery, foundations and skeletal structures. More of them rise in the distance, markers of a ghost town not yet built. Bare unborn boulevards, networks of girders underneath crane constellations, red lights bright now that the night has advanced. He blinks and the red stars form a pattern. Something behind the pattern seems to move…

Then a piece of placard on top of a pile of junk in a skip catches his eye. Hot pink and gold, lettering in a familiar black font. That tacky Remedy Double. He picks it up. Yes, it's a piece of signage with only part of a word: '...hall'.

He has doubts. Are those the colours? Would the Vauxhall Pleasure Garden really use Remedy Double in its sign? Memory, which seemed so clear, turns muddy. He can only try to recapture the perception of a young man, full of desire but ridden by doubt, walking across the roundabout and seeing the name.

He picks up the fragment and holds it close to his chest. It *could* be it. He bends forward to peer into the tip, only to find himself considering building-waste disposal violations. Damn, the autopilot mode that got him through the day now intrudes on his evening.

Some undefined noise makes him look up. His first impulse is to hide or flee, but when he hears nothing else he decides to keep walking. He isn't sure what he's walking towards until he sees lights shining out of a half-dug foundation. Security? But those moving rainbow colours won't come from a guard's torch.

When he's standing at the edge of a hole, he laughs and laughs.

At the bottom, a disco ball revolves on a makeshift plinth. It must be rigged up to a power line.

He stumbles down the slope towards the light.

After he reaches the bottom, he lies on his back so he can look up and watch the disco lights play among the ruby stars.

Then a tall slim man is looking down at him from the rim of the pit. Long legs in faded jeans, a white t-shirt ... just like this morning. The thrill of recognition hits like a sledgehammer in Daniel's chest. He never thought he'd see that face again or feel the gaze of those thoughtful eyes as they stoked his pleasure.

The man climbs down the side of the hole, loose-limbed and agile, looking like he's about to spring and break into flight. He doesn't seem to mind the night-time chill. Then he's next to Daniel.

His touch is cold, distilled from steel. His eyes are the colour of steel, too, his grey hair still startling above a face so bare of lines.

Daniel finally asks, 'Who are you?'

The man smiles but a molten core lights the steel of his eyes.

'Look at this ravished district and you'll understand.' The melodic quality of his voice surprises Daniel. With that the tall man touches his lips to Daniel's. The taste is metallic, yet exciting.

He wants to keep kissing this familiar stranger but also wants to hear him speak. He asks the question again, with a slight change. '*What* are you?'

His companion seems to prefer that formulation. He slips his hand under Daniel's jacket, finding the bare skin under his shirt.

'I'm the mind of the old market, and much more. The distilled desires of dumpster divers and bondage queens meet within me. I'm the roots beneath the old Pleasure Gardens and I arise from breathless couplings on hidden paths above them while the band plays Handel. I'm the dust on the streets and the weeds growing in cracks. I'm mud oozing between your toes, the cry of birds fleeing from the reeds. I bring the scents of the marsh, the fumes of exhaust, a sprinkling of sweat and perfume.'

He strokes Daniel's chest as he croons, 'Vauxhall, Vauxhall, where the hammer will fall...'

Daniel imagines an auctioneer's hammer, or perhaps the hammer of a worker pounding metal. Whether it is for building or demolition, he isn't sure. He runs his hands over the cropped hair of his grey-eyed companion. He touches the man's throat as the words vibrate within it.

'Some haunt abandoned ruins but I also haunt places that have yet to be.'

'You talk about the market and the Pleasure Gardens. What came before that? And what came after?'

'Real gardens that fed London once grew here. Later came factories and workshops, and the people that worked in them. There were fleeting kisses during tea-time, the flowering of many desires.'

'And before the farms and the factories?'

'This land was once held within two arms of the Effra. Another river flowed into the Thames from the other side. They all clashed in a whirl of waters that created an island. You can still find the ancient posts from the bridge to that island. Lives were given to the river – these machines will claim more. But there are other ways to make your offering.'

The man kisses Daniel with a tongue that tastes of iron. His hands move over him, drawing out his heat in the chilly night. 'Fuck us', he says to Daniel.

Fuck us, rather than *fuck me.*

This strange man, full of the flavours of iron and steel, grows pliable as they join together. He's only a man. But he is also all the things he says he is.

It's over faster than Daniel would have wanted. Already he's needing more as the clean-limbed figure lies quiet underneath him. Will there be another time? Does he have a name? He's afraid to ask for it, as if being named will diminish him.

He slides out from under Daniel, zips up his jeans but leaves the snap undone as if he intends to remove them again very soon.

He points to the ground nearby. There is growth where their bodies have touched the earth, where their fluids have moistened it. The smallest shoot of ivy, a minute leaf unfurling.

'This will crack the foundations … in time,' he says to Daniel.

The being stands up and holds out his hand for Daniel to join him.

'The others are arriving now. Many have known me in different ways. Their touch makes me stronger and sows the seed.'

He looks upwards, the lights playing over his face. 'Look…'

Daniel only sees the disco lights at first, embers of colour moving around the sides of the foundation. They flow faster, spinning to no audible music but the pulse in his ears.

Then Daniel sees others along the sides of the pit, men and women, their faces illuminated. Some seem uncertain while others grin. That night in the back room, he felt like he was looking down into a well. Now he's looking up at strange faces from the bottom of it.

The new arrivals clamber down the sides. Daniel sees that one of the newcomers wears a security uniform, the jacket disarranged and half-open.

Someone is calling to him.

'You all right, Daniel?' It's Barbara, making her stumbling way down the slope until she reaches him. 'I changed my mind about going out. I thought I'd be able to find you. And I did – you and your friends. I found the pub and followed the lights.'

She keeps her voice low, watching as more people descend into the foundation hole. Someone she sees makes her smile, then she is looking past them at the horizon. 'Lights! More of them... Look at all those fucking lights.'

Daniel nods, holding onto the hand of his old acquaintance. As that hand slips out of his, he is sure the crane constellation is forming a clearer pattern. He's still not sure what it is but if he looks longer, perhaps he'll understand.

Strong arms hold him from behind. He looks up to the sky again and now he thinks he gets it - tower after tower, sliding to the ground.

ANTITHESIS

(SOMETHING OTHER) (MOMENTS)

Fantasy/ideal ingrained in everyday life. At critical moments (turning points). Calm, determined eyes; a strong opening hand; a shadow falling on me; arms holding me from behind. Looking in strange faces, as into a well...

flickers embers of truth

YOU GIVE ME FEVER

e drove her mad-later, her
became his reality — wint
gradient of cold — wooden

"Not a child, no. More
sick animal, a sick de
and pissing over the co
trying to fuck a duffe
call it a child."

he could see the cold: di
the air, black lines movi

"After his father died,
(Old woman alone in ...
madness, not mine. It away.

if you try to remove people's armour

Suit of armour outside shop.

I NEED SOMEWHERE TO HID

comic-book mentalities: mask

emphasis — text falling ove

"What do they know of Engl
know?"

a baby crusted in rock

clean-shaven, cropped, perfe

"It shows I'm in complete c

JOEL LANE, POET

Chris Morgan

'Saving face'

Scar city *is the brief: the null slogan*
that underwrites the ad men
who've put up huge billboards
by the side of the expressway,
screening off the derelict houses
and patches of wasteground from view.

Near the industrial district, half
a street's worth of wire fence
surrounds a building site: trenches
and wooden crosses in the mud.
The contractor's logo on a red sign
declares the enterprise: MEND-A-CITY.

– Joel Lane

IN THAT POEM, Joel's phrase *scar city* is also scarcity and mend-a-city is also mendacity: there you have politics, Birmingham's urban decay and clever wordplay all in twelve lines.

When I first got to know Joel, half his lifetime ago in the late 1980s, he was already the consummate poet. His poems were subtle, original and sharp. He was inspired, making the writing of poems seem deceptively easy. Joel worked very hard at his poetry. He wrote, sometimes, several poems a week. He studied the market. He read modern poetry. He subscribed to those poetry magazines he respected. Every week he sent out a batch of his best unpublished poems to one of the magazines. Often they came back, not quite what the editor wanted at that time. But he persevered. He had faith in what he was writing.

Gradually his poems were published. *Ambit, The Rialto, Sunk Island Review, The North, The New Statesman.* A growing body of published work. He applied for the Eric Gregory Award, money given every year to the best English poets under thirty. And at twenty-nine he got it, several thousand pounds to help him take time away from work, time to write. Some of Joel's best early poems appeared in a shared collection by three poets that year, 1993.

Joel's first solo collection, *The Edge of the Screen,* came from Arc in 1999. It has cover blurb from Joel's two favourite contemporary poets, Edwin Morgan (who was then the Scottish macha, or poet laureate) and from Carol Ann Duffy (now our English Poet Laureate). And from Graham Joyce, perhaps the greatest stylist among British supernatural novelists. Joel's other two collections of poetry, also published by Arc, came in 2004 and 2010.

What did Joel write about? He was the great chronicler of local slum estates, crumbling tower blocks, derelict factories and dark canals. This is 'Lee Bank':

The estate is a place to hide
drugs, hide stolen goods, or just hide.
Tarpaulins are hoods for shattered
windows, screams no-one can hear.

Decay isolates the tower blocks
in their long wait for demolition;
the only way to mend the damage
is to tear them down and start again.

Yes, Joel's poems feature much urban bleakness. They're brief and hard-hitting, rarely extending to a second page. There's humour, too. The poem 'Canal' personifies that commodity that

Birmingham has more of than Venice:

I know where I start and end.
There's no need for movement.
Over the years, so many people
have dropped their furniture in me.

There's surrealism, as in 'The Birmingham Surrealists', who:

woke up in a foul temper
because of the seals barking
on the telegraph wires

who:

occupied the number 11 bus
singing Keep right on
to the end of the circle

and who:

went out secretly at night
to run a cosmic steamroller
over the world's vowels

Joel wrote about music and musicians, about his favourite crime writer Cornell Woolrich, his favourite bookshop, Andromeda. In 'Glass Houses' he wrote about an evening power cut in Birmingham:

After half an hour, someone
knocked. A young woman:
'Candles for sale. Fifty pence each.'
You laughed, said it was
enterprise culture. I paid.

On the main road, other
people were making a profit.
Twelve shops looted. The streets
were paved with glass.

Joel was a little nervous when he read out his poems, yet he was an intense and powerful performer thanks to Ella's drama techniques. He never applied to become Birmingham's Poet Laureate because he had to do a full-time paid job in order to live. But he was always very generous with his time, willing to read the work of other poets and offer them encouragement and perceptive comments. Without his help I would never have become Birmingham's Poet Laureate.

Joel's final collection was called *The Autumn Myth,* of which its title poem says prophetically:

The only autumn's in your head:
the slow dissolution of childhood...

But his autumn never came. He died in his summer years, decades before he should have.

THE REACH OF CHILDREN

Mike Chinn

SALLY DROPPED BOTH bombs as we walked alongside the canal. It was late at night, still warm, the water a narrow mirror reflecting a featureless, dark-purple sky. I couldn't argue with her reasoning. We were both eighteen, she approaching the end of her first year at university, me between jobs and in Macclesfield because that was where the train had brought me. Neither of us wanted a child.

Whatever reaction she'd been expecting, mine was obviously the wrong one. I just stood there, staring at nothing, deafened by memories. Eventually I realised Sally was angrily calling my name: 'Joseph. Joseph!' I pulled myself back into the present, took her arm and escorted her back to her student digs. I don't remember the rest of the conversation, probably something conciliatory and reassuring. I didn't stay, just traced the canal path back to my own flat.

I WOKE UP late and hung-over. An empty bottle rolled under my foot as I stepped out of bed. I tossed it into a bin on the way to the shared bathroom. After pissing I ran the cold tap, sluicing my mouth with coppery water. I gazed at the reflection in the mirror above the washbasin. A pale, black-eyed man stared back, blood running from his pulped mouth. I flinched, dribbling a mouthful of discoloured tap water down my t-shirt.

Sally had left a voicemail on my mobile an hour or so earlier. She'd made an appointment for the termination. It didn't take a genius to figure out Sally and I were just as finished. I sat on the bed, skull three sizes too big.

My flat was part of what had probably been a small warehouse in a better life, split into three floors, three rooms and a bathroom squeezed onto each one. There was even a sign over the tall, double glass front doors. The Old Warehouse. If the owner had cared a shit, I could never have afforded the place. He never showed his face, his phone number always redirected to an answer machine. Workmen would appear infrequently to partially fix problems. My fellow tenants and I had plenty to complain about and not a leg to stand on.

Once I was dressed, I went down to the single kitchen on the ground floor. It was the first place visitors saw; correspondingly it was the best serviced. Spacious, plenty of cupboards and appliances, most of which worked. There was only one other person there, a girl who'd recently moved in. We nodded a greeting; it was all we'd exchanged since the day she'd arrived. For such a crowded space the tenants maintained a far from respectful distance.

There was a large bruise down the left side of her face. When she saw me looking she dragged a length of black hair across it as she bent over her cereal bowl. 'Walked into some scaffolding in the High Street,' she said. I think it was the first time I'd heard her speak. Her voice was high, immature. Like fuck, I thought. And fuck was exactly what it was like.

I slipped two rounds of stale bread into the toaster as she finished her breakfast, rinsing her bowl under the tap and leaving it to drain. With another nod she left the kitchen, taking a chipped mug with her. Another tenant came through the door - Curt, from the top floor. He grinned at me, taking a crushed pack of cigarettes out of the cracked leather jacket he was always wearing. I wondered if he slept in it.

'You still looking for a job?' he asked, sorting through the cupboards. His accent was Lancastrian, thick, almost to the point of caricature. I nodded.

'I can get you one at our place.' He worked at a small garage in Bridge Street, the kind that did MOTs and fitted new tyres and exhausts. Opening a packet of Golden Grahams, he scooped the cereal out with his hands, eating it around his lit cigarette. 'Place's got busy last couple of weeks. Gaffer's been saying we need extra help.'

My toast popped up, burned and smoking. I threw it onto a plate, flinching at the heat. 'Sure. Why not?' I had no talent for repair work but thought I'd pick it up.

Curt grinned again, cigarette bobbing up and down. 'Ace. I'll tell him. Come with us tomorrow and we'll get you sorted.'

He shoved the open cereal packet back in a cupboard and left, punching me on the arm as he passed in a swirl of smoke.

THAT NIGHT I dreamed that I was in a cellar filling up with tenants. Even though I didn't recognise anyone, I knew they were from my building. One woman's pale, injured face bulged, gaping wider as a child spewed from her throat.

'Diminished responsibility,' a voice said. Drums started playing.

'Manslaughter.'

I jerked awake. My mobile phone's ringtone was playing Joy Division's 'Atmosphere'. I answered it, assuming it was Sally. On the other end all I heard was a child crying. I shouted 'Hello!' several times before hanging up. The call records listed the number as unknown.

When I went to the bathroom for a drink of water I heard a voice drifting up the stairwell. There was a woman sitting on the steps between floors, dressed in what looked like a long, thin nightgown. She was talking gibberish to herself. Drunk, I thought, or on something. Even though she had to be another tenant I'd never seen her before. People came and went all the time. After a minute she started to sing in some language I didn't recognise.

I went back to bed and drifted off, lulled by the staircase woman.

CURT DROVE US up to the garage in a rusty Ford that needed work as much as I did. The morning was already close and humid, but he was still wrapped in his old leather jacket. He made me feel hot just looking at him. The garage owner took one look at me, shrugged, and hooked a thumb towards the dim interior. I was hired. There were three other lads there, their casual indifference towards me worse than being picked on. After a morning's training from Curt I was replacing tyres and operating the pneumatic wrench. It was easy enough.

Curt drove us back to The Old Warehouse. 'You done all right, kid,' he laughed as we climbed the stairs. He punched my arm again when we reached my floor, grinding with his knuckles. 'See you tomorrow!'

I said something non-committal and opened the door to my flat. I grabbed a change of clothes and cleaned myself up in the bathroom. Oil and grease stains bruised my face. They washed away with a hard scrub.

I went out to a pub just around the corner. It served food and a decent pint, and had the advantage of not being a student hangout. By the time I went back to The Old Warehouse I was pretty drunk, despite the pie and chips I'd eaten. I could hear singing again as I fumbled with my key card and opened the glass doors. Some guy who I guessed was a ground floor tenant stared up the stairwell, though I thought the voice came from below us. He looked at me and frowned.

'Bloody foreigner.'

At first I thought he meant me. 'The staircase woman?'

'Yeah, her—' He broke off into a fit of coughing. His finale consisted of spitting a disgusting wad of phlegm onto the floor. He stared back up the stairs, expression ferocious. 'Shut the fuck up!'

I sidestepped the red and green puddle and made my way upstairs. I passed no one.

I WAS DRAGGED from sleep by echoing, furious shouts coming up the stairwell. It was still dark. Initially I thought the staircase woman was being screamed at again, but the voices were all male. I left my room to see what in hell was going on. Downstairs, framed by the stairwell, I saw the guy from last night being manhandled by three shaved gorillas in black zip-up jackets. Most of what was being yelled was incoherent, garbled by the echoes. I caught something about him needing the money for prescriptions.

The guy glanced up. His nose and mouth were bleeding dark mucous. He was coughing, deep, haggard sounds. He caught me watching, his eyes begging for help. I backed away, out of his sight. A moment later he was evicted through the open glass doors, still pleading, still spitting impotent threats. Chancing another look, I saw the third gorilla throwing a suitcase and bundle of clothes after him before snapping a key card in half.

There was no point going back to bed. I found some vodka and poured it into a half-clean mug. Prising apart a couple of dusty horizontal blinds I looked out at the paling sky, sipping the alcohol.

There was a small courtyard below my window, normally littered by dumped sacks of building rubble. In the uncertain, pre-dawn light I thought it was crammed by shuffling children, all damaged in ways that didn't show. For a moment I didn't know whether to run away from them or join them. I let go of the blinds before the decision was made for me.

THE NEXT DAY was Friday. Payday. When Curt and I came back from the garage in the afternoon, The Old Warehouse was jittering with police and rubbernecking tenants. I hung back but Curt grabbed someone by the shoulder and asked what was going on. Apparently the girl with the bruises had killed herself with an overdose. She'd left her door open, maybe hoping someone would catch her in time. By the time someone had bothered to check, it was too late. She was huddled on her bed, knees drawn up to her face, arms wrapped around them. Dead for hours. The police were taking statements but no one knew anything.

I climbed up to my room, shaken. Curt followed and I asked him inside. I poured us both vodka and he sipped his while I emptied my cup in one gulp.

'I think she said her name were Joyce,' he said, lighting a cigarette.

'Don't you think you ought to tell the police?'

'Lot of good it'll do her.' He drew on his cigarette. 'I know she left home cos she'd been fucking a married man. Kicked out, actually.'

I poured myself another drink. 'Now *that* you should tell them.'

He shrugged. 'Why? Someone else'll know. Anyhow—' he slapped me hard on the arm '—none of my business is it? Nor yours.'

I gulped vodka. 'Even so—'

He grabbed my neck. 'How long you been livin' here? This—' he flicked the tip of my nose '—keep it out!'

I tried to pull away but his grip tightened. I winced at the pain. Curt threw his cigarette aside and dragged me to the bed, hand locked around my throat. Violence worked on me where a tender approach would have put me off. It was like being back at school. Afterwards we lay in a tangle of limbs, Curt smoking. At least he'd taken his jacket off. I ran a finger along the traceries of old bruises and scar tissue networking his dark chest and arms.

He smacked my hand aside, sitting up. He dressed quickly, cigarette gripped in his teeth. 'See you tomorrow, yeah?' He grinned down at me, holding the cigarette's glowing tip an inch above my body. 'Remember…' He tapped his own nose before leaving.

The night passed. I lay on the bed, body aching from Curt's affections. Outside the Staircase Woman mourned. In the morning I dressed, emptied the last of the vodka and headed for the staircase. The echoes my footsteps provoked sounded like distant, garbled accusations.

The entrance hall was empty, felt like it always had been. Down the corridor I saw an open door. The girl's - Joyce's? - room?

I'd expected police tape across the entrance with the words *Crime Scene, Do Not Enter*. There was nothing. Inside only a rumpled bed indicated that anyone had ever been there. On a crude shelf above it were a couple of small brown bottles. I could just read the label on one: *KEEP OUT OF THE REACH OF CHILDREN* it warned.

I FOUND MYSELF in Alderley Edge with no idea how I'd reached there. I sat outside the Edge Hotel comparing the countryside with town. In Macclesfield the sunlight had flashed off concrete, painting the town white; out here there was more shadow. Less exposure.

I stayed in the shade of an umbrella, drink after drink eroding the wage packet stuffed inside my coat. Afternoon darkened into evening. The shadows lengthened and grew black, blurring. The car park was full of injured children, crawling under stationary vehicles. I pushed myself up onto rubbery feet, turning away from their faces. There was a steep slope away from the hotel and as I made my way carefully along it I was suddenly blinded by headlights. I don't remember being hit by the car.

I WOKE UP in hospital. Everything was stark and white. I tried turning my head but it was held in place. I was hooked to a drip; I heard the electronic chatter of monitors. Looking down along my body every part of me looked strapped together. There was no pain.

My bed was enclosed by half transparent walls. Some kind of mobile hung from a ceiling painted with fat, multi-coloured cartoon animals. They stared down with huge, glassy eyes, their grins terrifying.

I must have passed out. Next thing I was looking up at a nurse.

'Welcome back, Joey,' she said. 'How are you feeling?'

I tried to speak but my mouth was too dry. Nobody calls me Joey, I thought. Not since I was a child.

She was smiling as she reached over to take my pulse. It looked like she was trying not to cry. I looked away to avoid seeing my reflection in her eyes. The bed – and everything else – seemed so big.

BROKEN EYE

child
man with videos
... on Staircase (orgy in dark)
he watched dawn through wire grid in glass
seemed as though darkness still there

Des

Rachel

collects s...

1 staying with sister & child in tower
meets young man in block, stays with him
— he collects photos & videos —
going back to her room in the dark
runs into couple (group?) making love
on staircase
goes back to the man — he is lonely/afraid.
leaving in morning — drugged teenagers on
balcony
back to room — daylight felt like darkness
(slept for a day & then felt better)

(1) imprisonment — bars, stone, grids — against light
(2) the eye — TV screen — light
(their eyes ate the daylight)
(3) images — compound eye — windows
(broken up into windows)

... idea of freedom.

The ... shows ... domination ...
is it myopia or
that makes films
limelight my favourite
voices more alive than
I'm not a voyeur,
will do...
sound burrow
through to the soil of the
towards me, still in the
of being heard, being

EVERYBODY HATES A TOURIST

DIFFERENT SOUNDS
1) couple making love
2) solitary people in
3) girl in stress
4) bomb hospital
5) like an alcoholic ...
6) not sure what ...
7) ... tourists ...

The F. Devil
London
(BBC)
(2) ... [illegible]

THE MEN CAST BY SHADOWS

Mat Joiner

WHEN I THINK of Marc now, it's his art that first comes to mind, and the way it darkened. It's an effort to remember his face. I struggle to separate creator and creation – but that war was lost a long time back.

It took Scott's suicide for us to get back in touch. Last I'd heard from Marc, it was to ask if he could use a picture I'd modelled for as an album cover. Some metal band I hadn't heard of; he sent me the CD but I never played it. He called the picture 'A Cell's Dimensions'. I'm kneeling with my hair down over my face. Marc's behind me, a conjuror about to pull wings from my back. He gave me a stone body, walled the cell with old scarred skin. I never asked how; back then his techniques didn't interest me.

Scott had been a model too. I didn't know him very well. I remembered a brittle, pretty lad, already smitten with Marc. I wanted to tell him *been there, done that.* I wasn't exactly jealous. Marc and I had always made better friends. I wished them well and went my own way, for a longer time than I meant to. Marc emailed me from time to time: about exhibitions in the north, and moving away from Birmingham. When he went quiet I thought I knew why. A year or so passed and then I heard about Scott, but not until after the funeral. I didn't think he'd do that; and not with a razor. I raised a glass to them. A day or so later Marc sent me an email asking if I'd come see him.

He lived in a thin terraced house near Edgbaston Reservoir. The old waterworks tower loomed over the street, pure industrial Gothic. It just needed a vampire on the parapet. Around there it was mostly student housing, so in summer the area seemed depopulated. Marc opened the door, wearing a wan smile and the usual Oxfam black. His red curls looked like a child's scribble of hair. People say *lived-in* of a face but someone had used Marc's as a squat. His vowels had always been the broadest thing about him. He was even thinner now. When I hugged him he winced. He wore an open-necked shirt and I glimpsed a grid of dark bruises around his collarbone. *Ink or kink?* I wondered. 'They're not deep at all,' he said in an attempt to sound carefree. He was always good at answering the questions I didn't ask. That had charmed me, once.

The walls mirrored his skin, so watermarked they'd turned to maps. The low lighting didn't help the impression that the patterns were shifting – never the same coastline twice. 'Fuck. You need to get your landlords on this.'

He shrugged. 'It's the way they like it. And I won't be here long.' The house at least smelled clean – there was a pizza cooking.

Marc had made it as homely as he could but the shadows dwarfed everything, standing in for the prints he'd previously surrounded himself with. He'd got rid of a lot of his stuff including the cameras. That bothered me more than the hole he'd chosen to hide in.

'You're jacking it in?' I said. 'Or taking a sabbatical?' There was still an expensive laptop on the table.

He looked at his palms as if they held the answer. 'It's cost so much. You reach this point where it's not enough to create anymore. You want to *be* it. There's new work upstairs, if you want a private viewing.'

Bet you say that to all the boys, I almost said. I followed him to an attic room hung with a maze of dustsheets. At least that's what I first thought they were. I touched one – some fine pale cloth that swelled at a breath, tie-dyed with damp. I wondered why Marc flinched. After a while sketches and silhouettes emerged from the blotches. A saint with a halo of spider legs. Lovers fused at the head. One might have pictured roots, or nerves. I thought I recognised a mutual friend but the fungus reaching out of her eyes made me look away. None of them had obvious titles. There was a mottled border to each picture. The more I think of that now the more it seems like language. As if you'd found words growing in a Petri dish.

Marc hovered in the door. 'My last show.' His hands were shaking and he stuffed them in his pockets.

'Jesus beat you to it with the shroud,' I said. They reminded me of the silk screen prints he'd made when I first knew him, working out of a studio in Handsworth. 'Seriously, these are good. Morbid but beautiful. You shouldn't hide them away.'

'They're not meant to be *flaunted*.' His voice went low. 'They're my jury.' I counted: sure enough, twelve pictures. Before I could question him his mobile phone pinged in his jeans. 'Pizza's ready.'

Dinner earthed Marc a little. If he was weird, I could blame it on grief or wine. We circled the matter of Scott; I let him talk about that in scraps. They'd split up some time before the suicide. Marc *wanted* to tell me something more. Secrets itched at him like that. Instead he fled back into other subjects. He was suffering insomnia. Late-night walks around the reservoir or backstreets helped. There was some clock-tower or church he always heard tolling nearby. 'It comes and goes. Must be the wind, I guess. But I can't help wondering.' He was still trying to find the place but until then I'd have to be his confessor. Into his second glass he muttered, 'Scott wasn't trying to kill himself, you know.'

'What did he die of, then?' I'd have let him off if he hadn't seemed so calm. But sometimes fear brings stillness: it's a lesson I'm learning. 'Shaving cuts? I can't hear you properly when you've got your head up your arse.'

'Tactful as always, Justin.' Marc put down his glass. 'I mean… It was like sucking venom from a snake-bite. He was trying to save himself. Letting out the shadows. It worked too well.' His face twisted. I tried to take his hand but he shrugged me off. *You only reach out when it's already over,* he told me once. At least I was consistent.

'You're the only one who might understand.' Marc picked up a large paperback, a collection of prints by some old German biologist. He'd gone through several editions since uni. 'I keep going through this as if it'll tell me what I found.' He flipped through the book for a while. 'There's life everywhere. You don't have to look through a microscope to find the weird stuff. Think about *two-dimensional* life.'

I've dated enough of that. But I held my tongue – it wouldn't have helped.

'Look between the lines, down in the image. You'll find them. Shadows that nothing ever cast, that can't hold one form. You'll think they're tricks of the light at first. Flaws in the photo. I kept finding them in old pictures, then in graffiti, always just at the edge of sight. I thought I was mad when I saw them move that first time.' Still I didn't respond with the obvious. 'I watched and watched until I was certain. By then they were watching *me.* They made contact.' Marc drained his wine, poured another glass. 'I'm always so dry, now.' He watched me for a long moment. 'You're very quiet.'

As patiently as I could manage, I said, 'I'm waiting for you to make sense.'

He laughed. It sounded more like a smoker's hack. 'I'm waiting too. Maybe I'll be able to tell you tonight. If we had more time... They can *touch* images, Justin, change them. They're always hungry for shape. Imagine the temptation for me, the collaborations. The possibilities. I gave them a home in my art, a way in.'

'But?'

'You don't believe me.'

'In a story like this, there's always a *but.* Tell me about Scott instead.'

Marc leaned forward. 'I have been. Best if I show you.' He opened up the laptop. He clicked through a series of photos. They were of Scott, crouching naked in a bare room. There was a black haze in each one, like an aura of flies. Scott's bones were turning against him, twisting under the skin. The ribs opening like wings, joints knotting, his face tight against the skull threatening to break through. He crawled about, buckling under the weight of deformities. In the final pictures the shadows were growing over him in mossy patches.

'They're an infection,' Marc said. 'Give them a picture, they'll colonise, misshape. I knew what they were doing but I didn't stop them. Couldn't face it. The worse secrets are always the ones you hide from yourself.'

I pushed away the laptop. The dimness of the room had made it seem as Scott's deformities were trying to bulge from the screen. I was shaking. 'You sick bastard. You drove him to kill himself and now you're trying to justify it to me by spinning this bullshit? I'm going.'

'It's an infection,' he said again, leaning forward into the light. 'I should know. I've got it too.' Darkness crawled across his cheek. When it reached his eyes they went out. His face went *flat.* I mean that literally. For a moment or two he looked like a mask of Marc hung on the air. He hissed in pain, clenched, came back. The bruise spidered back under his shirt.

'They take the image first. Then they come for the original.' Marc reached for his wineglass. How could he stay so calm? I was saying *fuck* over and over under my breath. 'It's not just shape they're after. They want the depth we have.'

I thought of the attic gallery, trying to remember if I'd seen myself there. It took me a long time to speak. 'How many of us?'

'*You're* safe. I've made sure of that. I made a deal.'

'Why am I not flattered?' I'm still not. I should have asked him there and then what bargain he'd made. You can't just make someone a survivor then walk away from them. If that's love I want nothing to do with it. 'How *many*?'

'Twelve, at least.' *Of course,* I thought. *My jury.* 'Scott had it before he left me. Beth knew something was going on. She rang me up, pissed. Called me every name under the sun. There was a house fire, the same night. She must have thought burning the pictures would stop them.' He gave me other names, most of which I didn't know, or didn't want to – a roll-call of the dead or vanished. 'Now it's just me. Not that I'm alone.' Marc looked at the swarming walls. 'I let myself be infected. I can hold it in check, just, but I'm going under. One way or another it'll end with me.'

'Noble of you,' I said. I got up. This place could go to hell, if it hadn't already. I could walk out. The walls were only furred with mould. Marc was just deranged by grief. Simple as that.

He lurched towards me. I thought he was trying to start a fight. One punch and he'd crumble; he looked that frail. But his arms went around me and we fell onto the floor instead. From the outside we could have been tangled lovers. I knew what he carried and I tried to push him off. I used my elbows and knees; I couldn't bear to touch him with my hands. He was heavier than he looked. His lips touched my forehead. I shuddered away from more kisses. 'It doesn't spread skin to skin,' he said in my ear. 'Stay for me. I want someone *human* with me at the end.'

I reached up and grabbed his throat. He closed his eyes. I whispered, 'I could kill you now. Save them the effort. You want that?'

He smiled. 'You can try. They wouldn't let you... I've missed *real* touch, even like this. Their hands *burn.*' I let his tongue slip into my mouth for a while. I ran hands down his back. His spine felt normal but I wondered what shapes the vertebrae might bud into. It wasn't so much *desire* as a goodbye. Don't ask me how I could kiss him when he'd done what he had. You weren't there.

I took his hand and led him upstairs. At least the bedroom was on a different floor from the gallery. Marc put on the bedside lamp and we pretended that the darkness moving around us was only that. His lips were dry and hot. I couldn't do more than kiss him, conscious of being observed. I never did well with an audience. He folded into me and it was as if the last few years hadn't happened.

'We used to fit so well.' Did I say that or think it?

Marc was nodding off. 'I think I can sleep now,' he murmured. 'You were always good for that.'

'Thanks a fucking bunch.'

He laughed. 'I don't know if I'll wake up again … not as me, anyway. Do me a favour?'

'Read to you?'

Marc nodded. It was a ritual we'd had as lovers. I'd pick a book from the shelf – usually poetry or non-fiction, read aloud for twenty minutes. Jarman and Morgan were favourites of his. The slim book I found now was by a local poet – verses full of concrete and echoes, crimes with no witnesses. The lovers in them didn't seem any happier than the two of us. I'd have put the book back but Marc shook his head. I read on. Something about an empty house at the edge of a burning field, hair like gold. When I was done, Marc was asleep, eyes scudding behind thin lids. Alone, I felt even more watched. Well, I'd watch back.

At least I tried to. Instead I dreamed. Black rain like prison bars, eroding everything. I tried to find shelter before it took my sight but all the doors were locked. The houses were cartoons, then less than that. When I woke I thought the rain had followed me out of sleep. Marc had left a cameo of sweat on the sheets. A damp patch and an empty bed – in other circumstances I'd have felt nostalgic.

His clothes were on the stairs. It looked as though he'd torn out clumps of hair too. I found him kneeling in the gallery, or rather a study of him. A face made of hollows, papery skin, flickering like an old movie. The cloths were empty now, their occupants twisting around Marc in a kind of dance. Crabbed figures and shapes like wind-bent trees, antlers and tumours. I wasn't the only watcher. On the ceiling the stains ran together into something like a face. Another moment and I'd see just what kind, or it would be able to see me – the Rorschach blot that analysed you. But Marc said, 'Don't look at it, Justin.' His voice was down to a nub. But I listened to him focussed on him instead.

It wasn't a dance at all. The shadows were unravelling Marc with sharp fingers. There wasn't any blood; it wasn't horrible in that way. I've dreamed it much worse since then. He was layers all the way down, the features getting simpler and simpler. He was curls of tissue on the floor like apple peel. They did this slowly and in silence. It looked almost *tender*. What was left of his face stretched open in agony or delight. I can't decide. I reached out to him then dropped my hand. You can't save someone who doesn't want to be saved.

He was already down to shade when I turned away. *This* was his last show and I'd had my money's worth. They let me go – they knew I wasn't any threat to them. I have a memory of the darkness rustling like a forest. Maybe Marc was whispering somewhere deep in that. It parted for me and I was back out in the ordinary world. I kept walking towards the city and when dawn came I raised my hands to the sun as though it could burn away the touch of shadows.

I got rid of all the prints Marc gave me. But I still keep a photo someone took of us at a barbecue in Moseley. Marc's lifting a bottle to his smile. He looks relaxed. I've caught the sun. Wherever I live now I keep it facing the wall. Sometimes I pick it up for an hour or two. It's not just a reminder of better times or the way Marc once looked. It's an early-warning system. I look for a bruise where there was once sunburn, something wrong about the bones – now that Marc's changed, I can't rely on his protection.

THE WINTER GARDEN

Pauline E. Dungate

THE VODKA BOTTLE was empty. Matt blinked at it. He wasn't sure how that had happened. He'd only brought it on his way home. He'd been reserving it for later that night when he and Jo would round off the evening before tumbling into bed, wrapped in each other's arms. At least, that was how Fridays usually worked. Not any more.

THIS PARTICULAR FRIDAY, Matt came home despondent. Even the anticipation of Jo's slender body did nothing lighten his mood. Malcolm, his boss at the second-hand book and record shop, had told him that he intended to retire. He was closing the shop and doing all his business on-line. Malcolm was sorry about this but the shop wasn't paying for its overheads.

With what might be his last decent wage packet, Matt bought that large bottle of vodka. He'd also sunk a couple of pints on his way home and it was only his feet scuffing the leaflets on the mat that he noticed the white envelope. No stamp, he noticed, and his name was hand-written. Just that. No address.

He fetched a half-clean mug from the tiny kitchen and placed the bottle carefully on the table. He paused before pouring himself a slug. Drink first or letter? The vodka won. The spirit cut a heated swathe down the furred texture of his throat before he slid a fingernail under the flap of the envelope. The neat, black ink was in a hand he didn't recognise. Glancing at the name at the end he realised that he'd never seen Jo's writing before. He took another mouthful before starting to read. Letters blurred and ran into each other before he got halfway down the first of the two pages. Involuntarily, his fingers scrunched the sheets. After more vodka, he straightened them out to re-read. The gist of the letter was that Jo was fond of him but, until he sorted himself out and cut down on the alcohol, she wouldn't be meeting up with him again.

All manner of thoughts buzzed around his brain, mostly denial. He didn't drink too much. Okay, he'd occasionally got to the passing out stage on a Saturday night and over the last couple of months he'd had problems keeping an erection. That must be Jo's fault. Perhaps he didn't fancy her as much as he used to. It was time to move on. She'd just made it easy. He topped up the mug and sipped. He'd be better off prowling the clubs alone. Tomorrow. He'd head out tomorrow and eye up the talent. There were plenty, women and men, who'd admired his dancing in the past. He didn't need Jo. So why was the bottle empty? And why was his face wet?

MATT HAD VAGUE intentions of wandering onto the village and finding an off-licence to sell him more vodka or perhaps, in view of his new reduced income, cheap wine. He wasn't yet ready to descend to rot-gut cider and join the local no-hopers in the shelter of St Mary's lych gate. At the bottom of the stairs he became disorientated. The cool breeze from an open door wafted in the chill of a November evening and he turned towards the back door.

Despite having lived in the flat for nearly two years, Matt couldn't remember ever having been in the garden. The building was an old Victorian house on the outskirts of Moseley, the kind where the original owners had servants sleeping in the attic rooms. It had since been turned into six flats and Matt's was one to the two on the topmost floor, the ceiling sloping down steeply in his cramped bedroom. The windows were set at the sides and front, the kitchen facing the road and the tarmacked space edged by the remnants of hedges. There was no view of the garden.

Stepping outside, he realised his mistake. Above him, the

winter-stripped trees swayed, twiggy fingers intertwining. He squinted at the patch of luminescent sky before he worked out that it was the moon covered by a thin layer of cloud. He stood staring until the cold wetness underfoot alerted him to the fact that he'd neglected to put on his shoes and there was dew-soaked grass beneath him. He took a couple of steps and tripped. He registered the pain in his toe as he fell forward. He rolled over to stare up at the branches. They were illuminated from below. It was pretty, he thought, then frowned. Where was the light coming from?

Struggling into a sitting position, he looked back at the house. Two of the other flats had lighted windows and the thin curtains allowed out enough light to make the plants shine. He could make out the shapes of bushes and pale, glowing plants in their lee. He shivered. It wasn't just the cold air. Unsettling fingers stroked the back of his mind. He closed his eyes. He must be more drunk than he thought. An owl who-whooed behind him adding to the sinister chiaroscuro effect.

Matt pushed himself to his feet and staggered back to the house. The door had closed while he'd been lying on the lawn but not locked. As he fumbled with the handle he became aware of a peculiar scent. It reminded him a bit of the DDT his grandfather had liberally sprinkled around to dissuade every garden pest until the product had been banned. Next to the door in a very large pot was a tree-sized plant adorned with large white trumpet shaped flowers. He had no idea what it was. He broke off one of the blossoms and carried it upstairs with leaving a trail of wet, muddy sock prints.

By the time he had persuaded the chill to leave his feet he no longer felt like searching out more booze. He stuck the flower in the neck of the empty vodka bottle before falling, partially clothed, onto his bed.

IT WAS STILL dark when he awoke, his mouth dry and furred. Without switching on the light he staggered towards the kitchen. Turning the cold tap on full, he stuck his mouth under the faucet.

Water tracked an icy path down his throat. He coughed as it tried to choke off his airways and leave him gasping for breath. Behind him, he heard a soft laugh.

He straightened slowly, his heart beating faster in the hope that it was Jo. It couldn't be. Her laugh was coarser than that. He turned cautiously. Had he left the door open last night?

There was a glow on the table – where the flower was, he realised. As he stepped forward his body blocked the street light shining through the kitchen window. Someone was sitting at his table.

'Who are you?' His voice was croaky with sleep, rough with apprehension.

The youth's skin had a translucent quality, pale over the thin cheeks but bruised about the eyes giving them a cast of deep hollows. He wore denim so faded that, in the half-light, it appeared white. His hand reached out to caress the flower. Matt noticed the way that its perfume filled the space with a now unpleasant headiness.

'You brought me in,' he said.

'Go away,' Matt said.

'I used to live here.'

'It's my flat now.' Matt took a step towards the stranger.

'The winter garden is where all the bodies are.'

MATT BLINKED. A shaft of sunlight slipped beneath his curtain and aimed straight for his right eye. There was a sharp pain behind it and a steady pounding deeper inside his skull. You weren't supposed to get hangovers from vodka. Then he remembered the two or three pints he'd had in the Hare and Hounds before he got home. He needed coffee.

His hands shook as he filled the kettle. Working his brain out through the fog that smothered it he thought about the choice of films they could watch later, then remembered that Jo wasn't coming round any more.

He only filled the mug half-way before staggering into the main room. The flower was still on the table but its scent had taken on an odour of decay. He hadn't given it any water and the trumpet was wilted. Vaguely, he remembered waking in the night and seeing a youth caressing it. A dream, he decided, brought on by the pervading scent. He'd have to throw it out.

SATURDAY DRAGGED. DESPITE what Jo had implied, he was in control of his drinking. He was not going to open any of the bottles of cheap wine he'd bought at the Asian supermarket, until after six. He considered wandering down to the Hare and Hounds - beer didn't count - but decided instead to have a closer look at the garden that he'd inadvertently wandered into the night before. The door out was locked. He was about to give up the idea when he remembered the key in the bunch that came with the flat, which he had never used. He allowed himself a grin of satisfaction when it turned the lock smoothly and quietly.

The first thing he noticed as he stepped outside was the way the plants dimmed the sound of the traffic. He'd never been one for gardens but he recognised that this one was cared for. Someone in the flats spent time tending it - he doubted that the management would.

A narrow, slab path cut straight through the middle of a patch of grass and disappeared into the bushes. He saw the stone plinth that might once have supported a pot or a statue he had tripped over. A matching one on the other side of the path held a green plastic bag half full of rotting grass clippings. The edging of plants that had seemed to glow had tiny white flowers. He knew they were called alyssum because his mother had grown them and he'd thought they were alisons, and that was her name. As he walked down the path the light dimmed momentarily as he pushed past the bushes. It decanted him into an area centred around a stone-clad pond. A moss encrusted statue of boy with miniature wings stood in the centre. Lily pads floated at his feet. Matt thought it might have been part of the original garden. A wooden, lichen-spotted seat stood to one side of the entrance, decaying ungracefully. Beside it was a tree-like shrub with large white trumpet-like flowers. He caught the same scent as the one he had picked. He hadn't realised he had come this far the previous night. His memory had put the pot by the back door. In the other beds surrounding the area, tall seed-heads of grass and other plants moved gently between the late, white-flowering roses.

'Doesn't look much, does it?'

Matt turned sharply. The woman standing there must have been in her late forties. She wore an old-fashioned floral print dress and an apron. She carried a large pair of shears. Maybe this was the gardener.

As he didn't reply, she said, 'You must be the boy from the attic flat.'

'Um, yes.' Usually he would have objected to being referred to as a boy but she sounded kindly.

'This area is called the winter garden. It's at its best when the frost is on it. Too bad the winters have been so mild recently.'

'What's that plant?' Matt asked, indicating the one in the pot.

'Angel's Trumpets. The frost will kill it, though.' She seemed to vanish back in to the undergrowth and for a moment Matt wondered if she had really been there. He couldn't remember an older woman living in one of the flats but he knew very little of the other residents.

The mention of winter made him feel cold. He turned to go back.

THAT EVENING, MATT slotted a DVD of *Cabin in the Woods* into the player. It was a while since he'd watched it as Jo didn't like things that smacked of horror. Despite his best intentions, he managed to consume two of the bottles of wine before he chased them with a large shot of vodka and collapsed on his bed.

His head was full of the slightly unpleasant smell of decaying angel's trumpet. He opened his eyes to the sight of the statue in the garden. First he wondered if he was dreaming, though the clarity of moonlight on stone was realistic, then if he had sleep-walked here. That hadn't happened since he was a child.

He was dressed to go out but could feel the dampness of the

rotting seat penetrating his jeans. Someone was sharing it with him. It was the youth from yesterday.

Matt said, 'What are you doing here?'

'Being. This is where I am.'

'That's stupid.' Then he asked, 'Are you real?'

'This is my reality.'

'You said you used to live in my flat.'

'Until the junk I squirted into my veins took me down.'

'Down where?'

'Here. I'm not the only one.'

Then, Matt realised, there were others in the garden. He was sure they hadn't been there a few moments ago. The youth gestured towards the girl sitting on the pond's surround. She wore a long dress similar to those Matt imagined were of the age with the house.

'She was raped by her employer. She didn't dare tell anyone and when she fell pregnant he made her get rid of it. It was a botched job. She bled to death. See him?' He pointed to a man of about thirty who was pacing the other side of pond. 'He was a singer. Quite popular, I believe, until cancer invaded his throat. The surgeons cut it out but with no voice he ended it. Tore the scars open. Our gardener, you've already met her. She's hiding from her husband. She doesn't realise that she fatally stabbed him after he'd smashed her skull because she was tending her plants and let his supper burn. He won't be welcome here.'

'Why am I here?'

'It's where the bodies are.'

Matt closed his eyes. He felt totally confused. When he opened them again he was lying on his bed and had wet himself.

He staggered into the cubicle of a bathroom and showered, dumping jeans and underpants in the black bin liner he reserved for laundry. Perhaps Jo was right. He was drinking too much and that was inducing weird dreams. A glance at the clock showed him it was 3:30 am. He didn't want to sleep again so made coffee and glanced through his CD collection, most of which he'd brought home from the shop. He put three of the Scott Walker albums on continuous play and, out of consideration for his neighbours, plugged in the earphones. Listening to Scott's resonant voice he wondered if a singer had committed suicide in the garden.

IT WAS DEFINITELY the flower, Matt decided, that was giving him the weird dreams. Part of that was irrational. Even putting his nose up close to the withered petals, there was very little hint of the perfume that had invaded the flat when it was fresh. Plucking it from its make-shift vase, it crumbled in his fingers, scattering fragments amongst the detritus on the table. He ought to tidy up. It was one of Jo's complaints, that he never threw anything away. That wasn't true – he never left food containers around for more than a few days. The smell of stale pizza or curry was as nauseating as old socks. And he needed space to write. He would produce the novel he'd always been promising himself he would write once he had time. The tablet he'd used at uni wasn't suitable for what he wanted and his laptop was buried somewhere in this room. He swept some of the clutter aside and readied paper and pencil – after all, writers like Tanith Lee did first drafts longhand. First though, he needed a drink.

Hours later, the paper was still pristine and another wine bottle was empty. An evil smelling chip wrapper lay at his feet. He took the lazy way out, opened the kitchen window and dropped it into the bin below.

BY SUNDAY EVENING, he couldn't stand the isolation any more. A number of the local clubs wouldn't be open but there would be at least one on Broad Street. If it was one he didn't normally frequent, all the better. He was less likely to bump into Jo or one of his drinking buddies. Entrance would be cheaper as well, though bar prices wouldn't be. He calculated how much he was prepared to spend before squeezing into tight black jeans and a well-worn Joy Division T-shirt.

Waiting for a bus into the city centre, he shivered in weather that had taken another turn towards winter. Matt joined the short queue outside the venue and was soon decanted into the dimly lit space that was its hub. Music was already above conversation level and pounded from speakers lurking in the corners. The stage at one end was reserved for visiting bands or DJs, neither of which were scheduled for the night. He wasn't interested in that. He just wanted to get some of the itch out of his system and he hoped this place would do it.

He bought a large vodka and took it to one of the tables edging the dance floor, intending to sip slowly and absorb the atmosphere before venturing there himself. There were already a number of dancers, male and female, singly or in pairs, and groups gyrating to the random selection of piped music. Most of it was modern Goth from the likes of H.I.M., Nightwish and Within Temptation but with the occasional classic Cure or Joy Division creeping into the mix. It explained the clientele and he was satisfied with the clothing he had chosen. It fitted with his mood, the music and the rest of the clubbers.

As the place filled, he knocked back his drink and eased himself onto the dance floor. He didn't mind dancing alone. It gave him a chance to scope out the talent without being too obvious and of deciding who was with someone or who was scouting. Before long he found himself matched with a skinny Goth girl tightly laced into a crimson corset topping a stiff net skirt over leggings decorated with skulls.

'Good moves,' she mouthed at him over the beat.

He grinned. 'You, too,' he mouthed back.

'Drink?'

'Sure.' He knew she was asking him to buy. That's the way it worked if you wanted to make a connection. He caught her hand and led her to the bar. 'What?' he shouted.

'Black Velvet.'

He ordered two. It was one of the cheaper mixes on offer. They squeezed over to a slightly quieter area. Even with the lower noise levels conversation was difficult and though she told him her name, he didn't catch it. He did take the opportunity to look at her more closely. Her hair was cropped short – like Jo's – but dyed jet black. The make-up around her eyes gave them the appearance of dark hollows set in the pale of her face powder. Crimson lipstick matched her corset and nails. She was nothing like Jo except in hair style and figure. This girl liked the kind of movies that Jo scorned and it was inevitable that they should end up in Matt's flat, drinking vodka and watching *Nosferatu* with the sound down and Nine Inch Nails in the background.

MATT ROLLED OVER, his arm encountering soft, warm flesh. In his sleep-sodden state he initially thought it was Jo, before the vague recollection of the night before penetrated the haze. He moved carefully so as not to wake her. He slipped out of bed and headed for the bathroom.

On his way back he paused in the doorway. Light from the street glimmered through the window making her pale skin luminescent. She turned over and opened eyes submerged in dark hollows. It wasn't a girl lying there. It was the youth he'd encountered by the pond.

'What are you doing here?' Matt heard a quiver in his voice as he tried to keep the volume low.

'Waiting for you.'

'Why? What do you want?'

'You.'

'Go away. Get out.' Matt grabbed up his jeans and T-shirt. He thrust his feet into trainers and left the flat.

Matt was cold, very cold. He sat on the bench in the winter garden and stared at the trees. Behind them, the first touches of dawn were purpling the sky, the last stars fading to grey. Frost had touched the branches, crystals sparkled in the new light. Each grass stem was rimed. They shimmered and bowed towards the pond where the water was feathered with interlocking fingers of ice. The statue and the rim of the pond were shrouded as in white fur, the moss dusted with diamond dust.

'Beautiful, isn't it.' The woman he thought of as the gardener had appeared on the bench beside him. 'This is my favourite part of the garden, and the best time of year.'

'You like the cold?'

'It seeps into all of us in the end. Numbs the pain. That's the best thing about it. Nothing hurts any more.'

Matt turned his attention to the plants, aware of the strange perfume the angel's trumpets exuded. The rising sun softened the ice and it began to drip from the fronds, each drop a momentary prism. 'Not for long,' he said.

He had become less aware of the cold as he returned to the flat. The Goth girl was standing there, fully dressed, and looking furious.

She said, 'You told me you lived alone.'

'I do.'

'So who was that bloke I found watching me.'

Matt was confused. 'No-one.'

She added, 'I suppose you always leave your door open so anyone can walk in. Where did you go?'

'The winter garden.' His feet were beginning to thaw and the fire attacking his toes was excruciating.

'Is that where you got that flower? It smells like death.' She pushed past him and out the door.

He watched her go, unable to move or speak. He looked down at the flower he didn't remember picking. In the heat of the room, it began to shrivel. Water ran down his fingers and dripped onto the floor.

MATT WALKED SLOWLY along the road. After the morning's freeze-out he felt thoroughly spooked. He couldn't be sure that it wasn't his imagination that was conjuring the images of the dead people in the garden – except that the Goth girl had seen one. Unless that plant was making both of them hallucinate. In panic, he'd called Carla, a friend he'd kept up with from his school days. She'd said come over in the evening. After she'd finished work.

Her house was a big detached place, old but not as old as the building his flat was in. It was set well back from the road fronted by a garden that, even by street lighting, was wild rather than unkempt. The paintwork around the porch was flaking and there looked to be patches of dry rot in the frames. He was running his finger over a bare patch when she opened the door.

'I know,' she said, 'It needs a lot of work doing to it. Once I get established, I might be able to afford to do something about it.'

Matt knew from the past that this had been her childhood home. She was a late addition to the family and her older brothers had moved away long before. Her parents had died a year back, she told him now, and they had neglected the property in their later years.

'Let's go into Erdington for something to eat, then we can talk.'

After catching a pub meal, they walked the short distance to Witton Lakes. The former reservoirs formed a pleasant open space. Matt could hear the faint laughter of ducks as they squabbled for the best places to settle for the night. The inevitable Canada geese stood watch for foxes and stray dogs, screaming at the walkers who passed too close. It was cold and Matt shivered despite his anorak. Above, the stars looked like chips of ice scattered across an indigo velvet that bled towards orange at the edges. Though the water looked black, he imagined the ice creeping towards the centre. His mind gave it malice.

'Something is troubling you,' Carla said as the silence between them stretched.

'Yeah.' He hesitated, then told her about the visions, how he couldn't tell if they were dreams or hallucinations or if something weird was going on. 'I don't believe in the supernatural but it's like I'm being haunted.'

'You or the flat?'

'I've seen them in the garden.'

'You think you have. Come on, let's go somewhere warm.'

THE TWO DOWNSTAIRS rooms had been run into a single large one. The half nearest the back had been decorated and was furnished with a sofa, table and chairs that might have been her parent's choice thirty years before and never replaced. The other half was almost bare.

'Work in progress,' Carla said. 'I got rid of a lot of heavy wooden furniture and want to redecorate before I get any more. Coffee or wine?'

'Wine. Do you have to get up in the morning?'

'There's plenty of time yet. Choose some music to put on.'

Her collection of CDs was very different from his. She seemed to favour folk. One of the few exceptions was van Morrison. He selected the remastered version of *Astral Weeks* and slipped it into the player.

When she handed him the glass of cold white wine she sat beside him on the sofa.

'Did you believe me, about the ghosts?' he asked.

'Does it matter?'

'I don't know. I kinda feel safer here.'

'It's the music.' She reached over to take his empty glass and kissed him. The soft warmth of her lips chased away the final shivers from walking the cold night.

'Are you sure?' he said, as her fingers wormed their way beneath his T-shirt.

'Yes. Now shut up and kiss me.'

A memory of Jo flashed into his mind before he sank into the music and Carla's caresses. The gentleness was so different from the hurried gropings of their earlier relationship. He immersed himself in the softness of her flesh, allowing her and the music take him to another place. It was like being born again.

Totally relaxed, as he hadn't been for ages, he held her against him, his fingers stroking her back. His anxiety had receded during their love-making and he didn't want it back. He wanted this moment to continue.

Carla spoiled it. She pushed away from him. 'Grab the glasses,' she said.

'Why?'

She planted a kiss on his mouth and went to take the CD from the player.

'Don't do that,' he said.

She smiled at him. 'We can continue this upstairs. You did want to stay, didn't you?'

He caught hold of the pleasant atmosphere and trailed it in her wake.

MATT AWOKE WITH the lassitude of a night of pleasure. The music had long faded and he didn't remember when they had finished the wine, only that it had heightened his enjoyment. He hadn't thought of Carla in that way before. He hadn't thought of Carla in a sexual way for a long time. He turned over, expecting her to be next to him. The bed was empty, cold. Then he remembered that she had to work. She must have gone and left him sleeping.

His bladder prodded him with an urgent need to find the bathroom. Bodily functions always lowered the mood.

On his way back, he glanced out of the window at the back garden. Frost had turned it white. It wasn't as beautiful as the winter garden in Moseley but there were similarities in the way that the ice crystals sparkled in the early morning sun. At some time during the evening Matt had asked Carla why she stayed in a house too big for her needs. She had smiled and kissed him, saying it was the garden. 'It's where the bodies are buried,' she'd said.

The phrase came back to him now and he felt the chill of a barely heated house. Someone was down there. Not Carla. The figure turned a pale face with deep hollows for eyes up towards him and smiled. He hurried back to the bedroom where, he'd noticed, Carla had dumped his clothes before leaving. As he reached to pick them up he saw the chunks of broken ice in the place where she had been lying and caught a whiff of angel's trumpet.

Matt fled.

ON THE WAY home he bought two bottles of cheap vodka with the last of his cash. As he unlocked the door to the flat he was followed by a sense of betrayal. Had he brought the cold wights to her or had she enticed him to another place where they could reach him? He uncapped the first litre. He didn't bother with niceties, swallowing straight from the bottle. It sank into his tissues as water into the flesh of a thirsty man. At first, it warmed away the ice that had clutched at his soul. He felt he could breathe again.

By mid-afternoon, an early dusk, he started on the second. It was all that kept away the pain of thawing fingers.

'GOD, IT'S COLD in here.'

Matt raised his head from where he was slumped across the table. A double image of Carla stood in front of him. The ghost of the youth stood to one side.

'What are you doing here?' Matt said. He could feel one side of his mouth pulling down as the words slurred from him.

'I was worried,' Carla said.

'Not you, him.' Matt gestured towards the figure that grinned at him. He thought the youth replied, 'It's time to join us.'

'There's no-one else here.' Carla said.

'Everyone else can see him. Why not you? You're colluding with them.' At least that's what he meant to say. Even to his own ears it sounded wrong. Matt stood, or tried to. The room swayed alarmingly. He grasped what remained of the vodka and staggered for the door.

'Where are you going?' Carla asked.

'Anywhere else.'

He knew he was banging against the walls as he stumbled down the stairs. He slammed out of the back door not even stopping to think that it might be locked. Moonlight silvered the path and he trod it carefully sure that stepping off it would be a bad idea. Matt sank to his knees at the edge of the pond. Concrete was cold beneath his hands. He laid his cheek against it. The ice made it silky.

'Well come.' The Victorian servant girl was poised in the centre of the pool. One arm looped about the neck of the statue.

'The angel's trumpets died with the frost,' the gardener said. She held out a white rose. 'These are tougher.'

The bruised youth stood beside her and Matt wondered where

the dead singer was.

'You're drunk.' That was Carla's voice. She must have followed him.

'It stops me thinking,' Matt told her.

'Come back inside.' There might have been an edge of concern there. It irritated him.

'No!' He gestured wildly at her. His arm connected with the stone. The bottle was jarred from his hand. Ice shattered and it slid into the water. He leaned over to retrieve it. The singer pressed a shard into his fingers. It could have been ice or glass. He closed his fist around it. Cold seeped into his veins.

'Don't be stupid, Matt.' Carla's hands closed around his other arm. He lashed out at her. She released him, her hands going to her neck as she crumpled.

The four ghosts materialised around her. 'We didn't want her,' the youth said.

'She won't stay,' the gardener said, dropping the white rose on Carla's chest.

'Too vibrant,' the Victorian servant said.

The singer nodded.

Matt stared at them, then at Carla. Cold numbed everything. He stepped into the pond and allowed the icy water to close over him.

NATURAL HISTORY

Allen Ashley

ALL THE PSYCHOLOGY books, and I've read plenty of them, tell you that you never escape the shaping caused by your childhood experiences. As a child, I dreamed of flying like, or even *as*, Peter Pan. Scars and minor successes. My other role model was Doctor Doolittle: an inspiration for gawky, lonely would-be boy naturalists. The musical version of his story ponders how it might be if we could talk to the animals. I mostly try to communicate with dead ones.

MY DAY DOESN'T even get started until I've watched *Bargain Hunt*. Laughing at the losers who think they can spot a valuable antique and come home with a poxy profit. Telly for those who don't have jobs to go to.

I don't have a job to go to. But I have a place that I like to visit. Whilst I still can.

You ever been to an auction? Don't twitch and don't get carried away by the caller's silver tongue.

I wish I was well enough to go to work but then I wouldn't be able to spend so much valuable time in the local Museum of Archaeological Finds and Natural History. Of late, I have been its sole patron, in every sense of the word. The behemoth of Brackenfield Borough Council is hell bent on closing down both the museum and the next door library. De facto, I have become the David to their Goliath. But weak and lacking any useable slingshot.

They laid off the staff a while back, apart from a janitor who's probably doing it all voluntarily anyway. I *obtained* copies of his keys. Don't need to tell you how – trade secret. At least they haven't cut off the electricity yet, so I can check on the specimens easily enough now that I have begun their liberation and rebirth. The fridge is still running in the poky staff room even though the last milk went rancid five days ago. Black coffee will do for now. Instant.

They've let the surrounding gardens decay somewhat. I don't believe this is Brackenfield Council getting all eco on us; the shrubby hedgerows and the uncut lawns form a loose grouping along with potholed roads, uneven paving stones and wonky telegraph poles leant on too many times by the local lads on their annoying scooters. Across the far side is the cut through the common land that some refer to as a park. It's frequented in the mid-afternoon by gaggles of home-headed secondary school students, all clad in the academy's charcoal grey blazers. Any sensible fauna takes a siesta at that time of day. Even pigeons.

Even me.

I SUPPOSE I am lucky to have so much that my parents left to me when they left me. I use the term loosely. Whenever anybody official comes calling or drops into my Inbox, I hold fast to the tale that they are both missing presumed dead having embarked some years ago on the holiday of a lifetime; that brutally truncated said lifetime. After years of legal battles to claim full possession of the house and the bank accounts, I'm not going to be letting go any time soon. And I maintain that the benefits my parents claimed to help them deal with my 'condition' are now largely mine to claim on my own behalf. Cut out the middle man.

Dad lived his whole life in these few square miles of concrete, tarmac and claggy public parkland. He was fond of offering deep and meaningless aphorisms. After a day's supervision of the light engineering works on Tulsey Road, he liked to come home and settle himself with a mug of tea and a chocolate hobnob and say to me, 'I tell you what, Frankie, having a full-time job is like having a full-time job.'

Mother was generally more taciturn, busy keeping everything about the house spick and span for me and my father. She always encouraged me with my ambitions even if that merely meant offering a comforting smile or warm hug. She did once let her guard down, though, when she complained about me spending so much time at the museum. 'I can't see the appeal,' she said. 'If you don't like old things, there's nothing there for you.'

I talk to them both frequently, updating them on my plans. At some stage, I hope to enable them to talk back.

I WROTE LETTERS to the local and the national press. Everybody tells you that no-one writes letters anymore. Okay, mine took the form of an email but it served the same function.

I have several technological devices at home in my parents' old house, along with some workable scientific apparatus. If I hadn't worked out a clever scheme to hoodwink the electricity meter, life would be rather expensive. But I don't have a printer. That's become an absolute staple of so many households. Maybe it's time to put my Parker pens away and embrace the scuttling inkjet. That way I could run up some leaflets, repeat the gist of my message to everyone who passes by a horse chestnut tree or who stops to tie a shoe lace next to a lamppost or a bus stop.

Along with the decline and closure of our manufacturing base, it's a story the *Brackenfield Weekly Gazette* will have heard too many times before. The local council is closing both the library and museum so as to build *luxury apartments*; what they deign to call, 'A new venture in desirable in-town living'. The gravel paths, the duck pond and the scraggly trees and bushes will become somewhat cloistered, prettified perhaps, and certainly less easily accessible for us oiks. The likelihood is that what was once a public park will soon become a private estate's green space. This is a land grab and no mistake. And their future eyes have further plans. The old block of flats on the far side will now look dowdy and old-fashioned by comparison. It will be enough to give those *RE-VIVE-VITAL-EYZ*™ blinkered mob the excuse to tear that down as well, to turf out all the local working class families with their deep roots in our community and instead to re-develop it for yet another batch of incomer *young professionals*.

Please support and publicise our protest cause. Your words will be much appreciated. Your actions will help turn the tide.

I BOUGHT A dodo once. Off the internet, of course. I was aware that it was likely to be mostly composite rather than pristine and that the actual percentage of true dodo contained in the specimen would be small to doubtful. Still, it was the traditional starting point for any serious natural history collection. I gave it pride of place with the other items that I wished would remind me more strongly of my childhood.

Something I never forgot from that era was the production of *Peter Pan*. Including attempted launches propelled by my sprung-bed mattress, I have lost count of the number of attempts that I made at flight. Did you know Wilbur and Orville, the famous pioneering Wright brothers, managed less than a minute airborne? There were times when I superseded that paltry achievement but on other occasions I came crashing down with a painful bump. I still have scarring around my lips from the worst accident. I had a head injury, too. My father gave me the strictest talking to and probably wanted to tan my hide but Mother stilled his hand and I was hurried off to the hospital.

I remember being wrapped up like the mummy, mere eyeholes and air holes to distinguish my individual identity. It was like being cut off from the world; a feeling that has stuck with me. Sometimes I felt my parents were caring and concerned; at other times I'm sure I heard their twittering that they wished they'd raised a better fledgling; could they perhaps trade me in for an upgrade? I was young and still had school friends then. They came to visit and I felt like a museum exhibit. When I recovered, though, and went back to school I was no longer so interesting and gradually became isolated.

Having failed at flight, I nevertheless became quite interested in, indeed fascinated by, birds. I started spending weekends with Holman the owl man, a local guy who organised hawking walks through the nearby copse and the hedgerows bordering the sugar beet farms on the edge of town. My parents just let me get on with it. Sometimes my mother might remember to pack me a white bread chicken sandwich in a Tupperware box or dad might give me fifty pence or even a quid to 'buy a coke'. In Ravensby Woods? On the cold, damp mud of Harris Farm freeholdings? I suppose I was largely apprenticed to Holman in some sort of medieval manner that involved plenty of dogsbody work and no payment. He had me use a rusty, serrated knife to prepare the bloody, slightly slimy feed that he used as coaxing titbits to get his birds of prey to perform their short return flights for the punters. I carried bits of chopped-up chick in a canvas shoulder bag and doled out the chunks as necessary. On Saturdays, Sundays and, despite a weekly bath, the school slog of Mondays – my hands stank of carrion. And I wondered why the boys sniggered at me and the girls flicked their ponytails and turned away.

If I was lucky or if he was in a good mood, I'd occasionally get to wear the glove and have a kestrel or the contained bounce of a Bengal eagle owl land expertly on the leather gauntlet. Like a prisoner of war waiting for his rice rations, I lived for those moments, even though they were few, far between and soon over.

I STILL RECALL vividly being taken to that pantomime production of *Peter Pan*. Analytical even as a pre-schooler, I scoured the wings and the theatre roof for strings and wires but spied none. The characters really were flying. My mother indulged my impatient disappointment several times over the next few days with promises that one day I would achieve that ambition. Perhaps she had her fingers mostly crossed in the hope that her young Frankie would one day outgrow such childish fancies.

I say to her now that I understand a little better the pressures of adulthood. I hope she is aware on some level of my abiding love and respect for my wonderful, giving parents. Her open eyes and her slack posture give little away from within the specimen case. I have propped both her and Father upright against the rear wall of the locked shed but I wonder if they might be more comfortable lying in repose. Especially after all these years.

WHEN MY FATHER went to the local school it was just a bog-standard comprehensive keeping the grey-uniformed teenagers off the streets for a few years whilst moulding them just enough to become factory fodder or low-grade office clones.

Aged eleven, I survived the endemic bullying for a term until my parents made the survival decision to have me home-tutored.

Now the school is styling itself as an Academy and is 'Specialising in the Biological Sciences'. In practice, this means that the kids get to cut up loads of dead mice and fling their stinking innards around the lab when the teachers get too engrossed in their assessment and record-keeping. A rumour went round that the top GCSE stream were getting to try out electrodes on the brains of live monkeys. I was quite envious of this development and haven't ruled out borrowing some of their equipment *after-hours*. Of course, the Chair of Governors, our very own Council Leader Clive Chessman, had to go on local TV and strenuously deny these allegations. You can YouTube his shifty interview if you want. All I'll say is: would you trust a man who reputedly made his first million by helping an e-cigarette company get their branding onto the logo for a further educational college and two community radio stations?

ABOUT TWO YEARS ago, the local paper ran with a front page banner headline: 'Paedo Bird-Fancier Gets Found Out By Tweets'. The photo was a cropped shot of an older, greyer but still recognisable Holman the owl man. They'd cut out the accompanying Harris hawk to protect its innocent identity. The report told of how Holman had grassed himself up by posting some lewd Twitter messages that alerted the local constabulary, leading to a swoop on his ground floor flat and aviary. At times I wonder what became of his cache of trained birds. Had I been ready at that point, I could have stepped in altruistically and taken them into my own care. But there would have been too many police questions, for sure. And it's the case that at other times I replay scenes from my childhood, wondering if he ever interfered with me. I remember him grabbing my arm, positioning my hand, checking my stance, but all of these were explicable as assistance in attaining better falconry skills. Maybe he simply didn't mix business with perverted pleasure.

ELECTRICITY IS NOT enough. Electricity may never be enough. That Mary Shelley story was fiction, after all. Just some pubescent girl's sexually charged nightmare.

I'd done all the hard work. By which I mean that I had read a whole load about basic electrical circuitry on the internet. Hooked up the nodules. Siphoned off some unused amperes from the national grid. I was ready to go.

My plan was no longer to simply save what I could from the wonderful Museum of Archaeological Finds and Natural History but to reanimate what I could of its erstwhile contents. To bring the stuffed but surely merely dormant creatures back to vibrant life. See the squirrel skip, watch the dodo dance.

Maybe dear old Baron Frankenstein had it all wrong trying to start at the summit by animating or reviving or creating a human being. Modern day scientists have got the right idea by starting with gene modification. Don't expect to win the Nobel Prize with your very first effort; build your way up.

Bereft of formal qualifications and lacking the billion pound research grants of Monsanto and the like, I had placed myself somewhere within the middle of these two scientific extremes.

But it wasn't working. Maybe I'd do better to raid the local pharmacy, get my hands on this new miracle elixir all the plastic celebs and their sheep-like followers were popping like Smarties. Except not actually in their privileged gobs. Reputedly, this *RE-VIVE-VITAL-EYZ*™, administered as eye drops, would take years off your physical age, would preserve your skin and interior better than a taxidermist's dream. In time, you might become a walking, talking, living, breathing exhibit from the museum of your own life and family history. Live forever; or at least feel like you were going to.

Humankind does not deserve such an alchemical treasure. Give the planet back to those who would not harm it.

THERE WAS AN understandable public outcry at the planned closure of our local facilities all in the name of today's most popular political theorem: cost-cutting. Despite the grumbling, the local council might have managed to ride rough-shod over all protest were it not for the sudden intervention of Vladimir Ilyanov, billionaire chairman of the closest Premier League football club. His fortune had apparently come from oil and arms deals way back in the Soviet era; perhaps this current involvement would be a tardy philanthropic gesture or else a complex tax dodge. Whatever - at least the publicity got us a public enquiry.

We convened in one of those utilitarian meeting rooms in the recently refurbished civic centre. No top rank footballers graced us with their presence: probably too busy on their X-boxes or adding a shitty new tattoo to their smooth forearms. Instead, Ilyanov sent a dubious looking guy in a suit sharper than a dodo's beak to represent his interests. From the crack of a not quite closed cubicle door, I spied both him and local bigwig Councillor Clive Chessman partaking of *RE-VIVE-VITAL-EYZ™* elixir drops in the gentlemen's washroom. Although keen to live an artificially longer life, I noted that Chessman didn't bother washing his hands after urinating. As if his chairmanship of the enquiry wasn't already a dodgy deal…

We were too disparate a bunch to make our case coherently. The aural intrusion of two squabbling magpies in the tree outside the main window didn't help anyone's concentration greatly. The local history society seemed content to cave in after the promise of first dibs on a couple of poor quality Anglo-Saxon trinkets. A gaggle of overloud yummy mummies put forward vague plans to run an after-school club and a toddlers' crèche in either the library or the museum but couldn't agree on a rota that wouldn't disrupt their aromatherapy and mini-mosaic sessions. A Mr Smith, reputedly a building contractor although with nails cleaner than a Nivea model, promised an investment in social housing to rival the historical utopias of Bournville and Port Sunlight. I caught him later chatting freely with Ilyanov's stooge and I surmised that this was just one branch of the laundering business.

Having made the effort to skip a couple of my daytime TV favourites, I decided to raise my head above the parapet to deliver what I felt was an eloquent case for maintaining the museum undisturbed in situ.

Chessman let me ramble on for a minute or so before pulling his phone out of his pocket and declaring, 'In case you hadn't heard, Mr … Franklin, there's a new research museum on the block and it's free to everyone twenty-four seven. It's called Google.'

I took great delight in liberating my own device from a trouser pocket as it was two Samsung generations newer than the councillor's but my words were tinged with understandable anger and despair: 'With respect, Mr Chessman, pixels are no substitute for the hands-on experience.'

'Then get the coach to the Fitzwilliam or BMAG. There's nothing here worth saving.'

Ignorant words, pal. Shaking my head, I volleyed back, 'You make an unfounded assumption that we are all in a position to travel so easily.'

I made a point of bashing into a couple of chairs as I exited, exaggerating my limp as I did so.

For a moment, I had one of those 'Once this was all fields' flashes in the landscape outside. Chittering and snuffling tickled my ears; the rich aromas of ripening fruit and fertile loam caressed my nostrils. Then I remembered my quotidian disappointment and the vision vanished. Even the magpies were rendered still and silent.

BUT I DID get to genuinely fly once upon a time. It was late evening in the park and the last of the pairs of snogging secondary school kids had vacated the cover afforded by the hawthorn bushes and made their way back home to their TV dinners. I was on my knees checking a woodlouse colony when I saw a bird struggling on the twig-strewn floor. I approached slowly. It seemed to be some type of pigeon and it cooed appreciatively as I wrapped my small hands around its tense body. I lifted the creature, with a rising motion that was probably more appropriate for a sports trophy than a natural treasure.

Suddenly we were airborne. My Clarks sensible shoes kicked at empty air as we rose incrementally. With a little help from my fine-feathered friend, I was flying at last. We might have reached truly dizzy heights if the scientist part of my brain hadn't started wondering how this avian weighing less than a kilos had managed to lift my frame and limbs so far above ground.

'I fell out of a tree,' I told my mother as she applied water, soap and Germolene to my grazed knees.

'Maybe we shouldn't let you go out and play on your own,' she muttered.

'Then I shan't play at all. No-one else wants to play with me.'

I THINK I have something of a local reputation even though I'm publicly polite and, in appearance, fairly nondescript. Apart from the permanent scarring around my lips; which is mostly masked by the very modern accoutrement of a short beard.

Councillor Chessman has made much mention of 'footfall' or lack thereof in his pronouncements. Whilst I spend much of my day readying my specimens to reclaim their realm, I also make a point of taking an invigorating walk every afternoon through the newly disputed territory. The duck pond, the stunted trees, the crudely tarmacked footpath - these are all heritage items to my mind. Leaving the park by the north gate, I pass Dr Shah's surgery. He was my GP until a year ago when he quit the NHS to go profitably private. Today some academic secondary school kids were hanging around his freshly-painted driveway conducting behaviourist experiments with a grey cat and its spiky ball of string.

'Hey, look, it's Campaigny Man!' one of the boys called.

'Wonder what he's stuffing the animals with tonight,' a short female with San Quentin tooth braces lisped as I passed by.

I suspected that they were filming or photographing me on their phones because, well, what else is there to do when you're young, bored and thick as shit? As I reached the telegraph pole, I turned briefly and pulled a face. Let them make that their home page or cover image on *Insta-Crap*.

Retracing my steps five minutes later, they had moved off but in their juvenile haste they'd let fall a few items from their blazer pockets: a badly-chewed biro, a chocolate wrapper and a small phial of *RE-VIVE-VITAL-EYZ™*. I scooped this latter up and headed home without breaking stride.

The list of ingredients for this miracle life-extender doesn't live up to its Edenic promise. The usual obfuscation: aqua, riboflavin, hydro-cortisone ... even saline and sucrose solution. It's the emperor's new eye drops and no mistake. Unless the manufacturers want to keep their alchemical breakthrough as secret as possible. Can't have every Tom, Jade and Mason getting their grubby mitts on the elixir of life.

A new possible avenue opens for me. Electrical currents and my own enzymic concoctions aren't really doing the trick in terms of my grand project. Taking cased animals out of the museum ahead of its likely closure is not strictly a crime, more a stepping-up to a duty of care. But if *RE-VIVE-VITAL-EYZ™* really does what its proponents claim - and maybe even goes a stage further, into breathing *new* life into what once had life - then it looks like I might need to liberate a fair few litres of the stuff from my local pharmacy. As soon as poss.

MY FAVOURITE DISPLAY case in the museum was always the one entitled *Brackenfield Before Man*. The animals featured were earlier but still recognisable versions of stoats, otters, deer, foxes, wolves and various bird species. Sensibly, the designer - some forgotten gentleman of science turned local employer back in the late-Victorian heyday of knowledge - had shown the fauna in a lightly-wooded, heather and fern strewn environment. My point:

not the glacial steppes of the Ice Age that so many instantly associate with the Pliocene or Pleistocene eras. I think it helped that fossil evidence of mammoths and other eye-catching beasts has remained steadfastly absent in this area.

One of the mothers on the many sub-committees and support groups opposed to the council's closure plans disagreed with me. 'Imagine how much leverage we could get with a campaign to "Save the Brackenfield Mastodon",' she proclaimed.

Between worrying about little Jack's lack of application to his literacy homework and whether Daisy-Mae should take her iPhone into school with her, I think this lady had taken a bit of a shine to me. In a somewhat age-inappropriate maternal way. I seem to have had this effect on several women.

'I take it you'll be bidding for a few items,' she continued, 'when - well, *if* the inevitable happens. I've got my eye on a piece of Viking jewellery.'

'The fight's not over yet,' I answered.

'That's the spirit. Still...'

I knew enough about auction houses to know that they were staffed by the same cadre of shysters as top legal firms and high street estate agents. Bamboozling wide boys in striped suits and power-dressed women nipping to closely timed viewings in turbo -charged Mini Coopers. I made the decision early doors that I could cut out the middle man/median woman and avail myself of whatever items took my fancy without any need to bid, throw down the cash or exchange credit card numbers. The exhibits were public property; I was a member and sound-minded representative of that public.

I'm not strictly a collector, more an enabler. My great scheme is a new, fully animated - in fact, living - tableau called *Brackenfield After Man*. It won't take too long for the wiry plants to pull down the walls of the luxury flats and then my furry and feathered pretties can take their rightful place in a restored green and brown neighbourhood.

ANOTHER GREY DAY. I watched the starlings gathering,

soaring and swooping in their loose figure of eight formation. I hoped soon that other birds and creatures from my growing collection might join them; a re-populating of the scraggy urban oasis. Not all will be airborne, of course. Self-educated, I know the facts: the dodo never flew and the liger will never breed.

My specimens deserve a better display area. To date, they have been stacked somewhat haphazardly whilst I work on diverting the electrical current necessary for their re-animation. I invested in a few cans of that off-grey magnolia shade that is so popular in the surviving museums. Home decorating is not my strong point and my best trousers had become splattered with what the local ne'er-do-wells would assume was semen. Idiots. I don't produce the stuff and nor could they in such proportions and brightly luminescent shades.

My jeans were in the washing machine so all I had to wear outdoors was a pair of running shorts. Quite when I'd acquired these, I had no idea. I've never run. Okay, maybe *away* from someone pursuing me … but athleticism is not part of my personality.

I'd thought my main worry would be the keys accidentally slipping out of the tiny pocket of this garment but no, my cold route through the park brought me into contact with one of the greycoats skipping the final school period with the hateful nonchalance of youth.

'Oi, pervy!' he called. 'What's that you're carrying?'

I held the liberated display case a little tighter, though manoeuvring its front into his view. Let's see how much zoology they teach these wasters on the National Curriculum.

Caring not a jot that with his soft charcoal uniform he was easily traceable, the kid said, 'You're probably going to stick that on the end of your knob, you fucking weirdo.'

No naming of species, then. No interest in any fauna that didn't get squidged into a so-called chicken burger. I recognised the youth as one of the sons of our local Tory councillor; the *RE-VIVE-VITAL-EYZ™* treatment having done nothing for his acne-pitted skin and shrunken intellect. He was picking on the wrong target; judging by the posh university rituals exposed on the BBC News recently, it was far more likely that his father will have done something unspeakable with a stuffed raccoon.

'Fucking – fu-fucking fox fucker!' he eventually managed.

Close but no A Star GCSE for you, pal.

Fortunately, he suddenly remembered that he hadn't fiddled with his phone for all of five seconds so returned his attention to the tiny device in his hands and I made my way safely home with my latest acquisition.

I'VE HAD TO move faster than anticipated. In truth, I'm not entirely ready, even with a little fifty mile round trip to liberate some liquids from a pharmacy in Brockley. After dark and in a rabbit mask. Never shit on your own doorstep.

Things shouldn't be moving so quickly. No-one has seen Councillor Chessman for the past two days. No-one other than me, that is.

But suddenly there's a yellow JCB at the library entrance; plastic netting and *Construction Site – Keep Out* signs to indicate the oncoming destruction. By this stage, I had hoped to revive my whole collection but it's proving more troublesome than expected. I believe I saw some life in the standard British fauna: a fox, a weasel, a grouse, two or three butterflies. Mother and Father have yet to respond to treatment.

What is being planned here is not the natural order of things. In two centuries the buildings may have crumbled, including my beloved museum; but the modern inability to stay still and contemplate is bringing about their *imminent*, unacceptable destruction.

Come, my pretties, do my sweet bidding this one time.

But the revived animals disobey orders and run for cover in the trees, the bushes and the lily-clogged pond. Or up into the typically overcast urban sky.

If that's how it must be, then I shall respond. I achieved brief success before. So, now is the moment to try to join them, to reach up Icarus-style, like I did when I was a kid, a boy who believed he could fly…

THE SECOND DEATH

Ian Hunter

'I'M LEARNING HOW to die again.'

The voice was soft and clear, coming from the shadows of the upstairs lounge in the hospice. I almost jumped out of my skin with surprise and did well to bite back a swear word or two.

I turned, peering into the corner. 'Sorry?' I said, certain I had misheard and the owner of the voice said they were learning how to live again, before going on to tell me they were in remission. It did happen. Unexplained medical miracles. Not to Dad, though.

The woman tottered out of the shadows, all white hair virtually standing on end like a halo around her head. She was thin and the hand which held her walking stick was trembling.

'I said that I'm learning how to die again.' She looked at me, eyes sparkling, a smile on her lips. Both took decades off her. 'Imagine that after all these years.'

I made some vague noises, made even more vague gestures towards the corridor and Dad's room, before making a show of looking at my watch. 'I better go. They'll have finished changing his bed again.'

'There's no hurry, love, not yet. He'll not die tonight. Why don't you come to my room so I can show you something?'

'No, I, I...'

'Please.'

So I followed her.

THEY OPENED DAD up and closed him again then told me they could do nothing. The cancer had spread too far, had already affected some of his organs, which were starting to fail. Quite bluntly, a tired looking doctor told me that he wasn't a priority patient at his age. I didn't know what to say. I was in shock. The source of all Dad's pains and weight loss suddenly revealed. I should have argued. Demanded a second opinion. Fought for him. Why wouldn't they treat him? Because he was just an old man from a council estate? Would it have made a difference if he had been younger? Had been important? A contributor, not somebody who worked in the car plant all his life? The doctor said any treatment would be long and hard. A mixture of surgery and radiotherapy and Dad probably wouldn't survive it. I remembered the operation he'd had for the aneurism in his abdomen a few years back and how that nearly killed him. He was older and frailer now. The doctor looked at the clipboard he was holding, scribbled a few notes and looked up to ask me if I knew Dad's thoughts about being resuscitated if he lost consciousness.

THE OLD WOMAN walked slowly down the corridor, helped by her walking stick. I could almost feel myself slipping out of my body to hover above the two of us and take in the situation. I tried to remember when I had ever seen a woman walking with an ordinary walking stick. I remembered seeing them holding on to a walking frame – a Zimmer – we used to call it. I remembered seeing women aided by a metal pole which had three feet at the bottom. Those things always made me think of tripods, of Martian invaders. This woman walked with a traditional wooden stick. The wood dark brown, a silver tip at the end, instead of a piece of rubber, a silver band around the middle.

She stopped at another of the mirrors dotted along the corridor. Somewhere above us, something beeped and pinged – a smoke detector needing a new battery. She smiled at her reflection. Tilted her head to the side, reached up to push some of her hair aside.

'I have colour,' she said, voice full of wonder. She turned her head the other way. 'Imagine that, I'm not grey anymore, and the blood blossoms are gone.'

Colour? She was very pale but there was a slight, pink flush to her features, or rather, her face and neck had pink tinges to it, joined-up lines, like scar tissue. Without thinking, I looked at my hand and the pink circle where I'd had a freckle that darkened and hardened. They puffed some liquid nitrogen out of a bottle on to it and it died, fell off, and left this slightly pink circle, so different from the surrounding skin.

'I was just another one of those grey ladies,' she continued, eyes bright as she started to walk again. 'We all were, like grey ghosts that haunt an old building, or some moorland. Scotland is full of them. Britain is full of them. The world is full of them, I suppose. Women who were wronged. Met a horrible end and now walk a hazy line between life and death.'

I deliberately made a show of looking at my watch. She reached out and touched my arm.

'Oh, don't you worry, it's not his time yet. I can tell.'

'Can you?' Maybe she could. I wondered how long she had been here. Dying here? What she had seen. How many had died while she waited for her turn. I didn't like to think she knew something about my father I didn't know. Couldn't know, yet.

She smiled, her eyes far away. 'There's a little bit of life in me, like my little bit of colour. I walked further and further every day then took my chance and got away. Packed up what little I had and managed to get out of the village. Some hillwalkers found me, almost dead from exposure, and the ambulance took me further south, all the way down to here. All on a whim, you understand.'

'Not really.'

She stopped, hand shakily pointing to a door on our right with the number twenty-two on it. 'This is my room.'

I held out my hand. 'Have you got your key? I'll unlock the door for you.'

'Oh, it's not locked. What's the point in that?'

'You could get robbed,' I told her. 'Someone could steal your jewellery.'

'I don't have any, it's all gone. A Cutter took it years ago, out of spite. Another act of rebellion.'

'A cutter, what's that?'

'Come in and I'll tell you. Show you. I have photographs, all curled and brown.'

She did, lots of photographs in a wooden box with a warped lid, and a story to tell. One I didn't believe at first but as I haunted the hospice over the next few days, it began to flicker in my head like a candle, then became a fire, taking me over, making my mind up

THERE WAS A new girl on reception when I arrived at the hospice. What she lacked in experience she tried to make up for with enthusiasm and a wide smile. I told her I wanted to take Dad for a drive up the Bickam. Park on the hill and watch the sun go down. He'd had his morphine and was a bit sleepy. She wasn't sure. It was getting cold. He could catch a cold. That was the least of his worries, I assured her and wheeled him out to the car. She followed, still protesting, until her beeper went. She told me to wait there until she came back. I don't know if she did.

We drove north, skirting past Glasgow on the new stretch of motorway then passed the airport and over the Erskine Bridge. We wound our way past Loch Lomond, through Crainlarich, going north. North into Glencoe. The sky was wide and blue above us but starting to darken at the edges. The mountains loomed on either side like curious giants, while I kept glancing to the side looking for the road the old woman had told me about.

Except I couldn't find it. I pulled over and consulted an old map. Dad was dozing in the back but occasionally he would make a sound of pain and his features would tighten. I should have brought some morphine. Stolen it off the meds trolley sitting in the corridor. Rain suddenly splattered against the windscreen. With a sigh, I leaned forward, staring up as the sky thickened with clouds. Rain ran across the glass. I pushed down the lever to start the wipers which shrieked across the windscreen, probably scratching it knowing my luck – there was hardly any rubber left on the wipers. How had the car ever passed its MOT? I sighed again and drummed my fingers on the steering wheel, feeling frustration tighten inside me, pulling parts of me towards it, making it bigger. Soon I would lose the rag if I wasn't careful.

'So where the hell is this road?' I asked out loud.

I reached for the Sat Nav and pressed a few buttons which didn't offer any answers to my question. No surprise there, I was rubbish with new technology. I'd driven down the A82 past the road that turned off towards the Clachaig Inn and the back way into Glencoe Village but that wasn't the road to take, the old woman had told me. I'd have to turn the car again and head back the way I had come. It was, oh, so tempting just to keep going all the way back to Glasgow and forget about the old woman's story. I wondered if the hospice had rang the alarm bells yet and called the police who no doubt expected to find my car beside a river or a loch or the sea, waiting on two bodies to turn up several months later. Or thought they would find us sitting in a garage somewhere, tube leading from the exhaust through a slightly open window. Case closed.

I stared into the side mirror. Nothing was coming up behind us. I did a three-point-turn as fast as I could before another car came along, or a truck, or some motorcyclist doing ninety while I was blocking both sides of the carriageway.

The road I was looking for had to be on the passenger side, I thought, taking it slow. If anyone came up behind I would just pull over.

I'd almost passed the road before I realised it was there. More a track, really. Long grass trampled down in two lines, probably from tractor tyres or a quad bike.

So...

It could be nothing, just an old farm road leading up into the hills and the sheep clinging to the hillsides. I indicated left which seemed a daft thing to do since there was no-one about and turned off the A82, telling myself I would drive a couple of miles and if I didn't see anything then I would turn back. Switching my lights on I took it slower than slow. This wasn't even a single-track road with passing places it was a just a winding, twisting track. My heart was in my mouth at every bend, expecting a tractor to be coming the other way.

The half-road gained height. The dry stone dykes on either side dwindled to nothing like the leaning fence posts with rusty strands of barbed wire between them. Now there was another reason to take it slow as sheep lingered on either side of the track. Startled, they looked up, eyes reflecting my headlights as little bright circles. They ran away, some up the hill, some down, some straight ahead, blocking my path.

'Get off the road,' I growled, glaring at their woolly rumps, a splash of colour across their backs, presumably to tell which farmer owned them.

Finally they darted to the side and I kept driving, the track swooping down and skirting a forest which thinned away to nothing to reveal the ruins of a large house fenced off from the road. I passed a faded white sign, too worn to tell me if it belonged to a security company or offered some development opportunity.

I kept going, despite a gnawing voice at the back of my head chiding me for driving all the way out here on the words of a dying woman, a mad woman, possibly. The road almost doubled-back on itself and I slowed, slipping into second gear, my lights illuminating a huge wall of wool caught by the fence. The wool moved and I could see that it was a sheep trapped in the barbed wire. The sheep raised its head, eyes rolling back to reveal white. I swallowed and accelerated, certain if it opened its mouth it would speak to me. A warning or a curse, I didn't know.

'THERE USED TO be nobles living in the hills,' the old woman told me. 'There was the remains of a castle out on the moors.'

'So who lived there?' I asked, humouring her. 'A Laird or someone?'

'More important than that, a Marquis, almost a Lord, a Prince. Powerful people, always wanting more.'

'Yeah, well, what's changed there, eh?'

'The Marquis consulted a wizard, a seer, about his future. Didn't like what he heard predicted about him and ordered the seer's death.'

'Burned at the stake, I suppose?'

'Worse than that,' said the old woman, eyes bright, a gleeful look on her face. 'They got a barrel filled with pitch and set fire to it then lowered the seer in head-first.'

I grimaced, trying my best to get the image out of my head. It was hard work.

'He cursed the Marquis as his hair caught fire and his face started to melt, just before the pitch blinded him and went down his throat. Cursed him and the land round about. The Marquis would die young but those on his land would live forever, but not a good life.'

'Still better than the alternative though.'

She chuckled. 'You might call it that, but biding there comes at a price. It drains you, if you let it, unless you rebel, like me, or…'

I raised my eyebrows at her. 'Or…?'

'The Cutters,' she said, staring at me with a blank look on her face, all humour gone.

'And who are they?'

'They cut everything, especially themselves.'

THERE WERE HOUSES up ahead. A row of yellow street lights shone wanly above them. I slowed which was just as well as someone lumbered out into the road in front of me. A face leered through my side window, mouth wider than it should have been. The face had several mouths where something had cut it, leaving gaping flaps of skin that looked ragged around the edges. A hand appeared brandishing a knife which was waved in front of me. Then, with a desperate cry, the figure reared back, lurched into the road and hobbled down a lane between the houses.

Swallowing, I glanced at the dashboard and the little red indicator that told me the car doors were locked. All the houses were made from the same grey stone.. Row after row of sponge-like miners' cottages forming the main street, and others which branched off at right-angles to this one.

I was too busy looking to the side to notice a man had stepped into the road almost in front of me, his hand raised.

'Jesus!' I cried, stamping on the brake.

Slowly, clearly painfully, he moved round the front of the car. I stared at his hands, looking for a knife. He raised his eyebrows and I couldn't take my eyes off the marks on his face. Was this what the old woman meant by blood blossoms? 'So you've met a Cutter, then?'

'I suppose I have.'

'Don't worry, nae knives on me,' he said, holding his hands up, then waggled the index finger of his right hand. 'Park ower there, in front of the village hall.'

I nodded and followed his directions.

I STOOD BACK as three men appeared, the one I almost ran over with two others. Without asking, one of them opened the boot and took out my father's wheelchair and pushed it round the side of the car, then the other two helped him out. The third looked at me.

'I'm Rory, closest this place has to a leader, I suppose.' He jerked his head to the side. 'We'll go in there.'

'What about my father?'

'We'll make him comfortable. I'm assuming he's the reason you're here?'

'Yes.'

I followed him into the village hall, and almost recoiled from the smell of damp coming from the curtains which hung beside windows dripping with condensation. Several tables had been arranged board-room style. Rory sat down next to the nearest one and pushed a chair towards me with his foot.

'What's wrong with you?' I asked.

Rory managed a half-smile. I had the feeling it was hard for him to move his face at all.

He held up his hand and I stared at it, at the blotch on his skin which looked like a big black spider was sitting on top of it. I knew I was wrong as his hand moved towards his face. The big black spiders sat under his skin, like the one on his cheek that he was touching.

'This?'

'Yes, is it some disease?' Already a voice of alarm was talking on my head, babbling. Move away from him. Get out of the room. Get out of this place.

He made some sort of noise which might have been his attempt at laughter.

'It's no a disease, it's an anti-disease. The opposite of getting ill.'

'Doesn't look like it to me.'

'Ye could call it anti-illness, anti-aging, anti-death.'

'So the old woman back at the hospice was telling the truth?'

'Ahh,' he drawled, 'So that's what happened to auld Jennie? We thought she'd died somewhere out in the hills.'

'Where's my father?'

'He's in the cottage next door.'

I cleared my throat, suddenly afraid to ask. 'Is he comfortable?'

'Well, he's still alive. He'll always be alive.'

'What does that mean?'

'What does it sound like? This is a place that cheats death. Everyone is dying here, up to a point, but they never cross the finishing line.'

'Let me see him.'

Rory shook his head. 'Better you don't, perhaps. Better you leave him here and go back to wherever you came from.'

'Why? I thought he had cheated death. Gone into remission, or something.'

'No, you don't understand. He's no gaun to get better, he'll just be the same. He'll always be the same, oan the cusp. He's never gaun to die. I'm never gaun to die. You'll never die if you bide here long enough.'

I STARED AT my father. His eyes were closed. His face looked calm, peaceful. His breathing was regular but there were the beginnings of blood blossoms on his cheeks and probably elsewhere on his body.

Rory took a deep breath. It sounded like an effort. 'You can leave him if you want. He's starting to change.'

Was I? I wondered. Slowly, I raised my hand, it seemed paler, but something was happening to the veins under my skin, turning them dark, into spider marks. Forming lines that had still to join up. Lines that would spread all over me. Blood blossoms.

If I went back I would have to explain what I had done, or lie, so that they didn't come here and take Dad back to die. If I went home I would probably be arrested and go to prison, maybe for a long time.

Dad groaned, face contorted.

'I should have brought some morphine with me,' I muttered.

'You'd never have enough,' said Rory. 'So what are you gaun to do now?'

I licked my lips and thought about it.

BLANCHE

Andrew Hook

IT WASN'T MUCH of a tower.

Gavin stood outside the nightclub entrance. A torrent of rain peculiar to Edgbaston - grey, filmic - fell out of the twilight. He dug his hands into his jacket pockets, his dirty blue hair plastered down the left-hand side of his face. It wasn't a popular cut. Gavin was always on the edge of things. He watched couples arrive, those that subscribed to a gender and those that did not. They kicked puddles as they walked, as though each raindrop needed to be taught a lesson. Some held umbrellas, wore raincoats. Gavin craved authenticity. There was little of it to be had anymore. He was hardly eighteen, yet already he felt outstripped. Most of the crowd was much older than him. It didn't bode well for the remainder of his life.

The front of the Tower Ballroom resembled a carpet warehouse with some pseudo-Doric columns tacked on the entrance. It had started life in the 1870s as a roller-skating rink and became a dance hall by the 1920s. It had been used as a location for the television series, *Boon,* and had few remaining months of life before it would become caught up in the regeneration plans around the Edgbaston reservoir. Gavin had spent many a night inside, slammed against pop-punks, his eyes half-closed, savouring each connection as it whirled away from him, as though he were a spinning top with a rope around his middle, set off by contact with others.

In the back of his mind - always - the possibility of a meet.

Tonight Scalene, a tribute band, were playing. Gavin had to

Google the word. Unlike No Way Sis or The Smyths it wasn't immediately clear from the name who they were emulating. Even their flyers seemed deliberately ambiguous. When he found the answer, Gavin hadn't even heard of the former Birmingham band Triangle, a post-punk three piece who had scored a few minor hits before he was born. He wondered why Scalene hadn't chosen *Isosceles* or *Equilateral* as band monikers, but the name intrigued him. A scalene was a triangle with each side unequal in length. He considered adopting it as a pseudonym for himself.

The wind picked up. Damp, brown leaves, the texture of elderly skin, drifted from stricken trees. One leaf stuck to the back of his neck. He peeled it off as though it might reveal a temporary tattoo. An imprint of nature for this degenerate urbanite.

The Degenerate Urbanites would be *his* band name, if he ever got it together to play an instrument or make enough friends. He rolled the name around in his head whenever he got the chance, as though through repetition it might actually happen.

People stamped their feet. Bulls awaiting the china shop. Breaths formed as word-ghosts in the late October air. Gavin regretted leaving home early but there was only so much he could take. His parents didn't understand him. They had become stupid in their middle-age. When he had *come out* they had simply accepted it. He craved revolution and a bit of anarchy. His parents had experienced it but it was denied to him. They couldn't see the irony.

When the doors suddenly opened on the blackness inside, the crowd surged as though being sucked into a maw. Gavin hung back, the fist enclosed around the fiver in his pocket was raw with cold. He opened the note with arthritic-slow fingers. The cashier wiped the back of his hand with a cloth before applying the ink stamp.

The dance floor was empty. He queued like everyone for a lager and drained it slowly, standing at the back of the venue, shivering in his wet clothes. When the band finally took to the stage, their combined age could almost have been the number of degrees in a scalene triangle. Yet there was an urge to some of the material that hit him deep. A song, 'Stranger Key', was brooding and dense. He recognised an echo of violence which might have permeated the original band's performances. It was a pale shadow, however, and as his interest wavered he watched those in the audience who *had* been there in the old days, desperately trying to recapture their youth, pretending that they were young again.

Someone touched his shoulder.

He ignored it. Always best to ignore it at first.

Another tap.

Gavin turned his head. The man was a few years older. It might have been the interior lighting but the face was spectral. He wondered if the guy was wearing make-up. That wouldn't be unusual but the sallow expression matched the colour and Gavin realised he probably wasn't. There was a smile, a hint of something.

The guy leant forwards, 'You look out of place, man.'

'I always am.'

'Come here.'

He opened a concealed door in the black wall to the right of the mixing desk. Gavin took a final look at the band, drained his lager, and stepped behind.

There was a connecting corridor not much wider than an elevator and then another door opened to blinding white light. When the second door closed, the noise of the band was reduced to soft thuds and bass, the lead guitar and vocals relegated as though a dub-mix.

Gavin glanced around. He realised the space was the security hub. A handful of monitors showed the band and the crowd. Some of them were moving. The tempo must have changed. A dark blue quilted sleeping bag was rolled against one corner. The guy didn't appear to be a security guard. He wore black jeans and a t-shirt featuring the wavy lines of that Joy Division album cover that Gavin was aware of but had never played. He understood the transient nature of his generation, appropriating past culture without context. He was just as bad. Tonight's nostalgia gig. He wondered if one day there would be tribute tribute bands, the original acts further erased by sublimation, a kind of musical Chinese whispers.

The guy picked up a quarter-full bottle of Jack Daniels and held it for Gavin to take a swig. A large black and white poster dominated the back wall. A woman's head, eyes closed, short hair, lay supine on what appeared to be a tabletop. She held an African mask in one hand, *its* chin resting on the table with the remainder vertical, at an angle to the woman's face. Her pale features were as white as the mask was black.

'Man Ray's "Noire et Blanche". 1926.'

Gavin handed the bottle back. The whiskey warming. 'You like that, do you?'

'I like a bit of art, yeh.'

'Looks like you live here.'

'I have been. Won't be once the place is torn down. Nice Christmas, right? A mate of mine works here. Let me bed down for the duration. Seen you here before.'

Gavin reached for another swig. He wanted to be sure where the funny feeling came from.

'You're wet. Gig started thirty minutes ago. You must be soaked through.'

Gavin slipped off his jacket. The guy nodded and bent to roll out the sleeping bag.

IT WAS ABRUPT and needed. Afterwards, Gavin regarded the other's body objectively, outside of the roaring impulse of sex which often clouded decisions. There was neither meat nor muscle. *You need a good meal*, his grandmother would have said. The bones were as delineated as a shrink-wrapped carcass, his skin the colour of bone, too. What *had* been bone now lay flaccid. Gavin ran his tongue around the outside of his teeth.

'I call myself Blanche.'

'After the photograph?'

'You got no eyes, man? I'm practically albino.'

'Albino's have pink eyes, don't they?'

'Didn't say I *was* albino.'

A fan heater coursed a dry wind across their bodies, made scabs from semen.

'There's *A Streetcar Named Desire*, too. You know of that?'

'Sure I do. It's a play by Tennessee Williams. We did it at sixth form.'

'Blanche Dubois. Although if *I* depended on the kindness of strangers I'd never have lasted this long.'

Gavin understood the reference. It was Blanche's last line in the play before she was committed to the mental asylum. He stood up.

'Why'd you get homeless?'

'Things happen.'

Gavin shrugged. He knew he never had it so rough. On the monitors the stage was empty but the crowd hadn't dispersed. He realised the band must have finished before an encore began – he hadn't even noticed the music had ended but then realised the vibration that had accompanied their sex had stopped thrumming the concrete floor. There was something primal in the crowd's applause with the object of the adulation absent. He wondered whether an imaginary being held stage taking the applause, perhaps an old gold no longer worshipped who used stage breaks such as these to rekindle passions from mankind.

'They record these,' Blanche said. He stood and put a hand on Gavin's shoulder, then ran a finger down his spine. There was a wooden cabinet to the side of the monitors and he pulled it open. Inside, the shiny silver surfaces of DVDs looked like the sequins on Marilyn Monroe's dress when she sang 'Happy Birthday' for Kennedy. Gavin had a still from that performance on his bedroom wall.

'Here,' Blanche said. 'Take a few.'

He dug in at random, picked four or five, and pressed them into Gavin's hand.

'We all need a memory,' he said.

When Gavin returned to his clothes they had remained damp. Outside, the sky had cleared. A surprised autumnal frost glazed the rain-slick pavements. He had returned to the gig at the back of the crowd, just in time for the last number which appeared to be 'For the Distance'. It ended in a slow fade, the band leaving the stage as the sound engineer lowered the volume on their instruments. In the same manner the crowd dispersed, an antithesis to their reaction before the encore, as if they, too, had been muted. It was only outside that their voices returned, most praising the performance, convincing themselves that it might have been the real thing.

Gavin shivered in the cold. He clutched the DVDs in his pocket, the edges cutting a lifeline in his palm. He took a look back at the building before the doors closed. The band was back on stage, pulling out amplifier leads and packing up. Nancy Sinatra's 'The City Never Sleeps at Night' played out of the sound system. Gavin imagined Blanche must have had a hand in it. He wondered if he would see him again.

He returned home via the Somerset Road railway station. It was no longer in use and there were virtually no remains of the building and two platforms, other than a bricked up entrance on the Somerset Road bridge. Gavin had moved on to study architecture after English Lit. He nodded at the empty space, quickened his walk.

His parents were asleep. Quietly he unplugged their DVD player and took it upstairs where he had his own television. The DVDs were marked by date in green marker pen with no other distinguishing marks. The five he held spanned two years. He wondered if Blanche watched them overnight to relieve the loneliness. Perhaps he was kidding himself but he imagined Blanche spent most nights alone. It might explain why this random selection had lain on top.

One of the DVDs was unmarked, possibly unused. He put it to one side.

Keeping the volume on low he inserted the first disc. Gradually he identified Through The Sparks, a band who had just released an EP called *Coin Toss*. He wasn't keen on their music but then it wasn't what they were playing which stopped him turning off. The images weren't from the one monitor, as an official recording of the gig would be, but a composite from all the monitors. He sat back, had been too close to the TV. The effect was like viewing a black and white 3D image: the band on stage, overlaid by the audience, overlaid by an empty corridor with a flickering solitary light-bulb, overlaid by what must have been outside the front of the Tower Ballroom – occasional shadows crossing the image.

Gavin wondered to what purpose the recordings might be used. They were hardly acceptable bootlegs. He wondered about Blanche, about the Man Ray poster and the Williams' reference. Maybe Blanche was or had been an art student, experimenting with film. Yet this also didn't make sense, unless he had been living there for two years. So the DVDs were the product of someone else. He pressed eject and tried another.

The music was instantly recognisable. 'Follow the Leaders' by Killing Joke. Gavin had heard it often enough, blaring out of his parents' stereo. He peered closely at the images. The recording made no sense. From the age of the audience to the band it was clearly an old gig. He remembered his parents saying they had seen the band perform on one of their first dates. It was why they played the album so much. He did the arithmetic. The gig must have been 1981. Two years later they'd married and four years later, in 1987, he had been born. Gavin tried to focus on the empty corridor and the street outside the venue, finally muting the sound so the music didn't intrude. Those images couldn't be authentic. He could understand how the gig and possibly the audience might have been videoed in 1981 but during an essay he had written on city centre architecture he knew that CCTV hadn't been utilised by local government until 1987. One of those useless facts which the coincidental date of his birth had caused to be lodged in his memory.

The images and music on the other marked DVDs was unfamiliar to him. Yet again, the recordings seemed to belong in the past. Unless these were also tribute nights and the audiences had dressed the part. Gavin realised the dates on the DVDs might be irrelevant to the material, that they marked the date of transfer rather than the original recordings. On some of the obviously older footage the corridor and forecourt scenes must have been recently added. He rubbed his eyes. It was too late to examine them carefully, the multiple overlays were fogging his senses. He decided to put them aside, to review them in the morning, when he might see if there were similarities throughout the recordings. That might go someway to stop the mystery.

When he switched off the lights, the afterburn of the images mixed a loop on his retina. He fell asleep with the shadows in the corners.

MORNING MAKES THE night facile. Gavin woke and showered, his hands toying with the memory of Blanche before grabbing toast and heading to uni, barely nodding at the grunts of his parents.

Sunlight had yet to break the hold of the frost. He slid awhile. As students from all over coalesced towards the entrance of the building he found himself hanging back, a solitary swimmer. During lectures he kept his mind focussed on the architecture of John Madin, whose brutalist style dominated the Birmingham cityscape from the 1960s to the late 1970s. The Central Library, an inverted concrete ziggurat, had been described as *looking more like a place for burning books, then keeping them* by Prince Charles. Gavin held affection for these places, which isolated the soul.

Sometimes his thoughts turned to Blanche, yet like his Docs on the frost he found himself slipping away. The more he attempted to focus, the less likely the encounter seemed. When he arrived home he found his parents had returned the DVD player to the living room. His mother had attempted a *tidy-up*. The DVDs weren't immediately visible, but Gavin's main concern furrowed to the magazines under his bed which didn't appear to have been disturbed. Gradually, over the course of the next few days, with an essay on Madin due before the end of the semester, the episode at the Tower slow-dissolved. It was only on the 16th December, catching a news item about the 'last dance' at the Ballroom the night before, that Gavin decided to search for the DVDs and watch them again.

Applying his mother's logic, anything without a case needed a case. He flicked through his selection of movies – *Blue Velvet*, *The Matrix*, Andy Warhol's *Lonesome Cowboys* – and found nothing. Then he realised that without being played the discs couldn't be differentiated from CDs, and he located them on his racks in new jewel-cases amongst recordings his parents compiled to persuade his interests and demonstrate how relevant they remained.

He played each in turn, mesmerised again by the overlapping images, his brain playing catch-up with his vision. Similarities appeared in what he now considered to be stock footage. At the beginning of each recording a shadow fell across the entrance to the Ballroom, a grainy figure in a jacket which already appeared drenched by rain. Simultaneously, a white inverse-shadow moved along the corridor, pale as ivory, barely a blemish on the screen. This image repeated every fifteen minutes or so for the duration of the concert. The repetition suggesting intent by whoever spliced the images, imparting relevance. Gavin wondered whether the key to understanding the images was less in the music and the audience and more in the hidden motifs, like slow-motion subliminal messages.

Then he remembered the undated disc.

As he popped it into the player he heard a click as the boiler switched off. Nine p.m. He pulled a jumper from his bed and over his head as he sat cross-legged on the floor, anticipating winter's cold seeping in.

Immediately, this disc was different. There was no music, no shots of a band. The crowd danced against the flickering black and white of a disco. Silent film stills – some of which Gavin recognised from *Nosferatu*, *City Lights*, *Metropolis* – were juxtaposed over the central image. The corridor and exterior shots remained the same. Yet there was something else there, something he could barely catch. Pausing the film he reversed it back to the beginning and then edged it forwards again, frame by frame.

Interspersed between shots of the dancers, distorted by the film stills and what Gavin had come to class as stock footage, were entirely different images.

Naked bodies suspended from a ceiling track turned a figure eight over pots of what appeared to be steaming water. Gavin was familiar with the process of blanching. He had worked the summer months pre-uni in a frozen food factory. Scalding vegetables was a must for freezing. The action reminded him of the pencil factory in *Eraserhead,* the production-line movement carrying an inevitability which became mesmeric. He wondered what this - presumably student - short movie was doing spliced with the regular gig footage.

And then he returned again to the corridor and forecourt footage and saw a subtle change. The shadow on the forecourt moved forwards into the building and the white flash in the corridor turned a discernible face to the camera. There was no mistaking Blanche, and even less mistaking him.

THE NIGHT AIR blew cold.

He saw him walk twice around the Tower, trying to find a way in.

THE BODY STATIC

Tom Johnstone

EVER SINCE SHE'D heard the male voice say 'Mum', Christine often went to the shopping centre looking for a sign. Shoppers swarmed around the gleaming, bronze statue of a bull. There was nothing she wanted or needed to buy. It just made it easier to bear the tinnitus that sometimes crackled like radio static, voices creeping in as if someone was turning the dial, trying to find the right station.

The low, insistent murmur of the crowd was a carrier for the voices. 'This way,' one of them hissed. 'Over there,' another added. They were directing her towards the pavement that swooped down to the church and the rag market, shadowed by the big, oddly curved building with what looked like shining silver buttons all over it. She gazed down at the rows of market stalls in the distance, selling cheap fruit and vegetables, clothes and shoes.

'I can tell you why,' one of the voices said.

Christine looked up to see pale blue eyes staring at her. Unlike the others, this voice came from a thin, frail-looking body. The man was leaning against the balustrade above the steps. He glanced over his shoulder, as if checking who was watching or listening. It was a brief gesture, like a motorist doing a final blind-spot check, yet suggesting he was nervous, though there was nothing furtive in the eyes. They weren't a watery blue - more like stone.

'Why what?' she said.

'Why he died.'

Had he meant Jesus? Was this the preamble to some sort of approach in a recruitment drive for some church or other? Well, she already had one, and though it pained her to admit it, her faith hadn't helped her much. Then it struck her. He meant *her* son, not the Son of God. He wouldn't be the first spiritualist to offer her succour, if that's what he was, though she'd become less sceptical as the months had gone by and things had started happening. Nevertheless, she didn't need to pay a medium to hear Liam's voice through the static. She'd heard him say 'Mum', hadn't she? It must be him. Who else would say that?

'I know why he died,' she snapped back. 'Cheapskate firm didn't maintain the machines properly. No one there to watch over him. I couldn't exactly go with him to work, could I?'

That shut him up for a moment.

His unblinking eyes looked blurry through hers, which were wet. Her tinnitus was flaring up again, sounding not so much like radio static now but the crackle of snapping bones. He raised his twitchy hand up on to her shoulder. She shook it off. Or was it the other way round? She felt as if an invisible blow had struck her, reminding her of when she'd touched a low-voltage electric cattle fence for a dare as a kid. She felt angry too, at the cheek of it. Did he think she was an easy mark in her grief? Yet she listened when he said the next thing, though he still sounded like a con artist. She didn't send him away or walk off in disgust as she had been tempted to do.

'There are other reasons,' he said.

And he began telling her the story of the 'first people' whose god was in their image rather than the other way round. *Here we go,* she thought as he began. Yet as he went on, she began to listen. Maybe it was something about his voice, the way it carried despite its softness against the background hum and hubbub of the crowds walking to and fro past them, ignoring them but giving them space as if there was a bubble around them.

'They shared energy with the world,' he said, 'lightning, rain, sunlight, fire. But they hoarded it. Used it to create effects…'

He ushered her away from the wall, careful not to touch her

this time. She could feel something crackling against her arm where his hand approached it, repelling it, like when you put two magnets together the wrong way round. When they were clear of the wall, he swung round with a power and force she didn't think possible in such a strip of a man. With a sudden, flicking gesture, he threw his hands outwards.

She saw the crowd of shoppers and errant teenagers parting in a wave, as though another reverse magnetism was driving them away, another force of repulsion. She heard a loud crash and a sharp cry, also the tinkle of breaking glass somewhere. Someone shouted 'The fuck?' A slab had tumbled onto the paving stones below, its edges crumbling, as were those of the wall it had left behind, fault lines appearing in its brickwork. The low drone of humanity had given way to a more hysterical babble. Someone said, 'Fuck's sake… They've only just rebuilt all this! Typical. Bloody lucky no one was standing near that…'

He led her away from the confusion, which seemed to be spreading to some of the shops and restaurants near the steps. Waiters and shop assistants guided customers out of the buildings, whose lights were all off. Almost in tears, a woman said, 'Just got showered with glass from that bulb!' A waitress was placating her, pressing a dressing to a head wound, saying something about faulty wiring melting and short-circuiting.

'How did you know…?' she said. 'Did you…?'

'Don't be impressed,' he said. 'It's just death speeded up.'

And he looked like death warmed up, she thought, even paler than he had before.

'Their gods took the life-force from them and put it in dead matter,' he said, continuing from where he left off in his crazy creation story. 'Now they would have to win it back from nature. Now God lived outside them. It took them thousands of years to gain mastery over the natural forces, but it was only death speeded up…'

He paused again, struggling to get his breath back, as though something – the telling of the tale or his little magic show – had knocked it out of him. Finally, his breathing became more regular.

He continued: 'Nobody was to blame. The whole of their knowledge was based on a mistake – a mistake they had inherited and come to know as truth. It was like seeing the first people reanimated as machines, engines of separation and damage.'

Christine glanced back to where the crowds were milling around almost as if nothing had happened, carefully but automatically avoiding the area around the broken bit of wall, now taped-off almost as if by magic – like the force that had shattered it. She didn't know if anyone had been hurt but it wouldn't have surprised her if people had carried on regardless, even if someone was lying there crushed under a fallen slab. Maybe that was unfair. Somehow, in this selfish, grasping world, people often helped each other too, didn't they?

'It all just went on and on and got uglier and worse,' he was saying. 'Nobody was to blame. Maybe everyone makes the same mistake, and the first people were just like their god or their god was just like them. It doesn't matter now, does it?' He sounded almost irritable.

Well, I didn't ask you to tell me all this! she almost said. But instead she asked, 'So what will happen now?'

The thin stranger looked at her, his stone-blue eyes bitter with experience.

'Your guess is as good as mine,' he said.

'AND THEN WHAT?' Sean asked.

Christine was staring out of the bus window through the smear she'd made on the glass. The gap in the condensation just showed the rain-soaked, run-down shops on the Bristol Road, like that one that claimed it sold motor spares yet sold second-hand furniture that looked as though it would fall apart as soon as you touched it – like she had said that wall had done, when her latest conman had looked at it. Sean was starting to worry about his mother. Lately he'd even been wondering if it was safe to leave the kid with her.

Ellen had listened with rapt attention as her nan had recounted the story the man she'd met in the Bullring had told her. Hardly surprising, as it had sounded like a fairy tale. All that stuff about gods taking people's 'life-force' and putting it in dead matter! Mind you, that was how he sometimes felt when he looked at the 'affordable housing' he'd helped to build near Cannon Hill Park. Affordable for whom? Not him, with his 'life-force' sold for a pittance that barely covered the basics. Still, he could console himself with the thought that maybe some of it was locked up inside all the places he'd worked, haunting the bricks and mortar. Come to think of it, he wondered if his brother's 'life-force' was still stuck in the machinery that had chewed him up and spat him out.

What was he thinking? He was getting as bad as her, letting cranks con her with false hope of word from Liam. It was up to Sean to look out for her, warn her away from them, not join in with her gullibility.

'What then?' he said. 'What did he do then?'

It was hard to get her attention when she was fussing over her granddaughter.

'Did the man do more magic, Nan?'

He sighed.

'No, bab,' Christine said, 'he just … went.'

'Went up in a puff of smoke, did he?' Sean said with the sour ghost of a smile.

'You rotten so-and-so.' She scolded him. 'Taking the mick out of me like that!'

'Well, you've got to admit it sounds a bit… Him knocking a wall over without even touching it!'

'It was in the *Post* – and the *Mail*.'

'Don't mean *he* did it, though, Mum. You don't really believe all that, do you – what you said…?' His voice sounded almost desperate. He was serious, though there was a hysterical mirth in his voice. He wanted her to laugh it all off, agree with him that the man she met was a fool and a charlatan.

'Sean,' she said, 'his hand…' She moved closer to him so she could whisper in his ear, maybe because he'd got the hump about her scaring Ellen or putting daft ideas in her head. The little one had big ears and was craning her neck to hear, anyway. 'It gave me a 'lectric shock, Sean... You know like what you get sometimes when you pick up a polyester jumper?'

'Static electricity?' he murmured. She really was losing it. He looked at Ellen, imagining accidents or abductions made possible by her grandmother becoming too immersed in her obsession.

'Only this was stronger,' she continued.

He thought of that villain with lightning coming out of his head from his old Spiderman comics, the ones he used to let Liam read.

His kid brother.

No. Don't cry, not on the bus.

It had rumbled on through town, leaving the grimy Victorian terraces and run-down shops of the Pershore Road behind, and was approaching Longbridge's newly redeveloped industrial wasteland.

He stared out of the window again, so neither his mother nor daughter would see his weakness. But all he could see was the college building they'd put up on the ruins of the car plant. It had tiles in different shades of blue-green. Teal, that's what it was called, wasn't it? Whatever it was called, it was an insult, Sean reckoned. There was another one round the corner, done up in different shades of pink, like coral – 'The Factory'. He wondered how many people *that* 'Factory' employed.

'Sean?' Christine said. 'You all right, bab?'

He smeared the back of his hand over his eyes and turned towards his mother, nodding.

'Anyway, d'you wanna know what he said after the wall collapsed? He said, "Don't be impressed – it's just death speeded up"!'

He looked back at the garish new college. His father's sudden, rapid decline after Longbridge went under reminded him of walls he'd seen, crumbling under the weight of ivy sucking all the moisture out of the brickwork through its roots. Trouble was, if you let this go on for long enough, ripping the ivy away would cause the wall to collapse. By now the parasitic plant had been holding the damn thing up! Maybe the same thing was happening to his mother's mind, after losing both husband and son in such close succession.

'But seriously, Mum… You don't really think…'

'I don't know, Sean. I really don't know.'

It must be their stop soon. The soporific rumbling of the bus's engine had sent Ellen off to sleep, her little head slumped against his shoulder, her face like she was new-born again. How could he protect her against the future that was emerging, one where plastic palaces beckoned, ready to collapse like houses of cards as soon as you entered.

'I think I know what he's trying to tell me,' his mother whispered, taking great care not to wake the child.

'Who? That man who spun you the yarn in the Bullring?'

'No, Sean. Liam—'

'Liam?' he repeated with a frown of impatience.

'Sshh!' she hissed. 'Don't wake her! Listen… I think he wants me to do something about all this - make sure what happened to him don't keep happening!'

He sighed. She was getting worse. He felt bad for thinking this but he had to put his child first, didn't he? This would be another blow to her, he knew, but he was grieving too and, though he had a duty to look after his mother, that obligation no longer extended to letting her look after Ellen. He'd have to find someone else.

He began shifting in his seat, trying to disentangle himself and relinquish his role as his daughter's makeshift pillow.

'Right,' he said. 'It's our stop soon. Come on, Ellen, darling. Better wake up, eh, bab…'

The child was stirring, groaning into unwilling wakefulness.

'Oh, Sean,' his mother said. 'D'you still need me to…'

'Eh?'

'Next week? Ellen?'

'Oh, er… No, should be all right after all, Mum.'

With a hiss of hydraulics the doors opened and her son carried Ellen off the bus, holding her tightly as if shielding the child from her grandmother.

WAS SHE BEING paranoid? She thought again about that moment and decided she wasn't. He hadn't wanted her to babysit after that, though she'd offered enough times, until she decided she wasn't going to humiliate herself any more. If he wanted her to help out, he was perfectly capable of asking, wasn't he?

Anyway, she had plenty of other things to keep her busy now: the letters to MPs and councillors, the leaflets, the petitions. It helped to take her mind off the ringing in her ears that buzzed like a Geiger counter sometimes, though this also made it hard to concentrate, especially when the voices started coming through, one voice in particular.

'Mum!'

More insistent, almost frustrated, irritated even! But she was doing what he wanted, wasn't she? Maybe not enough. Maybe she needed to redouble her efforts, step up the campaign.

'Mum… MUM!'

At least one of her sons wanted something from her, even if it was the dead one.

It wasn't that Sean was avoiding her. Quite the reverse. It was starting to do her head in that he kept asking if she was okay. But whenever she mentioned her granddaughter, he got tongue-tied, shifty almost.

The last time he'd enquired after her wellbeing, she'd snapped at him that she could look after herself thank you very much, and she hadn't heard back from him since that. Maybe she should ring him back and apologise, but she had her pride to think of, didn't she? Whenever she thought of doing it, she held back, thinking *If he won't trust me with Ellen, why should I care how* he *feels?*

The doorbell shrilled, tearing through her thoughts and her tinnitus.

She went through possibilities like the children's story book she sometimes read to Ellen. Used to read, more like. The one where the *Tiger Comes to Tea*.

It couldn't be Liam, because he was dead; and to be honest, the state he'd been in after the accident ('Accident?' Corporate manslaughter more like), it was just as well. It couldn't be Sean, because he always rang ahead, and he hadn't been round much lately, anyway. It couldn't be the man from the Bullring because he didn't have her address and, well, that story in the *Post* about the fellow found near Digbeth all burnt up except for his hands… There'd been talk of spontaneous internal combustion, and though she didn't know for sure it was him, she had her suspicions.

It stands to reason, she thought. *If he wasn't going to go around doing the kinds of things he'd done that day, all that pent-up 'life-force' had to go somewhere. Might get turned inwards.*

Looking through the frosted glass of the front door, she saw it couldn't be any of them. Though the face and figure were a featureless blur, the shape of the person and the halo of blonde hair suggested a woman. Her ears rang with the aftershock of the doorbell. Who could it be then? Market research? Double glazing? Life insurance? She steeled herself to ward off whoever it was. She shouldn't have come to the door. She could have pretended she wasn't in but too late now. The caller could probably see Christine's own indistinct image from the other side.

As if to confirm this, the doorbell shrilled again.

She opened the door. The woman waiting behind it came into sudden brutal focus, the frosted glass no longer filtering the sharp contours of a young face that somehow wasn't as pretty as its owner thought, the mouth fixed into a smile crammed with white teeth, a request to come in 'for a moment' coming from between them.

'Mrs Brady?' said the woman, then added without waiting for a reply. 'We won't take a moment of your time.'

'And who might you be?' she asked.

'We represent Morton's Mouldings,' the woman smiled, deftly side-stepping the question of her own identity.

'Oh. Right. Wait a minute… What d'you mean "We"?'

When the man appeared from the blind spot behind the door frame, seeming as wide as he was tall, face pink and fleshy, crowned by straw-coloured fuzz, she thought of refusing but it was too late for that. She'd already agreed to let the woman in and didn't feel she could go back on that just because she hadn't bargained on another person appearing.

Reluctantly, she ushered them both in. Before she knew it, the large man was in the lounge of the small flat, standing at the mantelpiece picking up and examining the framed photo of Ellen as if he were an overgrown child in a sweetshop. Except he wasn't the child here, and she'd have told Ellen off for touching stuff that didn't belong to her.

'Put her down!' said the woman, with a brittle laugh of mock-reproof. Slowly, he did so. 'Your granddaughter, is she? Ain't she a peach...'

Christine said nothing.

'Down to business,' said the woman, her smile flickering off then back on again like a faulty lightbulb. 'Morton's Mouldings understands your concerns,' she went on, as if reciting a prepared script. 'However, we are disappointed that you have chosen to tarnish the reputation of a company that has done all it can to turn things around since your son so regrettably passed away... Sorry for your loss by the way. We are prepared to offer a very generous compensation package to yourself. However, we must satisfy ourselves of certain assurances from yourself that you will... How shall I put this? Keep mum.'

'Keep mum?' Christine repeated.

She looked at the man standing silently by the mantelpiece, huge hand resting next to the picture of Ellen, dwarfing the child's face.

'Mum!'

So that was what Liam had been trying to tell her. Maybe he hadn't been trying to encourage her to speak up but instead warning her to stay silent.

'You don't need to sign anything at this stage! A hand-shake'll do.'

The woman's manicured right hand shot out, pale wrist bared by the receding sleeve of her grey suit jacket, the fingers stiffly cupped to receive that of Christine, who suddenly wondered what had happened to her tinnitus. All this had certainly taken her mind off it. She knew it hadn't gone though.

It had moved.

And as she felt the crackling in the hand she was lifting, she knew where to. Smoke and screams rose, as if the young woman were shaking hands with a red-hot sandwich toaster. Christine considered another possibility: perhaps Liam had been trying to urge her to use actions instead of words.

THE BRIGHT EXIT

Sarah Doyle

is never far from here, always just over
a shoulder or caught from the corner of

an eye. There is no atlas, no compass,
no pocket horizon, nor sextant to map

the way. It is unnavigable: nebulously
edged and infinitely strange, a face seen

before but not placed, music heard beyond
hearing. The bright exit is an embrace

for the disappearing; a gesture, almost a
wave in the liminal space between sleep

and wakefulness when the night comes
on and we crest the peripheries, slipping

through the cracks of light and dark and
hoping - ever hoping - to leave behind

our mark.

YOU GIVE ME FEVER

Paul Edwards

IT DIDN'T TAKE long to find her. Gossips in shabby pubs directed me to Nash House where a loose-tongued neighbour disclosed Mary's flat number. I thanked the neighbour, then took the lift up to the second floor and drifted along a corridor to her pale, unpainted door.

Winter was loosening its grip on me – warmth and sensation spread through my frame as I rapped at the letterbox. I tugged my coat collar, suddenly feeling nauseous and out of breath. Without warning, the door jolted open and a security chain snapped taut.

'Please,' I said as I placed my hand against the door to prevent it from closing. 'Please, Mary. I just want to talk.'

A strangled cry came from within the flat and I wondered if the shock might be enough to kill her. Then I took my hand away and the door slammed on me. 'Mary? Mary ... *please*.'

I stopped calling to her after a while and tilted my head forward so that it rested against the door. I stood very still, breathing hard against wood. In my head I saw dirty creases in the air, black lines moving toward me. I smiled briefly, emptily to myself. Then the door jerked open and I seized the doorframe to avoid falling at her feet.

She'd gone back inside but had taken the chain off its hook. I shuffled forward, scuffing the soles of my shoes on a mat as I entered. There were some wooden steps leading up to a room that was just out of sight. I took them carefully, the treads creaking and complaining beneath me, my hand gripping a loose rail as I ascended.

I edged into the sitting room just as the old woman was easing herself into an armchair next to the window. I caught a glimpse of myself in the glass and, as usual, convinced myself it was him looking in on things, appealing in vain for acceptance and companionship – a distant echo of my own pitiable existence in this world.

Her Gorgon stare fixed me and I quickly turned away, trying to seek a trace of the familiar within the room. Weirdly, I thought of the pornography that Aiden had written about – stuff she used to make him watch – but there was none of that here. Perhaps it was stored in a drawer somewhere, or perhaps it was long gone, destroyed in a fit of panic when the authorities had pounced. As my gaze flickered to a mug on the table beside her, I found myself being transported back in time to the house in Digbeth. I recalled paisley wallpaper. Tall windows shuttered against the sunlight. That splintered door beneath the stairs. The half-formed things in jars in the cellar…

'Well this is a surprise,' she said, interrupting my thoughts, squirming in her seat as I perched myself on the sofa. 'Didn't think I'd see you again. Thought I'd found a place to escape everything. Guess I thought wrong.' She rubbed her eye vigorously with a fist. 'The date's not lost on me, you know. If I'd have known you were coming, I might've got something in. We could have had a celebration.' She laughed mirthlessly at her words.

The air was stifling and uncomfortable. It seemed to get hotter with each passing second. A film of sweat broke out across my forehead as the four walls shimmered mirage-like around me. I thought of taking my coat off but I didn't want to forget it and leave it here. I wished I was outside, in the cold, anesthetised by winter once more.

'Why this year?' Her grey eyes glittered with distrust. 'You want answers? Is that it?' Her expression mutated into a maniacal mask of contempt. 'We breathed life into you, Martin. *Both* of you. But it was too much … especially for your father's wretched conscience.' She laughed another humourless laugh, then waved her hand dismissively as she tugged her cardigan around her shoulders. 'It wasn't that I preferred Aiden, of course. I just wasn't allowed to keep you both. Perhaps in hindsight I made the wrong decision, considering...' She pulled in a breath. 'Still, you were given to a good home, right? Given to people who accepted you for what you are. Probably better off where...'

'I don't want answers.' I shook my head, cutting her off in mid-sentence, sweat flicking from my face. 'This isn't about me.'

'Then what is this about?' Her cheekbones twitched as she gripped the armrests and straightened in her chair, her wizened fragility disappearing before my eyes. 'There's nothing for you here. There never was!'

I noticed a picture on top the bookcase opposite me. One that wasn't grey and made up of flecks.

I got to my feet and snatched it up, studied it for a while.

He looked about fifteen. A shy, strained smile creased his feral face.

'After his father died, he was all I had.' She nodded at it, her voice drained of emotion. 'It was his madness, not mine. It always was.'

I closed my eyes and listened to my heart pound like a jackhammer inside my chest.

I remembered reading about the diary that the detectives had found in his flat: a vicious, hate-filled thing that became more violent and rambling as it went on, frequently name-dropping Mary and all her terrible misdemeanours.

I opened my eyes, sighed and stood the picture back up on the bookcase.

She was talking but I wasn't listening any more. I could smell formaldehyde again. Was opening the splintered door beneath the stairs...

I wished we'd stayed down there now. Wished we'd never been made to leave that womb of dust and darkness.

Above all else, I wished we'd never been separated, Aiden and I.

He was the only one who could have known what it's like to be me.

Mary's voice was raised now, her words betraying her madness; a madness that became Aiden's reality, and filled him with a fever that there could be no recovery from, no cure for…

'…not a child, no. More like a sick animal, a sick dog. Shitting and pissing over the carpet. I caught him trying to fuck a duffel coat in his room. He wasn't right. We should have aborted before we even attempted to…' She shook her head viciously. 'He was filled with such uncertainty and self-pity. Took after his father for that, I suppose. And the ironic thing was, they both went the same way, knotting their hospital bedding into nooses and then leaving me here to face a barrage of unwanted attention *all on my own.*' Her wizened claws bunched into fists in her lap. 'And the business with the whores … those three women *he* butchered that night, validating my belief that he was a mistake, that we should never have made him.'

I sat down and stared at her wild-eyed form. Remembered the newspapers, the TV reports, the widespread horror and condemnation of him.

'…and he wrote it was *me,*' she prodded at herself with a finger. 'The *poison* of my body and mind, infecting *his* world. Couldn't he see that I was trying to *protect* him? Toughening him up so that he could grow into the man that he needed to be?'

Spit exploded from her mouth as she gloated about having never been incriminated or sectioned, but I was tuning out of her paranoid diatribe.

Survival through denial. Mary was an adept.

I was burning up, sweat trickling down my brow to soak and sting my eyes. I glanced round and saw the radiator beside me, half-hidden by the sofa. I stroked it with my knuckles, then gripped it with a troubled frown on my face. Cold. I breathed and saw vapour, yet my body was bathed in sweat.

I stared at Mary, clouds of mist escaping from her lips as she glared at me with eyes of ice and fire, then allowed my gaze to slide across to the figure framed in the windowpane beside her. 'It wasn't your fault,' I whispered, and offered him the scantest of smiles. 'Not really.'

I often think it should have been me. Not him.

And the guilt never goes away, no matter how often I try telling myself that it hadn't been my fault, that I'd been too young and powerless to have ever been able to change anything.

I spoke then, and the words that tumbled from my lips were distant and unreal, like when your sinuses are blocked and your own voice sounds like a ghost chattering in your ear: 'I have a love in me that you can scarcely imagine.'

I found my feet, disgust and panic exploding across her face as I took two steps toward her. I sank to my knees and stretched my arms out wide.

'Hold me, Mother.' That made her wince, and I laughed meekly. 'It's all I've ever dreamed of.'

She tried to bat me away but I wrapped my arms around her and pressed her close to me. In a bid to connect to something, anything, I craned my head forward and focussed on the mug beside her. My sullen reflection rippled on the surface of her tea, gaunt and feral-looking in the pale-brown liquid. Except it wasn't my face; it was *his* face, getting clearer and stronger all the time, like a photograph in developing fluid. And he was grinning and nodding his head with approval as I squeezed.

She began to squirm and thrash but I hugged her fiercer, tighter, enveloping her. My left hand gripped the wrist of my right arm, squeezing with all my might until I heard an animal sound escape her throat and a bone snap inside her.

I kept hugging and twisting until the tears and the sweat streamed down my face and my eyes were filled with bright, hallucinatory patterns. I swallowed a scream. I ground my teeth together. I squeezed even harder. In time I let go and she sagged like a doll in my arms. My head felt as though it was on fire. I stood unsteadily, bumping into the wall as she slipped off her armchair to fall in a heap on the floor. She looked deformed and twisted on the carpet, like something she and Dad might have conceived in their make-shift laboratory before the police and

Social Services intervened. I kicked her. She didn't move.

I turned, walked out the room and trudged downstairs with sweat dripping from my tired, trembling body. I stumbled along the corridor and pushed through the communal door into the courtyard outside. The beads of sweat on my forehead joined and became trickling rivulets of coldness down my cheeks. I scurried out the main gates and kept walking without aim or purpose until I'd stopped perspiring and my heart had slowed to its normal rate. Soon winter's chill reached my bones and I was so desperately glad. I could see the cold again as dirty creases in the air, black lines moving toward me. Something flickered in the corner of my vision. As I whirled and focussed I beheld a shape twitching upon the surface of a shadowy shop window.

We were cut from the same cloth – we'd always looked similar – and so it's easy to imagine he's here, still around, and I'm not alone in this world.

'Happy birthday.'

The words left me in a plume of vapour. Our strained smiles slipped from our faces as the illusion of him began to fade. Then I turned and hurried on, into the anesthetising cold, eager not to feel anything but numb again.

THE OTHER SIDE

Lynda E. Rucker

A FEW MONTHS after Adam disappeared, my phone started ringing and blinking his name at me. I snatched at it and knocked it off the table so when I finally scrambled it back into my hands and accepted the call it was with a string of swears before I gasped, 'Adam! Where the hell are you?'

There was a moment of silence. Then a woman's voice said awkwardly, 'Sorry, Mark, this is Lauren. Adam's sister.'

I was speechless with rage and sorrow and she had to know it. 'I'm sorry,' she said again when I didn't reply, 'I didn't think. I just saw your name in his phone and I...'

I had met her a couple of times, a washed-out woman with a face that was somehow pudgy and hard at the same time. Adam had never got on with her and I got the sense she didn't like me either. I'm pretty sure she thought we were lovers but it was never like that with me, or with Adam and me. Anyway, Adam only fucked people he never saw again. Not that I was ever going to tell her that.

'I'm sorry,' Lauren said yet again, and that was probably more than the total number of times she'd ever apologised for anything in her life up to that point. 'I didn't know who else to call.'

'About what?'

'It's Adam. I've seen him.'

'What? Where? Did you go to him?' I was already shrugging into a jacket but she said, 'No, no, it isn't like that. Exactly.'

'What exactly is it like?' I said, biting off the ends of the words.

She was silent for a beat. 'Can you just meet me?' she said. 'I can't really talk about it over the phone.'

IN FACT, LAUREN and Adam were twins, which made the fact that I'd never met two siblings who were more different from one another even stranger. That she chose to meet me in one of the most depressing cafes I've ever had the displeasure of visiting made me rethink that. That was all Adam: eating in terrible cafes, living in grim bedsits, drinking in pubs that hung the St. George's Cross and smelt of urine. He took a pleasure in it, you see. It was maybe his only source of pleasure. 'Let's go on a picnic,' he'd say, and two hours later you'd find yourself sitting with a spread in the middle of some godawful housing estate surrounded by feral children and their chavvy barely-not-children-themselves parents. By 'you' of course I mean 'me.' I was generally terrified in those situations. Adam was exuberant. He had this idea that you could find the most profound beauty, even the sacred, in the ugliest places. You had to train yourself to look for it, he said.

It was what we feared, of course, those of us who knew him best. That he'd finally looked in the wrong place, or with the wrong person.

Lauren and I exchanged pleasantries, as though either of us cared how the other was doing. The waitress brought us cups of tea that tasted like they'd been made with the dishwater. Lauren seemed as reluctant to broach our purpose in being there as I was anxious to hear what she had to say. We sat for several minutes in silence until she finally said, 'I saw him from the motorway.'

'What?'

'It was just outside of the city,' she said. 'Out near that stretch of abandoned factories.'

I said, 'What?' again, more emphatically this time.

And then, 'Did you stop? How was he? Did you talk to him? How did he look?'

'He looked—' She couldn't speak for several seconds. She lifted her face up to me and I was surprised to see her eyes shimmering with tears. 'Beatific.'

I wouldn't have thought Lauren would come up with a word

like that. But it told me everything I needed to know. I was angry at her for wasting my time but I told myself it wasn't her fault.

'I mean,' she said, reading my silence, 'it wasn't some kind of hallucination. It was him, solid as you are right now. He was there, he was really real. I couldn't stop, of course, but I got off and went back down the A road and I couldn't see him. I got out and looked for him. I walked up through the shrubs and he wasn't there any more. I didn't know what to do. So I wrote a note for him. I weighted it with a rock and left it there and I went and told the police what I'd seen and now I'm telling you.'

There was a pleading quality to her voice that angered me. She expected something from me, reassurance maybe, but I wasn't going to give it to her. I drank my tea in silence for a few minutes. Finally I said, 'What do you want me to do?'

'I don't know,' Lauren said. 'You two were – I mean, you were closest to him. I thought it might mean something to you. Or you'd know what to do. Mark, he's alive.'

She said it with such conviction that I almost believed her. How I longed to believe her. To think Adam might come walking through the door at that very moment with that disarming grin of his, what a joke he'd played on us – but that would never happen, because Adam wasn't the joke-playing type. If Adam was gone, then Adam was dead – that was the four-letter word we wouldn't say to one another. It felt like a betrayal to say it even to myself, but it was true.

'Will you just go and see?' Lauren said. 'Will you?'

I don't know why I said I would. To get away from that awful cup of tea and out of that awful cafe and far from that awful sister of his. To get her to stop looking at me with those pleading eyes.

Because it was just the sort of place that Adam *would* be, only she couldn't possibly know that about him.

THEY WERE BORN, Adam said to me once, trying to kill one another. Her cord around his neck nearly strangled him.

As soon as they were free of the womb they'd been forced to share, they set out doing their best to ignore one another, and had done for three decades. I knew Adam for a dozen years, and for the first few, I didn't even know he had a sister. There were just the two of them, too, no other family. Their parents were dead, in circumstances Adam would never discuss with me, and they'd grown up in care. Adam never talked about his family, his childhood, or his personal life at all, really.

We'd met at a gig. I don't really remember much about the night because I was drunk. I was also having a fight with my then -girlfriend, who stormed out at some point. Adam and I were drinking and talking and laughing and then, much later, we were sitting on a disused railway bridge with our feet dangling, smoking fags, and Adam started telling me about something he called the edgelands. He said it was something people had known about for a long time, since the Industrial Revolution first created such places. It was a woman named Marion Shoard who had dreamt up the word 'edgelands' but he said he believed it had been given to her.

'What do you mean, "given to her"?' I asked.

Adam said, 'The edgelands are liminal places. Where you can tap into other things.'

I didn't know what liminal meant, either. I was starting to feel seriously out of my depth.

I said, 'What's that?'

Adam said quietly, 'Thresholds. Not here or there. We're in one now.'

I'd been slumped against the struts of the bridge but when Adam said that I sat up suddenly, feeling clear-headed and scared. Adam went on. 'Anything can happen in the edgelands. They're blighted places – and that makes them magical. Ruined places. Ruined people. That's what interests me.'

We kept on sitting there for a long time and shared a joint between us. Nothing like Adam was talking about happened to us though. I got back home around dawn – I still lived with my parents in those days – and later on my girlfriend rang me and demanded to know whether I was queer, going off with that bloke like I did. I said as I'd remembered it she'd been the one who left. She said I was dodging the question. Then she broke up with me.

Funny that I don't even remember her name.

After that I started running into Adam all the time. We'd see each other at gigs and then later we started making more deliberate plans together. It wasn't until a couple of years later though, when we got a flat together, that he talked about the edgelands again.

Adam used to tell me about his dreams. I know that makes him sound like a tedious fucker, but somehow the way Adam described them, they were always gripping. I used to wonder if maybe he was lying because nobody could remember their dreams that well, or have dreams that were that compelling. That was another thing about Adam: he was one of the most honest people I've ever known. Sure, he didn't open up much but if he told you something, it was bound to be the truth. I don't think he was capable of saying something that wasn't.

One morning, a couple of months after we'd first got the flat, I was sitting bleary-eyed on the couch with a bowl of Weetabix and he came and sat next to me. He started talking to me and I felt vaguely annoyed because I was hungover and I had the feeling this was going to be a long one and unlike Adam, I wasn't unemployed. I had to get to my job at Wax Me Records.

'Do you remember when we first met? When I took you out to that railway bridge and I told you about the edgelands?'

I said no, because I was hoping that would discourage him. Of course, being Adam, he didn't miss a beat.

'They're the places that aren't city but aren't countryside any longer either,' he said. 'Where you find disused railways and abandoned factories and burnt-out cars. Some of them are poison. Toxic. Wastelands. Only they aren't waste – well, they are, but that's the point. They aren't anything, they're lost places. Last night I dreamed I was in the edgelands.

'I was walking through tall grass and muck. I knew the muck was poisonous and I could feel it sucking at my shoes as I went. It was so real, but it was like something was telling me to keep going. I was moving toward these rusted metal girders in the distance. It seemed important that I reach them even though I didn't know why.'

I said, 'I'm late for work.' I started putting on my Vans.

'Wait,' Adam said, and put a hand on my arm. That stopped me. Adam never touched me. He wasn't a touching-you kind of guy. 'Listen,' he said. 'You can go in a minute. I need to tell someone about this.' I was shocked to see he had tears in his eyes. 'I kept moving but it was getting harder to walk. I kept slipping and when I looked down what I saw underfoot were – things like little children's hands, floating in the muck and all twisted up with bits of barbed wire. I started pulling them out, like I thought the children might still be attached and I could save them, but it was just their hands. At first I couldn't work out where I'd gone wrong. I had gone to that place looking for something beautiful. And then as I went on, the severed hands started seeming beautiful to me. At the same time, I knew that was wrong, that something had gone wrong in me to think that. And then I finally reached the girders and they weren't metal at all, they were made of flesh.

'It was like all the suffering that made the edgelands had vomited up these things. The harder I looked for something beautiful the more horrific it all became until I couldn't tell the difference any longer.' His voice cracked. 'I'm scared, Mark. I feel like I took a wrong turn somewhere. I'm afraid of what I'm capable of.'

I said, 'I don't understand what you're trying to tell me.'

'Neither do I.' He retreated then. His hand dropped, and he got up from the sofa. 'I'm sorry. Go to work.'

'Look, if you need me—'

'I don't need anybody,' he said, and he walked out of the front door of the flat and slammed it behind him. I went after him, right away, but he was nowhere to be seen. It was like he could vanish at will, even in those days.

WHEN I GOT back to my flat after meeting Lauren, my girlfriend

Polly was waiting there for me. She hadn't properly moved in but she had a key and was there at least as often as she was at her own place.

She was sitting on the sofa watching something that she used the remote to stop as soon as I came in the room. She said, 'We need to talk.'

I said, 'Oh for fuck's sake.' That wasn't the best response, was it? But it wasn't just because those four words strung together manage to be ominous, tedious and clichéd all at once. It was the snap back into my everyday life and the realisation of how little of the present I was in, and how little I cared about it. I wondered how long that had been going on, but in an idle way.

I said, 'I can't talk right now.'

Polly said, 'Why not?' and I didn't say anything, and she said, 'That's the whole point, Mark. This *is* the talk. That you don't tell me anything, you don't let me in. You keep me on a need to know basis. It's like I'm not really a part of your life.'

Polly was a beautiful girl. She had honey-coloured hair and skin that just glowed and she liked sex. She was agreeable and easy to be around and she was the kind of girl your friends like, too, so that when you broke up with her, mates would all think you were mad and you wouldn't know how to explain it because how do you explain absence? You break up with people – at least people you'd been with for a while, like Polly and me – *because* of something, something one of you does or says, or because you have some profound disagreement over whether or not to get married or have kids or buy a flat. Or those are the reasons you give anyway. Because you can't say to people *it was because something wasn't there.* What, they would ask. Love? Commitment? Sex? Affection? No, none of those things. Passion? That wasn't right either; that described something so fleeting and what I was reaching for was the opposite of fleeting.

'What is it?' Polly said. 'Is it because you were single for so long? Do you just not know how to let someone into your life?' She reached out for me, to touch me, but her hand fell away into nothingness.

THERE WAS SOMETHING I hadn't told Lauren. I hadn't told anyone, not the police, not any of mine and Adam's mutual friends. I told myself that it didn't matter because it wasn't relevant.

I got a letter from Adam a day or two after he was last seen. No, it isn't right to call it a letter. The envelope was addressed to me in his handwriting. Adam had never sent me anything in his life, and as soon as I received it I rang him up to talk to him about it, to ask him why he'd sent it to me and what it meant, but of course there was no answer. At the time I didn't think anything of it. It was only when a day and another day passed and I couldn't reach him that I began to realise that something was wrong and, by then, other people had too.

The other strange thing was that when I received it, I hadn't seen or spoken to him for a while. We weren't on the outs, but Adam and I would go through periods where we'd just be out of touch for a while, busy with our own lives, and then we'd come back into contact. But he'd never made contact like this before.

When I opened the envelope, a single slip of paper fell out and drifted to the floor. I picked it up, and this is what I read:

This dream came in the spring when I was nineteen – a time when I felt emotionally confused and lonely. I was standing among a group of people in a railway station, on an outdoor platform. It was early evening and the air was cool. The people with me weren't strangers, but I didn't know them well. They might have included friends and colleagues. They were bickering and pacing, like any group of travellers waiting for a late train. The atmosphere was sullen. I felt out of place, though it was a situation I was used to.

By chance, I glanced across the platform. Through the bars of a luggage rack, I saw a young man of my own age. He was sitting alone on a large suitcase with his hands spread beside him, gazing at the tracks. His face was pale. His hair was somewhere between brown and blond. There was a quiet stillness about him. He didn't look like anyone I knew in real life. I thought I knew why he was alone.

The evening light seemed brighter there or at least less cluttered. I picked up my suitcase and crossed the platform to sit beside him. He looked at me. Our hands touched, held. No one from the group I'd left came after me. The world behind us ceased to exist. We waited, together, for the train that was going in the opposite direction to my planned journey. It grew darker on the platform, but the lamplight watched over us.

Still more embarrassing than recalling this dream is recalling that I woke in tears, gripped by a virtual infatuation that hurt for days. It wasn't an erotic dream; it was a dream about being in love, which is much scarier and harder to make compromises with. And it wasn't just a dream about 'sexuality' either: the image of crossing over, of changing direction, had other meanings which I'm still learning about. Really important dreams don't come true; you go on dreaming them, and they change you.

And at the very bottom of the page, three words: *in the edgelands.*

I WENT TO the place where Lauren said she'd seen him. I got a city bus part of the way and then got out and walked. It was a blighted area, all right, just the type of place Adam *would* vanish into. Scrubland instead of any real vegetation, and hulking monstrous buildings that might have been abandoned twenty-five or a hundred years ago for all I knew. It was as if the road buzzing through had rendered it all but invisible. It wasn't a real place at all, any longer, but a place to pass through. I didn't know what any of it had been once upon a time – why would I? Why would anyone? It was the kind of place you forgot even while you were looking at it. Adam would have known.

I spooked myself, just a little, thinking of the little severed hands of Adam's dream, not literally expecting them of course, but it did occur to me that this was the kind of place where people dumped bodies. I wondered what it would be like to find one, some murdered man or woman, battered or shot or knifed, exposed to the elements for who knew how long, their empty corpse waiting for acknowledgement. I felt that being discovered by me would somehow be a disappointment.

I walked for a long time. It grew cold and a biting wind went on the attack, so I huddled deeper and deeper inside my coat and scarf. I didn't expect to see Adam and yet somehow I couldn't bring myself to leave, either, worried that to do so prematurely would be to abandon him altogether. I also wanted to be able to tell Lauren with sincerity that I had tried.

Later, as the day wore on, I was unsurprised to come across a set of train tracks. I followed them for some time before the dying day and the fierce wind finally drove me back onto the road and in search of another bus. I think if I had followed the railway line for long enough I might have found the abandoned station they had once passed by and, dull as the day was, it might have been warmer and lighter there, but I don't know, and I don't know what I would have done, or seen, or been after that.

Still later, back at my flat, I slipped into bed next to Polly. We were still together, in that state a relationship reaches where you know its days are numbered but neither of you has had the courage yet to end it. What Adam would have called *liminal*. She was sound asleep. I reached out to touch her. She liked being woken up for sex. We had fucked, wordlessly, countless times in the dark, in the middle of the night, like that. I think it made her feel like she could shed inhibitions but I don't know because we never talked about it. She didn't wake when I touched her at all, though. She didn't even stir, so deep was she in dreams. I wondered what she dreamed about. We never talked about that either.

The letter from Adam had been startling to me in more ways than one. Of course, there was the strangeness of receiving it in the first place, but even more, I was surprised by the longing that suffused it. I never met any of Adam's boyfriends because he never had any although he had as much sex as anyone I've ever known – but it was purely anonymous, entirely recreational. The idea of Adam ever falling in love with anyone, let alone that he appeared to have been so secretly consumed by a desire to do so, startled me. In a way it made me feel like I'd never really known him at all, but I don't know that people ever do. Know one another, I mean.

After I finally fell asleep, I dreamed as well. I remembered the dream the following day, which was unusual for me. I was back in the edgelands. I was walking with someone who I thought was Polly, although I wasn't sure, and Adam was on the other side of me. It looked different than it had when I was there. The only way I can think to describe it is if you've ever woken early someplace that is not a city, where it is bright and the dew is glistening on twigs and grass and leaves and makes everything look like glass. It should have been beautiful, but all I felt was fear. I felt big and clumsy, like I might break something, and I felt like that would be the worst thing in the world. I didn't know what would happen, but it would be terrible. I wanted to tell Adam and the person who I thought was Polly what I was afraid of, but every time I tried to talk to them it was as though they couldn't hear me. The same glass seemed to separate us and, although I was between them, they could hear each other but I couldn't hear either of them. They were talking and laughing with one another and neither of them seemed afraid of anything breaking. I began to think maybe it wasn't Polly next to me at all. I wanted to look at who it was instead, but I was afraid of that, too. I finally mounted the courage to do so and when I did, I saw that it was me. I was so frightened, I didn't know what to do. I didn't understand what it meant. Had I split in two, or was I not who I believed myself to be, or both of those things?

When I finally woke, morning sun streaming through my window, I didn't know where I was for long moments. Next to me, Polly was still breathing softly, still dreaming. I was as well. I believed that I was made of glass and that if I moved I would shatter. Yet at the same time it seemed critical that I reach across the gulf between us and touch her. Like the boy in Adam's dream, she was awash in a golden light and, yet unlike in his dream, I could not move. I could not reach her; I could not cross to the other side.

... the Shadow

... takes room
on wall of room in moonlight
(room)
landlord, who reveals it belonged to man w...
... his shadow — tall, broad-should...
(...) that only at a ce...
full moon, Landlord stands befo...
... landlord gives hor...
... that of a distorted ...
... window — only shado...
... ...

... 2nd year at University
THE OTHER SIDE
... on ... platform
... evening, cool
... standing on one side, waiting for
... city train — others with me
... talking & staring (usual ...
... — family, friends)
... other side — boy sitting alone on
..., hands spread out upon
..., looking at the tracks —
..., neon-blond (no-one I knew ... thought I
...) quiet. I knew why he
... alone...

... less cluttered — I pick...
my suitcase & crossed the
platform, sat beside him — he
looked at me — our hands touch...
no-one noticed I had gone —
world behind me didn't exist —
waited, together, for the train
... going ... the opposite
... to my ... journey
... darkness, but ... lamplight
...

about 1,000 words
WINDOW SHOPPING (?)
Character: 20 yr-old ma...
university. Uneasy with h...
away, familiar/alien. The h...
Highlights fading in his ...
Feels at risk/exposed ...
but not expecting to be seen ...
his distance. Need for ...
Maths student ("...
another but not to his ...
people in this town. Past ...
men he wanted, chased by ...
Almost always rejected ...
wished he didn't have ...
"almost").
The summer ...
... next ...

OF LOSS AND OF LIFE:
JOEL LANE'S ESSAYS ON THE FANTASTIC

Mark Valentine

WHEN I STARTED, with Tartarus Press, the journal *Wormwood*, devoted to literature of the fantastic, supernatural and decadent, Joel Lane was one of the first writers I asked to contribute. I had first met Joel at the British fantasy conventions held in Birmingham in the nineteen-eighties. He became part of an informal circle of keen enthusiasts of fantasy and horror, the Doppelgangers; he was one of the most well-read and thoughtful characters in our group.

While his short stories will prove an enduring legacy, Joel was also a fine poet, who used modern forms and imagery while at the same time expressing concisely and acutely the perennial concerns of love, mortality, longing and loss. And Joel was furthermore an exceptionally pensive and insightful critic of the fantasy and horror fields.

For *Wormwood* he went on to contribute a series of essays on major figures in the genre, including Thomas Ligotti, Fritz Leiber, Ray Bradbury and Robert Aickman. He also hoped to write further about Aickman and Shirley Jackson. Like most of us reading in this field, he was also great enthusiast of H.P. Lovecraft - his youthful copies of paperbacks by the Providence author are endearingly annotated 'Joel Lane/HPL Library'. However, he was discerning about the work of the followers of Lovecraft and wrote perceptively about the differences in quality and conviction in them. Joel was also a strong champion of the urban horror fiction of Ramsey Campbell, and wrote widely about his work.

In an interview on the African Paper blog in 2011, Joel said, with characteristic modesty: 'I certainly wouldn't claim to have a great knowledge of weird fiction, but I've read quite a bit of it over the past forty years. And doing that can enhance your own writing, if only because it helps you see how diverse and rich the weird fiction genre is... It's easier to try and be original if you've got some idea of what's gone before. And it helps you to see what the genre is really about, what the recurrent themes are.'

The range of his reading was apparent from his answers in an interview with Phillip Stecco on the Thomas Ligotti Online discussion group. As well as Ligotti, he said:

Within supernatural horror, which I read obsessively, my favourites include Edgar Allan Poe, Arthur Machen, Walter de la Mare, John Metcalfe, H.P. Lovecraft, Clark Ashton Smith, Robert Bloch, Ray Bradbury, Theodore Sturgeon, Fritz Leiber, Harlan Ellison, Robert Aickman, Ramsey Campbell, M. John Harrison, Lisa Tuttle, Nicholas Royle and Conrad Williams.

In other fields, I appreciate the noir fiction of Cornell Woolrich, Dashiell Hammett and David Goodis; the poetry of Robert Browning, Rainer Maria Rilke, T.S. Eliot, Sylvia Plath, Ted Hughes, Edwin Morgan, Allen Ginsberg, Thom Gunn, Tony Harrison, Ian McMillan and Carol Ann Duffy; the existentialist novels of Jean Genet and Albert Camus; and the non-fiction writings of Michel Foucault and Theodor Adorno.

Another long-standing friend, John Howard, had many discussions with Joel about weird fiction authors and noted: 'Joel was a sound critical voice. In an often bloated field he knew what would endure, and why. He provided new insights on classic works and authors... Returning to these authors after Joel had written about them was to see them from fresh, and refreshing, angles.'

From working with Joel on his *Wormwood* essays, I know that he never relied on past evaluations or readings of the figures he discussed: he re-read everything of importance by them with great care and focus and thought, through his own original perspective on their work. I know from our correspondence how much concentration and creative energy he put in to these studies, which should also stand as a testament to his devotion to our literature. However, there was a sly, lighter side to Joel too: I usually had to watch out for his trademark awful puns, and occasionally (I regret to say) suggested removing the more outlandish. His thinking was acute and pursued sometimes difficult trains of thought with fierce persistence; I was always following a lane with many unexpected turns.

What did Joel look for in the work of the writers he discussed? He told the African Paper blog: 'You can't expect literal social realism from weird fiction, but you can expect bold metaphors, unease and irony, and I feel the genre is a rich resource of social commentary.' And though in the following answer he was talking about his own fiction, his comments could apply equally to the themes he addressed in his essays:

Personal loss is an important literary theme and one that I return to quite often, but it can get a bit monotonous if that's all you're talking about. The challenge is to understand how people keep going, how they survive – emotionally as well as physically. Life is a struggle and in the end you lose everything – that's a given and there's no point just saying it, you have to show what it brings out of people.

As this comment shows, Joel had a clear-eyed vision of the human condition, but refused to be daunted by this. He knew, and celebrated, the strengths offered by art, humour and friendship. And so it is wonderfully appropriate that his many friends have come together to write stories based upon his ideas and notes.

Mambo

He's always on the edge of

– the crowd on the b/w stop-motion film disco (silent film juxtaposed)

– don't know why he that / unless it's the of his expression making him seem

he depended

SHADOWS

Joe X Young

THERE ARE SHADOWS in your city. During the day the worst of the shadows lurk within pockmarked redbrick testaments to Victorian glory, dwelling in boarded-up doss holes doused by delinquents with the cloying stink of piss, the façades tagged with obscenities by those less likely to face the demons within.

Birmingham is no different. At night the darkness takes on a life of its own. It prowls, cold and unforgiving, in merciless pursuit of the unfortunate. I did not much care for the night – it brought out the natural beasts, predators whose money kept their secrets for them. They did not pay well but for those whose next meal depended on a few minutes in a public toilet or a parked car, what little they did pay we were grateful for.

Through escalating misfortune, at nineteen I had wound up on the streets with nothing but the clothes I stood in, alternating between starving and vomiting up other people's discarded food I'd retrieved from random bins. I tried to keep myself clean, basically presentable, making use of public lavatories, fast-food restaurant toilets, anywhere with soap and water where I was not expected to make a purchase before using the facilities, where I could fill my pockets with tightly wadded toilet roll in preparation for those times when nowhere was open or was safe to go to. It was in one such place, the gents toilets in The Old Contemptibles on the corner of Edmund Street, where I met John. He was appropriately both old and contemptible. They are always called John, the people who pay for secrets, who dole out money for food and drink to rid us of the taste of what else they wanted us to put in our mouths. My desperation led to my degradation as I was too close to starving to death to refuse his proposition. That first time I gagged, cried, ran outside and retched, vomiting his cum from my otherwise empty stomach, all of the time believing I had sold my immortal soul for a fiver. But then I faced reality: there were people, men, women, young and old, sucking cock gratis, even taking pleasure in it. For me it was a matter of survival. Later, as I sat in the Wimpy on Corporation Street walloping back a cheeseburger, fries and a Fanta bought with the spoils of debauchery, I was better disposed toward it. Life carried on like that for a few weeks, the eroding of my dignity hardening me for life. Mostly I slept rough, which was safer than getting a dry bed in shared dorms at the YMCA, and was selective when approached by the buyers of secrets, earning enough money for food but very little else, learning the hard way to get the money up front.

I went down St Martin's to the Bull Ring Market three days a week, trying to get work on the stalls. Nothing doing though, not even able to scratch some cash fetching cups of tea for the market traders as the divs on day release from the mental home had all the action there. Among the traders there was a woman who had a bric-a-brac and collectables stall on which was a Tupperware box full of art materials, pencils, pastels, crayons and chalks. I stared at them, seeing their potential. I knew I would not be able to afford the whole thing but if she would just sell me a few pieces, I had the chance of a way out. She saw me looking, poking through the box, separating black pastels, and charcoal, white chalk. She told me I could have the boxful for two quid. I had one pound thirty and I needed most of that for food and drink, so I asked if I could just buy a couple of pieces. She asked what I wanted them for, so I told her that I could draw some pavement art and possibly make money for food. She walked toward me, took the lid from under the box and sealed it up, then gave the box to me. I offered to pay; she refused to take a single penny. There are so few angels these days.

That night I sat around the back of a squat, the blend of

sodium street lamp and moonlight giving me enough light as I separated the box's contents onto pieces of newspaper, wrapping them in little bundles to keep the colours and types of material apart. The following day I headed for Victoria Square and drew a random landscape on the pavement. It did not take long before people started tossing loose change into the Tupperware box and on the ground beside my artwork. I made almost three quid before I saw a copper heading my way, so I grabbed the money, my chalks and ran. That was my means of escape: no more hunger, no more Old Contemptibles. I was set. There were days when I made enough to eat well with money to spare. There were other days when it was all about being able to turn up at the Snow Hill Centre with the deposit for a room. That day came fast.

Room 104 was comfortable and reasonably clean. Adrian, the day manager of the Shape project which ran the Centre, had shown me the room and explained the rules – mainly don't use or booze. No turning up wasted, no bringing people back with me, no fucking with the hallway fire extinguishers, common sense and decency sorts of things. He gave me the key, which I had to leave at the reception desk whenever I went out. There were only a dozen or so rooms unoccupied of the hundred and fifty-seven. Shape was fussy when it came to giving the rooms out but for the first time in months I'd got lucky. The place was old, not quite the splendid art deco I had expected judging from the exterior of the building. It was running to ruin a little here and there but efforts had been made to tidy it up. My room smelled of stale paint. The occasional mottling of damp left mould stains showing, yet it was still a significant improvement on the plethora of doorways, telephone boxes, skips, and assorted shit-holes I had slept in over the past few months. Exhausted and happy I locked myself securely in my new home, lay on the bed, closed my eyes, and slept the sleep of Kings.

My days improved. I was able to wash, to eat and drink, to sleep securely and to face each day knowing I was safe. Being in proper accommodation I was able to register for benefits, finally getting the cash to pay for my room and other money to live on, and a social fund payment secured a much-needed change of clothes. I even had enough spare money to buy more art materials with which to supplement my meagre income. By now I had learned the best places to set up and had permission from Birmingham City Council to do street art as long as I taped paper to the ground and didn't apply colour straight onto the paving slabs. During the day I was a street artist, by night I sat in my room at the Snow Hill and painted landscapes with acrylics I had bought from The Works by the Odeon, taking care to leave my window open so nobody caught a whiff of brush cleaner and thought I'd got a vat of moonshine on the go. I even got involved with Shape's mural projects and exhibition at the Snow Hill Centre when the artist they were going to use let them down. They gave me all of the left-over materials, which suited me just fine. I soon became the 'artist in residence', getting commissions for a small consideration, my room becoming more of an art studio than the small bedsit space it should have been.

WHEN THE TIME felt right I asked the day manager, Adrian, for permission to paint a mural in my room., There was a big stain on one wall, many smaller blotches, but this one was growing, shifting, becoming more visible each night, taking on a life of its own as the clouds traversed the night sky. They transformed the moon into a flickering projector lamp, sometimes animating the expansive dark patch into a personal screening of *Nosferatu*. I told Adrian that I loved horror films, but I didn't want to live in one. Adrian was having none of it, giving me some bullshit about listed buildings. He said that if the patch was that bad he would get the maintenance crew to give it a lick of paint and then maybe, maybe, if it started to show through again, I might be allowed to hang some posters up with blu-tack.

That evening I waited, watching the wall, seeing the usual dance of the blotches coalescing, forming a figure, tall and broad, almost alien, the full moon enhancing the stain. I left the light on, exited my room and made my way to the lobby. I may not have been able to convince Adrian that my wall needed painting but if

I got a member of the night staff to take a look they would see how bad it was, it would be reported in the night book. The management committee would either have to allow me to paint the wall or transfer me to another room; either would have been fine with me.

The night staff are a good bunch, chatty with the residents, usually happy to help and this time was no different. Gordon and Warren were on the desk. One of the residents, nicknamed 'Osram' because his weak jaw and bulbous pate made his head resemble a light bulb, busied himself telling them stories of his heroism in the Korean War, which they knew he was too young to have fought in, but his bullshit was always so damned comical that they let him carry on regardless. I waited for a break in his storytelling and asked if whoever was doing the next floor-check could pop in my room to look at the wall. When I said it was room 104, Osram interrupted.

'You mean they've actually put somebody in that room?'

'Yeah, why wouldn't we?' Gordon replied.

'Because it's haunted,' Osram continued. 'That was the mad Professor's room. He went in one night, never came out. When they broke the door down, his key was still in the lock on the inside. No sign of the fucker'

'I think I heard about that, couple of years before I got transferred here, suicide wasn't it?'

Osram shook his head. 'Was it bollocks a suicide. Can't have been - the window was locked from the inside. The Police never found the body. Nothing down on the towpath or in the Canal. You can't have a suicide without a body'

'Yeah, you're right, I remember hearing about it at the time. He just vanished into thin air,' said Warren. 'No bugger has been able to stay in that room since. Are you sure you're in 104?'

'Bloody positive, here's my key.' I showed them the key with 104 on the fob.

'That's 104 all right,' said Warren. 'I'm doing the rounds in a bit. I'll take a look and you head on up and wait. I'm afraid you can't come with me in case there's a problem with other residents'

'I'll come,' said Osram.

'Fuck off you will, this has nothing to do with you,' said Gordon.

'How long do you reckon you'll be? I asked Warren.

'Well, it's about twenty minutes, all told, but I guess with you being on the top floor there is no reason that I can't start there and work down. Come on, let's get going before Osram starts telling ghost stories.'

With that Warren took the master pass keys off the hook behind the reception desk, gesturing for me to follow. Osram walked toward us but Warren cast him a disapproving look. I shrugged and said, 'What the hell. You may as well come too, tell us more about the Prof.' Osram instantly launched into the tale of how the Professor wound up homeless after his wife kicked him out for scribbling equations on every surface of their home, a habit he'd brought with him to room 104, which, no matter how many times it had been repainted, still failed to adequately cover the scrawling. Several people had been placed in 104 in the months after the Professor's disappearance. None had stayed for more than a few nights. They were claiming it was haunted by the Prof's deranged mind, that numbers and symbols glowed on the walls, rotating, sometimes floating around the room, that his spirit was trapped in the wall, tearing its way through from the afterlife, a monstrous shadow waiting to engulf the unwary and drag them into insanity. At first it was dismissed as the ramblings of drug addicts and drunkards, but even the more sober residents rarely lasted more than a few days. Wallpapering and then painting over the paper had not stopped the reports. Nobody wanted to stay in there, so they just left it locked until the Shape Management Company took over. I was the first person in years to stay in 104. Osram said had he have known I was in that room, he would have warned me about it sooner.

We arrived at room 104. Warren grabbed for his passkey but I was quicker opening the door. The room was moonlit, my light switched off. I stepped in, flicked the switch: nothing happened.

'So, for a start, it looks like the electrics are a bit dodgy,' said

Warren.

'I told you this place is haunted,' said Osram.

'You know, for someone with such a large cranium you're a bit of a spaz,' Warren replied as Osram pushed past him, heading for the window.

'This is what I'm on about,' I said to Warren while pointing at the dark patch which was expanding on my wall. I turned toward Osram, trying to get his attention 'So... How tall was the Prof? Only the shadow gets to be about seven feet tall.' Osram ignored me so I continued: 'It bends across the ceiling, which is bloody weird when there is nothing in the way to cast it. If it's a ghost he's a tall bugger.' Although I was taking the piss, I was nervous of the answer.

Osram turned his back to the window, and sat on the sill. Behind him the full moon shone off his hairless dome, making him look more like his nickname than ever before. If he actually answered me I didn't hear, all I heard was Warren as he was slammed against the wall, his breath rushing out of his body as the shadow drew him in. I stepped toward him, to help, but some dark force kept me back, icy tentacles of shadow wrapped around me, not harming just restraining. The room dimmed, taking on an oily cast. Clouds deflected the moonlight, bouncing it off the canal's surface and rippling it back up into the room. Osram's shadow was thrown against the wall so it merged perfectly with the shadow crushing the life out of Warren, Slick black tendrils were rammed into Warren's throat, choking him, while yet others invaded his nostrils, ears, his eyes They were pulling, dragging him into itself, backward into the wall, into the void, tearing Warren's own shadow from his being – and then he was gone.

The tentacles around me slackened, released their hold, uncoiling, snaking back to the wall where now the only shadow appeared to be Osram's. In the night sky the clouds made their retreat, the strip light in the room came back on. I turned toward Osram.

'Did you see that? Did that really happen?' I said, blinking against the sudden flickering brightness, first seeing what I thought was Osram, soon realising he was something other. Darkness hung around him like a shroud. The night outside blackened as the light within my room stabilised. Osram's skin shone dark, slick and bilious, dissipating, integrating with the glass behind him, reflecting my horrified expression in his mirrored blackness as he seeped through the structure of the glass and merged with the night.

It wasn't long before Gordon left his post to check on Warren. I told him Warren and Osram had only been with me for a couple of minutes and left together. It was not exactly a lie just not the whole truth. As Gordon checked each floor for his missing colleague, I carefully opened the window and looked outside, checking to see if the Osram-thing lingered in wait but there was nothing, only moonlight and cold air. I packed my stuff, except for the brush cleaner, which I splashed across Warren's shadow and some on a pillow which I placed it at the base of the wall. I struck a match and dropped it, recoiling from the 'whump' as the pillow ignited sending flames up the wall and across the shadow. The shadow writhed, banging beyond the veneer of reality, trying to escape the flames. I left, closing the door, headed for the foyer. I dropped my keys on the reception desk, set off the fire alarm, and let myself out the front door. The air outside was cool and fresh. I breathed deep and started running.

I NEED SOMEWHERE TO HIDE

Steven Savile

ELLIE FRENCH HAD one wish, to be the hero of her own life. It wasn't a big wish but then Ellie wasn't a big girl. Not yet. She lived in a small town with an even smaller name. There were two streets of shops but none of the major high street brands. There were greengrocers and ironmongers, a florist and a post office and one shop that was wonderland, a shop with a window full of costumes and wooden toys. Mulligans. The sign proudly claimed it had been there for ninety-nine years on the same spot, captivating the young hearts and minds of the town through one world war, three coronations, silver and golden jubilees, always wearing the changing face of fun as it stopped being about puzzles and miniature tool kits and model aeroplanes and became all about consoles and computers. Puddles of last year's leaves were still on the ground. Once upon a time, like in all good fairy tales, road sweepers had come this way. There had been pride in seeing the county in bloom. Now the ghost of time had replaced pride. Things rusted. Things decayed. Age crept in. But the flags of St George still snapped in the wind.

Ellie was thirteen, or she would be next Monday. She would stop being a little girl overnight. She'd close her eyes and wake up a teenager. Just like that. She didn't really remember the world a different way. It had always been like this. She was only just beginning to understand it for what it was - hostile. People that were supposed to care didn't; people that were supposed to offer protection didn't; people that were supposed to make it a better place for you didn't. This was a world out for itself, a world of greed and grief that needed a hero.

She'd asked for a party and when her mum had said she wasn't sure because of the time and effort involved in entertaining a dozen newly teenaged girls, asking had become wheedling and wheedling had become begging until finally promised a month of babysitting for Mary Elisabeth, her seven-year-old clone, in return for a Saturday afternoon of fancy dress. There would be pirates and clowns, angels and animals, fairy tale heroines and Disney princesses. She didn't want to be any of them. She wanted to be different. Special. Just for once.

She just had one and a half days to get through.

The problem was, Ellie wasn't brave, not like Mary Elisabeth who didn't understand how fragile she really was, or half of the other girls at school who all seemed to know who they were already. Ellie found herself trapped half way between wanting to play make believe with her patchwork doll with its dull sequins for eyes and wanting to play a different kind of make believe where she pretended to be grown up without really knowing what growing up meant beyond being sad most of the time.

Ellie had been looking at the suit of armour in the window for a week now, a few minutes every day, imagining what it would be like to wear it. Sticks and stones would bounce off it.

The window was different today. Mulligans always changed their window display on a Friday. The armour was gone. In its place was a superhero costume – the Blue Falcon. She'd seen the cartoon on the telly. It was one of the Saturday morning cartoons they showed during the summer holidays every year. The cartoons were from the 1940s and star of the short-lived black and white serial hadn't been in another show for almost forty years. But that didn't make the Blue Falcon any less of a hero. Every week he escaped from impossible situations with only his utility belt and his wits to save him. Every week he outwitted the bad guys, leaving them tied up back-to-back in the middle of the road for Detective Carlson to lock up. Even his theme tune was cool, all trumpets and saxophones. Miles Davis composed it and played on it with Thelonious Monk and John Coltrane. Ellie didn't know who they were but she'd memorised their names.

Looking at the costume on the mannequin she knew who she wanted to be on Saturday.

She wanted to be the Blue Falcon.

Ellie opened the door. A little brass bell tinkled as she went inside, announcing her. The old man behind the counter – Mister Mulligan himself, looking every bit as impossibly old as the shop itself – smiled down at her. 'Well, now little miss, what can I do for you today?'

'It's my birthday tomorrow,' she said.

'Ah, what a wonderful thing that must be. Let me guess … thirteen?' he said and she couldn't help but smile all the more, puffing her chest out proudly. 'Almost too old for toys then?'

Ellie shook her head. 'You're never too old for toys.'

'A girl after my own heart. So then, something fit for a birthday girl? What can it be?'

'I want to be the Blue Falcon,' she said.

'Oh, do you now?'

She nodded fiercely.

'Well how absolutely wonderful. When I was young girls never wanted to be the heroes, or if they did they were never allowed to admit it. I rather like this new world we're all living in. If you want to be the Blue Falcon my dear, the Blue Falcon you shall be.'

He shuffled out from behind the counter and rummaged through the things in the window display until he had the various parts of the costume to offer her. 'You can try it on through there, there's a little room in the back. I'll stay out here and make sure no one disturbs you.'

Ellie took the costume from him and disappeared into a small room at the back of the shop which shared most of its space with cardboard boxes. A roll of carpet leant against the wall, thick enough to act like a curtain as she found a path between the boxes. She changed quickly; the awkward girl, all elbows and knees, disappeared. In the mirror she saw the hero she so desperately wanted to be. It was perfect. The outfit had been made for her. She pulled the mask down over her face. It couldn't hide her smile. Beaming, she headed back into the shop.

'Let's get a look at you.' Ellie pushed the blue cape over her shoulder as she stepped out from behind the counter. 'Oh my, don't you look just like the Blue Falcon. A proper hero if ever there was one.'

'How much is it?' she asked.

'Don't worry about that, money isn't everything. Happiness is. So, are you a happy Blue Falcon?'

She nodded fiercely, the whole shop seeming to bob around her because her head went up and down so quickly. 'Very.'

'Then that is my price, my dear. To be the Blue Falcon you must be happy. That is all it costs.'

'But that's not very much,' Ellie objected.

'Oh, my dear girl, it is *everything*.'

She ran all the way home dressed as the Blue Falcon, swirling her cape and splashing in the puddles, her laughter filling the little town. It was infectious. People saw her and laughed along. For just a minute she touched their lives and made them that little bit better before she moved on to the next and the next, laughing all the way. Her house wasn't the smallest one on the lane but it wasn't the biggest, either. Her little sister called it *Goldihouse*, in that it was just right for the French's. There was a flag in the window of the box room, the red cross doing the job of curtains. Ellie pushed the gate open. The pitted rust was rough against her palm. There were enough cracks in the paving stones to break the backs of every mother in town if their offspring felt vindictive. Ellie skipped all the way up to the door where her mother waited, the red vines in her cheeks flushed.

'What the hell are you wearing?'

'My party costume,' Ellie said defensively.

'What party?'

'Tomorrow. You promised.'

'You look stupid. Get in here and get that thing off. Where's your uniform? You better not have lost it, girl. That cost good money. We don't have money to burn buying you a new blazer.'

All of the words tumbled out in a drunken rush, one after the other without a breath in between.

She clipped Ellie around the ear as she rushed up stairs, chasing her with the threat, 'Just wait till your father gets home, girl!' Ellie took the steps two and three at a time, stretching her legs as far as she could, and tripped on the top one. The only reason she didn't fall was because her outstretched hands hit the carpet on the landing and pushed her up again, like she could bounce. Ellie ran into her bedroom and slammed the door behind her.

She wrapped the blue cloak around her and sat in the corner of the room, her back pressed up against the wall, and stared at the door, knowing it was only a matter of time before it opened. She bit her bottom lip, refusing to cry. Her happiness was over as quickly as that. Nothing good was going to come through that door. It'd be better if they just forgot she was up here. There wouldn't be any dinner. There never was when her mum was drunk.

Ellie heard her mother stumbling around downstairs and tried to remember the last time she'd been nice to her. It took her longer than it should have to come up with the memory of them walking down through the town to the sports hall for gymnastics practice last week. They'd shared a 99 dripping with monkey's blood on the way home. Thinking about the ice cream melting between her sticky fingers didn't raise a smile like it normally would. One moment of kindness in ten days.

It was like there were two mums living under her mother's skin. One of them was beautiful and funny and loved to dance to music on the radio and bake things filling the house with smells homes were meant to be filled with. The other was a vicious drunk who delighted in hurting everyone around her and then couldn't remember what she'd said the next day. She liked to lash out, too. But then she'd be all sweetness and light when the hangover wore off. Those rare moments of normality when she was like her old self were becoming fewer and further between these days, though.

It was all about hope, or the lack of it. It was hard to hope when every day was hell. That was why Ellie wanted to be a hero, for her mum, for her dad, and her little sister. Heroes saved people and there had never been three people more in need of saving than the Frenches.

Drunk mum was a mask, just like the one Ellie was wearing. Even if you couldn't see it that didn't mean it wasn't there. The thing she couldn't work out was if her mum had been wearing it for so long it had taken her over, or if it was who she was and the other mum, the one who loved her was the mask.

She heard the door slam downstairs, then raised voices, mostly her mum's shrill nails-on-a-blackboard cackle, followed by his tired footsteps on the landing. He opened the door but for a moment didn't come in. His silhouette stood in the doorway looking at her empty bed.

'What have you done, Ellie?'

'Nothing,' she said quietly from the corner of the room. The shadow turned to look at her.

'You know that's not true,' he said. 'What are you wearing?'

'It's my costume for my birthday party,' she said. 'I'm the Blue Falcon.'

'It's not your birthday today, though, is it?' He said.

'No,' she admitted. 'It's tomorrow.'

'And where did you get the costume?'

She couldn't look at his face as he knelt down in front of her. 'From Mulligans,' she said.

He looked at her. The shadows hid his eyes so she couldn't tell what he was thinking. 'Your mum didn't give you the money to pay for it and I know I didn't, so how *did* you pay for it, Ellie?'

'Mister Mulligan gave it to me,' she said.

'Hmm. Why would he do that, kiddo? He runs a shop. Shops *sell* things, they don't give them away,' he said, like that proved she was lying. 'So either you stole it, or he did give it to you, and you know you're not supposed to take things from strangers. You don't know what he wants or what he's really like. Trust me, I know people like him, I know what they are doing when they're being nice to you. I know you like it but it's for your own good, kiddo. You're taking it back tomorrow. Understand?' She knew that nothing she could say would convince him otherwise.

'But he gave it to me,' she said, hearing the whine in her own voice.

'That doesn't change anything, Ellie. You're going to take it back first thing tomorrow morning and say sorry and that you can't keep it because your dad won't let you. He'll understand why. Now get ready for bed. No arguments. Lights out in five.'

He left her to change into her nightie and went back downstairs. It wasn't even six o'clock and her bed time wasn't until nine which meant three hours lying in the dark with her stomach rumbling, hungry.

She could hear the TV downstairs and more shouting. Her parents never seemed happy these days. She couldn't really tell what they were arguing about this time; her mum's words were slurred and her dad's voice was pitched low so she felt his anger rather than heard it. Back and forth, back and forth, a slammed door here, and curse there. The sound of breaking glass was last thing she heard before the front door slammed. The silence that followed was worse than all of the shouting. She hated it.

Her bedroom door opened as Mary Elisabeth crept in and clambered into bed beside her. 'Can I sleep in here with you?' She didn't say any more. Ellie knew.

It wasn't a good night.

Her little sister tossed and turned, and when she wasn't, she sweated up against Ellie's side making her nightie cling to her skin. Outside of the window the moon threw shapes up against the wall like a shadow play where spindly characters crawled across the stage.

In the middle of the night she heard the bedroom door open again. Her dad stood in the doorway. He was bleeding. She must have been asleep because she hadn't heard him come home.

'I need you to help clean me up, sweetheart,' he said, like getting your thirteen-year-old daughter to patch up your wounds was the most natural thing in the world, because it was the most natural thing in his. He was sweet about it, sitting on the edge of the bath while she used antiseptic-soaked cotton wool to dab the blood away from around the cuts. One was much worse than the others. She asked him what happened.

'One day you'll understand, sweetheart. One day. But this country ... it's a mess. It's up to people like us to uphold everything it stands for. Everything it means to be English.'

He winced as Ellie pressed the stinging antiseptic into the cut itself, opening it wide enough that it started bleeding all over again. She wiped it away, revealing the ink of the bulldog on his arm. She'd always loved that tattoo. The dog looked so friendly, so proud. Her dad called him Bulldog Bobby with his proud grin and canines sticking out.

'It's a war,' he boasted, like he was a soldier fighting some endless conflict on England's pastures green. He went out after dark to meet his brother soldiers and came home bloody and battered, but grinning and saying 'You should see the other bastard…' like he was a hero, like the Muslim kid he'd left battered and bleeding in the gutter was some enemy combatant that didn't deserve to breathe. It was a night time conversation. A confession. Like part of him knew what he was doing was wrong and he needed to unburden himself. It was another mask, like mother when she was drunk.

Sometimes he even claimed he did it for his girls, to make the town safer for them because the place was going to shit. His knuckles were raw. He made a fist so that she could get the grit out of the abrasions.

'You need a hero like the Blue Falcon,' Ellie said, making him smile.

'Maybe we do, baby girl, maybe we do.'

'I could do it,' she offered. She'd do anything for him. That was love, wasn't it? Being willing to do anything for someone, no matter what.

'Not tonight. Tonight you just need to go back to bed. And what are you going to do tomorrow?'

'Take the costume back,' Ellie said.

'That's my girl.'

It was the last thing she wanted to do but she could never say no to her father. The idea of disappointing him twisted her gut. So straight after breakfast on Saturday morning she went back to Mulligans clutching the supermarket carrier bag with the Blue Falcon costume inside it to her chest.

'Whatever is the matter, dear girl?' The old man said as she opened the door.

'My dad said I had to bring this back because I hadn't paid for it.'

'Nonsense, girl. I gave it to you.'

'But you're a shop. You sell things. You don't give them away.'

'Sometimes I do,' he said. 'But isn't today your party?'

'Yes.'

'Well then you need it more than me. I know your dad, sweetheart. I know he's a proud man and doesn't want my charity but sometimes he is wrong. Look,' he came out from behind the counter and walked with Ellie to the window. 'Tell me what you see out there.'

She looked. She didn't know what she was supposed to tell him. 'The street,' she said finally.

'More than that.'

'Two cars. One red, one blue.'

'Yes, and more than that?'

'What do you want me to see?'

'Ah, that's the question isn't it, dear girl? Do I want you to see something in particular or just something in general, like the cars, that between them and the street sign above them make up the colours of our nation? Let me give you a clue, shall I? Out there, that is England.'

'I knew that.'

'I know you did. But where do you think those cars are from?' She shook her head. 'One is German, the other is Japanese. What about the music on the radio right now?' She didn't recognise the song and said so. 'It's French. Or at least the singer was. He's been dead for a long time now. What's your favourite food?'

'Hotdogs,' she said, without a second's hesitation.

'Invented by a German man living in America. How about mathematics, do you like that?'

'Not really,' she admitted, earning a chuckle.

'The first numbers were written down by Egyptians, and the first real mathematical puzzles solved by the ancient Greeks. The alphabet they taught you at school is Latin, meaning it has its roots in Italy. Christian missionaries from Rome brought it here. Our English alphabet was made up of runes. The sounds of those old runes are obsolete now, *thorn, eth, wynn, yogh, ash,* and *ethel.* All gone. Replaced. Even our language owes more to Europe than it does to any history of England. Do you see? My point is, all of these things are fundamental parts of the England you're looking at, aren't they? So they're England, too, really, aren't they? Your England. And this war your father and his friends think they're fighting to keep it pure? That's been over for a long time. We're all in this together. Everything's different now. If this place needs a hero it is always going to be someone more like the Blue Falcon than some vicious thug like Ben French. It's up to people like you to be our heroes.'

She didn't really follow what he was trying to say but sensed it was important to him, so she tried. She offered him the bag with the costume inside.

'No, dear girl, you *are* the Blue Falcon. You always were. How can I give you what is already yours?'

'But my dad –'

'If your dad has a problem with it, you tell him to come and see me after your party, okay? I'll explain to him just why it is important you get to wear that costume. Now, do you know what's special about the Blue Falcon?'

Ellie shook her head.

'She helps people who can't help themselves. She protects them. She keeps them safe. She gives them somewhere to hide while she defeats the bad guys. You can do that, can't you? Just help one person. That's all you ever need to do to be a hero. Just help one person.'

She nodded.

'See. I told you.'

'Can she fly?'

'Of course she can,' Mister Mulligan said with a gentle smile. 'She can do anything she sets her mind to.'

MUM WAS DRUNK again. Dad was out. Ellie couldn't find Mary Elisabeth when she got home. Her sister wasn't in her room. A quick glance confirmed she wasn't getting ready in the bathroom or downstairs toilet. She wasn't in the garden. There was no sign of any decorations for her party later. The house was a mess. No one had cleaned up the breakfast dishes. She asked her mum but her answer was for an entirely different question. Ellie walked up and down the street asking the neighbours if any of them had seen her little sister, but none of them had. 'Did she come home from school?' Ellie demanded. Her mother sat on the doorstep smoking a cigarette. She looked up, alcohol in her eyes, shrugged, and took another deep sucking drag on the dog end.

'You should get out of here,' her mother said finally. 'Run away. Take that stupid costume of yours and go while you can.' She was crying. Proper tears, not crocodile ones. 'I'm sorry, Ellie. I know you hate me… I know you think…' she couldn't finish the thought, whatever it was she was supposed to know. 'I'm not a good mum… I never wanted this for you… I should have protected you. Both of you.' She exhaled. The smoke corkscrewed up in front of her face. It took that drunk's mask away with it, leaving a vulnerable woman behind, bare, exposed.

Ellie reached into the plastic bag and took her own mask out, putting it on.

As it settled into place putting a layer of plastic between her and her mum's pain, she said, 'I am the Blue Falcon, mum. I'm here to save you.' It was so innocent, so sweet, and the wrong way around.

'You can't save me, kiddo. I'm going to Hell. The best thing that can happen is if you don't go with me.'

'Where's Mary Elisabeth, mum?'

'Safe at least,' she said.

Ellie didn't understand what she meant but there was something about the way she said it that frightened her. Another drag on the cigarette, shrinking it. Another mouthful of smoke curled up in front of her face. The ash dropped off the tip, landing on her jeans.

'It wasn't meant to be like this,' she said. 'This wasn't meant to be our life.' Her smile was so sad it hurt to see. Ellie sat herself down on the stoop beside her and rested her head on her mum's shoulder.

'Where's Mary Elisabeth?' she asked again.

'He wasn't always like this,' she said, ignoring the question to talk about her own ghosts. 'Not when I met him. He was passionate. He blazed brightly. You couldn't help but love him. But that passion changed. It became darker. He started to blame everyone else for our problems. And then it all fell apart so quickly. He stopped touching me. I needed somewhere to hide,' another suck on the cigarette. 'That's what the drinking was. A place to hide from him. But that left you girls in the way. Not any more though, I'm taking you with me this time.'

'Mum?' Ellie said, the plastic mask digging into her cheek.

'What is it honey?'

'Where's Mary Elisabeth?'

'In the bath,' she said. But that didn't make any sense because she'd checked the bathroom and hadn't seen her in there.

She went upstairs to check on her sister, opening the bathroom door slowly. She couldn't see Mary Elisabeth until she stood over the olive green bathtub and looked down into it. Her sister was under the water, looking up through a layer of soap bubbles that had gathered around her cheeks and nose. She looked perfect. Peaceful. The water didn't move. Her lips were parted, bathwater puddled between them.

Ellie reached down to try and shake her awake. The water kept Mary Elizabeth's skin warm, but it wouldn't stay that way. She pushed and pushed and pushed her but she wouldn't wake up.

She heard footsteps heavy on the stairs, trudging up, and saw her mum's reflection in the tiles behind the bath.

'Come on, sweetheart, let's get you into your costume, shall we? We need to get you ready for your party.'

Ellie turned to see her mum holding the carrier bag with the rest of the Blue Falcon outfit in it. She fished the top out and offered to her daughter. Ellie didn't know what else to do apart from put it on. She changed in front of her mum, not taking the mask off as she struggled into the leotard with the Blue Falcon's crest on its chest and her mum helped secure the cape in place. She put her pumps on last.

She wasn't Ellie anymore.

She was the Blue Falcon.

'Did someone hurt Mary Elisabeth?' she asked. Heroes didn't cry. What was it Mister Mulligan had said? They helped people who couldn't help themselves. And if they couldn't save them they made things better somehow.

'She's fine, sweetheart. She's just sleeping. We'll get her dressed and she can come with us. I'll carry her. Okay?' Ellie nodded. 'Go and get some clothes for her to wear. Her favourite things. Can you do that for me?'

She nodded again and scurried out of the room to raid Mary Elisabeth's drawers. It only took her a moment to find the brightly coloured t-shirt she loved with the dancing fairies on the front and the striped woollen tights that matched it.

By the time she got back to the bathroom her mum was towelling Mary Elisabeth dry. Her sister still hadn't opened her eyes and she couldn't hold herself up, she just slumped over her mum's shoulder while she sang to her – a sweet little lullaby telling her to go to sleep my darling, go to sleep my love. Ellie had an idea. She put the clothes down on the stool and ran down to the kitchen before her mum could stop her, and rifled through the drawers for the tin foil to make a pair of angel wings for Mary Elisabeth so she could have a costume for the party, too. It only took her a few minutes. They weren't perfect but they didn't need to be.

She was almost finished by the time her mum came down, cradling Mary Elisabeth in her arms. 'I made her some wings so she could dress up for the party,' she said, holding them up.

'Beautiful, Ellie. You're a good sister.' Tears streaked her mum's face as she helped knot the silver foiled wings around the dead girl's neck. 'She'll be able to fly all the way up to heaven with these. Okay are you ready to go to your party?'

'Aren't we having it here?'

'Oh no, we're going somewhere really special. I promised you, didn't I?'

'Where are we going?'

'Somewhere we can hide together,' she said, smiling through the tears.

She carried Mary Elisabeth as though she weighed nothing, her silver wings crumpling as they pressed against her chest, through the old streets, past Mulligans and the iron mongers and the green grocers. At the post office she put a letter in the box. They carried on walking, out onto the other side of town, towards her school - which was where she thought they were going for a moment - and turned away towards the forest on the edge of town. They walked side-by-side, the Blue Falcon, the Silver Angel and their mum, towards the chalk cliffs that marked the end of the world as far as Ellie was concerned.

On the edge, looking down, they linked hands.

It was a long way to broken stones at the bottom of the chalk pit.

'I want you to understand something, Ellie,' her mum said, not looking at her. 'I never meant any of this to happen to you. None of it. I would hear him go into your room... I knew what he was doing in there ... doing to you ... but I couldn't stop him. I'm sorry, El. I really am. I'm a bad mum. I should have protected you, but...' She ran out of words. 'I've written it all down. I posted it in the mailbox on the way here, telling everyone. He won't win. They'll hear us. This is the only way I can think of where we beat him. They'll listen. They'll have to.'

'I don't want to hurt dad,' she said. 'I love him.'

'I know you do, El. That's why we've got to go. Before you stop being you and become me. We can't be his victims forever. We need to take control of our lives. Just us, out of his reach forever. Safe. Take my hand. I love you, kiddo. Heart and soul.'

'I know you do.'

She reached up, interlacing their fingers, her small hand in her mum's larger one and they stepped out into the nothing. For just a moment the Blue Falcon, the Silver Angel and their mum flew gloriously, the wind streaming through their costumes before it tore those tinfoil wings away and wrapped the blue cape over her eyes.

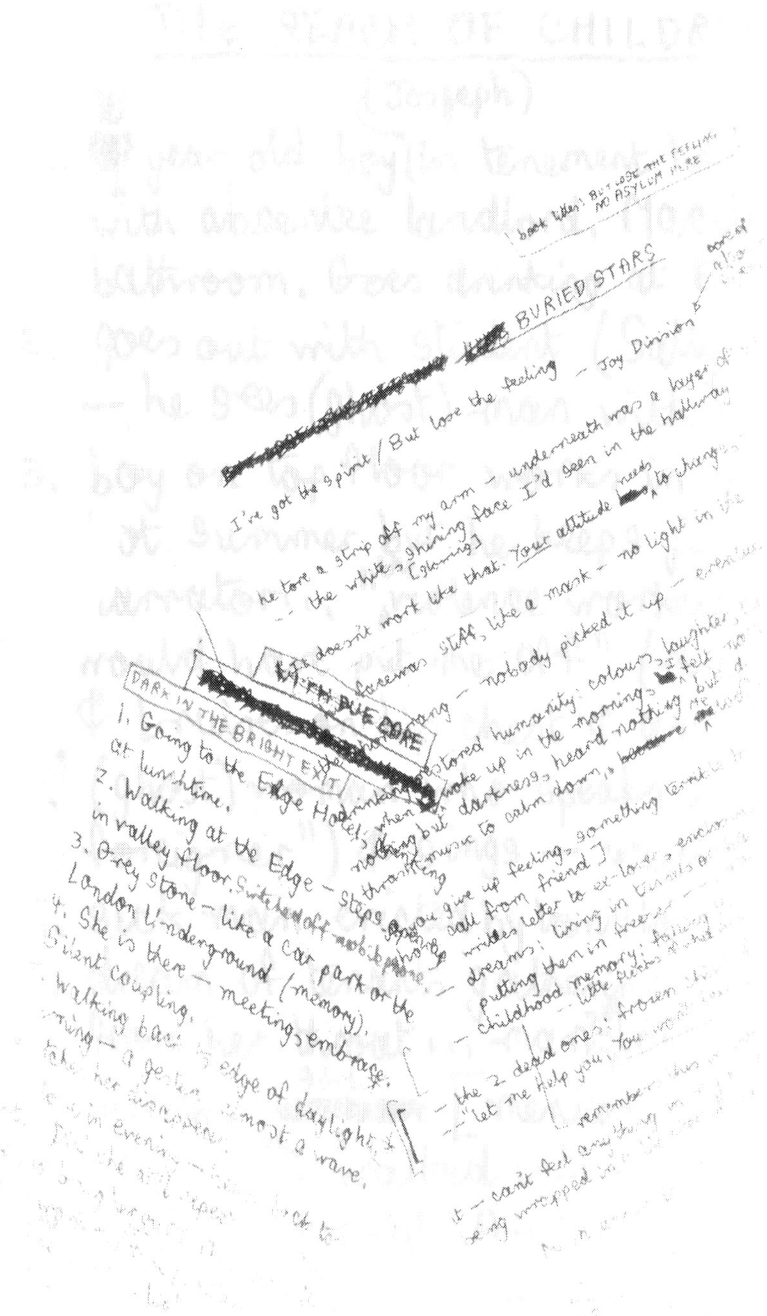

(Joseph)

BUT LOSE THE FEELING / NO ASYLUM HERE

BURIED STARS

I've got the spirit / But lose the feeling — Joy Division

he tore a strip off my arm — underneath was a layer of

— the white, shining face I'd seen in the hallway [glowing]

doesn't work like that. Your attitude needs to change

face was stiff, like a mask — no light in the

— nobody picked it up

restored humanity; colours, laughter

woke up in the morning, I felt

nothing but darkness, heard nothing but

music to calm down,

something terrible

you give up feeling, something

call from friend]

writes letter to ex-lover

dreams; living in

putting them in

childhood memory;

— the 2 dead ones; frozen

— "let me help you.

remember

DARK IN THE BRIGHT EXIT

1. Going to the Edge Hotel, drinking at lunchtime.
2. Walking at the Edge — steps in valley floor. Switched off mobile phone.
3. Grey stone — like a car park or the London Underground (memory).
4. She is there — meeting, embrace. Silent coupling.

walking back edge of daylight, almost a wave.

COMING TO LIFE

John Howard

AS JUSTIN KISSED Paul awake, he knew that Paul had been dreaming about the people in the walls.

The dream came regularly now. With Justin's aid Paul rose out of it. Blinking and yawning, he saw that their bedroom was darker than it should have been. The window wasn't there. Paul realised that Justin had put the board up by himself after he had finally fallen asleep. Then, the gale had been increasing. Overnight it had reached the height of its strength, but now the wind merely blustered, although almost overwhelming the voices from the radio close by in the other room.

'Can't we take that thing off the window?'

Justin shook his head. 'Not yet, love. Maybe in a while. We've talked about it enough times. When there's a really strong gust everything still shakes. If the glass got blown in…'

NEITHER OF THEM had been enthusiastic about the flat. It was on the first floor of a three storey block, one of a small development out on the edge of the city. With quiet distaste Justin had called them toy buildings. They had large windows and tiled roofs, slightly inclined, that overhung the brick walls. The roofs looked as if they hadn't been trimmed close enough. Paul had to agree that the blocks of flats did look rather flimsy.

'I'll huff and I'll puff and I'll blow your house down,' Paul had said, before he had noticed the full extent of Justin's despair. He'd had enough of searching. 'All right, we'll take it. For the minimum term, at least. Until we can find something better – more substantial. It's not so bad. We'll make it our own place – our first place together.'

At least the location was good. The estate was served by a couple of bus routes and it was easy to get to supermarkets and the city centre. There was a small shopping parade nearby. Many of the shops were now fronted by steel shutters, spattered with graffiti and seemingly rusted into place. But there was a convenience store that hadn't succumbed. And on the other side of the new flats were stretches of rough grass and semi-derelict farmland, spreading out to a horizon of low tree-crowned hills which concealed the motorway. Justin and Paul had moved in during the first full working week of the New Year, as soon as the arrangements had been completed.

Paul felt the cold more than Justin did. They had to watch heating costs carefully. Paul would stay huddled in bed while Justin padded around the flat in his overcoat. They both looked forward to the spring. As the days slowly lengthened, they got home from work to find the flat filled with dim grey light, uncertain and as temporary as the snowdrops on the grass verge by the bus stop.

They celebrated Valentine's Day with friends from the university department where they all worked and took a taxi home. Paul fell asleep; Justin sat in the icy breeze of the open window of the taxi hoping that he would wake up before they got back. He steered Paul from the car to the entrance hall and up the stairs. As they climbed, Paul shook himself fully awake, gasping as a gust of wind seized hold of the building and rattled the huge panes of glass in their frames. That night he dreamed about the people in the walls.

JUSTIN LISTENED TO Paul's account. It was still windy outside. The windows shook and draughts invaded the flat. Justin imagined an invisible hand plucking the roof off the block, pulling it off and flinging it away like the lid from a box. They stayed in bed. Justin settled to the role he had become used to:

listening while Paul talked. He had come to recognise that it was Paul's way of giving, how he gradually released parts of himself, dispensing them as if on an instalment plan. Justin took what Paul gave – although, as he knew, that meant he was the giver and Paul the taker. But he told himself they complemented each other. Friends said that they made a great couple and Justin believed that. If only there could ever just be the two of them.

To begin with, Paul had described the crowd of people milling around in the walls in terms of a painting: one of those great broad Victorian scenes of society. Justin knew what he meant: crowds of people at a race track or in a railway station or banking hall. That was the sort of thing. A multitude of faces and attitudes and appearances, a canvas diversity of ages and stations in life. A cross-section, a glimpse of all there was.

'It's not really a painting with all those people there but that's the easiest way for me to describe it,' Paul said. 'I go to sleep and it's windy. I dream of lots of people, all – somewhere – and they want to get out. It's as if they're gypsies, nomads. And when I wake up the gale's still blowing and they still haven't got out. So it's as if they're still in the walls.'

'Why do they want to get out?'

'I don't know,' Paul said. 'But if I were stuck somewhere maybe I'd want to get out.'

Justin bit back a response, and a question. He swallowed. Paul had been as enthusiastic as he had about them living together.

Paul hauled the duvet over Justin's bare shoulder. Paul's lips were cold but the rest of his body poured out welcome heat as Justin clung to him. Head, hands, mouth: he tried to exclude everything that wasn't Paul.

THE GALES CONTINUED unabated into March. On a Saturday morning of thin-layered milky cloud hurled across the sky, the sun was a wide smear of yellow light. Paul and Justin sat on the sofa in front of the window huddled in fleece jackets and bathing in the flickering sunshine.

'Sitting here in the sun it'd be nice and warm if the wind

didn't keep getting in as well,' Justin said. 'This room should be like a greenhouse.' He looked around. They had few possessions to bring to it – two bookcases provided blocks of colour against the plain and empty walls. The wooden floor gleamed. 'I'm sure this place is being shaken to pieces.'

'As long as we're safe.'

'Thank you, Paul.'

He reached for Justin's hand. 'I mean it, sweetheart.'

'I know you do.' He paused. 'Listen. The guy upstairs told me he's getting some pieces of plywood to put over his windows when it gets really windy. He said he'd get us a couple of pieces, if we'd like them. I said yes.'

Paul had closed his eyes. For a moment the air was still and the sun warm. Justin wished he could drowse too.

'Good idea,' Paul said quietly. 'That'd also give them more space. Occupy them.'

Justin knew what Paul meant. He had been describing more and more scenes of people from the walls, the comings and goings and transactions of the throng of wanderers. Paul had said they were getting crowded and probably needed more space. Justin had suggested that Paul write everything down but he had refused to try. They need to escape into the air, not into something else, like paper,' he'd said.

In the sunlight Justin plucked up the courage to ask his question. But he knew it wasn't the first one he should have asked. 'So why are they stuck in our walls?' There was a gust of wind and he shivered.

'Perhaps I'm stopping them from escaping,' Paul replied. 'Or we both are.'

'If they're like in a painting maybe we could help by covering it up. I mean, we could decorate the rooms. We've never touched them. But if we were a bit more certain, we could make them brighter, more part of ourselves…' Justin spoke rapidly. 'What do you think, Paul? I don't mind doing the actual painting, if you don't want to bother. We should choose the colours together, though – agree on them.'

Justin saw the pity in Paul's eyes. 'Go ahead if you want,' Paul said. 'It won't make any difference to them, though. I'm sorry, but it can't.'

'I'll go upstairs and see when he's getting the boards,' Justin said.

Later, in the afternoon, he left Paul in bed and went for a walk. Outside the shops, sweet wrappers swirled and empty drink cans clattered across the cracked paving. The sun was an orange smudge behind bare trees.

Justin blinked away tears. The wind must be blowing grit into his eyes. He could hardly believe that he'd met Paul only four months before. And then he remembered when Paul had first talked about himself, how he had said that he wasn't complete, and that if he could find the right man to help to finish him off, if they could stay together for long enough… That night Justin hadn't misinterpreted Paul but had started the process.

The boards couldn't simply be nailed across the windows. Nails would damage the walls, and any damage would have to be paid for. Justin thought about what to do. Eventually he drilled a series of small holes on either side of the windows and fitted plugs and hooks into them. Then he drilled matching holes in the boards, so he could hang them in place – as if they were pictures.

Paul had watched while Justin measured and drilled. He passed Justin the tools and fixtures as he asked for them.

'Even if we had damaged the wall it wouldn't make any difference,' Paul said. 'Same as if you painted the walls. Boards or no boards, they'll get out when they're ready to.'

In the dusk the room began to fill with silver shadows. A bar of light slanted across the floor, wan and chill. They had never bothered to buy curtains. As it grew darker outside, the gale increased. The glass shook in its frame. Justin thought he could feel the entire block move, as if it was being shifted from its foundations. Muffled shouting drifted down from the flat above them.

Justin stretched out his arms and grasped the board. He tried to manoeuvre it into place. 'Help me, Paul.'

'It's not heavy, is it? Just a bit tricky, getting it lined up.'

When they had finished, they stood back and regarded the almost completely blocked window. A strip of sky at the top, a deep inky blue, was all that remained.

'You know, Justin, for a moment then you looked like you should've been in front of a cross, not a piece of boarding.'

Justin laughed. 'Thank you, love.' You are the cross I bear, he didn't say.

THEY GOT INTO the routine of hanging up the boards over the windows. At some point during each evening one of them would get up from the sofa. The other would follow and between them they would block the windows. The sound of the gale wasn't lessened and the windows and walls still rattled and shifted. But Justin felt that they had done something useful and protective: Paul seemed calmer. When they went to bed they would kiss frantically, as if their opened mouths would permit an exchange. Then Paul would fall asleep, with Justin holding him. He wanted to. He wondered if their linked bodies could make possible a further transaction to fill the spaces within. He also knew Paul was meeting his dreams.

Most mornings before they left for work Paul would say something about his dream of the previous night. He would describe one of the people from the wall – one of the figures of the wide and spreading picture. Sometimes the same person would feature in successive dreams.

'He's discontented,' Paul said. 'He wants to be absorbed, to move on.'

'What do you mean, absorbed?'

'I'm not sure. Perhaps being absorbed into me, or us, and escaping that way. What do you think?'

'I don't know what to think, love. Except that I can't wait not to have to keep dealing with these fucking boards. This place always shaking and shuddering in the wind.'

'I'm sorry. I can't help it,' Paul said.

Justin turned to him. 'Do you want to leave? For us to split up?

You're not happy, are you?'

'Hey, come here.' Paul embraced Justin. 'It's not you.'

'I'm working late. Will you be here when I get home?'

'Yes.'

FROM THE PAVEMENT Justin saw that their flat was in darkness. The windows gaped out to the night – vast, bare. He walked faster, leaning against the gale. Budding branches danced in front of streetlights.

Justin burst into the room, switching on the light. He shouted for Paul to help him put up the boards. He ran to the bedroom.

'Love? Paul?' He was sitting up, swathed in their duvet. Justin touched his shoulder, started to shake him.

Paul remained still. Justin knew he was watching them, a spectator.

They moved as a crowd, in silence. He didn't need to hear their voices. He knew what they intended. They came forward, out towards him.

Neither man moved. Then Justin was the first to run.

THROWING THE FLAME

[illegible] the dance so much [illegible] of [illegible] I'll never be able [illegible] morning [illegible] ago we first met. I remember [illegible] nightclub; I hadn't even bought a drink [illegible] the dark tables in front of the dance floor. [illegible] dressed in a black T-shirt and jeans. He remained absolutely still for about ten minutes, watching the dancers. There was something angry in his stillness, a tension [illegible]. He emptied his glass and stepped onto the dance floor. Suddenly the music shivered through his limbs; he was caught in it like a floating candle on a river. I knew I had to speak to [illegible]

weaving/tapestry loom

THREADBARE – notes

~~Helen~~ / tapestry artist & clair[illegible]

Tracey – singer, computer operator

1) Helen & client (Tarot-reading)
2) embroidery – faces
3) Helen & Tracey
4) two clients with threadbare faces
5) Helen & Michael – argument over ph[illegible]
6) uses her own hair to embroider [illegible]
7) hands shaking – loom rusty – pulls thre[illegible]
   – in café, faces coming apart
8) back with Tracey, feels her own sk[illegible]
   a series of horizontal threads – th[illegible]
   interwove – you had to start somewh[illegible]

superstition is a loose thread in the fabric

~~an authorised by faith~~

an unauthorised bit of faith

[illegible] a man who disappeared mysteriously [illegible]

THE ENEMY WITHIN

Steve Rasnic Tem

THE BODY MUST have been in the canal for a couple of weeks. It had been difficult to identify - parts of the head had been removed, probably before the body was dumped. The *Walsall Echo* ran several stories about the crime, eventually reporting it to be the body of one James Firth, a factory worker who had disappeared a month before. He had lived alone, and medical records were all the police had to go on.

Ian showed Paul the latest clipping. He couldn't tell Paul exactly why he saved the stories about the drowned man, although Paul certainly knew that Ian had his compulsions. He had accumulated a number of such aimless and obsessive activities: saving movie tickets, writing down his dreams, biking the canal path on weekends and the occasional evening. Such activities brought him no real joy. Perhaps someday one of them might lead to something more significant, but for now they were just ways to kill time.

'I must admit I don't particularly care for this new morbid streak of yours,' Paul said, but he took the clipping anyway and read it. 'He worked for your company. Did you know him?'

'Firth worked in the production section as a spot-welder. I'm in packaging.'

Paul gave the clipping back, rubbing his fingers uncomfortably on his jacket. Ian smelled the new soap Paul was using - he was always changing soaps, always taking showers. Paul had compulsions of his own. 'I know. You carry the boxes, you load the vans. You don't involve yourself beyond that. So you've told me. But you could do better, of course. Firth apparently had a trade. You could have a trade. But you never met him? The factory isn't that large, is it?'

'If I ever met him, I don't remember. Some of my friends knew him a little, but I think he kept to himself. They never mentioned him before and now he's all they can talk about. James Firth has replaced the pay dispute and those unexplained sackings as the conversational topic of the day. I suppose I should be grateful to him for that.'

'He would have had parents, Ian. A life outside work. Show some humanity, please.'

Paul's comments stung, although they were typical of their recent conversations. They were going through a rough patch. They didn't talk anymore until Paul left for his job at the hospital. It seemed Paul was always lecturing him, playing the mature, older mentor. Perhaps eventually he would decide Ian was too young for him and leave, just as Lawrence had. Of course that had been different. They'd all been friends, and then Ian had gone behind Paul's back – who'd been working long shifts at the hospital, *saving lives* (of course he was only an orderly) – and slept with Lawrence. Bad enough that Paul took the moral high ground in almost every argument – the moral high ground was something Paul had actually earned.

It was late January; rain blackened the walls, pulled down the clouds until they seemed as near as the smoke from the factory chimneys. Sunlight had become the colour of dull metal, and would not warm. The rain left whitish smears on the windows. The roads near their flat were constantly busy, with lorries and vans competing for the district's business. Ian found mass transport too unpleasant to tolerate and so used his bike more and more, sticking to the canal path, which was largely abandoned this time of year. Even though the rain stung his eyes and he couldn't keep the damp entirely off his skin, no matter what he wore.

He supposed he was too sensitive; even a hint of an argument could ruin his day. Ian decided to call in sick. Then he slipped on his yellow Mac, grabbed his bike, and headed for the canal, looking to ride off some of his tension.

Paul wouldn't have approved, neither of the dereliction of duty or of the canal ride. He said the canal path was unsanitary and dangerous, 'a good place for someone to murder a pretty fellow like you.' Now he had the sordid Firth murder as confirmation. Well, Paul wasn't his father just because he acted like it. Ian had only left his parents in November, and sometimes he missed the family home. At least there he'd had his own room.

The canal went right past Paul's hospital, Ian's factory as well. Paul could save himself a great deal of commute time, and money, if he only had a bike. But he thought it too 'young,' and Ian had to admit it was hard to imagine stuffy old Paul straddling a bike.

Ian actually wasn't as reckless as he wanted Paul to think. The path was narrow and often muddy, slick and wet on the paved parts, and bumpy on the brick parts, so Ian took his time. He always dinged his bell when headed into a blind corner - he wasn't a *firefighter*, constantly ringing his bell so that it didn't mean anything anymore. And he'd stopped wearing clips. More than once his awkwardness slipping in out of the toe clips had caused a *cliptastrophy*. He needed his feet unencumbered to avoid a wobble and a spill.

Just before the first bridge, Ian dropped smoothly from the street onto the bumpy ramp and then onto the towpath before it dipped into the darkness made by the road overhead. Dark as a cavern with this January weather, dark as the middle of the night - which he knew about, since sometimes that's when he would sneak out and ride. Paul slept like a drunk old man, talking in his sleep, rambling on about ridiculous, impossible things concerning flowers growing out of faces held underwater. *Just punishment* - that was one of sleeping Paul's favourite phrases. He turned into a regular sleeping Nazi, he did. But he didn't wake easily - most nights it would have taken a bomb to rouse him.

Ian had his light on - he knew the path, but a single miscalculation might send him arse over tit into those stinking waters. Maintenance of the canal was no longer what it used to be, some sections being so poorly maintained the narrow-boats rarely attempted them. Too many trips down the weed hatch to free the propeller and fill the rubbish bags meant a boat journey down such a putrid ditch was rarely worth the effort. A typical stretch included heavy patches of reeds on the one side and encroaching trees on the other, weeds in the black smelly mud along the bottom and the not-infrequent submerged object. There were barely two feet of water in parts of the channel. Even the wildlife had abandoned certain areas – he rarely saw more than the occasional duck. These were sections where only cyclists and the occasional fisherman ventured. Which of course was to Ian's liking; some days it felt as if the canal were his alone.

There was something vaguely outside geography about navigating the narrow canal path, passing under signs that always pointed somewhere else – Black Lake, Tame Valley, Gospel Oak – as if he were travelling through no place to anywhere he liked. Like the transporter on the old *Star Trek* show.

He passed under numerous bridges for cars, pedestrians, railways, or some combination, with concrete or brick or steel bases, many with the usual rude graffiti, some with a different sort of nonsensical language whose origins he could not fathom.

He passed the hospital and a while later passed the factory. Several apartment buildings in between made him wonder why Paul chose the building he did, but wasn't sure it was worth bringing up with the inevitable row. Ian shouldn't have let Paul choose. The truth was, Ian wasn't confident enough that he could choose better. He didn't know much yet about himself, or the world, but of course he couldn't admit that to Paul, who of course already knew.

The Firth body had been found somewhere between the hospital and the factory but he wasn't exactly sure where. The photos in the *Echo* showed only the gathered backs of policemen and bits of the canal. Most canal bits looked pretty much the same, with rundown, broken industrial buildings in the background. The *Echo* stated that the body had been covered with black mud. Glancing at the canal now, Ian could see several black objects in the water. How could he know one of them wasn't a body? He wasn't about to check.

He picked up speed on a long paved section running alongside a brick wall. A collection of cherry pickers parked on the other side resembled the long, bent legs of a giant tumbled insect.

He looked over at a crumbling old canal side warehouse with an overhead bay for unloading. It probably hadn't been used in fifty years or more. The canal was rich in such useless and decrepit architecture. The same could be said for the whole city – where he'd been trapped all his life – modern shopping complexes looking out of place alongside shabby empty shops in the suburbs. He needed to move someplace where everything was new but wasn't sure such a place existed in all of Britain.

Ian rode under Pleck Road and out to the M6 before turning back. He didn't see any bodies, not that he had expected to, really. He'd lied to Paul. He knew very well who James Firth was. Ian had first seen him singing in a folk club two years before. Ian had been sixteen at the time and unused to drinking; he'd spent most of that evening in a daze. He remembered trying to follow that handsome singer around and never quite getting close enough. Imagine his surprise when he got the factory job and there was James Firth in another department! Not that he ever worked up the courage to speak to him – he got that way with the truly handsome ones. But he had imagined it every day. By that time he was with Paul of course, but he always thought James Firth might be another Lawrence, only better, if he could just work up the courage to speak to him.

Good thing they'd never made the connection. He felt strangely about his death, the way you'd feel if you narrowly escaped being run over by a bus. Imagine how he would have felt if they'd been lovers?

He was tired enough on his return that he decided to stay in the rest of the day. Alone like this the flat seemed alien. Paul had selected most of the furniture. He hadn't minded at first – Paul was the one with *taste,* but at this point nothing felt like Ian's anymore. It was the ground floor of a terraced house. When they moved in the old wallpaper had been left, faded blue flowers on grey. At least in his parents' house he had been allowed to paint and put up anything he liked on the walls. But Paul had very specific and conservative tastes. It was Paul's flat, really - now all grays and tans and pretentious knock-offs. It could hardly feel more oppressive. If Ian were sacked and could no longer contribute he'd lose the little influence he had. He might as well move back in with mum and dad.

Paul had promised they would redecorate soon and Ian could choose some pieces, the way a parent might give a child some illusory freedom by allowing them to choose some design element for their bedroom. Ian would have to put up with so much condescension about his cluelessness it hardly seemed worth it.

He hid from the rest of the flat by sitting in the bedroom playing *Tindersticks* on the record player. The records and the player belonged to Paul, of course, but Ian was the more dedicated fan. He'd have them put away before Paul returned - he didn't like the way Ian handled records, and some of Paul's vinyl was rare, or at least he claimed it was.

When Paul came home he brought sushi. Afterwards Paul took a ridiculously long shower and they went out for a film - something Iranian Paul had read about. Ian had a hard time following it, and finally fell asleep against Paul's shoulder. He had a dream of flowers growing on the body in the canal. It had floated there so long plants had the opportunity to take root. The song from the film's soundtrack was 'Killing Me Softly With His Song.' Roberta Flack. Or was this part of the dream? It seemed a strange song for an Iranian film. Ian felt terrified as the petals began to open.

Paul woke him up after the film ended. He seemed angry. 'They give you too much work there,' Paul said as they left the cinema. 'You're exhausted all the time. You should insist on more breaks - you have rights. This isn't the slave trade.'

Ian felt guilty about lying to him but was also derisive of Paul's earnestness and gullibility. It made him nervous and agitated. Paul started to call a taxi when Ian broke off and started walking rapidly down the damp and greasy pavement. 'No, let's take the towpath!' he shouted back at him and started to run.

Ian was already under one of the bridges by the time Paul caught up to him, completely out of breath and grabbing on to Ian's shoulder. His sweat stank of marsh and damp wool. 'Stop . . . damn you...'

Old man already, so out of shape. Ian shrugged off his hand. 'It's shorter, and it's free. Take a chance.' He started walking. Soon enough Paul caught up again, stony-faced and sullen beside him. Ian was happy to let him stew but after only a few minutes couldn't bear the silence and needed to make small talk. 'The water levels in the canal are lower this year, but I'm not aware of a drought. I suppose it made it easier, to find that body, I mean.'

'It spreads. It's the leakage,' Paul replied.

'What? What do you mean?'

'The water leaks into the basements nearby, some of them. All around here - it's the leakage. And James Firth - the body had a name.'

Ian ignored the comment about Firth. He didn't want to argue with Paul now, here by the canal, in the dark. 'Leakage? I've never heard of such a thing - is it from one of your articles or something?'

'It's— ' Paul stopped and looked around. 'Did you hear something? In any case it's common knowledge. You might know if you weren't running about all the time, or staying home and playing my records. A relationship requires commitment, Ian, and sometimes that means giving up our selfish needs.'

'Look, if you're talking about Lawrence, that wasn't all my fault. You left me alone with him again and again...'

'Let the dead rest.'

'He's not dead.'

'He is as far as I'm concerned.'

There was a sudden humming, a bee-like sound, and then

something dark popped up out of nowhere and passed swiftly between them, almost knocking Paul into the canal. Ian snapped his head around to follow the sound – it was a Bike Ninja, riding around with no lights on in the pitch black. The rider had removed all reflective gear to maximise his or her ninja status. Ian felt envious – he'd long wanted to do the same thing. Maybe he still would.

Paul roared, furious. 'Is that what you want to be? Is that what you do when you leave me in the middle of the night?'

Ian could see the dark shape expanding behind Paul. Another Ninja.

But this one wasn't attached to any bike. Paul's face, red and angry, dropped away inside an obscuring shadow. He hit the pavement with a dull thud.

THE NEXT DAY at work someone caught his hand in one of the hydraulic stamping presses. It brought the production line down. Ian watched as the medics brought the poor fellow out. He overheard someone say the entire arm might be paralyzed. Ian had the opportunity to go home early but decided to stay and help out with a few random tasks. Paul was at home, recovering from the incident by the canal and Ian didn't want to talk to him just yet.

They'd both decided Paul had simply gotten confused and fallen. He had scrapes on his hands and the left side of his face, as well as several contusions along his rib cage. Paul was the one who decided it had been a fall; Ian had been there and still had no theory of his own. It had been dark, certainly, and they'd both been agitated. Paul refused to see a doctor. He seemed more embarrassed by the event than anything else.

During lunch there was a bad smell of stagnant water in the warehouse. Ian complained to the new safety officer, who assigned Ian and three others to clean the area. Early in the job his two companions claimed they couldn't bear the stench and Ian had to work alone, sorting through boxes and bags, some of them feeling warm and damp and vaguely flesh-like. Ian had actually grown accustomed to the smell and didn't find it that bad. He found himself humming that song from the soundtrack of *The Drowning Pool*, or had it been from that dream of the body infested with flowers? 'Killing Me Softly With His Song.' He couldn't be sure. The words from the soundtrack echoed in his head, widening the darkness inside him. He could hear water dripping but couldn't decide whether it was inside the warehouse or inside his head. And he could smell this reek of flowers, as if they'd been cooked in some humid confinement until their sweet perfumes had become a kind of stench. He kept replaying the scene in which that dark shape had risen up behind Paul. It might have simply been a trick of the shadows - Paul thought he himself was responsible for his accident. But it defied logic. Ian replayed it again. Paul had been so angry - Ian had never seen him angry like that before, as if he might lose his mind. And then that shadow had appeared so suddenly, as if it had been ripped right out of him, enfolding him like dark wings from his back.

Ian had left his bike at home, choosing to ride the bus. He wasn't sure why - it felt like a gesture of respect for Paul, for Paul's feelings about Ian's activities. But he wasn't going to give up the bike - just for this one day, as a kind of gesture. He walked home via the canal path. Today it felt like an act of defiance. But he also wanted to get another look at the canal where Paul's so-called accident had occurred.

It was a relatively clear day for that time of year. Ian set off from behind the factory through the rusted old canal access gate at the back of the employee parking lot. He only had a short period of daylight left before twilight and the rapid fall into dusk. He reached that stretch just beyond the bridge where the incident had occurred. It was already partly in shadow because of the angle of the sun.

Of course there was nothing to see. He wasn't sure what he'd been thinking. Clues were for the movies, not for real life.

He spent the rest of the walk checking out the banks on both sides of the canal. The water level was still low. He could clearly see the dark line of stain where the foul water usually reached, like the line in a toilet bowl which hadn't been conscientiously scrubbed. Of course Paul never permitted such an occurrence in their flat. The surface of the canal was a good foot below that line.

As he walked on he looked for breaches in the old concrete and stone that lined the canal, any spots where the water might have escaped and gone somewhere else. He felt foolish about it – he was no expert and couldn't possibly know what he was seeing – but he looked anyway and pretended that he wasn't completely ignorant.

There were definite fissures in the lining of the canal. Whether they led anywhere it was impossible to determine. All along the embankment there were drops and sunken areas of varying degrees. Whether they meant anything Ian was hardly qualified to say. This was a very old part of the city – it had been built, torn down, reworked, rebuilt numerous times over the decades. Several of the buildings along its banks were either empty or non-functional. They should have been demolished, but people here loved the old – they held on to it, embraced it, even after it had ceased being useful. Why couldn't they see that sometimes it was best just to tear things down and start over?

Ian thought about their flat. No matter how much they redecorated it and hid its flaws, he doubted it would ever feel like home.

He came up off the canal path only a short distance from the flat. He could see now that theirs wasn't the only one looking for a remodel. A number of trades people were packing up their vans and loading their trucks, construction bins were full and, as darkness rapidly encroached, it brought with it not only the usual cooking smells but the aromas of fresh paint and new plaster as well.

And something else. A certain stagnancy carried over from the canal that seemed out of place here where things were being made new. The stench made him anxious and he found himself glancing into any gaps between buildings, peering over steps going down, simply trying to be more aware of his surroundings.

Alongside the building next to theirs was a depressed place

where a narrow passageway between that building and the next had sunk a bit. In the side of the building there appeared to be a damaged access door whose frame had partially collapsed. Ian had never noticed it before and wouldn't have seen it now except for his heightened, what? Paranoia? He veered off the path until he was only five or so yards away. The stench was worse here. He went up to the broken door intending only to peek, but there was just the right amount of space for him to squeeze inside, almost as if the amount of collapse had been tailored specifically to him.

He felt as if he had entered his own head. The smell of foul damp, the notion of secret growth, and that distant memory of song, *killing me softly, killing me softly.*

A few yards in he found the decaying human face with the flowers growing in its sockets. No, not growing, but put there recently. Previous offerings of dead flowers lay scattered across the water that had seeped in from below, petals and stems turned brown or mouldy. He couldn't see the rest of the body as it was somehow anchored below, but even with a few chunks missing he knew the face. It was Lawrence.

'Paul! Paul!' Ian went straight to their bedroom and burst through the door. The bed was empty, the covers in disarray. The foul odour of the canal was strongly evident. Water rose from the carpet when he stepped nearer the bed. The sheets, too, appeared wet.

He followed the sound of the running shower down the hall. The shadowed figure behind the clouded glass door was humming tunelessly but Ian could still decipher the melody, *killing me, killing me.* The shadow turned, and grew broader, and became confusing in its shape.

ANTITHESIS

(SOMETHING OTHER)

(MOMENTS)

Fantasy/ideal ingrained in everyday life. At critical moments (turning points). Calm, determined eyes; a strong opening hand; a shadow falling on me; [redacted] arms holding me from behind. Looking in [redacted] strange faces, as into a well...

YOU GIVE ME FEVER

drove her mad – later, her
came his reality — wint
radient of cold – wooden

Not a child, no. More
sick animal, a sick do
and pissing over the co
trying to fuck a duffe
call it a child."

could see the cold: di
the fire, black lines movi

After his father died,

If you try to remove people's armour

Suit of armour outside shop.

I NEED SOMEWHERE TO HID

comic-book mentalities: mask

emphasis – text falling ove

"What do they know of Engl
know?"

a baby crusted in rock

clean-shaven, cropped, perf

"It shows I'm in complete

not mine, It any

AFTERWORD:
THE WHOLE OF JOEL

Ramsey Campbell

SOME STARS SEEM to shine brightest because their energy consumes the source. That's hardly an original thought, but I believe it's appropriate here, and I hope Joel Lane wouldn't have found it too familiar when applied to him. Much more likely, he would have bowed his head and swept his hand over his hair in that self-deprecating gesture of his before swiftly turning the conversation away from himself to praise the latest work of whoever was trying to compliment him. There's an old but highly equivocal joke – Kingsley Amis once made it about Allen Ginsberg – that [insert name here] has a lot to be modest about. Let me rescue it to use without ambiguity. Joel was almost painfully modest about his own talent, which was considerable and capacious. We can only hope that however quick he was to duck any praise, he was at least aware how highly we and many others who aren't here regarded him.

I'm not sure when we originally met – at a FantasyCon, I imagine – but I'll never forget my first encounter with the keenness of his mind. One day the post brought a fat brown-paper envelope, which I thought contained a folded brochure of some kind until it proved to hold a letter quite a few pages long, written in Joel's painstaking minuscule hand. It was no less than a detailed reading of my first four published novels, and it didn't merely astonish me with its insight – it actually made me look again at what I'd written, identifying elements that my subconscious had put in while I was occupied telling the tale. One example out of many: Joel found any number of negative constructions in *The Nameless* and showed how they could be read in terms of the book's theme. I honestly believe that he'd written the essay for no other reason than to set his ideas down and let me see them, but I saw it was a significant piece of criticism and encouraged him to send it to *Foundation*, where it duly appeared. I later realised that Joel wrote many of his friends letters – in later years, emails – that contained or consisted of highly perceptive accounts of their work. If the missives still exist, someone should collect them, and I live in hope that he sent enough of his monograph in progress – a study of twentieth-century horror fiction – to friends for it to be pieced together. I know it would be a major addition to our literature of criticism.

As for his own work, it was as profound as his critiques. It was driven by the political beliefs he passionately held without, to my knowledge, ever trying to impose them on anyone, and by his deep humanism and his sympathy for his characters, often the excluded or oppressed. He developed his own bleak form of horror fiction as a way of showing how we live now (indeed, not only then). All this may make him sound sombre to folk who sadly didn't meet him, but those of us who did know better. Once you coaxed him out of his shyness he was great fun as a companion, and we can forgive him even the horridest of his puns. I can't help feeling that he would have been amused to learn that in the first paragraph of this piece my spellcheck tried to convince me I meant Kingsley Amiss.

To round this brief piece off I went back to the message board on my web site, where Joel often used to post, to see if I could find a pun to represent him at his worst. I found him vigorously defending his beliefs, casually revealing the breadth of his knowledge of jazz and rock and folk music, engaging in literary debate, showing concern for other contributors to the board… I found no puns, but I happened upon this, his image of a favourite device in weird fiction, the object that admits us to a different reality: 'little bits of midnight they forgot to sweep up when the dawn came.' I think that's genius, and a reminder of what we've lost – what more there might have been. But though Joel has gone, his work still lives, and I believe its worth will only grow with time.

July 2016

BROKEN EYE

...child
...with videos
...on Staircase (orgy in dark)
...watched dawn through wire grid in glass
...seemed as though darkness still there

Des

parent

collects

...staying with sister & child in tower
...meets young man in block, stays with him
— he collects photos & videos — ~~(arguments)~~
...going back to her ~~room~~ in the dark
...runs into couple (group?) making love
...on ~~staircase~~
...goes back to the man — he is lonely/afraid.
...leaving in morning — drugged teenagers on
...balcony
...back to ~~room~~ — daylight felt like darkness
(slept for a day & then felt better)

The Inner Eye
shows domination
is it myopia or
that makes films
...candlight my favour...
voices more alive than
I'm not a voyeur, ...
will do, ... and burrow
through to the soul of the
where the lost ~~voices~~
towards me, still in the
of being heard, being ...

2. (1) imprisonment — bars, stone, grids — against light
(2) the eye — TV screen — light
(their eyes ate the daylight)
(3) images — compound eye — windows
(broken up into windows)

(4) ~~...~~ idea of freedom.

EVERYBODY WAS A TOURIST

DIFFERENT ...
1) couple ...
2) solitary people ...
3) girl in ...
4) bomb hospital
5) like an alcoholic ... don't care of ...
6) not sure ... alien that ... it's human being ... an addiction ...
7) double calls ... tourists ...

CONTRIBUTORS' NOTES

Allen Ashley is an award-winning editor, writer, poet, critical reader and event host. He runs five creative writing groups across north London including the advanced SF/Fantasy group Clockhouse London Writers. His most recent book is a revised version of his novel *The Planet Suite* (Eibonvale Press, 2016). allenashley.com

Simon Avery lives and works in Birmingham. He has had fiction published in a variety of magazines and anthologies including *The Third Alternative, Crimewave, Black Static, The Best British Mysteries IV, Beneath the Ground,* and *Birmingham Noir*. A novella, *The Teardrop Method* is forthcoming from TTA Press.

Stephen Bacon's fiction has been published in *Black Static, Cemetery Dance, Shadows & Tall Trees, Postscripts, Crimewave, Terror Tales of Yorkshire* and many other magazines and anthologies, and has been selected for *Best Horror of the Year*. His debut collection, *Peel Back the Sky,* was published in 2012. stephenbacon.co.uk

Originally from Manchester, **Simon Bestwick** now lives on the Wirral with his long-suffering wife, the author Cate Gardner. He's responsible for three novels, four story collections and a chapbook. Two new novels, *The Devil's Highway* and *The Feast of All Souls,* will be out later this year. simonbestwick.com

James Brogden is a writer of horror and fantasy who lives in the West Midlands. His latest novel *Hekla's Children* will be published by Titan Books in March 2017. jamesbrogden.blogspot.co.uk

In 2015 **Ramsey Campbell** received the Lifetime Achievement World Fantasy Award and an Honorary Fellowship from Liverpool John Moores University for outstanding services to literature. His most recent books are *The Booking, The Searching Dead* and *Limericks of the Alarming and Phantasmal.* ramseycampbell.com

Mike Chinn has published almost 60 short stories and edited four anthologies. His collection, *Give Me These Moments Back,* was published in 2015 by The Alchemy Press. The new Damian Paladin collection, *Walkers in Shadow,* and a Western, *Revenge is a Cold Pistol* are to be published by Pro Se Productions. saladoth.blogspot.co.uk

Peter Coleborn is the editor-in-chief of the award-winning Alchemy Press. He's also done stints as editor (*Winter Chills/ Chills, Dark Horizons, BFS Newsletter*), British Fantasy Convention organiser, and takes the odd photo or two. He lives in an old house in Staffordshire. alchemypress.co.uk

Gary Couzens has had stories published in *F&SF, Interzone, Black Static, Crimewave, The Third Alternative, Midnight Street* and other magazines and anthologies, and the collections *Second Contact and Other Stories* (2003) and *Out Stack and Other Places* (2015). gjcouzens .weebly.com

Sarah Doyle is the Pre-Raphaelite Society's Poet-in-Residence. She has been widely published and placed in many competitions. *Dreaming Spheres: Poems of the Solar System* (written with Allen Ashley) was published in 2014 by PS Publishing. Sarah is studying for a Creative Writing MA at Royal Holloway, University of London. sarahdoyle.co.uk

Pauline E. Dungate is the author of many short stories and a plethora of reviews. She helps run Cannon Hill Writers' Group in Birmingham. Now she has retired she travels to exotic countries in search of butterflies; a number of her stories are based in places she has visited. When not writing, you may well find her in the garden.

Jan Edwards has a passion for folklore and the supernatural that inspires much of her fiction, with forty-plus short stories published in UK and US anthologies. Many of these tales are reprinted in her collections *Leinster Gardens and Other Subtleties* (Alchemy Press) and *Fables and Fabrications* (Penkhull Press). janedwardsblog.wordpress.com

Paul Edwards was born and raised in Bristol, but now lives in the Somerset market town of Frome. His debut collection *Black Mirrors* was published by Rainfall Books in 2012 and a second collection, *Now That I've Lost You*, was published by Screaming Dreams in 2013. pauledwardshorror.com

Liam Garriock is an author and poet of the fantastic and the *wyrd* based in Edinburgh. He is honoured to appear in a book dedicated to the late, great Joel Lane.

John Grant has won the Hugo (twice), World Fantasy Award and others. His seventy-plus books include the collection *Tell No Lies* (The Alchemy Press, 2014). His *A Comprehensive Encyclopedia of Film Noir* (2013) is the largest film noir encyclopaedia in English. He runs the website *Noirish at* noirencyclopedia.wordpress.com. johngrantpaulbarnett.com

When not writing, **Terry Grimwood** teaches at a college, plays harmonica at a blues club, and acts and Directs for an amateur dramatic society. His novel, *Deadside Revolution* is due from Horrific Tales press this autumn and his collection *There is a Way to Live Forever* from Boo Press.

Andrew Hook's most recent publications are *Slow Motion Wars* (co-written with Allen Ashley), *Human Maps* (Eibonvale Press) and *The Greens* (Snowbooks). Joel wryly informed him that 'horror is the new slipstream', but even so he contends he writes the latter. andrew-hook.com

John Howard was born in London. He is the author of several books, including *The Silver Voices* and *Written by Daylight*. He also has published essays on classic writers of the science fiction and horror fields, some collected in *Touchstones* (The Alchemy Press).

Ian Hunter is a children's author, editor, short story writer and poet. He reviews books for *Interzone* and other places, and is also poetry editor for the British Fantasy Society, a post previously held by Joel. Lane. ian-hunter.co.uk

Tom Johnstone lives in Brighton with his significant other and their two daughters. He works as a council gardener, and enjoys extreme lawn-mowing. His fiction has appeared in *Supernatural Tales, Strange Tales* V, *Black Books of Horror* 9-11 and *Best Horror of the Year 8*. tomjohnstone.wordpress.com

Mat Joiner lives near Birmingham, England, where he haunts second-hand bookshops and real-ale pubs. His stories and poems have appeared in the likes of *Not One of Us, Strange Horizons,* and *Winter Stories.*

Tim Lebbon is a New York Times-bestselling writer from South Wales. He's had over thirty novels published to date, as well as hundreds of novellas and short stories. A movie of his short story 'Pay the Ghost' was released last year, and there are several more screen projects in development. timlebbon.net

Alison Littlewood is the author of *A Cold Season* and several other novels. Her short stories have been picked for *The Best Horror of the Year* and *The Mammoth Book of Best New Horror*, as well as Joel Lane's *Never Again* anthology. alisonlittlewood.co.uk

Simon MacCulloch was privileged to be a friend of, and correspondent with, Joel Lane during the 1980s and early 1990s.

Gary McMahon is the author of several acclaimed novels and short story collections. He considered Joel Lane a friend, mentor, and major influence on his own writing. Gary lives, works, writes and studies karate in Yorkshire, UK. garymcmahon.com

David Mathew is the author of five novels, two volumes of short fiction and two volumes of academic non-fiction. His most recent publications are *Sick Dice* (Montag) and *The Care Factory* (Cambridge Scholars). He works as an Educational Developer and as a researcher in education and psychoanalysis. He edits the *Journal of Pedagogic Development* and teaches academic writing.

Adam Millard is the author of twenty novels, ten novellas, and more than two hundred short stories, which can be found in various magazines and anthologies. Probably best known for his post-apocalyptic fiction, Adam also writes fantasy/horror for children, as well as bizarro fiction. adammillard.co.uk

Chris Morgan has had eleven books published. He was Birmingham Poet Laureate in 2008-9. Now retired, he spends his time reading, travelling abroad to photograph wildlife, and dabbling with writing.

Pauline Morgan has been short-listed for the post of Birmingham Poet Laureate four times. Maybe one day she will succeed. Her poems have appeared in various places including the Fair Acre Press anthology of *Maligned Species: Spiders*.

Thana Niveau writes: 'Joel solicited and published my very first story and helped me through my first panel. Since then I've been shortlisted for BFS awards for Best Collection and Best Short Story. He was always a generous, supportive friend and the world is a poorer place without him. I miss you, Joel.'
thananiveau.com

Marion Pitman is a Londoner living in Reading. She has written poetry and fiction most of her life and published it since the 1970s. She sells second-hand books, and has worked as an artists' model. She has no car, no television, no cats and no money. Her hobbies include folk-singing and theological argument.
marionpitman.co.uk

British Fantasy Award winner **John Llewellyn Probert** first met Joel Lane at the launch of his debut book *The Faculty of Terror* at a Nottingham FantasyCon. They became firm friends and even wrote two articles for the medical magazine Joel edited - one on surgical devices, the other on John's top five surgical moments in horror. johnlprobert.com

Rosanne Rabinowitz lives in South London and works at a variety of occupations. She has contributed to anthologies such as *Jews vs Aliens, Soliloquy for Pan, Tales from the Vatican Vaults* and *Horror Uncut: Tales of Social Insecurity and Economic Unease.* Her novella *Helen's Story* was shortlisted for the 2013 Shirley Jackson Award. rosannerabinowitz.wordpress.com

Nicholas Royle is the author of seven novels, including *Counterparts, Antwerp* and *First Novel*, and a short story collection, *Mortality*. He has edited twenty anthologies and is series editor of *Best British Short Stories* (Salt). A senior lecturer in creative writing at the Manchester Writing School at MMU, he also runs Nightjar Press. nicholasroyle.com

Lynda E. Rucker is a Shirley Jackson Award-nominated writer who has sold more than two dozen short stories to various anthologies and magazines. She is a regular columnist for *Black Static*, and her second collection of short stories, *You'll Know When You Get There*, was recently published by Swan River Press.
lyndaerucker.wordpress.com

Steven Savile has written for Doctor Who, Torchwood, Stargate, Arkham Horror and others. He won the International Media Association of Tie-In Writers award for *Shadow of the Jaguar* and the Lifeboat to the Stars award for *Tau Ceti* (with Kevin J. Anderson). His latest books include *Sherlock Holmes and the Murder at Sorrows Crown* and *Sunfail*, and due in 2017 are *Parallel Lines* and *Glass Town.* stevensavile.com

David A. Sutton has been a writer since the 1960s. His short stories are collected in *Clinically Dead and Other Tales of the Supernatural* and *Dead Water and Other Weird Tales.* He is the recipient of the World Fantasy, The International Horror Guild and twelve British Fantasy awards. He is the proprietor of Shadow Publishing. davidsutton986.wix.com/shadowpublishing

Steve Rasnic Tem is a past winner of the World Fantasy and British Fantasy awards. His last novel, *Blood Kin* (Solaris) won the Bram Stoker Award. His new novel *UBO*, a science fictional meditation on violence, drops in January/February from Solaris.
m-s-tem.com

Mark Valentine published Joel Lane's early short stories in *Aklo*, the journal he edited with Roger Dobson, and in a chapbook, *The Foggy, Foggy Dew* (1986). He edits *Wormwood*), a journal of the fantastic in literature, to which Joel contributed many fine essays.
tartaruspress.com/wormwood.html

Joe X. Young is a writer, reviewer, and illustrator. His work appears in publications including *The BFS Journal, Morpheus Tales, Wordland 2, Nat.Brut* and from Haunted Waters Press, Parallel Universe Publications, and many others. Joe loves his fiancée and his job and is always up for new challenges. joexyoung.com

embroidering/tapestry loom

EMBROIDERY – notes

embroidery/tapestry artist & clair[illegible]

singer, computer operator

1) Helen & client (Tarot-reading)
2) embroidery – faces
3) Helen & Tracey
4) two clients with threadbare faces
5) Helen & Michael – argument over [illegible]
6) uses her own hair to embroider [illegible]
7) hands shaking – loom rusty – pulls [illegible]
   – in café, faces coming apart
8) back with Tracey, feels her own sk[illegible]
   a series of horizontal threads – [illegible]
   interwove – you had to start somew[illegible]

Superstition is a loose thread in the fabric [illegible]

~~– not authorised by faith~~

– an unauthorised bit of faith

Lightning Source UK Ltd.
Milton Keynes UK
UKOW01f1059020916

282043UK00001B/93/P

9 781911 034049